DARK VESSEL

Series by D.I. Telbat

The COIL Series

The COIL Legacy Series

The Resolution Series

The STEADFAST Series

The Last Dawn Series

Never Lost Series

The Leeward Set

Other Books by D.I. Telbat

Arabian Variable

Called To Gobi

God's Colonel

Soldier of Hope

†

COIL Short Story Collections

Christian Short Story Collections

DARK
VESSEL

A CHRISTIAN SUSPENSE NOVEL

Book Four in The COIL Series

D.I. Telbat

In Season Publications
USA

Printed in the United States of America

Dark Vessel/D.I. Telbat. -- 1st ed.
The COIL Series, Book 4, Christian Fiction

ISBN 978-0-9864103-4-5

Book Layout ©2013 BookDesignTemplates.com
Cover Design by Streetlight Graphics

~

To my brother

~

~

Acknowledgements

Thanks to everyone who supported the efforts it took
to bring yet another COIL novel to completion,
particularly my editors, Dee and Jamie.
Also, many thanks to my reading friends.
To God be the glory.

~

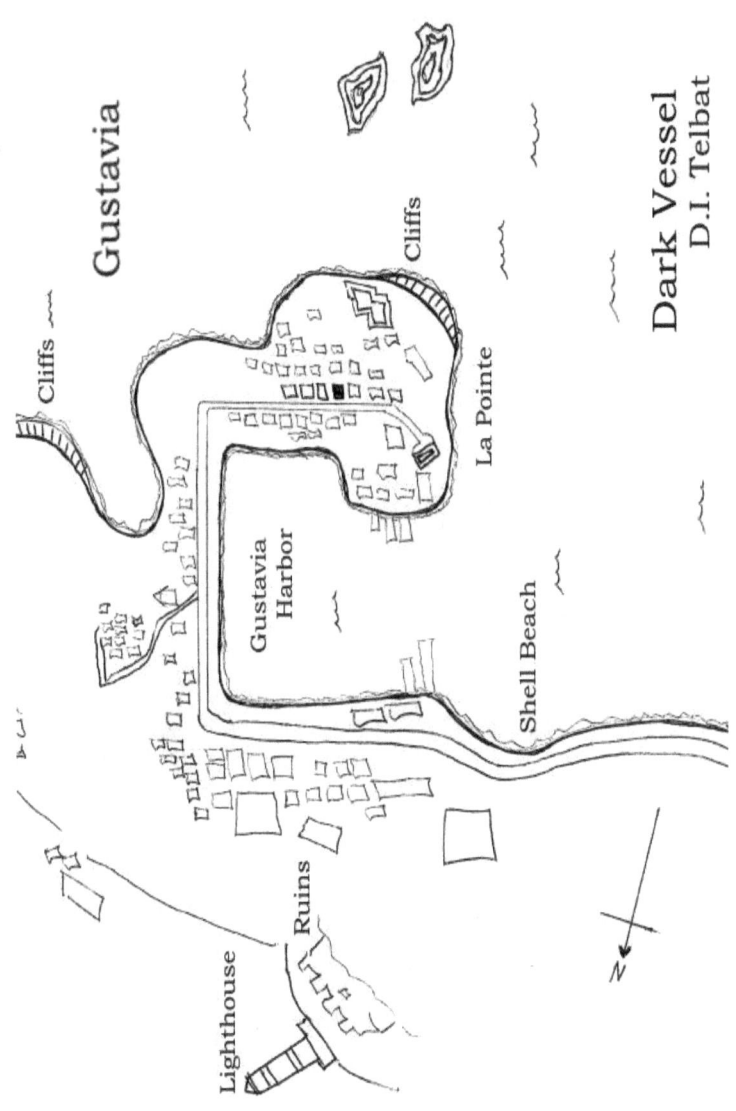

Gustavia

Dark Vessel
D.I. Telbat

Forglade's Cottage

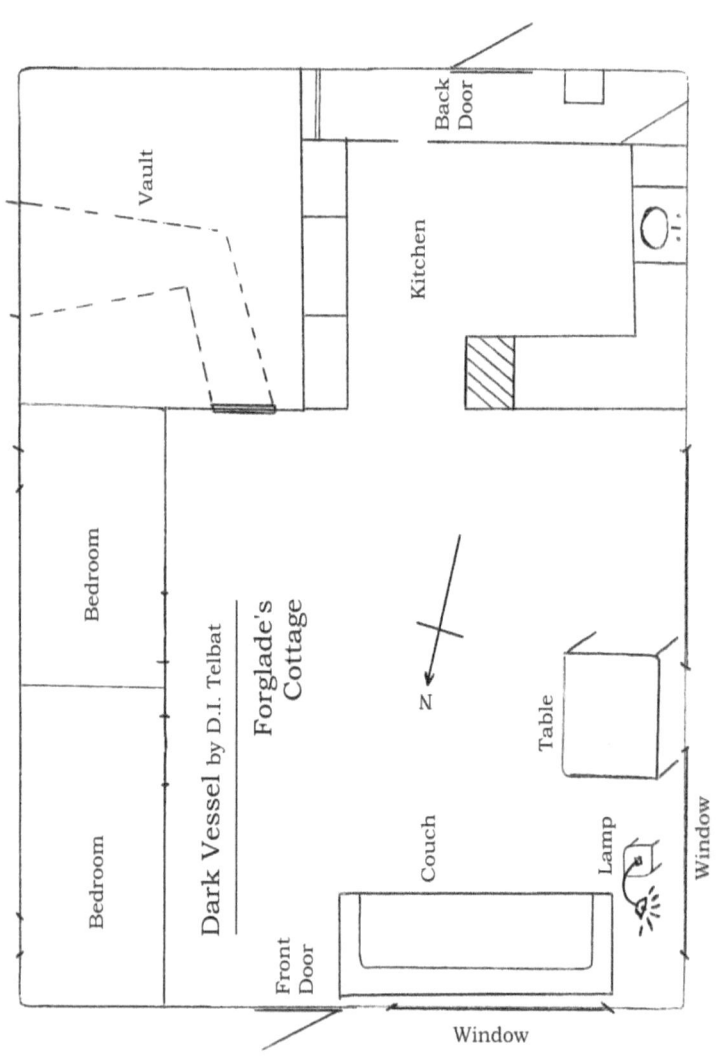

Dark Vessel by D.I. Telbat

Forglade's Cottage

Vault

Kitchen

Back Door

Bedroom

Bedroom

N

Table

Window

Couch

Lamp

Front Door

Window

Manhattan

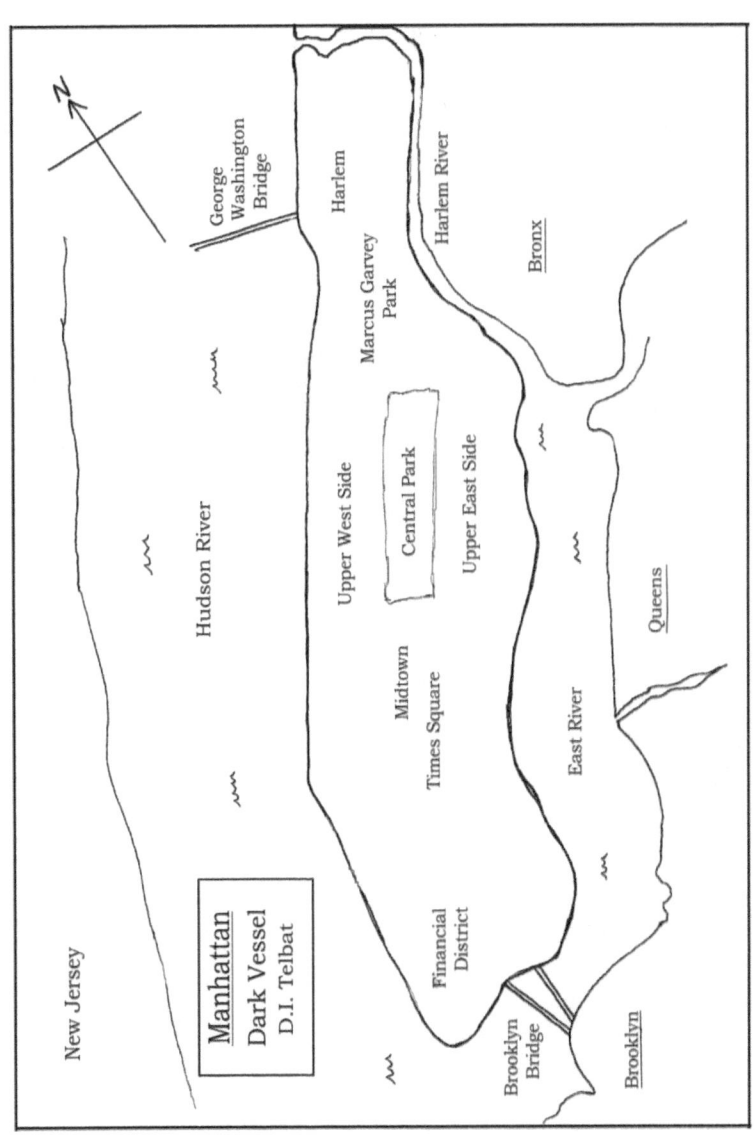

~

Psalm 72:4
"He will vindicate the afflicted of the people,
Save the children of the needy
And crush the oppressor."
(NASB®)

~

PROLOGUE

The man in the expensive suit faced the man dressed in casual jeans. The parking lot was empty except for their two cars. The affluent man had arrived in a limo, his driver remaining behind the tinted glass. The one in jeans had arrived alone in a sports car.

"This will be the last time we meet." The man in the suit turned up his collar against the evening breeze. "I need a mess taken care of, and you've been laying plans to remove Corban Dowler. In one little explosion, my problem disappears along with the CIA's biggest liability. We both win with this conclusion."

"The ordnance is ready for tomorrow, sir." The man in jeans checked his cell phone, dismissed a call, then pocketed the device. "Don't forget, once Corban Dowler's out of the way, we'll still have to face his friends—some in the COIL agency, and others we can't yet foresee. A few in the government have hesitated to remove Dowler, but he's an easy target."

"You mean, because they use tranquilizers instead of bullets?" The suited man chuckled.

"No, because they're the best at what they do. I can cover my end. It's what I do. But the way you live—you're not

1

exactly clandestine material, sir."

"Just take care of Dowler and his people, and I'll handle the rest. I don't need to graduate from Langley's spy school to squash a few gnats."

"Then we ride this to whatever finish we find."

"The only finish is my peace of mind and your mountain of cash."

"See you on the other side, then."

Both men parted and returned to their cars. As the suited-man reached the door, his driver jumped out and opened it for him.

"Hey, Coleman," the affluent man called. The other man paused. "Those Christians—they're not better than the rest of us. Put as many in the grave as you have to. Not many will care, least of all me! Earn your money."

"I always do." The man in jeans smiled wickedly, then climbed into his sports car.

PART I: CORBAN

CHAPTER ONE

The explosion lifted me up and threw me backwards. I felt the searing heat against my skin as bits of shrapnel pierced my flesh in a dozen spots. When I landed on the lawn of a Bronx townhouse, it took me a few moments to recover from the jar to my skull.

Quickly, I lapsed into years of training: first, assess the situation. I was alive, though barely. If I'd been two steps closer to my four-door Lexus, I would've been a smoldering mass of flesh. Roy Turpin, however, hadn't been so blessed. Flames flickered from his charred corpse in the front seat. The bomb was surely not meant for him, but who would be trying to kill me?

The night was pierced by sirens. I rolled over and crawled into the hedges of the townhouse. Had anyone seen me survive the blast? Once again, God had kept me alive for another purpose. My heart leaped at the possibilities—at that which He intended for me!

With no more than a couple minutes before emergency personnel arrived, I had to decide whether I would run or stay on the scene.

Still on my mind was a set of identifications for Roy Turpin, one of COIL's most recent recruits. The townhouse on my left was one of my stateside safe houses—apparently not so safe. The veteran field operative inside was responsible for at least a hundred identification packages over the last ten years. It wasn't possible that he'd tried to kill me—not in front of his own residence.

And where was my own wallet and identification? It had been in the Lexus, in the pocket between the front seats. For now, Roy Turpin would assume my charred identity, until tests showed that he wasn't me at all. For now, Corban James Dowler was dead. Rest in peace, I thought to myself, then climbed out of the bushes. There was nowhere to go but underground—if I was to survive.

I'd been recruited by the CIA when I was only nineteen. Now, thirty-eight years later, I was familiar with personal attacks—and no stranger to death squads and assassins— though I'd officially left the Agency five years earlier. As any retired agent, I'd maintained ties with old contacts for security purposes.

But I had another level of concern on my mind as I limped into the back yard of the townhouse. I ran COIL, a private agency that assisted Christians under international threat. The Commission of International Laborers had survived many attacks in the five years since I'd founded it, but this was something different. This was a premeditated terrorist attack, blatant, and on American soil. Not only did I have a handful of potential agencies to suspect for the bombing, I also had to consider my own more recent dealings with anti-Christian militias and governments overseas. COIL protected Christians so the gospel of Christ could be shared. Many would do whatever it took to shut down COIL, or me.

After climbing two fences, skirting three houses and two barking dogs, I could go no further. Two blocks behind me, the dark sky was lit by flashing lights. I seemed to be safe at the moment. Next to a mailbox, I plopped down on the curb to rest. Blood matted my scalp above my left ear, and a piece of metal rubbed on the ribs in my right side. If I continued moving without medical attention, my injuries would become worse.

From my pocket, I palmed my phone, but I didn't dial. Whoever had blown up my car had close access to my life, maybe even my phone. If I called someone now, they'd know I was still alive. In a quick motion, I took the phone apart, disabled the power, and shoved it deep into the lawn against the curb.

My wife, Janice, would be in turmoil, along with our blind adopted daughter, Jenna, now ten. It wasn't likely that they'd been attacked as well, but my old contacts in the Agency, or friends from COIL, would see to my family's immediate safety. That was standard procedure. For the moment, I could focus on whoever had tried to kill me.

The death of Roy Turpin was a big loss for me. Not many had known I'd been in contact with the recently paroled ex-convict. After twenty-nine years in prison for murder, he'd been released. For two years, I'd corresponded with him. Since he'd received Christ twelve years earlier, he was open to service for God, once released. I'd been preparing him for a dangerous operation into Iran. That mission was now on hold.

A car drove up the residential street. Gritting my teeth through the pain, I used the nearby mailbox to pull myself to my feet. I didn't want to involve anyone else, but my options were limited. God was obviously watching over me, so holding onto that faith, I waved at the headlights.

The yellow color of the cab was apparent as the car stopped. I climbed into the empty back seat.

"Manhattan," I said. "Tenth Avenue. Chelsea."

I spied the driver's ID. Pakistani. My Urdu was fair, and on any other night, I might have engaged him about his homeland, then directed the conversation toward the purpose of life under God's loving hand. But on this night, I shrunk down in the seat to get out of his sight in the mirror. Surely, he'd already noticed I was hurt and bleeding. I was counting on his cultural custom as a Pakistani to help a man in need without a fuss.

With some effort, I pried off my right shoe where I carried a few folded bills. I offered the driver a fifty-dollar bill, then sat back. That would keep him quiet, I hoped. All I needed was a few hours head start, and whoever was after me would become the prey instead of the hunter.

As we crossed Harlem River, the events of the night perplexed me more and more. Someone had gone to the trouble of strapping a bomb to my car. But they hadn't made sure I was in it when it exploded. Perhaps it had been triggered by the radio or the window? Since picking up Roy Turpin at the train station, I hadn't turned on the radio or opened the windows. Perhaps Roy had done so while I was in the townhouse fetching his new papers.

It hadn't been a rocket or a missile. I'd remained conscious throughout the explosion, but I'd heard no zip or whoosh of a projectile. That meant it was a self-detonating device with a trigger mechanism. For certain, it wasn't the type of device a professional would use, which meant whoever had done this thing had underestimated me and overestimated their bomb. There was no room for estimating in our world, so I was looking for recent enemies, maybe, who wouldn't know better. A novice. A few came to mind.

By the time we reached Chelsea, all my wounds had clotted, but I wasn't anxious to move, which would begin the bleeding again. After thanking the driver, I got out near the High Line rail and walked a block east. It was now after midnight, and the sidewalk was quiet. However, I'd been a spy too long not to pause and search the street for danger. Parked cars crowded the curb. Two men stood in a doorway, smoking a cigarette. There seemed to be no danger. Even if someone knew I was alive, no one could guess I'd come here. No surveillance team would be set up yet.

Entering the front door of a red brick building, I studied the apartment labels. Doctor Mick Rhogtill. Yes, that was the new name I'd given him. I pressed his apartment button three times before he answered.

"Mick, it's Corban." I glanced over my shoulder. No one was in sight. "Buzz me in. It's an emergency."

"Corban who?"

"VES KDO SEM," I said in Slovenian. You know who I am.

The door buzzed and I tugged on the handle. My strength was fading fast, so I was happy to see Mick Rhogtill's shaggy head peek down at me over the third story banister. There was no way I'd be able to climb three flights unassisted.

"You have seen better days," he said in English. After descending the stairs, he carried half my weight over his shoulder. I was a few pounds heavier and past my prime, but Mick Rhogtill was an ex-mercenary, and in apparent excellent condition. "But you have also seen worse. How long has it been, brother?"

"Since you last stitched me up, or since we last talked?" I tried to chuckle, but gasped instead.

"Too long, my friend."

Once inside his apartment, he closed his door softly and braced the door with more security locks than I had on my own home in Queens.

"Let us see what you have done to yourself." Clearing his dining table, he helped me to climb up and lay on my back. With scissors, he removed my bloody clothes, then covered me with an army surplus blanket as he studied my wounds one by one. He prodded my ribs. "This one is the worst. Good thing you did not try to remove this yourself. You could have bled to death or suffocated on a punctured lung. But I will fix you."

He went to work sewing on me. I dozed between sharp pains as he stitched, and the plunking sounds as he dropped shrapnel into a container.

"Plastic and aluminum," he said. "That is all. What was it? Something blue and . . ."

"My car was blue."

"Enough said. Well, I will tell you to stay in bed for two days, no less, but is that really an option?"

I sat up with his help and checked his needlework on my skin.

"How's the couch till morning?" He supported me to a short couch in faded flowery upholstery. "I had to go to somebody, Mick."

"Stay as long as you want and return whenever you need to. I may have saved some blood from seeping out of your flesh, but you rescued me from a life of murder and bloodshed. If we were keeping score, I would say I owed you." He knelt next to the couch. "To keep up appearances, I will go to work as normal. That window opens to the roof, then the fire escape drops to the garage. A silver Buick under another name is parked there. The keys are under the front bumper."

"Thank you, Mick." My eyes began to droop. Had he given me a shot of something? "I'll sort this out in the next day or two."

"What of your wife and daughter?"

"Can you make sure they're safe, Mick? Please use discretion."

"I will make sure of this. No one will know you are here with me. Now I will pray for you, Corban. God knows what is happening, even if we do not . . ." As he prayed in his native tongue, I fell asleep.

†

CHAPTER TWO

I woke around noon the next day. Mick hadn't left me a note or message, which was best since neither of us wanted to leave any sign of my presence if an adversary were to prowl around. But he'd left me a suit of clothes at the table that looked like it would fit me well, and he also left me enough cash for a few days. Mick was a general practitioner who lived meagerly. He had spending money, which would be called on-the-run money in our trade.

In the bathroom, I found a new razor and fashioned a goatee from my two-day growth. Using a beard trimmer, I cut my hair into a longer crewcut, giving my short stature an extra inch in appearance. I needed a shower, but not with the stitches so fresh. Minutes later, I checked myself in the mirror—plaid trousers, blazer, tie, and a white shirt. A thick camel coat and patterned scarf for the fall weather completed my costume. I'd never worn this style of clothing before, as I was a slacks or suit man in the city, and a jeans and flannel man when in the field. The only thing I wore that was my own now were the shoes—used cap-toes that had never been shined. If my problem wasn't soon sorted out, I'd need boots for what lay ahead, but the shoes would do for now.

Mick Rhogtill's Bible was on the kitchen counter. As I munched on two bowls of cereal, I read from Psalm 69. It was a fitting passage for my situation with unknown enemies on every side. My faith remained in God's lovingkindness. The road ahead seemed very daunting at that moment, and though I was tempted to rush ahead to face my suspected foes, I was a Christian now. I'd received Christ nine years earlier, and later left the Agency. My wife and my conscience had urged me to leave behind my blood-shedding ways. Now, I relied on the Lord's counsel. How would I proceed? That, I didn't yet know.

In the sink, I washed the bowl and considered what I'd read. Coincidences are nonexistent for the believer. Thus, I didn't mentally approach my situation as one of loss, but one of gain. Living for Christ didn't end when contrary circumstances seemed to overwhelm. Rather, I had to be aware of what doors might open for God as He guided me ahead.

Of all the people I could call, Chloe Azmaveth was the one I was most tempted to contact. She ran COIL in my absence. Having been a Mossad agent for twelve years, the pretty Syrian-born Jewess handled stress and danger like a veteran warrior. By now, she would've received word that I was dead. No doubt, she'd been one of the first to offer help to my wife and daughter. Even if others like Mick Rhogtill had wanted that privilege, Chloe would insist on the responsibility. My wife Janice would prefer Chloe's safe-keeping as well, rather than faceless government agents asking her questions she didn't know answers to. Chloe and her husband Zvi had become personal friends to us.

Dozens of other contacts in and out of the country came to mind. Only a nitwit would try to kill a veteran agent and not make sure he was dead. Fools! If I'd been the old Corban, I could've called in a couple of domestic strike teams and sorted all this out in hours!

Or could I? Checking my arrogance, I went to the back window that Mick Rhogtill had identified as an escape route. Whoever had made the attempt on my life wouldn't be so careless next time. I had to carefully sort this out or risk offering up my family or myself in the aftermath. The head of the snake had to be located and cut off, and that meant going into operational mode. It meant slipping into my most-practiced and subtle skills, wherein I was most comfortable, though I didn't intend to compromise my Christian standards.

Could it be done? Could I fight alone against the grand enemy I suspected, and win? I had to. And I had to do so quietly. At the first sign of an offensive by me, the trail could disappear, or my loved ones would be targeted. If the enemy discovered I was on to them, they'd panic. Panic meant unpredictable behavior. But I had too many resources to not cause someone panic, even the organization that I suspected for this mess.

Holding my ribs, I climbed out the window and onto the roof. Even if the enemy—and I had a possibility in mind— guessed I was alive, they'd expect me to come for them diplomatically, probably through old CIA channels, like retired Deputy Director William "Chip" Buchanen. Instead, I would do the unexpected. I'd do as I was trained to do, as a spy, as an infiltrator, as an inside man, as a ghost, as a mole. I could wear many masks.

Slowly, I climbed down the three flights of fire escape stairs to the garage. The keys were under the bumper of the silver Buick as Mick Rhogtill had said, and for just a moment, I froze before climbing into the car. My enemy could be anywhere, be anyone. Any car could contain a bomb. Any phone could be traced. Any person could be an assassin. With an infinite degree of possibilities, I was seemingly defenseless. Thus, I climbed into the driver's seat with a scoff at myself. The safest place to be was always in God's will, no matter the situation. Instead of praying for no more bombs, or perfect safety, I prayed right then that I'd be bold and wise enough to do whatever He directed me to do.

From Chelsea Avenue, I drove north on Broadway and looked up to my right when I reached Times Square. The COIL offices were up there, mostly just Chloe Azmaveth and caseworkers behind plated glass. With one phone call, they could summon any of nine COIL special ops teams— whichever weren't already deployed around the world. Their operative status knew no borders, much like my own authority even outside the CIA now. I'd built too many covers, recruited too many active agents, and retired too many exposed assets for the Agency to merely forget about me. Some of my aliases were still so important that I'd made minor concessions to accommodate Agency requests. The payoff was the liberty to run COIL unrestrained.

And that's where my mind journeyed as I drove through the Upper West Side. I still had no plan exactly. The driving helped me to think, and wherever I did end up, my winding route wouldn't lead back to my trusted Slovenian doctor in Chelsea.

Recently, a branch of Homeland Security had been initialized, called the Tactical anti-Terrorist Division, or the T.a.T.D. The TaTD had made a request to the Agency that a specific Middle Eastern alias be surrendered to them to use at whim and will. The alias was Muhammad ibn Affal, an Egyptian arms dealer. It was my alias and a cover I'd built during my Agency days, and continued to use for COIL. Through Muhammad ibn Affal, I'd gotten into Middle Eastern countries where no one else could go. I'd smuggled Bibles, collected intel, and saved lives. For men to know this and yet demand that I give them the alias—was a crime against Christ Himself. I couldn't hand over the cover.

To my knowledge, the TaTD hadn't known initially who was behind the Muhammad ibn Affal alias. When the first request had reached my eyes, I filed a counter-request, reminding the CIA that they still used the alias themselves periodically, through me, officially and unofficially, depending on the operation. The alias couldn't be shared. It could compromise the lives of hundreds that Muhammad ibn Affal had secured in the past. My negative response had alerted the TaTD of me, the holder of the alias.

The Agency had received one more communication from the TaTD after that, which they'd passed on to me. The TaTD director, four-star General Logan Forglade, was furious that his request had been denied. He vowed to pursue it until he was given full rights to it, as his own superiors assigned him to do. Resources were to be shared, he argued, and that alias was needed for purposes of national security.

I'd believed the general's request was important, but I hadn't considered his threat genuine, until recently. He now knew who owned the alias—me, a retired agent pushing sixty. Getting intel out of the Middle East was as urgent as ever, and a solid alias—over twenty-years-old—could make or break an operation. But my work now with COIL, regardless of my sideline with the CIA, took precedence over any war efforts the general intended to pursue through that identity.

Driving clockwise around Central Park, a plan took shape in my mind. The TaTD wouldn't expect a full-frontal infiltration into their offices. To them, I'd died in the car. They wouldn't know it wasn't me for another few days. DNA tests took time. And besides, they had my identification from the car—my car. The assumption would be that I had died. The younger agents now with the TaTD had never seen me. Even five years earlier when I was part of the Agency, I was usually deployed overseas. Mingling with interagency spooks wasn't my pastime. No one would know my face except those directly related to the bombing in the Bronx. That would be a very small number of people. Two or three, tops. I knew this because, in my darkest years, I'd been among that small number of people who knew and made such ultimate decisions.

Unless I was mistaken, the TaTD had left the front door open for me, and I was going in. My alias and the people it sheltered couldn't be abandoned!

✝

CHAPTER THREE

In south Harlem, I pulled the car to the curb and paid a street vendor for a newspaper. On page seven, there were three sentences about a car fire in the Bronx the night before. It said a gang had targeted the wrong vehicle by mistake and killed a New Yorker, name not released.

So it began. The spin-doctors—probably deployed by TaTD—were hard at work. They surely believed their mission had been successful. Thus, I confirmed that it was indeed a rogue division trying to kill me. If I didn't act responsibly and definitively, they would use my alias to the point that it would put families around the world in danger—and close doors no one else could open for years, if ever. Muhammad ibn Affal needed to be protected. But how?

I had one safe house in the city, and though I didn't want to visit my old haunts, I couldn't avoid East 72nd Street, the Upper East Side. It was an apartment in a nine-story building that faced the Queensboro Bridge. The apartment door lock, like the whole building, was digitalized, and I punched the code into the keypad. Besides me, only one other man knew the lock combination—Nathan Isaacson, one of my first operatives recruited into COIL. And since he was on an overseas mission in Zalzuna, I'd be undisturbed.

Without touching anything for a few minutes, I walked around on the wood floors of the spacious rooms. Was anything out of the ordinary here? Except for the dust, it was unchanged.

Nathan Isaacson's clothes were hanging in the bedroom. He was a taller man than me, but with a little needlework, I could make his pants work. After removing his things from the closet, I tapped the back wall, searching for a nearly indiscernible crease in the drywall. I pressed hard until a panel clicked, then I stooped low to crawl through a narrow passage.

The passage opened into a large bedroom, this one facing south. A small adjoining bathroom completed the hidden area. One wall was covered with COIL non-lethal weaponry. There were also two trunks of COIL and Agency gadgets, some of which I'd developed myself. The secret room could easily become my refuge for months, but I wouldn't use it yet, not unless I was forced to. It would be my fallback apartment, if I were too severely wounded to go elsewhere, or too exposed to live anywhere else. The armaments, however, were another matter. I needed equipment for what lay ahead.

From the first trunk, I filled a backpack with all the necessary items I imagined I'd possibly need. Tech and weapons. In New York City, I needed to remain incognito, so I didn't take any of the carbines or machine pistols off the wall. Two months earlier, I'd added a few cell phones to the second trunk. I took two of those now.

Closing up the hidden bedroom, I replaced all the closet items, with the exception of one suit, complete with black jacket, trousers, a polka dot tie, and a white shirt. The backpack of gear and clothes, along with a sleeping bag, a New Testament Bible, and twenty TV-dinners from the freezer, all fit into one duffel bag.

From 72nd Street, I drove five blocks south and parked in the underground parking lot of a failed office-building project—perfect for squatters but a good place for me to lay low. I shouldered the duffel bag and trudged up the stairs from the parking garage to the lobby, which was lit by one lamp at the desk.

Various failed building projects could be found in any big city, from San Francisco to New York City, but not all were completely abandoned. Many, like this one, were manned by a supervisor, hired by the owner, until investors helped to complete the construction. The supervisors often rented space to illegals, or the homeless, all subject to heartless eviction at any moment. But I was willing to take my chances.

An unshaved, dark-haired man in a stained tank top sat at the desk. What may have been a crimson uniform blazer that once represented his security status was now draped across his desk.

"I want to rent a room," I said loudly in my best Russian accent. Glancing about, I noticed a plain young woman enter the building through the street access. She carried an infant in one arm and a trash bag in the other. The trash bag, I guessed, contained her possessions. "How much for one room?"

"Last room. Twenty bucks a week." He scribbled on a notepad. "Apartment 1722. Pay first. I catch you on any other floor, I deal with you personally. Get it?"

Digging into my pocket, I pulled out the cash that Mick Rhogtill had left me. The woman elbowed me aside to push up to the desk.

"Not the last room, Wilbur!" she said. "You promised me!"

"Hey, cash is king, princess. He can pay now. You got twenty?"

The young woman, no older than twenty years, with pale skin and black, greasy hair, glared at me. The baby appeared to be sleeping, bundled in a cotton-white blanket—white enough for me to see that she cared more for her baby than for herself.

"I got half. I'll get you the rest tomorrow." She kneed the desk. "Come on, Wilbur! I can't sleep on the street again!"

"You've slept on the street before. None of the others have trouble raising money. The brat shouldn't stop you from raising money the usual way."

"We will share." I slammed my bill on the desk. This was the type of moment I'd prayed I would recognize. My enemies might be looking for a washed-up single man, but not a Russian grandfather with a girl and a baby. And regardless of my familiarity with strife and struggle, I was a family man, and actually preferred the company of others.

"Three in one room?" Wilbur had greed in his eyes. "Thirty dollars total. One week for the happy family."

The young mother took a step back, eyeing me cautiously.

"It is good," I said, my accent extra rich. "I am Russian."

That was something my COIL friend, Fost Ivanovich, would've said, had he been in my place—as if the mere fact that he was Russian meant he was honorable.

Instead of waiting for the young woman's refusal or the offer of her own hard-earned money, I slammed down another ten.

"Good! Apartment 1722!"

With my transaction complete, I went to the stairs. Seventeen flights? In my condition? As I was still gazing up at the zigzag structure where I-beams remained unpainted, the woman brushed past me and started up.

I contemplated taking my duffel bag contents up in intervals, but it wasn't wise in that environment. Squatters weren't known for protecting the rightful property of others. It was true I was stepping into a gray area where legal and illegal merged. However, I was a man who'd worked for the government in various capacities, accomplishing jobs by whatever means necessary. Where a solid line existed for some, a dotted line existed for me, and my conscience was clear. To protect others, remaining off the radar in this way was the best route for now.

By the fifth flight, I felt a couple stitches stretched to their max. Though I probably didn't look it that day, I was healthy. Just a few months earlier, I'd jogged with a full pack across a Sudanese desert to ensure that a refugee camp received their provisions.

"Are you having a heart attack?" the young woman's voice called from many flights above. "Do you want me to get someone for you?"

"No, no." I waved her on without looking up. "I am Russian!"

It took me an hour of stopping and starting to get to the seventeenth floor. One stitch did tear from my calf, but it was nothing a little Superglue wouldn't fix.

Entering apartment 1722, I found an actual living area and not an office suite at all. It had one room, divided by a counter to house a spacious kitchenette. The woman exited the bathroom as I leaned against the wall. She'd washed her face, making her pale skin now blushing-red.

"Water and plumbing, but no power," she said. Since I'd taken so long to arrive, she'd claimed one corner of the empty carpeted room closest to a sliding glass door that accessed a balcony. "We'll take this side, and you take that side."

"Yes, it is good." I closed the apartment door. It had no lock, but where the handle should've been, the woman had stuffed a rag into the hole to keep out peeping eyes.

After setting my bag on the floor against the opposite wall, I went to the tall glass door. There were no shades, but the runners along the ceiling would work well to hang a curtain or blanket. It was the fall season and was certain to grow dark early. Without power, we'd have only the lights of the city to light the room. I made a mental list of items we'd need to turn our apartment into a home, however briefly for me.

The baby started to cry, but the noise didn't bother me since I'd slept through detonating ordnance in war zones more times than I could remember. It was only three in the afternoon, but I was exhausted. Without unpacking, I used my camel coat as a pillow to lie on my back. I prayed for wisdom in how to proceed. Much had to be done for my living quarters, and much more to clear my name. For my own cover, I'd taken on two more lives, potentially placing them in more danger; but with me, they were probably safer than sleeping on the street.

Tonight, I decided, I'd begin to hunt. I fell asleep to the baby's cries, missing my own family.

†

CHAPTER FOUR

Gently, I pressed a black pair of bushy eyebrows over my brown ones. From the backpack of gear, I used quick-color gel to shape my hair in a one-inch spike. My goatee was already growing in thick and dark. Janice preferred me clean-shaven, but I figured she'd understand if I just showed up alive.

I furrowed my fake brows, creating a glare that even I didn't recognize in the apartment 1722 bathroom mirror. For many years, I'd admired God's faithful servants who faced death with courage. Socrates once philosophized that the afterlife was affirmed by the boldness with which men faced death in battle. Well, I believed in the afterlife, but I wasn't feeling too bold. In truth, I was questioning my tactics.

Chloe, as my right hand at COIL, had often criticized me for recklessly handling catastrophes all alone when she and others could burden some of the headaches. Was I just being stubborn?

A plan had formulated in my head to infiltrate the TaTD and get close to General Logan Forglade. It was an old scheme we'd used in East Berlin to infiltrate the Foreign Intelligence Service—a bold-faced bluff no one would expect, I hoped. Could it be done in Washington or New York? The new generation of clandestine personnel wouldn't remember our Cold War methods; they weren't even alive then. Those undocumented stunts could be my ticket.

Exiting the bathroom, I went to my duffel bag. The young woman hovered protectively over her sleeping child, and glared at me as if she were seeing a demon. My disguise was surely frightening her, but I couldn't risk sharing the truth with her. Instead, I set all of my frozen TV dinners on the floor between our two sides of the room.

"These will stay frozen while stacked," I said in my Russian accent. "Eat what you want. Stay away from my bag. You understand?"

She glanced at my duffel and nodded. I pocketed and sleeved various tools of my trade and walked to the door.

"I'll be back in the morning."

Seventeen flights later, I found the building lobby empty and Wilbur no longer at his post. Several misplaced hip-hop artists had been on the stairs, but they'd left me alone. The door to the garage locked behind me when I passed through. I paused to examine the lock. If I needed to get back inside during Wilbur's off hours, I could manage the it.

Instead of driving, I walked down First Avenue. I was in my element—nighttime with a disguise on my face. And best of all, no one knew I was alive.

At the end of an alley, I bought two more cell phones from a street vendor in a cheap suit. They were probably hot phones, but I needed them for whatever was to come.

In a twenty-four-hour Internet cafe, I logged into an Isle of Man bank account and dispersed enough funds around the world to start a new life if I had to. The money had been seized in years past during arrests or deaths on behalf of one government or another. Usually, such accounts were confiscated by the country of record, but some operations were too sensitive for the US to claim even one cent. Such accounts helped me finance COIL, and to give new lives to people who needed to flee from their pasts. One of those people was Mick Rhogtill. I prayed he'd looked in on my family. It would be unwise for the two of us to communicate further.

After visits to a dozen ATM machines, I had enough cash on me to conduct a little business. I took a taxi up to Harlem and started street shopping. Right on the street, I made my needs known, and it came to me, item by item, outside Marcus Garvey Park—a solar generator for five hundred dollars, two hundred feet of nylon rope for sixty dollars, candles, blankets, propane stove . . . By three o'clock in the morning, my pile of gear was laid out on a tarp at my feet. One hoodlum still lingered nearby. He'd been particularly resourceful in locating several items.

"One last job for you, Terry." I gave him a piece of paper and a fifty-dollar bill, interrupting his count of other bills I'd already given him. "Here's cab fare. All this stuff should fit in the trunk and back seat. I need everything delivered to this address, the underground garage. Wait one hour for me there."

"What's in it for me?" He was a hustler. There was a chance he'd simply resell my stuff and I'd never see him again.

"Five Benjamins."

"It's your money." He shook his head as if I were insane, and started to bundle the items in the tarp. The generator was by far the bulkiest item, but all of it weighed probably no more than one hundred and fifty pounds, I figured.

I hadn't walked through Marcus Garvey Park for years, and since I hoped to use its sparse trees and scattered bedrock terrain as a meeting place later that day, I decided to scout the area. The pathways were empty, though an occasional pile of clothing here and there identified a homeless person lying off the path against boulders or under bushes.

To get close to General Forglade, I'd have to go over his head for the bluff I had in mind. That meant I had to get close to New York Senator Nettleton, the man who held the purse strings to everything from airport security to the Coast Guard. This chairman of the Subcommittee for Domestic Oversight was a powerful man, levels above whoever had carried out the TaTD attack on me. The senator's name was fresh on my mind since Senator Nettleton had recently replaced the late Senator Shannon Griffin as chairman four months earlier. Everyone knew who held the money.

Getting close to Senator Nettleton would be difficult to do quickly as myself, and next to impossible as an anonymous and supposedly deceased ex-spook. But God managed the impossible every day, so I anticipated His guidance and merely looked ahead.

In the distance, I saw a man in a business suit sitting on a park bench. As I drew closer, though, I could tell the man had a strange stare off to the side, and he didn't look at me as I approached. Perhaps he was a husband who'd blown his check on booze, and was too ashamed to go home to face his wife. Or maybe he was a Wall Street broker contemplating suicide after an unsettling day on the trading floor.

These hypotheticals reminded me that my own problems weren't so terrible, and that God had equipped me with the tools from His Word to manage through this life. But some lacked the faith or skills, and I was there in that park on that dark morning for a reason. I had an hour before I was to meet Terry downtown, so I stopped at the bench.

"Hard to imagine," I said in my natural voice, "that millions of people live all around us. How peaceful this spot is, huh?"

I sighed as I sat down beside him. From the corner of my eye, I saw the wind ruffle his hair. The man had a one-hundred-dollar haircut, and his navy suit was nothing cheap, either.

Leaning forward, I noticed even in the reddish glow of lights through the fall trees, that his cheeks were deathly gray. And then I realized . . .

Feeling a little foolish, I checked the pathway for walkers. Someone could come over the knoll any second and see me with the dead man. I didn't need that trouble!

Rising, I checked the bike path again. Maybe I needed to look at this as an opportunity.

Before I could argue against my impulse, I once again strained against my stitches as I drew the dead man over my shoulder and carried him into the trees. I dropped him gently into the leaves and searched his pockets for a wallet. Holding his ID up to a sliver of park light, I saw his name was Tom Channing. Fifty-seven. Business cards for an upholstery shop in Morningside Heights. And faded pictures of a wife and two grown boys.

My mind reeled at the possibilities. It really was just like Berlin all over again when the US had used a bluff to develop a cover. This man had evidently died from a heart attack, from the way his left hand was clutching his chest. With the right spin, I realized Tom Channing could be my ticket into Senator Nettleton's good graces. I was trained for this moment.

It was the second time in as many days that I'd hoped a dead man could provide me some advantage. First, parolee Roy Turpin, and now this man, Tom Channing.

I dialed one of my disposable phones before I over-analyzed the situation. After twenty minutes and three phone numbers, I finally heard a human voice on the line.

"My name is Peter Mitchell," I said quickly, as if in a panic. "This is an emergency for Senator Nettleton. Connect me, quickly! Please!"

This time, I was transferred, and a sleepy-sounding man answered after two rings.

"This is Chang."

"Chang? Who's Chang? I asked for the senator! This is an emergency!"

"Easy, easy! I'm Senator Nettleton's assistant and advisor. No one gets to him except through me. Now, what's going on?"

"My name is Peter Mitchell with the Weltersand Operation."

"The what?"

"The Weltersand Operation. Come on! For four months, I've been hanging out here, waiting for you guys to make contact!" I coughed into the mouthpiece. "Now they've started to kill us off. They got Tom earlier tonight. I'm standing over his body right now! And it all points back to the senator!"

"Whoa! You have a body there? Where are you exactly?"

"Marcus Garvey Park, near the—"

"Don't say another word. I'll be there in twenty."

Shutting off the phone, I knew that a dead body would always get a politician's attention. I had twenty minutes to fine-tune my plan—forty minutes before I had to meet Terry for my gear. It was going to be a busy night.

✝

CHAPTER FIVE

I waited on the bike path in Marcus Garvey Park and prayed for guidance as men in overalls and some in suits approached me from various angles. Three of the five who were advancing in the early morning darkness had drawn firearms, though they had them aimed at the ground.

One of the lead men was a short Asian—probably Chang, Senator Nettleton's personal assistant. During the twenty-minute wait, I'd looked up Rod Chang in the CIA's database. I didn't need a back door into their servers to access intel; I had only to recall past agents' passwords or old covers of mine that had yet to be deactivated. Sometimes mismanagement could be an asset.

With a subtle nod, I let Chang know that I was indeed waiting for him. Understanding, he approached me directly as his four men established a perimeter. Chang had been a research analyst for the CIA's subversive logistics division. He was no fool.

"Mitchell?" he asked. As I had researched him, he'd surely done the same with the name I'd given him. This Peter Mitchell was an ex-Green Beret from Alabama. I'd used the cover off and on for twenty years.

"That's right." I glanced over my shoulder. "Sorry if I seem skittish. That's two of our guys dead inside a week. I haven't showered in two days; been too afraid to hole up anywhere."

"You'd better explain yourself, Mitchell. I know who you are. Years ago, you trained down in Birmingham with the 21st. Take your time and tell me what's happened."

"Actually, it was the 20th in Birmingham," I corrected, appreciating the test. "Senator Griffin had my boys and me tracking personnel under an op called Weltersand. Weltersand was initiated to investigate the Tactical anti-Terrorist Division. The senator had evidence that the Division had been compromised."

"That's General Forglade's baby." Chang turned his head and I followed his gaze to see two more men emerge from the trees. One was pushing a wheelbarrow. "You said something about a body?"

"This way." I led him and his men off the path to where I'd left the dead man. "Senator Griffin said if I couldn't get hold of him, I could trust Senator Nettleton. When Griffin died and you guys never contacted me, I realized Nettleton's office might not know how to contact the Weltersand operators."

We reached the body. Chang knelt and studied Tom Channing's face and position.

"I'm not familiar with Weltersand," Chang said, "but Griffin and Senator Nettleton were friends. This guy was one of ours? Expensive suit."

"His name was Tom Channing." I knelt next to Chang, shoulder to shoulder. His men remained paces away, keeping the area secure. "His cover was an upholstery shop in Morningside Heights. He had a wife and two grown kids. We were hiding in plain sight, but when Senator Griffin died, we all got jumpy. Our investigation into the TaTD continued, but my daily activity reports were no longer logged by a handler. That stopped almost four months ago."

"Get me copies of those DAR's," Chang said.

"We've been burned." I shook my head. "My network's shattered. Everything we had was in Tom's upholstery shop, or maybe he had it on him tonight. He told me he needed to clean out, just to protect his family. They knew nothing, of course."

Chang searched Tom Channing's body until he found the wallet I'd replaced. He studied the ID then pocketed the man's wallet.

"Looks like a heart attack."

"Yeah, looks like it. My guess is ricin." I touched Tom Channing's cold cheek. "Whatever it was, it's probably untraceable. Our rendezvous was for midnight, but he's been dead for hours."

We stood and backed away as Chang's men in overalls loaded the body into the wheelbarrow, covered it with leaves, and wheeled it away. It was a much more efficient cleaning crew than I'd anticipated. Chang and I walked slowly along the paved path past the bedrock.

"You said two deaths in a week. Who's the other?"

"Just a contact we had. Corban Dowler. Died in a car bomb in the Bronx two nights ago."

Stopping, Chang stared at me.

"There's been a lot of buzz about that. Dowler was a CIA man. One of the best, it's said." He bit his lip and browsed the park. "A lot of details will be missing about his life if I dig into his past. I should know because I was with the Agency at the end of Dowler's career."

"Well, we know the TaTD was behind these deaths," I said. "Tom Channing was just a minor asset for the investigation into the Division, but Dowler was no slouch."

"The TaTD recently petitioned for next year's budget. It's on Senator Nettleton's desk right now. He'll want to know everything you have on this investigation—Operation Weltersand." Chang offered me a business card. "Extension 421. Memorize it. You wire me everything you have by noon. Got it? Even if it's been stolen and you have to spew it from memory. Unless I need to bring you in to debrief you?"

"I'll probably be safer in the shadows for now." We shook hands. "If General Forglade knows you're onto him for these deaths, he'll do whatever he can to protect himself."

"Let him try," Chang said. "There's nothing else important on my desk until this TaTD issue is sorted out, but I need to hear from you later today. I can requisition Dowler's body, but your intel can link this all together. We'll burn down General Forglade's little empire if we need to, but I want everything verified first."

"You'll get everything I've got by noon. If I do need to come in officially, you might think about assigning me as a Department of Defense agent. I'll be in touch," I said, then turned and walked away. I didn't have to look back to know that I was being followed.

...✝...

By the time I lost my tails by swapping taxis throughout Manhattan, I was thirty minutes late to meet Terry in the underground garage. It was four-thirty in the morning when I walked up to Terry and my tarp of gear. However, Terry wasn't alone.

"Terry, I appreciate you waiting." I drew out a wad of cash and counted the bills in the view of four other thugs, presumably Terry's friends from Harlem. "Promised you another five hundred, right?"

"It was more trouble than that." Terry stepped around the gear and glanced at his pals, who began to surround me. "We'll need everything you've got on you."

"Everything I have on me?" I chuckled, playing the naive suburbanite until the real me was required. With an unsuspecting itch to my left elbow, I dislodged a pen-shaped device from my forearm under the sleeve, which then slipped into my palm. "If you need more cash for food or rent, I'm sure we can work something out."

"Well, it's been worked out already. Hand it over."

I didn't see any weapons. They probably didn't want my blood on their hands, but I wasn't taking any chances in the isolated garage.

A youth in a hoodie on my right reached for me first. I grabbed his arm and roughly drew him stumbling across in front of me. As he passed, I poked him once in the back through his clothes with the tranquilizer.

Two came at me at once, from the back and front. I kicked blindly at the one behind to buy time, then parried a punch from Terry. The pen jabbed into his forearm, then I let him go. The first man to receive a drop of neuro-inhibitor into his bloodstream was seizing on the ground, but the others were blinded by adrenalin, seeing only me in their tunnel vision.

Terry fell, and I went on the offensive. One man backed away, but I caught his jacket and pricked his neck. Before I could face the last two, a blow glanced off my left shoulder. The camel coat absorbed most of the impact, but I was still bruised to the bone. While he frantically slapped and jabbed at my face, I stepped closer and kneed him in the side. The pen poked him in the shoulder as he twisted away.

The last man, with fear on his face, held a knife leveled at my gut.

"Your friends aren't dead." I retracted the needle tip of my pen, then stowed the weapon up my sleeve again. "I'll give you one hundred dollars for that buck knife, and you can walk away. Your friends'll be awake in twenty minutes."

He shifted his feet, his eyes on my handful of twenties.

"Terry said you'd be easy money."

"Nothing is free, buddy. Cash for your knife. Drop it."

"Maybe you'll . . . do something to me." He gripped and re-gripped his blade.

"I'm a Christian, you understand? Even though you have assaulted me, I'm willing to forgive and help you. Look, I'm offering you money for your weapon. This is a crossroads for you. You and your boys can take this opportunity to undergo some changes. The next guy you try to rob may not be so gracious."

"Yeah." Hesitantly, he set the knife on the concrete. I handed him the money. He gave one final look at his friends, then ran away.

Checking my watch, I set the timer for fifteen minutes, when the first of the thugs would start waking up. I needed to be out of sight—with my gear. My car was parked a few spaces away, but that was no hiding place. Somehow, I needed to get upstairs to the seventeenth floor apartment, with over one hundred pounds of gear.

✝

CHAPTER SIX

"One . . . two . . . one . . . two," I said in cadence. "Good, Ruth. Steady. One . . . two . . ."

My roommate's name was Ruth Holland. With the promise of household provisions, she'd agreed to help get the gear upstairs. Using my nylon rope, I'd hooked the tarp of gear to the other end, and we were hauling it a draw at a time up the side of the building to our balcony.

"Almost there," she said through clenched teeth. Since I was heavier, her one-hundred-and-ten-pound frame was in the front and I anchored the line. "There! We got it!"

A moment later, I dragged the bundle over the balcony railing and dropped it onto the floor. Almost greedily, Ruth unwrapped the tarp to see what goods I'd brought us.

"This way, Wilbur won't know what we have." She laughed. "He'd probably charge us more if he knew you had money for— Whoa!"

I slid the solar generator aside.

"Let this charge for a few hours here on the balcony, then we'll have electricity. Here are some candles, a cooler for our food, more blankets, and other things."

"Can I . . . ?" She looked up at me, her brown eyes watering. "Can I use some of this stuff?"

"Anything you want, Ruth. It is for you and Jenny. How about this: you are in charge of everything. Situate it, then tell me what else we might need before I go out next time."

By the time I'd set up the generator and battery pack on the balcony, the sun was above the East River. Though I was exhausted, and feeling my bruises and wounds, I'd committed myself to Chang's investigation into General Forglade. I sat against the wall on my side of the room as Ruth fussed over the provisions. Using the keypad on the cell phone from the safe house, I typed a lengthy report to Chang.

The body of Tom Channing had created an opening for my bluff with Chang. A dead body and a story—mixed with shreds of truth—had a way of convincing people to believe. Yes, I'd bluffed Chang and Senator Nettleton's office like a fisherman baited a hook, but it wasn't all bluff. Already, General Forglade and the TaTD might be feeling the heat. Though the death of Tom Channing would never be decisively tied to the TaTD, with people poking around my own supposed death, my enemies would certainly be getting concerned.

With a careful eye, Chang could've even discovered by then that I was indeed Corban Dowler, if he'd compared my old service photo with that of my cover identity, Peter Mitchell. Chang had been the only one in the park close enough to see my features. Even then, my black, spiked hair, bushy, dark eyebrows, and goatee might've thrown him off. It didn't matter now. The investigation was rolling. If Chang did figure out who I really was, he'd spoken highly of

Corban Dowler, the deceased ex-agent. I doubted he'd blame me for my improv.

"Look, honey!" Ruth juggled a bottle in front of the wide-eyed baby. "Shampoo! You get a real bath! Yes, you do!"

I connected to three international proxy servers to send my report to Chang. The text detailed General Forglade's request to use the alias, Muhammad ibn Affal. When the general had been denied access to use it for whatever operation he was working on, he'd retaliated by targeting the possessor of the alias, the ex-agent named Corban Dowler. These were serious accusations against a general.

My moves thus far had been risky, but the next one would be even more precarious. Nothing, I imagined, would be more destabilizing to my enemies than for them to see their plans fall apart without understanding why.

Since I guessed their whole plan had been to use the Muhammad ibn Affal identity, I needed to stop them before irreparable damage was done to that cover. Lives and livelihoods depended on it—people whom General Forglade had so casually dismissed—but I wouldn't let those lives go so easily.

The following day, I strategized in earnest. I counted three primary moves I had to make before I could surface safely and rejoin my family. First, I had to unsettle the TaTD. If I could successfully throw them a curveball without announcing the fact that I was still alive, they would halt all operations to discern what was happening. That would buy me time, as well as create radio chatter, to which Chang in Nettleton's office could eavesdrop.

Second, I needed hard evidence to go with the circumstantial evidence I already had. Technically, I was just a civilian now. My word against a four-star general—and whomever he was working for or with—wouldn't amount to much without certain evidence of the plan to assassinate me for my alias. Obtaining that evidence would be dangerous because I'd have to prowl into the lion's den itself, but I'd been using disguises for most of my professional life. Lord willing, I wouldn't be recognized.

And third, I had to expose myself to Senator Nettleton's office once and for all, if they hadn't learned of my true status beforehand.

Each step was increasingly more risky since I didn't know where General Forglade had spies, or even how loyal Chang was to Senator Nettleton. A misstep could mean death for me, for which I was prepared, but more critically, it could mean death for my wife and daughter, for which I wasn't prepared.

"Dinner, Fost." Ruth offered a plate to me, which I gratefully accepted. She'd heated two TV dinners over the propane grill. On my side of the room, she sat cross-legged facing me. "Jenny's finally sleeping. Sorry for her crying so much."

"It is no bother," I said, still playing the Russian bit. I'd introduced myself as Fost, borrowing my Moscow friend's name for a while, which he'd neither know about nor care. No doubt, he'd used mine over the years as well. "Tomorrow I will leave for two days. I have seen the type of people who live here on the other floors of this building. You will be safe?"

"I have mace." She shrugged. "It's not as dangerous here as it was on the streets. If we had a door lock—"

"Good. I will get one tonight."

"Fost, I'm so grateful to you. Most of the people I meet are ugly inside."

"It is a matter of the heart." I eyed her cautiously over my plate. "You know this. . . . Jesus?"

"Jesus?" She stopped eating. "You mean the Christmas Jesus?"

"Yes. What He did for us is important to know. None of us is worthy. He came and died for the sins of mankind."

"Will Jesus give me back my home, my job, and an honest man?" Ruth scoffed and continued eating.

"The message of Jesus is why I am nice to you. You seemed surprised at my sincerity. I tell you why."

"This is America, Fost. Jesus is just a name a lot of rich people use to put on fake smiles and drive nice cars on Sunday. It's not real."

"True, some people are not real, but the gift from Jesus is real." I set my plate down. "How much money do you have?"

"Why?" Her eyes narrowed. "Ten dollars. You already know that."

"The same ten dollars? You have no more than that?"

"No. So?"

"But you have been eating, drinking, and feeding Jenny in peace? Sleeping, showering, and reading your romance novels in safety?"

"Yeah, until I get . . ."

"You have not spent a dime, and you have not been sleeping on the sidewalk. And you do not see God's hand in your daughter's life? Is this real?"

"It was you who helped us, not God."

"No." I shook my head. "You cannot be that foolish to think it is coincidence that you and I came to Wilbur's desk that night at the same time. God does not promise in the Bible to give you a wonderful life, but He does promise to forgive your sins, if you come to Him. Because He forgave mine, I am a man without burdens; I am willing to help others because I am free in my heart. Only God can forgive sins. Right now, I am without a home. I run for my life and hide from enemies. But I am innocent before God and I believe He cares for me. This is why I share with you. So, you see why I say you are foolish to say it is not God who helps you. Do not thank me. Thank God."

Her eyes focused on her plate for a few seconds, then she silently stood and returned to her side of the room. What I'd said had stung her, but she needed to be stung. A lot of people needed to be stung. I would care for her regardless. God had paired us together. And I wouldn't neglect my responsibility to lead her in the way of the cross.

✝

CHAPTER SEVEN

Twenty-four hours later, I stepped off a plane in Paris. After leaving the airport, I called a man in Le Mans, a contact who had disguises for sale. I bought a beard, nose, and chin from him, paying him well for his silence, as was customary in his business. In a public restroom, I applied the disguise as I had a hundred-plus times before. From my carry-on, I completed the facade with a pair of thick-rimmed glasses.

Once again, I was Muhammad ibn Affal, and I rented a car under his name.

Back at the airport, I walked up to a terminal gate and bought a ticket to Alexandria, which was rumored to be Muhammad ibn Affal's smuggling grounds. By the look on the attendant's face when she typed in the name given on my passport, her computer alerted her to call the authorities. As Muhammad ibn Affal, I'd been on a no-fly list for over twelve years. Usually, with that disguise, I required private transportation.

"Comment-vous applez voux?" she asked. What is your name?

"Savez-vous bien." I frowned. You know well who I am. "Je m'appelle Muhammad ibn Affal."

"Ah. Je suis detrompe." She smiled and dismissed her faked misunderstanding with a hand wave. "Vous n'avez rien oublie?"

"No," I answered. I'd forgotten nothing. Like the expert she was, she stalled as long as she dared, waiting for security personnel to arrive and arrest the wanted man, Muhammad ibn Affal. "Je t'attendrai la."

Gesturing to a row of chairs, I implied that I'd wait there for the call to board. Instead, I kept moving down the corridor, past dozens of ceiling cameras, and out the exit doors.

On the Right Bank, I dumped my rental car and sat on a bench with the Bastille in sight. With razor, needle, and thread, I sewed my Muhammad ibn Affal disguise and identity into my clothing. At that moment, I imagined digital memos being sent worldwide. Muhammad ibn Affal had been seen in Paris. Normally, I confined the identity to locales where the smuggler was much more welcome—the Middle East, Africa, and occasionally parts of Asia.

Next, I would surface in Athens. Again, I'd walk casually before cameras, attempt to buy passage elsewhere, then depart mysteriously. Then, I'd go to Berlin for my final stop. Any more flaunting than that would be asking for trouble.

The first stage of my plan—to unsettle the TaTD regarding my alias—was well under way. Whatever operation they had planned for my identity would surely come to a screeching halt. Their plans couldn't undergo scrutiny if someone they thought they controlled had been seen in Paris, Athens, and Berlin. It would certainly cause them to question my death.

I yearned to know what their plans had been, which was the second stage of my plan—if I survived Athens and Berlin!

...✝...

After two days, I was finally back in New York City. I picked the lock to my squatter building and ascended the stairs. A number of homeless teens were camped out on a couple of the landings, but Wilbur had done relatively well otherwise at keeping the place on the clean side. The lack of electricity discouraged most stereos from blaring and thumping, but a few in the building could be heard, probably powered by generators like we had in our apartment. Buying batteries all the time would be cost prohibitive for most.

Anticipating a shower and a full night's sleep, I felt God urging me instead to forego that comfort for a few more minutes. I passed the door to floor seventeen and continued up to the roof, four stories higher.

The cold wind tore through the city at that elevation, but still, a party of drunks was gathered on one corner of the roof. Avoiding them, I went to the north railing.

Though I was used to wearing disguises, applying and tearing off the adhesive from my eyebrows and cheeks had left my skin raw, and my eyebrows plucked thin. The cool wind felt soothing to my face.

At that moment, the death of Roy Turpin weighed on my heart. During my flights over the Atlantic and around Europe, I'd been too consumed with my tactics to consider the life that had been taken because of me. Roy Turpin had spent twenty-nine years in prison. Three days after his release, when his new life for Christ in the free world was to begin, he'd been killed. Meant to be God's vessel, he was now a corpse because of enemies who wanted me dead.

I knew better than to blame myself, for Satan and his cohorts were active. Rather, I was saddened that Roy Turpin had anticipated working for the Lord, yet he'd been taken before he could exercise his newfound faith outside the prison walls.

But, it was part of the journey of a believer. Persecution came in many forms. This reminded me that though I would continue to serve God even in hiding, my end goal wasn't only to return to my family, but also to my work with COIL, wherein my tradecraft could be employed to further the gospel of Christ.

For nearly a week, I'd been managing my emotions, but I was near snapping under the pressure when it came to my family. It was too dangerous to call Chloe or contact Mick Rhogtill again. That meant I had to trust God with my anxiety. Was Jenna safe? Was Janice worried? Had the authorities questioned them? What I couldn't know, I had to leave in my Lord's hands.

After twenty minutes of prayer, I returned to the stairwell and descended to floor seventeen. I heard a child's wild crying and wailing long before I reached our apartment. The sound was coming from next door. Since it was after midnight, I imagined the whole floor was furious over the noise. But it was the price of an illegal residence.

To my surprise, Ruth was standing and holding Jenny when I unlocked our door and walked in. A couple of candles were burning and she looked like she'd been crying, too. The room looked in order.

"Everything okay?" Walking past her, I set my backpack on my side of the room.

"Well, that was a long two days!"

"Ruth, I am sorry. I will not do that again." Had she grown so attached to me already? "Just a few hours here and there from now on. What is happening next door?"

"That kid has been crying for hours, since this morning!" Ruth shook her head, tears coming again to her eyes. "I even went over there and banged on the door. No one answered. I swear, when I get my hands on whoever lives over there . . ."

Since I wasn't conditioned to living such an impersonal life, I wasn't about to ignore a wailing child. A little sense told me that something was wrong, but apparently everyone on the floor was like Ruth—it was easier to get mad than try to solve the problem.

As Ruth was still complaining about her lack of sleep and Jenny's fussiness, I returned to the hallway. Two neighbors poked their heads out of their doors. One fat man with no shirt gestured with a flashlight at the neighboring door.

"I tried to get in to shut that brat up, but the door is jimmied."

"Ah, it is all right." I gave him a thumbs-up. "It is good. I am Russian!"

He watched as I tried the door, then applied my weight. It wasn't budging, as if it were braced by something heavy and solid on the inside.

From my room, I went out to the balcony. It was an eight-foot leap to the neighboring balcony—a distance I didn't dare until I'd secured myself with the nylon rope. Even then, it took three tries, two times leaving me swinging and flailing. And my injuries talking to me. Ten minutes later, I climbed onto the balcony and looked back at Ruth.

"That was the craziest thing I've ever seen."

"It helps if you cannot see anything looking down." I glanced at the dark void below as I untied the rope from my chest. "But I do not advise it for you."

Ruth tossed me a flashlight and I used the buck knife from Terry's hoodlum friend in the garage to pop the lock on the sliding glass door. A putrid odor wafted into my face and the child from within ceased crying.

"I'm coming in!" I announced to the darkness. My light played on a woman on the carpet lying face down—the source of the smell, at least in part. The child, not over two years old, sat in his soiled diaper next to her. "Hey, little buddy. What's your name?"

I patted the curly-haired child on the head and surveyed the apartment. Glass smoking pipes littered the counter. Beer cans on the floor. And a two-by-four had been wedged into place against the door, anchored on the adjacent wall. Removing the beam, I opened the door to air out the apartment, the open balcony door sucking much of the smell out in seconds.

"What happened?" the fat man in the hallway asked.

"The mother died. Needle in her arm. You knew her?"

"Nope. Better let Wilbur deal with her and the kid, though," he said. "The cops come here, they'll kick us all out. No refunds, either."

It was a selfish thought, but he was right. We had to be careful. Ruth took the child into the bathroom to clean him up as I searched the room for an ID. I finally found a piece of mail and used my phone to run a search.

Ilsa Olson was only twenty-nine. She was British; an illegal, it seemed. Her son's name was Earl. No father was listed on the hospital's digital copy of the birth certificate. He was twenty months old with no other relatives on record.

The fat neighbor and I used two garbage bags to wrap up poor Ilsa, then I collected any personal effects like clothes, pictures, and toys for young Earl.

"What do we do now?" the man asked me.

"Wilbur has probably dealt with this sort of thing before."

"Yeah." The fat man scratched his belly. "Wilbur dumps them in the East River."

"I will make sure he drops her at the hospital, but I am more worried about Earl, the little boy."

"Don't give him to child services," he said. "He'll just follow in his mother's footsteps."

"Well, I will sort it out. I am Russian." I shook his hand. "Das vidhania."

In our apartment, Ruth and I sat on the floor. She spoon-fed Earl warm pudding as I held him in my lap. With the night finally quiet, Jenny was sleeping soundly.

"Oh, I always wanted a little boy," Ruth whispered. "Now Jenny has a big brother."

"What? You can't keep him!" I gasped, nearly forgetting my accent. "You cannot! In the morning, I will take him to the authorities. It is the right thing to do."

"You'll be investigated." She pouted. "And maybe even arrested. Besides, you're just like the rest of us. So what if you got some money? You know you won't find a place this nice to live in, not in this whole cursed city."

Was it selfish to let her keep the child? I could easily produce all of his necessary paperwork.

"No," I insisted. "You cannot take care of one child. How will you take care of two?"

"With you!" She seemed shocked that I hadn't seen the bigger picture. "You said you wouldn't be leaving again."

I said nothing more on the matter that night. The child needed a home and real parents—legal parents. There were people I could speak to at my church in Queens, people who had experience with the foster program. But I couldn't contact anyone from my life until I could surface entirely.

Though I had yet to gain control of my own existence, I now had three depending on me. Again, I yearned for my own family.

✝

CHAPTER EIGHT

I waited in the dark living room of a Baltimore residence as a town car parked in the driveway. Unable to see past the headlights, I moved behind a potted plant and bumped into a baby grand piano. General Logan Forglade's house was too cluttered for a proper ambush, but I could work with it.

Two doors slammed. The general and his driver? A bodyguard? I dared not sneak another peek. Already, I'd tranquilized two people—the housekeeper and a security guard. They were flex-cuffed in a back bedroom. Except for his staff, the general was divorced and lived alone.

The front door opened. I'd come in through the back from the yard after taking a cab from the National Aquarium, where my car was parked.

"I'll pour us a drink," the general said. His voice was familiar from a sound bite I'd heard that afternoon while researching the military man.

The sound of footsteps approached me as General Forglade moved across the room to the bar. In his uniform, he didn't appear to be armed, but I assumed his driver was. Stepping from behind the plant, I chopped at the driver's throat—just hard enough to cause panic. As he turned from me, I moved behind the man to tranquilize him with my pen.

That's when my plan fell apart. Two men had entered with the general, not one! The other man, still in the foyer, drew his sidearm and fired instantly at me. I flinched, but then frowned as I realized the bullet had smacked into the chest of the man I held by the shoulder. With a kick, I sent my human shield into the arms of the alarmed shooter.

Before the shooter could raise his gun at me from around his partner, I stabbed him with the tranq-pen. Though disgusted with myself for drawing gunfire and wounding a man, I couldn't see to him yet. I darted quickly to the bar to find the general reaching into a cabinet for what I assumed was a weapon.

"Drop it, General." I aimed the bodyguard's gun at the aged officer. His cheeks were sunken and his hair was thinning. Though inches taller than me, I was heavier since he appeared to be frail and sickly. However, I knew the man was a marathon runner, and despite his drinking and appearance that night, he was a fit soldier a couple years older than me. "Don't make me shoot you."

He eased his empty hand from the cabinet and I moved up beside him. Even face to face, I could see in his eyes that he didn't recognize me. Such was my disguise of color, added cheekbones, and padding to my gums.

"What is this about? Who are you?"

"You killed my friend last week," I stated with a southern accent, and pressed my borrowed gun into his chest, though I wouldn't pull the trigger. Instead, I watched his face closely. "Corban Dowler has powerful friends."

Recognition. Yes, he grasped that accusation. I planted the tranq into his shoulder and caught him as he slumped to the floor.

Running back to the injured man, I checked his gunshot wound. A nine-millimeter slug was buried in his left pectoral muscle, fortunately slowed after passing through a leather notepad in the man's breast pocket. Using the house phone, I called an ambulance.

Five minutes later, I was driving the general's car toward the National Aquarium. Forglade's hands were bound by flex-cuffs in front of him with the seat belt securing him in the passenger seat. I checked the mirrors a couple times, but there seemed to be no danger. No one had known my plans. No one even knew I was really alive. And on my hands, I wore epoxy with various famous deceased persons' fingerprints. Figuring me out wouldn't be easy.

In a dark alley not far from a busy intersection, I parked and squirted bottled fluid on the general as he slowly gained consciousness. Torture wasn't in my plans, but it was proven that the prospect of torture gets better and more accurate results.

"No, no!" the general screamed. "What are you doing?"

"I knew you wouldn't talk," I said calmly, then flicked a lighter between my fingers. "What do you expect? You killed my mentor. This seems like a fitting vengeance."

"No! I mean, stop! Who are you talking about?"

"Corban Dowler was a good man. Sure, he had a past of darkness, but God had changed his heart." The flame moved toward his lap. "I can't say I've made those same changes . . ."

"Wait! Corban Dowler . . ." He squirmed away, gasping at the biting stench of what seemed to be lighter fluid all over his lap. "Please, I'll talk! I'll talk!"

"Talk," I said, flipping the lighter closed, "and you might not become barbeque, if your story makes any sense at all."

"Okay, okay. Listen, it's not real. None of it! I swear! We didn't kill Dowler! It was a ruse!" The man bowed his head and sobbed, certainly thinking he was about to die. "It wasn't my call. We set Dowler up to go on the run, to isolate him. He's still alive out there somewhere, honest!"

My jaw trembled in the darkness. How could this be?

"You're lying! My friend Corban Dowler was blown up in his car! They got his body. Corban was in his car!"

"No, I swear!" He sniffed and shook his head. "It was just some guy we got out of the morgue. Please! We just followed orders. I answer to others, you know?"

"Who? Tell me!" I flicked the lighter. "You'd better talk!"

"I can't! I'm dead if I do!"

"You're dead as possum on the grill if you don't! You smell that? You like the thought of hellfire? Talk!"

"All right! All right. It was the TaTD."

"From what I hear, you run the TaTD, General!"

"No, these guys are over my head. They wanted something from Dowler, an alias, for us to use in Lebanon to do something with Hezbollah. Dowler wouldn't hand it over, so we were told to put him on the run, set him up somehow. I don't know all of it."

"A name! Give me a name, General!"

"I can't! Look, Dowler's alive! He's out there somewhere. I'll call my guys off. Just . . . let me go."

"How is pretending to kill Dowler the same as setting him up?"

"Honest, I don't know. He's in hiding. I think the TaTD was supposed to force Dowler to use his alias to do what they wanted originally to be done in Lebanon. That's all I know!"

"Exactly what did they want to do with the alias? Talk!"

"Something with Lebanon! I don't know for sure!"

"Guess! Now!"

"A controlled terrorist attack, I think? And Dowler would get blamed, but his alias has Hezbollah ties. It would look like Hezbollah did it. With Dowler in hiding, he'd be the perfect patsy. It looks like he's guilty since he's not showing himself. He's alive, and it looks like he faked his own death. You're going to get me killed for this!"

"Quiet!" I checked the mirrors and tried to manage my own breathing. The whole situation—I'd read it all wrong. They'd known I was alive the whole time? They must've blown my car intentionally before I reached it. All in an attempt to force me into hiding to use my alias. It was possible, but my overseas stunt as Muhammad ibn Affal must've thrown them a curveball. "One last question to decide your fate, General. If you guys really planned all this, and you used a cadaver in my burnt car, then what about Roy Turpin? Only one corpse was found in Dowler's car."

Forglade turned and looked me in the eyes, the reflection of the flame on our faces.

"There is no Roy Turpin. It was just a cadaver."

My whole body went cold. No Roy Turpin?

I dropped the lighter into the general's lap. He screamed and squirmed, but there was no fire. The lighter's little flame went out against Forglade's thigh, leaving a scorch mark on his pants.

"Relax, General. It was just pepper and lemon juice." I squeezed some into my mouth. "You'd better clean this mess up within twenty-four hours or I visit you again. Next time, I won't be alone. Get it?"

"Yes, I get it." He hung his head. "You're gonna get me killed."

"The truth can keep you alive. If you're vocal enough, Corban Dowler can come out of hiding, and then the two of you can put the record straight together."

Leaving the car, I walked down the alley. From my collar, I tugged at a small lens and audio receiver. The evening's events had been recorded, from the ambush and shooting to the car seat interrogation, but that didn't mean I had all the answers. In truth, I was as scared as ever that I'd been predictable and manipulated.

Danger hovered closer than I'd imagined. Though I wanted to check on my family, I dared not for their own safety.

†

CHAPTER NINE

It was Sunday, and instead of racing around the East Coast to defend myself from an enemy I had yet to fully identify, I decided it best to focus my energy on the Kingdom of God. Regardless of her arguments against it, I convinced Ruth to attend church with me.

A few blocks from our squatters' building, we walked with the two babies to a basement chapel. I knew of it from a visit several years earlier. There was a mixture of lost and broken, homeless and wealthy sprinkled throughout the congregation of about two hundred.

Ruth and I sat toward the back on two folding chairs. At first, Ruth seemed very distracted. Her hands played with the hem of her faded dress and she kept glancing over her shoulder. I wasn't sure whether she was uncomfortable in her simple clothing or uneasy about leaving the two children in the crowded nursery room behind us. We were by no means the most impoverished-looking, nor was there any valid reason to be concerned about the children being left with three mothers who were seeing to the rabble of toddlers.

Finally, I set my Bible on Ruth's lap and put my arm across the back of her chair. She sat up straighter and touched the Bible's pages. At last, she started listening to the speaker—a sincere man in jeans and a collared shirt.

He spoke about Joseph in Genesis 41, how he'd been in bondage, kidnapped, and enslaved, yet he trusted God whether in prison or not. This was evidenced by how he named his two sons, born in bondage: Manasseh meant "making to forget," and Ephraim meant "fruitfulness." When we trust God, the man explained, He causes worldly concerns to be put out of mind, and regardless of our circumstances, He makes us spiritually fruitful. God was indeed the answer, not worldly circumstances.

I was pleasantly surprised to see Ruth listening attentively. She heard the message clearly that day.

After the service, Ruth made a move toward the nursery, but regular churchgoers kept intercepting us, wanting to know who we were, shaking our hands, and smiling warmly. I maintained my Russian facade and allowed Ruth to awkwardly fend off their greetings.

As soon as we could break away from an elderly couple, I guided Ruth toward a young man who I'd spotted earlier. He had a gold-colored pin in the shape of an "I" on his collar.

"This is Ruth Holland and I am Fost." I pumped the blond man's hand. He was in his late twenties and wore dusty clothes with a tape measure on his belt. Though his hands were rough and calloused, his face was bright and eager with the obvious love of Jesus.

"Ben Vitco. It's a pleasure." He glanced from me to Ruth, probably trying to make sense of our relationship. "You two are new here?"

"First time here together," I said. "Your pin—you are a Son of Isaac, yes?"

"Oh, yes!" He fondled his collar. "God guides me in my decisions, even the big ones like finding a job or a wife. You've heard of the Sons of Isaac, huh?"

"Yes, I have, and I agree with traditional courtship arrangements. It is very Russian." I threw an arm around Ruth. "Ruth is a single mother. She loves her daughter and is an excellent housekeeper."

"I see . . ." Ben Vitco grinned sheepishly and thrust his hands into his pockets. "The most important matter to me is, Ruth, are you a born again believer in Jesus Christ?"

"Well . . ." Ruth scowled at me, probably sensing I'd set her up. "I don't really understand what that means. I have no desire to be perfect because I've never been able to be. Actually, I'm exactly the opposite."

"You know, that's an important step, what you just said—realizing that you're not perfect. I'm the same way, imperfect." Ben looked at me. "Can we sit down? I'd like to show you both a few life-changing truths about God."

"Ruth will listen," I nudged her toward him. "I will check on the kids."

We were not the only ones lingering in the basement church. The regular parishioners had deployed themselves to interact with visitors in the crowd, and Ben was certainly doing his part in obedience. He led Ruth to a bench against the wall and opened the Bible that I'd left with her.

The nursery had thinned some, but the women assured me they'd stay as long as they were needed. Earl was waist deep in toys, and Jenny was somehow sleeping through the ruckus. I returned to the main room to watch Ben and Ruth from across the auditorium. Ruth seemed engrossed, and focused on this rough construction worker's words of salvation from sin. For ten minutes, I watched them and prayed that God would open Ruth's heart to see her need, and for Ben to share the message straight rather than sell her a bed of roses to get a false conversion.

To my excitement, Ruth nodded to something Ben said and she seemed to be teary. Then it appeared that Ben let Ruth pray to her Heavenly Father. Finally, they stood, embraced, and both approached me. I would've been hard-pressed to determine whose smile was broader—Ruth's, Ben's, or mine!

"Ben wants to know if we have a phone," Ruth said. I gave him the number of my second disposable phone, then Ruth continued. "And he wants to know if he can take us to dinner some night. He has a lot more to teach me."

"Of course!" We set up a date for Tuesday evening, though I had every intention of disappearing by then. I had to return to my own life sooner rather than later, or I'd have no life to return to at all.

On the slow walk back to the squatters' building, Ruth seemed deep in thought as she stared at the sidewalk in front of her. Finally, she looked up.

"What was that pin on his collar?" she asked. "You seemed to know what it was all about."

"It is a Christian fraternity of bachelors, the Sons of Isaac. They believe in biblical marriage concepts, even the idea of others in the church counseling and approving a couple before or during a courtship. They desire to serve

God in their marriages. In the Bible, Abraham sent another man to find just the right wife for Isaac, his son. They trusted God to find the right wife."

"What?" Ruth stopped walking. Her face was pale. "Is that why you introduced me as a single mother? To let him know I was on the market? I just made a very important decision in my life! And you just want to pawn me off to some stranger?"

"No, but I will be leaving you soon, Ruth." I shifted Earl in my arms as he squirmed to watch a clown on a skateboard zip past. "It is my desire to see you settled in a good church that can watch over you and disciple you in your new faith. Whether a relationship develops with this Ben or someone else is not the most important thing. For you to get to know your Savior is."

"You and I are supposed to be family, Fost!" She started walking again, this time too quickly for me to catch without jogging.

"Ruth, you know I am on the run," I reminded her. "Jenny needs a father. It cannot be me. I am old enough to be your grandfather!"

"What about Earl? He gets pawned off, too?"

"Well, no, but I have considered the situation. He will have to be turned over to the authorities eventually, and he is young enough that he will likely be adopted rather quickly. If you had a way to give him a good home, Ruth, then I would agree that he should stay with you."

"Fost, it's not your say!"

"It is my decision."

She threw the door open to our building and marched across the lobby to the stairs. Wilbur saw me coming and rose to his feet behind his desk.

"I dumped that body in front of the hospital like you said." He shrugged, wearing the same stained shirt I'd seen on him the day I'd moved in. "Remember, you said if I did what you said—"

"Of course, Wilbur. I remember. I am Russian." As promised, I handed him fifty dollars since he'd taken Earl's mother to the hospital instead of dumping her in the river. "What did you think about that paper I asked you to read?"

He pushed several newspapers across his desk to find a gospel tract I'd given him the day before.

"Honestly?" He handed me the tract back. "I didn't know exactly what the cross meant, but it's not for me. I'm not going to put my sin on Someone else. I'm fine with the hot place."

"Sorry to hear that, Wilbur." I pocketed the tract. "Well, at least you have heard the truth. You've proven that you love your sin more than you care for your precious soul. God will judge you rightly."

While his mouth gaped at my harsh words, I shook his hand and started up the stairs. It was my responsibility to share the gift of God. God's grace would draw the needy heart.

†

CHAPTER TEN

In the past, when serving my faithful God in one thing, He'd always prepared the next step for me to take. It was no different the following night. I had expectantly trusted Him with my predicament, and God continued to show Himself faithful. Without His guidance, I'd be lost. One wrong move, and it could mean my death, as well as my family's.

Regardless of my confidence that God would produce a result to my dilemma that glorified Himself, I felt then the loneliest I'd ever felt. By a strange twist, for the first time in my life, my enemies knew I was alive, but my family believed I was dead. This fact brought me to the back door of my trusted employee and COIL's finest operations manager, Chloe. I needed help.

Zvi and Chloe Azmaveth had recently bought a house on Staten Island. They had no children, and Zvi owned an international micron gold mining company, so he was often on the road, as he was that night. It worked well for Chloe since the COIL office downtown required her hard work, which she attended passionately.

Because of the risks involved in meeting someone I knew was under surveillance, as was Chloe, I returned to the safe house in Manhattan for a second-generation NL weapon, a machine pistol that fired non-lethal tranquilizer pellets. It held two-hundred-and-fifty pea-sized rounds with a maximum effective range of fifty yards, each pellet inducing a twenty-minute dose of sleeping toxin, if inhaled.

My caution in contacting Chloe was warranted. Both of our pasts with international agencies often brought security auditors into our rearview mirrors. As open as COIL's mission statement was, agencies still checked on us periodically. Were we a threat? Were we using our skills against the country? So, past operations and present conflict gave me reason to be extra careful.

From the hedges in the back yard, I aimed the NL-2 at the back door light of the Azmaveth residence. On fully automatic firing, the burst of water-soluble rounds shattered the bulb on impact. The back yard was shrouded in residential darkness, offering me shadows in which to approach the door, but not invisibly. Invisibility would've been nice since I'd already spotted two government agents in a town car out front.

Regardless of the agents in the car, I was more concerned about being tranquilized by the forty-six-year-old ex-Mossad agent I was trying to speak to. Chloe and I had a hundred ways to send secret messages during a field deployment, but our domestic system was somewhat wanting. With so much at risk, I couldn't enter the house and risk a directional microphone that could eavesdrop on our conversation—through dense walls or windows.

Anticipating these dangers, I set a disposable phone on the doormat and knocked loudly on the door. Without waiting to see how many lights came on in the house, I bounded over the hedges and vaulted over a neighbor's fence. After avoiding a doghouse that reminded me of my escape a week and a half earlier, I reached my car. Chloe certainly had the drop phone by then, but I needed to give the agents in front of her house more time to settle into their seats after seeing a little activity in the Azmaveth house.

The phone on her doorstep alone could've caused Chloe to suspect my presence, but such was her caution, I guessed, that she'd need to meet me in the flesh to be convinced I was really alive. And I couldn't wait for morning.

An hour later, I stood on the rocks of Jeffrey's Hook beneath the George Washington Bridge. The Little Red Lighthouse stood dark on my left, the narrow passage between Manhattan and New Jersey as calm as I'd ever seen the water.

I texted Chloe an encrypted message only she would know: "Meet me. Bait the hook. Miss. in Laos last year. - A.B. Leever."

It was clever enough to make me smile. We'd smuggled Bibles the year before to Jeffrey Parker, a missionary in Laos. A.B. Leever was a pen name under which I published a children's adventure series. The government would take days to track down our friend's name in Laos, but Chloe would figure out in a couple minutes that she was to meet me at Jeffrey's Hook.

Two hours later, she finally showed up—and not in her own car. It was borrowed, probably from a church friend or neighbor, someone whose car the Feds were sure to not consider bugging, if they were following her to that extent.

"Rumors of your death are greatly exaggerated, I see!" She stepped carefully on the rocks. Though she'd tried to appear wide-awake in a casual suit and her curly, dark hair tied up into a ponytail, her face was puffy from crying, or possibly from lack of sleep. "You missed your own funeral yesterday."

We embraced as friends who'd been through dozens of life-threatening operations together.

"You know I wouldn't want to spoil a nice ceremony." We both faced the drive above. No one could approach without us noticing. "Janice and Jenna need to be protected until I come in. How are they holding up?"

"Well, that's of some concern, Corban. They'd been with me, but after the funeral, some bald guy approached Janice and spoke to her in private. I couldn't get a good look at him other than see he had a shaved head. Janice insisted that she go with this man, but she wouldn't say who he was. Before I could do or say anything, they were gone. They didn't even have any clothes with them. Whoever he was, I feel just sick for not being more careful. Corban, I never thought they'd come for your family at the funeral!"

"This bald guy, was he gaunt with dark eyes?"

"Maybe, Corban, but it was pretty far away. He wasn't exactly mingling with the mourners. If he had, I would've noticed him." She cocked her head. "Aren't you upset with me? I don't know who this guy was."

"I do. It's fine, Chloe. He's a friend."

"The one who's looked after them in the past? Is he the one who chews bubble gum that Jenna told me about?"

"Yes, I think so. I can't imagine Janice going with anyone else." I forced a smile for her sake. "They're safe. My guy probably got wind of some nonsense and knows of a safer place for them."

"Well, I won't pretend to know all the spooks from your past. So, will you at least tell me what's going on?"

Starting from the beginning, I told her about the night of the explosion, and the man I thought was Roy Turpin in my car. The sun was rising by the time I finished.

"So, if Roy Turpin didn't die in your place, who was in the explosion?"

"Maybe just a cadaver. That's what I understood from General Forglade. Either way, I was set up to believe I was helping a recently-paroled convict. For two years, I wrote this man in the prison upstate. I did a little hunting this week. All signs of a Roy Turpin ever existing, of course, have disappeared."

"Is this the recording of General Forglade's admission?" She tapped a fingernail on the flash drive. "There hasn't been anything in the news, Corban. I guess he didn't come forward like you'd hoped."

"It was expected. Even generals answer to someone. We have to find who has him so frightened."

"This terrorist bit has me real concerned." Chloe growled under her breath. "There are probably a hundred people you've situated in dangerous countries under Muhammad's cover, and those are just the ones I know about. If it comes out now that it was you all this time, those people will have to be warned."

"That could take months, and by then, it'd be too late." I kicked at a rock. "We have to handle this delicately. Interrogating the general and giving Muhammad three appearances in Europe hopefully caused a hiccup, but I doubt I've derailed their plans entirely."

"So, how do we proceed? Senator Nettleton's office? You trust this Rod Chang character, the assistant?"

"Trust? No. Do we need him? Maybe so. He didn't seem very pleased to hear that the TaTD is up to something covert on the senator's watch." A siren blared on the bridge above. "Can you free up a couple days for me?"

"Sure. Zvi isn't due back until Saturday. What do you have in mind? Bring back Alpha Team? The boys would take this on like a hurricane."

"Nah. I'm thinking of a more subtle route. Just you and me. How about a bait and cover gig?"

"Fine, if you're the bait!" Laughing, she slapped my arm.

"Good. Do what you do. Catch up to me by noon at the apartment building on 67th."

"Okay, but I'd sure feel better if we brought in a couple of the boys for overwatch."

"Those COIL teams are trained for foreign countries, not for this country with its restrictions and scrutiny. Too many laws to be aware of, Chloe. I need you to do this without alerting anyone."

"All right. It's your neck. See you at noon."

I drove back to the squatters' building that morning with a nervous excitement in my gut that I associated with a feeling when I was about to face a superior adversary—and knowing I had the upper hand. Like walking through a Chinese border crossing with a suitcase of Bibles, or driving a carload of Christian refugees out of Syria. God had been watching over me for years. He was watching over us still.

My family had been abducted, in a fashion, by whom I was certain was the Italian Luigi Putelli, a deadly man whose life I'd delivered three years earlier. Ever since that blistering day in the Bekoa Valley in Lebanon, Luigi Putelli had been shadowing my family, returning to me the debt he insisted he owed me. Though he wasn't a Christian, I'd involved him in training clandestine operators, like Nathan Isaacson, but mostly it was to keep Luigi near, exposing him to the gospel lived out through uncompromising Christians.

Regardless, I needed to somehow confirm that Luigi did indeed have Janice and Jenna. My blood pressure was definitely running high right now.

Ruth fixed breakfast for me—waffles from a box—and I relaxed on my sleeping bag as the two kids squealed and played. I'd been waiting for Ruth to make the first move since her commitment to Christ the previous Sunday. Sure enough, she began asking questions about the Bible and reading the Scriptures every chance she got. To me, this was initial evidence that her conversion was genuine. She wasn't merely a believer in what Jesus had done; she was born again, repentant of her past, proving that a miracle had occurred in her life. If Ben Vitco played his cards right, he might even get a devout, Christian wife.

†

CHAPTER ELEVEN

Much of a spy's life of interaction with people involved ambushing the lives of others. I employed this tactic under disguise as I slipped into Senator Nettleton's building in Tribeca, a few blocks from Manhattan's financial district. The senator's staff occupied four floors above the twentieth story, and I'd already called ahead to confirm an appointment.

In Texas flourish, I emerged from the elevator to be received by the receptionist. She seemed to identify me right away by my cowboy hat and cigars in my leather vest.

"Mr. Herbert Ephron, may I take your hat?" The receptionist rose from her wide desk and took my hat, setting it on a hook. She was taller than I was, but I wasn't so insecure that it bothered me. I'd been infiltrating foreign regimes for as many years as she was old. "The senator is expecting you."

Giving me VIP treatment, the woman opened both doors to a spacious office that faced south. The New York flag and photos of family spanned the only wall that wasn't glass.

Senator Nettleton greeted me like an old friend, though we'd never met. He had a fixed smile and narrow eyes, seemingly made for politics. He was chubbier and younger than I expected.

"Always a pleasure to meet a contributor, Mr. Ephron!" He shook my hand heartily, which was expected since I'd scheduled the meeting after disclosing a fabricated bank balance. "How long are you planning to be in the Big Apple?"

"Not long enough to miss my Lone Star beef!" I laughed boisterously, feeling the glue on my bushy mustache holding sure. "More than a couple days here and I'd go insane without the wide openness of my ranch. You ever been there? I'll show you livin'!"

"I might take you up on that." He gestured to his left. "My trusted advisor, Rod Chang. You two spoke on the phone, I believe."

"Pleasure, young man." I shook Chang's hand and locked eyes long enough to allow him to recognize me, but he didn't. Before that day, he'd seen me only in the darkness of the park and on the photo ID where I appeared to be Peter Mitchell. Hoping to maintain my disguise a little longer, I turned from Chang and plopped down in a wide soft chair. Though tempted to prop my cowboy boots onto his desk, I decided that might be too much. "I'd sure like to hear how you're working on our country, Senator, especially after all the recent headaches in the Middle East. Those A-rabs just don't stop, do they?"

"Well, you understand, Mr. Ephron, that I'm chairman of the domestic oversight committee." Nettleton folded his arms. "While those disturbances impact this country, my job is to keep home-front agencies funded, as well as keep the public safe."

"Of course, but when I hear about our own people dying on the streets of your city, you understand my concern." The senator and Chang exchanged glances, but I acted like I didn't notice as I offered cigars to the men. They both refused politely, then I lit up without asking permission. "I read the papers. When an agent friend dies in a car bomb, I want to know how I can make sure that never happens again."

Chang sat up straighter and Nettleton studied me more closely. I didn't have time to court these men all day. The Texas way was to go straight to the mark, even if I wasn't really a Texan.

"I'm assuming you're talking about Corban Dowler who died a week and a half ago." Nettleton tapped his desk calendar. "It was unfortunate, but after an investigation, we found it to be a case of mistaken identity. A local gang already claimed responsibility. I wasn't aware that Dowler had many friends who knew he'd been an agent for the US. Were you two close?"

"Closer than most, I suppose." I blew smoke at the ceiling. "We all know that was no accident, boys. Top CIA agents don't die by accident. I'm interested in contributing to your efforts, Senator, but I want to make sure the good guys are safe before I secure your office for the upcoming election."

"The investigation is closed, Mr. Ephron. Dowler was purely a tragic accident." Nettleton's voice raised an octave, a sign that I took to mean he was lying. "Bad things happen to good people. It's very sad."

"So are you working with the TaTD to cover up their assassination of a patriot, or are you intentionally keeping me out of the loop?"

Nettleton's mouth opened, but he closed it quickly and looked at Chang. As intended, I'd caught them unguarded. I glared at Nettleton, the pressure mounting. He was surely torn between the promise of my supposed millions and his own committee's secrets. Something wasn't right, but I wasn't finished watching him squirm.

"How would a cattle rancher from Texas know anything about the happenings here?" Nettleton asked.

"How come my contacts here know more about the death of an elite secret agent, and you know nothing?" I ground out my cigar on a coaster on his desk. "The TaTD—are you in bed with them or not? You one of General Logan Forglade's people or not?"

"No, I am not!" Nettleton's face was red. Of course, I knew Forglade answered to him. "I need to know how you know about this situation, and I need to know how much you know!" He scowled at Chang. "I thought you said this was zipped tight!"

"It is from our end." Chang folded his hands in front of him. "General Forglade may feel us closing in. That night generated some unguarded chatter. If the general knows we're tracking him, he may erase any record of what we're trying to do. As soon as we have the pieces in place, we'll bury Forglade."

"Okay." I nodded and sighed, my Texan drawl gone. "I had to be sure you two were still working for the home team. I'm not who I told you I was."

Chang rose from his chair and leaned over to stare at me in the face.

"I knew it!" He smiled at Nettleton. "It's Peter Mitchell, the Weltersand operative from Marcus Garvey Park I was telling you about."

"Mitchell?" Nettleton's brow furrowed, probably at the evaporated prospect of funding. "This is a little elaborate, isn't it?"

"Not with the TaTD on the prowl. Besides, I couldn't be sure you were interested in helping me."

"It's a little hard when we don't have all the facts," Chang said. "Your report justified an inquiry into the TaTD, but they're blocking every query we throw at them. General Forglade's even left the country."

"Yeah, I figured as much. Well, it's a lot more complicated than that." My heart skipped a beat. I had to trust someone besides Chloe, who was somewhere outside the building at that moment, watching my back and listening to my conversation through my belt buckle microphone. "Corban Dowler is still alive."

This was my final test. If they already knew that fact, then I'd know they were involved. Only those directly involved in the car explosion would know it wasn't meant to kill me. However, their faces seemed to show genuine surprise. Or shock. I prayed I was reading their faces accurately.

"What?" Chang gasped and closed his fingers around a fistful of his own hair. "Why would Dowler do all this? How do you know he's alive? That explains why his family is missing. He's put them somewhere safe."

I studied Chang and the words he used. Something still wasn't right with him, as if he were trying too hard. But I was encouraged that he'd looked in on my family.

"Yes, I've put them with someone I trust." I peeled off my mustache, though with some pain, but I left on the thick eyebrows. "Corban Dowler, gentlemen. Peter Mitchell doesn't exist. Chang, you said in the park that you knew of me when you were in the Logistics Division at Langley. Do you recognize me?"

"Uh . . . I guess so. I can't say I'd remember his, I mean, your face real well. No offense."

"Are you accusing us, Mr. Dowler?" Nettleton asked. "Or suspecting we're involved in this web of lies with the TaTD? I'm a senator, and I'm outraged that certain men have attacked citizens of this fine country!"

"Senator, I'm looking at everyone carefully. Remember, I was just blown up in a car!" Nettleton's defensiveness made me cautious, but I had to keep going. "The TaTD is for certain behind this. I questioned General Forglade in his car, and that's probably why he left the country. Though they never intended to kill me, they meant for me to think someone was trying to kill me so they could set me up while I was on the run. Now, I don't know the status of their plans, but I'm certain that Forglade wasn't working alone. He was afraid of someone else."

It took me twenty minutes to share what I knew from the general's admission, but I left out details of my squatters' residence, my family's safety with Luigi, and the recording of our conversation.

"So, whoever is behind General Forglade is who we need to pin down." Chang clenched a fist. "Enough playing around, Senator. We need to shut down the TaTD headquarters once and for all. Who knows who Forglade has corrupted against us!"

"Not so fast," I said. "It might scare the puppet master away if we jump before it's time. We need to know why he wanted my Muhammad ibn Affal cover in the first place. I can do that if I go inside the TaTD."

Chang and Nettleton looked at one another, communicating with their eyes. The TaTD was the key, I thought, but these two had secrets.

"Mr. Dowler . . ." Nettleton shook his head. "You're clever, and thank God you are! But you're just a civilian now. I can't sanction something like that. That's walking into the viper's nest down there. The TaTD may as well be considered a rogue agency with this latest move. I have a number of younger agents who—"

"With all due respect, Senator, I was in Iran during the Revolution. I've brokered arms deals between Israel and Pakistan, smuggled prisoners out of North Korea and agents into Saudi Arabian nuclear sites. Your agents are up against a foe who knows how they think. I'm an outsider. To them, I'm running scared, but I know what to look for. Give me a DOD ID for a routine liaison briefing, and I'll find out what the TaTD is up to. Whoever is filling in for the general at their headquarters will know something."

"Just how will you find out?" Chang shook his head. "How will you get it out of them by only a visit?"

"Isn't it obvious?" I stood and pressed my mustache back into place. "Whoever was using General Forglade won't run away if they think they're undetected. They may even try to go after Forglade because they'll know he got scared and talked. The one who Forglade left behind will lead us straight to the culprit."

"Let me throw this out there, Mr. Dowler," Nettleton said. "Wouldn't it have been much easier to just give them the Muhammad identity at the beginning of all this?"

"Too many lives are dependent on that ID, gentlemen, lives that a dark heart wouldn't blink over when they're lost. But I'm a Christian now. God cares about every soul, and that means I need to care as well. If that doesn't make sense to you, then—"

"No, it makes sense to me." Nettleton stood and rested his hands on his hips. "I was raised that way. It's good to hear a man stepping out in faith, Mr. Dowler. Coordinate with Chang here. We'll back you, but only because I know you won't be killing your enemies. I've always admired COIL. Makes me feel a bit insignificant where the bigger picture is concerned."

"Change is a decision away," I challenged, then nodded to Chang. "You, too. God is looking for men who will admit their insignificance in themselves, and their significance in Him. That's what the cross is all about, saving us from ourselves, in Christ."

"Let's, uh, get to work," Chang said. He moved to the door, but when Nettleton and I looked at one another, we shared a knowing smile. At least I hoped that's what he was smiling about—that he understood the true impact the gospel could have on an individual's life.

†

CHAPTER TWELVE

B ecause I sensed my time living in hiding was ending, I stopped by the squatters' apartment and collected my few personal belongings. I was leaving the generator and household provisions for Ruth.

"It's just as well that we're moving on," Ruth said as she ruffled Earl's hair. "I've been convicted about living in an illegal place. There's an older couple at the church that has a small basement apartment. They said me and the kids could move into it until I find work."

"That's great, Ruth. I'm glad to know you'll be okay." I swung my backpack over my shoulder. When I looked at her, I thought of my own family in the hands of Luigi, who'd become my family's bodyguard of sorts. How I missed them! "What do you want to do about Earl?"

"If I go to child services, I'll lose him." She gave a rattle toy to Jenny. "But if I keep him, I could lose him at any time. I should pray about it, right? No, don't tell me. Now that I'm a Christian, I know to do the right thing, even when it hurts."

"I have waited for days to hear you say that." Scribbling on a notepad, I handed the paper to her. "This is a government friend of mine. She will help you. Say Corban sent you. That name is on the bottom here, too. Tell her everything, and she will make sure it is all legal for you to keep Earl, assuming he really does not have any relatives when she searches."

"Serious?" She threw her arms around my neck. "You've done so much for me, Fost! How can I find you again?"

"You will not find me, Ruth. This is where we part for good."

Ruth looked around the apartment. We'd been together for only two weeks, but we'd become like family. God knew to bring her into my life to give me focus as I dealt with my own problems. Maybe to distract me some, too. I was a man who could obsess over dilemmas.

She promised to teach her two children about their Russian Uncle Fost, and I promised to pray for God's will in her relationship with Benjamin Vitco. With that, we parted.

Down in the garage, I didn't drive away too quickly. One more final stunt required one more elaborate disguise. This one I applied with much artistry. Cheekbones and chin, teeth and nose. It took me an hour in the car mirror to get my hair just right—a lighter brown that I could wash out in any sink in sixty seconds.

"Okay, I'm ready to go into the TaTD facility," I said to Chloe, who still shadowed me. "If you can't get in ahead of me, I'll have to go in alone to finish this business once and for all."

There was no answer since my belt mic was only one-way.

The TaTD's secure facility was in Maryland a short distance from the Pentagon. I turned off Washington

Boulevard and into the packed parking lot of a building I'd never been in before. It was a new installation with a Plexiglas entrance where two armed officers sat at a desk. The rest of the structure appeared to be concrete, interrupted occasionally by narrow, tall windows that reminded me of archers' windows in the walls of an ancient fortress.

Rod Chang had provided me with a Department of Defense identity under the name of Eric Lando, a senior agent. Instead of fabricating a file in that name, the military file was sealed in confidentiality codes, which, if checked out, would fit my cover adequately. However, I was entering the wolf's lair. The amount of bluffing I'd have to do to get the information I needed was of more concern to me than my identity. It could even mean my life.

"I'm here to see the acting director of the TaTD," I informed the first officer in uniform. He scanned the digital tape on my ID, one that matched my new face. Chang's people were experts. As my clearance was run, I glanced at the second officer. His hand was on the trigger of his carbine, hanging on a sling across his chest. I couldn't read his face behind dark glasses. If I had to fight my way out of the building, I was up against some tough men. Hopefully, getting inside was the hardest part.

"General Forglade is out of the office," the first officer said.

"That's why I said I'm here for the acting director," I snapped. "Someone's filling in for him. Who is it?"

"A man name Karl Coleman, the general's right hand." He pointed at my side. "I need to check that briefcase."

In the past, I'd smuggled into North Korea micro-thread Bibles that were sewn into my clothing, so I wasn't concerned about these boys finding my weapons of choice. They were just doing their jobs.

At last, I received a visitor's pass, which was clipped onto the breast pocket of my suit. When I walked through a metal corridor, I was reminded of a body x-ray machine I'd seen in a Saudi palace earlier that year. To confirm my assumption, I heard a low whirring sound. I was being scanned for contraband, maybe even for bio weapons.

Arriving at the end of the corridor, I found an elevator with one button on the wall, but I didn't reach for it since two more armed men were there to operate the car for me. This status of alert was what I expected from the Tactical anti-Terrorist Division headquarters within Homeland Security. I couldn't imagine Chloe infiltrating the facility on short notice, but she was a pretty ex-Mossad agent. Not even I knew the extent of her resources. At the least, she was outside in the car, vigilantly listening to my communications, following my transponder on her little screen, tracking me.

My escorts knew exactly where to take me, and we descended several floors instead of going up. That made sense since the building appeared to be only two stories tall from the outside.

The next hallway was surrounded by glass walls through which I could see dozens of uniformed men and women hard at work at their stations. The glass reminded me of the government job I'd left years before; Big Brother and Uncle Sam were always watching.

We turned a couple corners and arrived at an office door still labeled with General Forglade's name. I waited calmly as a man punched a security code into a wall-mounted computer. The door popped open and I was motioned forward. Now I was left to proceed alone into the carpeted room with glaring artificial sunlight.

I stepped inside and the door hissed closed behind me. A mural behind glass windows gave the impression of a tropical beach.

"It's all solar-powered," a voice said, "but it still ain't the sun."

Turning, I faced a man I knew well. Or thought I knew. It was Roy Turpin, the very man I thought had been blown up in my car! He was alive! Instead of brown, wavy hair, however, he'd shaved it all off. Or the hair I'd seen two weeks earlier had been a wig. The man walked around his wide desk and offered his hand. Clearly, things were much darker, much more sinister than I'd ever imagined. I wished I'd worn glasses with video imaging to capture his face rather than just audio for Chloe to record.

"What's the DOD sending someone down here for? Is this about General Forglade?"

Shaking the man's hand, I hoped my eyes didn't give away my anger and accusation on the surface of my brain. All the time I'd spent on this man, thinking he was an inmate in need of a fresh start as a vessel for Christ! It wasn't the first time I'd been fooled, but what an elaborate hoax! All for what?

"I'm here under the guise of liaison for Homeland Security resources." My voice was raspy to throw him off. I took a seat as he returned to his side of the desk. "You do understand what I mean by guise, I trust?"

He licked his lips and studied me. Could he tell that my face was made up? Was my chin still in place? My teeth?

"Have we met?" He tossed a cashew into his mouth, but offered me none. "Tough to tell from your file where we might've met."

"Serbia in '91? I did field work there." I held his gaze, daring him, challenging him, like two cardholders on the final call. "Mogadishu, maybe."

Since his face betrayed nothing, it probably meant he knew I was misleading him intentionally.

"What do you mean you're here under the guise of some liaison?" He shook his head and leaned to one side, perhaps to check my face from another angle. I turned my head slightly to face him more directly. "You weren't expected. I don't take meetings like this."

"I was sent to clean up this mess. It's gotten out of hand. Dowler's not cooperating like the general promised." My words made him stop chewing his cashews. "What? You didn't think Forglade was keeping his plans to himself, did you? Muhammad ibn Affal and all that business— You-Know-Who isn't pleased with things."

His eyes narrowed slightly, and he may've tried to recover, but I glimpsed uncertainty there. And fear. Yes, I was bluffing. I had to bluff. Roy Turpin, or Karl Coleman, and General Forglade were working for someone too terrifying for the general to even remain in the country.

"Go on," he said.

"Dowler was underestimated." I stared my coldest, hardest glare I could muster. "And we overestimated your ability to control him."

"It wasn't about control!" He was ruffled. "It was about removing him from the picture long enough to . . . You know. We expected challenges."

"Of course." I didn't know what he was talking about exactly, but I needed to know before I left him. "How would you explain those challenges to date?"

"Are you here to take me out?" he asked, with more calmness than I would expect from a man wondering if he were about to die.

"Stay on subject. We want to know how you're explaining these challenges. That's why I was sent for face-time. Nothing else has been decided."

"Sure, Dowler made some unexpected moves." He scratched his ear, or adjusted a comm I couldn't see. Was someone besides Chloe listening? Could Chloe even hear my signal through all the tech and cement? I guessed not, which meant I was isolated, alone. "But we still have leverage. That's why Dowler still hasn't shown his face. It could still work. We just need a little more time. The general did his part. I promised to do mine, or clean everything up if I have to. Go back and tell our friend his money has been well spent. This is what I do."

I let my eyes drift, as if bored, over to the distracting mural. They had leverage? That made me shiver. Leverage in what form? Intel? COIL personnel in their pockets?

"How do you know that leverage will do what you intend?" I raised my eyebrows. They felt bulky under so much epoxy. "Dowler's anything but predictable."

"If I know anything about him—and I think I know him better than anyone—I know he cares for his family."

"His family?" I scoffed, an icy feeling in my gut.

"Yeah, this op has been my baby the whole time. Mine. Don't let anyone forget that. I'm not going to let it fall apart! No one else has put more time into it than I have. I don't leave any loose ends. Trust me: I'll get the general. Dowler corresponded with me for months, laying out all the things he cared about in plain terms. The man's a sap. He's got two passions: God and family. We had a need, and we're meeting that need—using a man who's no longer loyal to anyone but those two fragile passions. Don't tell me I don't know my business. Dowler's family was easy pickin's. It's what I do, remember?"

I stopped breathing. It was my turn to panic. My wife and daughter! How? It made no sense! Chloe had said Luigi Putelli had picked them up after the funeral, hadn't she? No. Wait! She'd said a slender, bald man had picked them up, and she hadn't gotten a good look at him. I'd assumed it had been Luigi, but Karl Coleman was bald too! Everything was crumbling around me. Feeling myself slipping, I tried to keep my composure, to manage my blood pressure.

"What if Dowler has already gone to the authorities? It'll blow up in our faces."

"We are the authorities. Besides, what would he say? There's nothing to say, and he knows it. That's why he went underground. Except for that game in Europe with the

Muhammad identity, he hasn't surfaced anywhere. He can't know what we're doing, what we're using it all for."

"Even after what Forglade confessed a few nights ago?" I asked. His eyes widened, and I didn't want to give him an inch. "What? Didn't he tell you about that before he skipped the country?" I sighed loudly. "See, this was a mistake. Forglade's practically out of the picture now. You wonder why? He had to know this was closing in on him and he left you to take the fall."

He cursed and chomped on his nuts.

"Who would've thought making a civilian our scapegoat would be this messy?" He pulled a drawer open and took out a small laptop. "I'll kill the general myself. It's not like I don't already have blood on my hands over this. Your boss isn't exactly untouchable, either. Keep that in mind when you throw your veiled threats around. It'd be real easy for someone to link us together, even if all I ever do is share my debriefs, or see only your face."

"What about this leverage?" I didn't care about whatever I'd been framed for, and I wouldn't until I understood in what way he was talking about my family.

"That's what I'm talking about." Coleman typed on his laptop. "Even dead, they're still leverage if Dowler thinks we're holding them. They'll be found in a day or two, maybe, but we're counting on the investigation on the whole other thing to run its course, right? Dowler's hiding out creates just the suspicion we're after. Forglade is in Gustavia, using our own tech to hide from us. Now there's a predictable man. He bragged about that place for years. Your boss sent him there himself. In a few days, I'll catch a flight and—What're you doing?"

The pen was in my hand almost without me thinking about it. I aimed it at him across the desk. My other pen with the tranquilizer serum was still in my pocket. But this pen contained a truth serum and a mild sedative with the ability to fire the toxin in projectile form. He was still within range.

"Don't move an inch. Keep your hands on the desk." I stood slowly. Panting, I could barely control myself from doing the unthinkable to this man. "You actually killed Dowler's wife and daughter?"

"That . . . was the plan. What are you doing?" His nostrils flared. "Don't do this! I won't fail you guys! Think about it! They'll investigate my death. You kill me, and you'll never get out of here. This place is a vault!"

With a clouded mind, all I could think about was that my wife and daughter had been murdered! Now I wanted to kill this man. My heart ached against my Lord's call to represent Him—to get vengeance for the blood that had been shed against me. It was all my fault! No, it was Karl Coleman's fault—this dark heart before me, this evil vessel who'd killed my family. Murderer!

I pressed the tiny tab on my pen, expecting a quick hiss of CO_2 to propel a water-soluble dart into his chest. But nothing happened. Trying again, the button seemed to be jammed. He saw my weapon had misfired and reached into his desk. An instant later, he was aiming a handgun at me.

"You're good, Lando, but not good enough." He walked around the desk and shoved me into my chair. As he tore the flawed pen from my fingers to inspect it, I didn't fight for it. "Clever weapon. The scanners upstairs didn't even notice it. What was your plan? Let me take the heat with Dowler? I told you I'd fix things, or take care of anyone left hanging in the wind. Listen, I'm not going down for this, not without taking you guys down with me."

"Your gig is up," I said boldly, my eyes trying to look around the muzzle. "It's all over!"

"Hardly." He reached over his desk and touched an intercom. "This is Coleman. We have a security breach. Secure the building and send a team to my office."

"This is a government facility, Coleman," I said as he walked behind me. "You can't stay here forever. It's over. Why do you think Forglade took off?"

"What? You don't think I can still clear my name? Remember, I know who I'm up against. And I'll still finish off Forglade and Dowler. I have contingencies in place." The door behind me burst open and four armed men entered. "Two of you prepare the west tunnel exit. Go! You two, secure him and come with me."

My arms were roughly bound behind me with something plastic around my wrists, then I was marched out of the office after Karl Coleman. If I hadn't been in such shock over the news of my wife and daughter, I might've tried to fight them off. Now bound, my options were limited. As soon as we surfaced above ground, however, Chloe would be able to detect and track me, as long as I didn't lose my belt. Besides the belt, I felt I had nothing else to lose. My family was gone.

†

CHAPTER THIRTEEN

Karl Coleman clearly didn't want me talking in front of the TaTD security agents who escorted me. This much was apparent when he battered me on the head when I tried to question him about his intentions. The fact that I'd so easily convinced him I was sent from someone higher up seemed to be of some hope for my survival. He didn't know I was Corban Dowler. I was in a tight spot, and my mind was spinning from being so deceived. If I could free myself and take Coleman into custody, there was a chance—

A concrete tunnel was exposed from behind a wall. It had a ramp down and to the west from the TaTD facility. If my bearings were right, we were headed to the southwest side of Arlington Cemetery, on the other side of Southgate Road.

When the tunnel began to ascend toward ground level, I knew I had to start thinking straight or I was a dead man. Two men still escorted us, with Coleman leading the way up the damp floor. I stumbled along but it was ignored as my two escorts roughly forcing me ahead. There seemed to be no stalling these professionals. Unsuccessfully, I tried to shut out my anguish over my family's demise. If I gave up now, or if I didn't live through the next few hours, I'd be the loser.

"Don't try anything!" Coleman rasped in my ear as we reached another heavy door. It swung upward, then we walked through a small, cluttered shed to an opening covered by flimsy metal. The hidden door behind us closed. Coleman unlocked then shoved me roughly ahead through the metal doorway. Sunlight made me squint. With my hands bound behind me, I struggled to remain upright lest I fall headfirst onto pavement.

When I seemed to be standing alone in a parking lot, I looked back at the small shed from which I'd emerged. Coleman aimed a silenced gun at the two escorts, then shot them dead. They fell inside the door of the shed, and Coleman closed and locked the door.

"Move!" He pushed me toward a row of vehicles. There seemed to be no cover, and with my hands bound, I didn't dare attack the frantic gunman. It was then I realized we were in the parking lot of the Arlington Memorial Chapel. Had we come that far from Washington Boulevard?

Now exposed to the satellites above, Chloe was certain to be tracking me. Though I faced seemingly insurmountable danger, I wasn't without hope. Chloe had bugged my belt for this very reason, and if all else failed, I knew my salvation was secured in Christ for all eternity. And I'd soon see my family again in heaven! My contempt for Coleman was loathsome to me, and I regretted it terribly. In light of my probable death, I prepared my broken human heart for a meeting with the King of Kings.

"Get on the floor and lay down!"

Coleman nudged me from behind as I stepped into the back seat of an SUV. When I seemed to be stalling, he jabbed his gun into my left kidney. I dropped face first, bloodying my brow, but I felt only the pain in my back. The door slammed, and I was trapped on my belly for a moment, struggling between the seats.

The engine started, and Coleman rushed us away from the lot. I couldn't think. Was there nothing I could do? My knife! On the floor behind the front seat, I twisted my left foot up to my bound hands. From the heel of my shoe, I picked at a tiny tab. Finally, I slid a composite knife from the heel. It was oddly shaped to fit snuggly in the sole, and razor sharp. As plastic, it hadn't been detected by the security screenings earlier. But now what?

Like a squirrel trying to right itself, I squirmed around until I was on my back. I dropped my shoulders low, one at a time, and shifted my bound wrists from under my back, below my legs, and to the front of me. My wrists were bleeding and the knife had cut me twice along the thigh and calf, but I didn't care about anything but getting free now.

Again, I paused. Now what? Was I willing to kill this man who'd so conspired against me? I truly wanted him to pay, but I resisted lunging over the seat and attacking him. Not only was I a Christian called for a higher purpose, I also needed answers from this murderer. Why such covert action against me and my family? For what purpose did the TaTD need the alias Muhammad ibn Affal? Who else was involved?

From my suit pocket, I drew the tranquilizer pen, the one with the needle tip. Coleman hadn't searched me at all to detect my other resources. Underestimating me had led to the demise of many enemies.

With the knife in one hand and the pen in the other, I took a deep breath and planted my knee on the floor to surge up and over the seat. Coleman was already driving recklessly. It wouldn't take much to push his panic to my advantage. All I had to do was tranquilize him, as I'd done a hundred times to others since designing the little weapon.

The SUV was suddenly smashed broadside. The impact threw me into the door nearest my head. My feet were nearly crushed by the crowding metal. For an instant, I saw the grill of another vehicle through the twisted body of our SUV.

We were spinning. I couldn't focus my eyes even when the SUV seemed to be still an instant later; my head was too rattled.

"Get out of the car!" a voice screamed from somewhere outside. I knew that voice. Chloe! She'd found me!

A moment later, I heard the pelting of tranquilizer pellets on the side of the SUV.

"Chloe!" I yelled frantically. Wedged between both seats now, I could only kick one heel at the twisted metal below me, trying to make as much noise as possible. If she heard I was trapped, maybe she could rescue me from my metal coffin.

The vehicle lurched forward, then we zoomed away. How could the SUV still be operable? It didn't matter. Chloe was on the case. My transmitter was obviously working. She'd track me down. I just had to stay alive!

The knife and pen were no longer in my hands but somewhere below me. Still bound, I couldn't search the floor.

The SUV swerved left, roared ahead, then veered right. By the shadow on the seat, we were headed west. Ten minutes later, we slowed and entered an enclosure. The sunlight was blocked out and the engine echoed strangely off solid walls. Then we stopped. My wife and daughter were dead. This man was responsible! I wouldn't go calmly; he'd have his hands full.

The door at my head opened. The silenced pistol tapped me on the forehead. I looked up to meet Coleman's eyes. Were they the last eyes my wife had seen? The same eyes that had watched my blind daughter shrink in fear and confusion before he—

"Get out."

"I can't. I'm stuck. You'll have to—"

Holstering his gun, he grabbed me by my blazer shoulders. I slid out and fell hard on the ground. It wasn't pavement, but weeds and earth. Some sort of forgotten, underground bunker, it seemed. Once again, I dismissed hope of my transmitter broadcasting through these walls.

Coleman tugged me to my feet. I glimpsed my knife and pen in the SUV, but they were left behind as I was pulled by the arm toward a metal door with graffiti painted all over it. After stumbling through darkness and beer bottles underfoot, I ran face first into another door. Keys jingled in Coleman's hand, and the heavy door opened.

We entered a room that was illuminated automatically. Metal desks and outdated computer consoles spanned from wall to wall. Passing these and a dusty room that looked like a conference room, we stopped in a hallway with linoleum flooring. Coleman looked up and down the dark corridor that had doors lining the walls in both distant directions.

"Seems like a good place." He kicked at the back of my knee and swept my feet from under me. I fell painfully onto my bruised shoulder. "Years ago I came here. It's an old presidential bunker. A White House staffer leaked its location to a reporter, so it was abandoned. What a waste, huh?"

He stepped away from me and drew from his pocket my pen that had malfunctioned in his office.

"What's this?" He unscrewed the shell. "Ah. Here's your problem. A piece of plastic blocked your trigger mechanism."

Kneeling next to me, he pressed it against my neck.

"Tell me who you are or you die." He seemed calmer now, but I shivered fearfully under his cold gaze and grip. "Talk! I doubt your name is really Eric Lando. Your boss had a special crew of us selected for different tasks. What was your job? To take me out if something went wrong? Then you go after the general? Huh?"

"You get an answer for an answer," I said, nervously eyeing the injector held against my neck. "Just don't shoot me up with that stuff!"

"Talk, or I will!"

"Kill me and you get nothing!" My boldness grew, my mind delving into survival mode. Lies and tactics came naturally at that point. Deception and counteraccusations. In truth, the pen held only a mild sedative with a truth serum, nothing fatal or too incapacitating. "You'll kill me anyway. Just give me some answers to questions of my own."

"Fine." He relaxed. "But if you don't talk, I'll give you everything in this vial. You get three questions. Make them count."

I nodded fearfully, but he was threatening me with a weapon he didn't fully understand. For one, it wasn't a syringe, but a six-shot tube with water-soluble projectiles.

"Where is Corban Dowler's family? You said you killed them."

"The landfill outside Paterson. My turn." He lowered his face until it was even with mine, perhaps to see my eyes to confirm the validity of my answers. If he looked too closely, he'd see the makeup that covered the seams of my disguise. "When were you brought into the operation?"

"From the start, I've been involved," I said. "We're all puppets, Coleman."

"Then how didn't you know that—"

"My turn." I set my jaw stubbornly as he shook his head. He was enjoying himself more than me, and he seemed to sense no threat.

"Why make Dowler think he needed to stay underground? I never understood that."

"Ah, that was the genius part—my part of the plan." Coleman smiled. "Flight 524."

"Flight 524? The airliner?"

"That's what it was all about, anyway. See? You didn't even know that? Dowler was retired. It would've been easy to pin the explosion on some terrorist group. But he and his Muhammad ibn Affal cover was a better patsy, more believable, setting him up as a traitor to his country—an embittered, Christian extremist. He was already on my list of Agency liabilities, and we had to take down Flight 524. Two birds, one stone. Clever, I must say."

"It would've worked," I said, "if Dowler would've cooperated."

"Yes, there was that. Now, my turn. Do you know how to find Dowler? Maybe I can't salvage this op, but he's the kind of guy I need to find before he comes for me. Or any of us, if you live."

"Sure, I know where he's hiding. I can show you right to his doorstep. I know everything about him."

"Where is he?" he growled. "Tell me! No more games!"

"My turn!" I said. "Who else besides General Forglade is involved?"

"Forglade, me, you, and your people."

"Who do you think my people are?"

Swallowing, I held my breath. A name! I needed a name!

"What are you playing? Do you know where Dowler is or not? It's the only thing that'll keep you alive." He threatened with the pen again, and I jerked away like it was the most deadly thing imaginable. At the same time, I shifted my right foot slightly to kick him away if needed. My hands were bound, but if I could keep him from using his gun . . .

"Get me out of here, and I'll take you to Dowler."

"Nah, I don't think so. That's all the questions. Now, Dowler, or you die."

"The only way you'll ever find him before he finds you is if I take you to him."

"That's not happening." He smiled. "I'm allergic to ambushes, and thanks to you, I'm already on the run. Oh, I'll just find him myself, before or after I go after the general. There might be some truth to him trying to pin the whole op on me. But I'll clear my name with your people, no problem. And you won't be around to put a sniper bullet in me in the meantime."

"Killing me and the general won't be enough," I said, stalling. "You took all the risks when you showed your face to Dowler, posing as a Christian paroled convict."

"How'd you know that? Who told you that? Tell me!"

"I told you I was close to Dowler. Let me take you to him." I prayed as he considered the idea. If I could just get above ground again, so Chloe could track me . . . "Don't do this, Coleman. Not that way."

"No, you obviously know too much. Time's up, old man. Can't trust you to leave you alive any longer. It could be months before anyone finds you here."

He pressed the tab. The projectile shot into my neck with enough force to feel like I'd been jabbed hard with a pencil tip. For an instant, I panicked, afraid the injection would cause shock, and my throat would close. That pen was meant to shoot its projectiles from a distance, not to be placed against the neck where the force could inflict actual internal tissue damage to a target.

But a moment later, the warmth of the serum seeped into my bloodstream. It was meant to cause severe apathy and have some cognitive effects, but I remained lucid enough to fake several convulsions and seize rigidly. I then breathed a long exhale as I stared at him, my consciousness fading slowly.

Coleman checked my neck for a pulse. I was partially paralyzed, so I knew my heartbeat had slowed considerably, and my breathing was nearly nonexistent. The poison swirled through my brain and I struggled to focus.

And then he was gone, leaving me for dead. Since I was unable to move enough to keep the motion-activated lights on, the fluorescents above me blinked off to leave me in darkness. My family's killer had escaped, and I had achieved nothing, except to create more questions. Knowing I'd been set up to take down Flight 524 helped me little since I didn't know for whom Coleman and the general were working in the first place.

When I was able to move again after an hour, I rose to my knees and the lights clicked on. With some effort, I tugged my belt out of my pants and threw it on the floor. When I surfaced, I decided I didn't want Chloe tracking me. I was back in operative mode, covert status. Karl Coleman and General Forglade would pay. Then, I'd go after whoever had set me up and killed my family. I wanted them dead.

PART II: LUIGI

CHAPTER FOURTEEN

Some animals fight to the death for others in their herd, and it's this protective nature that I, Luigi Putelli, felt rising within me. It's animalistic, even predatory.

That autumn when it was rumored that Corban Dowler might've been killed by a car bomb, I didn't fail his family. Though I'd been in Italy seeing to personal matters when the bombing took place, my heart told me I needed to be back in New York to watch over his family, so I'd flown there the next morning. Failing Corban again wasn't an option.

Though I've never told Corban Dowler, I'm his most loyal friend. I've not always succeeded in my attempts to be loyal, but I've tried to show him the honor I believe he is due. The failures of my past to care for Corban's family have haunted me for months, and I have exercised extreme measures to ensure their safety even more than my own.

While searching Corban's past, in the wake of his supposed death by bombing, I followed a trail from a Serbian covert operation that led me to Dr. Mick Rhogtill's New York City apartment one block east of the High Line. After accessing the small apartment from the fire escape, it took ten minutes to confirm my suspicions: not only had

Corban been at that apartment recently, but it was so recent, he had to still be alive!

During the three years since he'd brought me into his inner circle, I had time to discover truths about his years in the CIA that I wished were lies. Corban had been a spy hunter and a mole "cleaner," though many of those details were hidden from even my eyes. I'd uncovered enough, however, to find some of the men and women whom Corban had helped before and after he'd come to follow his God. But the years since he'd started to follow his God were of particular interest to me. No longer did he sacrifice himself for his country, as he had with the CIA; now he sacrificed for his God. In fact, he no longer seemed like the same man today. Such dedication to his morality and spirituality had saved my life, as he'd helped me depart from my own misguided existence as an assassin for hire. I was inclined to follow Corban to learn from this selflessness.

Though confirming that Corban was still alive had been my objective, when I heard the key turn in the door, I hesitated to flee through the apartment window for the sake of uncovering more of Corban's current status. Perhaps I would see Corban himself in the flesh? I preferred to work unnoticed at night, but there were moments when I had to show my face and actually speak to people.

Standing next to the kitchen counter, I slid a knife stand farther away against the wall as the door swung wide open and Dr. Rhogtill stepped in. His arms were loaded with a grocery bag and a briefcase. From years of practice, my thumb went to my waistline where I could whip off my belt. The buckle had shards attached that had been dipped in a knockout toxin called falaco. Yes, I was indeed tempted to subdue him, tie him up, and proceed with my usual methods of information extraction. But being so close to Corban, and now hot on his trail, I was compelled to reform my usual methods.

Rhogtill closed his door, then turned and saw me. He paused with a calmness only expressed by confident men who've faced and survived countless hostilities. I recognized the doctor from photos uncovered from Corban's past. The doctor was a wanted man—in Serbia. There were still questions about his involvement during the war, but I wouldn't betray him. It would dishonor Corban. And because of this man's past, I knew he was no stranger to aggression or threat, and I found myself admiring him for this—besides my draw to him as a friend of Corban. Corban must've come to him for help.

His eyes, under a shaggy brow, glanced left and right, perhaps to confirm I was alone. He was short and firmly built, probably more firmly built than I was since I was struggling with health complications from a lifetime of violence.

"I am a friend." I held my palms open, though it was merely a gesture. Men such as us have no need of weapons in hand to cause harm.

"Friends wait on the doorstep." His accent was Serbian, and I considered how flawless his new identity must be to hide in the States when his Balkans accent seemed so obvious. "An enemy is more likely to wait inside after breaking in."

"You are a doctor. Corban Dowler came to you." The man's expression—one of confidence—didn't change at the mention of the name. "He was injured from the bombing, I believe. I have information for him. It is information for his ears only. I know he was here."

"Crumpon? I do not know the name."

"Corban!" I fumed, then smiled. Of course, he was playing with me. "You know him well, if he came to you first. Everyone else thinks he is dead."

"This man is not familiar to me, my friend." He set down his grocery bag and briefcase on the floor. I wasn't about to underestimate his capabilities; I hoped he didn't underestimate mine, because I didn't want to hurt him. "I live here alone. No one has been a guest here since I moved in six years ago."

"A hanger in the closet is bowed and empty. I suspect a heavy coat was on it until recently. The sofa cushions were cleaned and turned over, but I found speckles of bloodstains consistent with a man who has received multiple shrapnel injuries from a bomb. You or he swept the floor, but in your broom, I found brown hair inconsistent with your own color. Shall I continue?"

"Who are you?" There was no bewilderment in his voice. He was a dangerous man—I would know, since I was one, too.

"Luigi." I gestured to a kitchen stool ten feet away from him. As I leaned on the kitchen counter, hoping he would sit down on the stool, I continued introductions. "Corban and I met three years ago. He changed my life, but not so much that I follow his God, though I am drawn to the power that surrounds Corban's life. Because of him, I try to live in ways that honor him."

"Of course." He walked cautiously to the stool and set a hand on it. "God Almighty is worthy of attention."

Faster than seemed possible, he flipped the stool at me. I had time only to raise my arms and bat it aside, but Rhogtill's attack had only begun. He followed the stool with a kick to my abdomen that threw me against the brick wall next to the fire escape window. As I fell forward, he was on me again, this time with his hands, rigid and unclenched, like an expert hand-to-hand fighter.

Desperately, I blocked a few blows aimed at my neck and face, then moved to my left. He followed, but now I was prepared. Taller with a longer reach, I employed a dozen lightning strikes with my feet and hands that sent him backing up to the kitchen counter. His bushy brow was bleeding, but I was only winded and a little bruised.

"Doctor, I'm not here to hurt you." I whipped off my belt. "But I will if I have to."

"Not the words of a friend." He reached back and took hold of two steak knives from the stand on the counter. Apparently, I'd not moved them far enough away. "The door is to your left and the window is to your right. You can leave without injury."

He reversed his grip on one knife while keeping the other pointed upward. One for defense, both for offense. This doctor hiding from Serbian antagonists knew how to knife fight. But my belt was forty inches long. He didn't have a chance.

If we made too much noise, which a prolonged fight would cause, neighbors would surely call the police. I had to end the conflict before that happened—or before I was killed.

I swung the belt in great vertical loops, a vibrating rhythm that he studied in a calculating fashion. When I stepped forward, so did he. He held up one knife to take a belt strike while he stabbed at me with the other blade. However, I whipped the belt buckle horizontally and slashed its needle-like shards across his shoulder.

Rhogtill instantly realized he'd been bested, and he backed off. Though he still stood, I began to lace my belt into my pants.

"Is this my end?" Rhogtill dropped his knives and fell against the counter as he appeared to feel the effects of the toxin. "Do I die not knowing what this is about?"

"Rest in peace, Doctor, but only rest. In twenty minutes, you will regain consciousness, and we will talk like the friends of Corban that we both are."

He fell to the floor, still trying to fight the drug, and looked up at me. I knelt beside him, ready to catch his head as he slumped to the side. His determination to fight the drug was keeping him conscious longer than anyone I'd seen.

"You are truly a friend?"

"Yes. Do not fear. No real harm will come to you."

Then he fell asleep. Or so I thought.

The instant I relaxed my guard, the edge of a steak knife was at my throat. I was about to die, and I reflected in that moment how afraid I was of the afterlife. To my shame, I'd passed by many opportunities to discover in a personal way what Corban's God and Savior could mean to me.

"If you move, it will be your end," Dr. Rhogtill whispered. He sat up and rolled to his knees, with no relief of the pressure of the knife at my jugular. How a man who'd just fought and been drugged still had a steady hand, I didn't know. But I was terrified. "This knife is not so different than a scalpel in my hand. Would you like to see the color of your lungs, Luigi?"

"No." I felt my face redden.

"During the wars I was a doctor of death. I have mixed nerve gases and created toxins you cannot imagine. You see a plain surgeon before you now, but there was a time when I tasted whatever sleeping potion you cut me with. I am immune. What was it? Something stale but sweet. It is familiar to me."

My eyes flicked to his shoulder where my buckle had slashed through even his jacket to reach his bloodstream. If I lived through the next few minutes, I determined to become immune to falaco as well, knowing now that it was possible.

"Falaco. Corban uses something similar."

"So he does." The knife didn't move. "If you are close to Corban, then you are a Christian, yes?"

Though I was tempted to lie, I knew if I lied, I could only bluff, and pretending to be a Christian in front of a real Christian wasn't easy to do for long. Besides, it came with dangers I couldn't face as a mere man. Only a fool wouldn't fear Corban's God.

"It is as I said a moment ago. I do not follow his God. I have been stubborn. Corban would say as much."

"Yes, he would." The knife left my neck. In the same motion, Rhogtill stood and stepped back. "I cannot tell you anything about Corban. If you know him, you know he would not tell me what is happening and I am not one to ask."

Slowly, I rose to my feet, aware that he still held one knife.

"So, he is alive." I felt a chill of pride; Corban had bested his enemies again! But I also felt dread. Corban had been attacked by an enemy so dangerous that he'd not yet surfaced. "He does not die easily."

"The best I can do for you is to take a message to give him, but I doubt he will return. It would not be wise to return, if I am now watched. Obviously, you found me. Others may also." Rhogtill pointed the knife at a newspaper on a coffee table. "Corban may not be dead, but I cannot say the same for his family. A week ago, they were safe. Someone has blood on their hands."

I picked up the newspaper. The front page identified Janice and Jenna Dowler's bodies found in a landfill. Since they were related to the recently deceased Corban Dowler, all three deaths were being more closely investigated. Corban still had powerful government friends, apparently, who were not willing to sweep his supposed demise into the shadows.

"It is a ruse that a man like you could appreciate." I set the paper down and smiled. "Maybe you can imagine the lengths I went to. Dental records and blood types, clothing and hair samples."

"Janice and Jenna are alive?"

"Of course. I am their bodyguard."

"Does Corban know they are alive?"

"That is what I must tell him. I must find him now, before he does something drastic without this information."

"If he thinks his family is dead," Rhogtill said as his face turned pale, "there is no telling what he may do to his enemies!"

†

CHAPTER FIFTEEN

Since I was never one to park in front of a residence, my older half-sister's apartment in Queens was no exception. For most of my adult life, I'd believed I was alone. But after meeting Corban, I'd reflected more carefully on my family, and found my sister, Anna Putelli, only months earlier. She'd been living in a shabby cottage outside Perugia, Italy.

I imagined that Corban would say that I found her exactly when God wanted me to, for she was poor, ill, and disabled. When she was on the verge of suicide, I'd knocked on her door, introduced myself, and moved her out of Italy to New York. Though I could afford a full-time nurse to take care of her paraplegia needs while in Italy, Anna would never be safe without me near her. My many enemies knew that I still remembered their secrets.

Moving Anna to Queens had been selfish of me. I wanted to be close to the sibling whom I'd never had, but for her, she was just as isolated in New York as living in a sickly state in Italy. In Queens, she had a full-time attendant living in the duplex apartment above, but Anna spoke only Italian. After eight months in Queens, she'd been outside just twice—a factor I contributed to her own self-consciousness of being seen in a wheelchair. It had been five years since her husband had wrecked their car and crippled her. Uninjured, he'd remained with her for only a few months, then departed, leaving her broke and shamed in a country where family tradition defined much of our existence. If I hadn't vowed to Corban not to kill any longer, I would've visited her ex-husband.

"Anna, I am here!" I called as I let myself in the back door.

She said something from the back bedroom, but I didn't move from the door. Instead, I studied the apartment. Two days had passed since I'd last visited. The apartment looked the same: messy, as if the private attendant I'd hired wasn't doing her job. Dishes in the sink. Dry soil in the flowerpot. Dust on the windowsill. Empty food wrappers on the kitchen counter. I swept the wrappers into the wastebasket as I moved toward the quaint living room. With Anna, it had been a fight to get her to move in furniture. "I am in a wheelchair!" she'd complained. "Why do I need furniture?"

My attempt to give her a normal American life hadn't been smooth. If I'd found Anna, my enemies could have as well—if I hadn't convinced her to change her name to Anna Scalia, a name she detested.

"I am coming!" she said from the back room.

Sitting on the arm of the sofa, I watched the television that had been left on a news channel. A scandal had erupted over a crashed jet from months earlier. Though I knew nothing of Flight 524, or the reportedly missing passenger manifest, the fact that General Logan Forglade was wanted for questioning told me it was connected somehow to

Corban. Though I was no longer the killer I once was, my network of intelligence contacts was still intact—as were my skills at information gathering. Especially when it involved Corban Dowler. Darkness was at work.

"Did you bring me cigarettes?" Anna asked. Turning, I watched her roll into the kitchen, pushing herself. "Luigi! Where are my cigarettes?"

At times, I thought about walking out and never coming back. True, I owned the duplex and Anna would live in it as long as I paid the property taxes, but did I really need to be around her? My own problems were sufficient. But then I considered Corban, the man who'd broken me for reasons I'd still not completely grasped. What would Corban do in such a situation as this? He'd had his own problems as well, but he had dropped everything to see that my old life ended, and he exposed me to his God.

"No, Anna, I did not buy you cigarettes." Two car doors slammed outside. I crossed to the window. "Go with me to the park, and afterward, if you still want to smoke, I will buy you cigarettes. Fresh air does sound nice, yes?"

The thought of smoking made me fumble for two pieces of bubble gum from my pocket. I dropped the wrappers in the pot of dying flowers. My own smoking habit had nearly killed me, but that was a story I'd not told Anna.

"Luigi, I know you are manipulating me! There is nothing for me at the park! Where is Stephanie? She will get me cigarettes if you will not!"

Indeed, I wondered where Stephanie was as well. I gently pushed aside the window shade, expecting to see plump

Stephanie with her two children. Instead, I saw four men with mini-machine guns approaching the front door.

"Anna? Have you called anyone lately? In Italia, perhaps?"

Leaving the window, I moved next to the door. My belt was already in my hand.

"I do not care what you say, Luigi. I still have a life back there! Yes, you rescued me, but I had neighbors who—"

The front door burst open. These men were there to kill Anna, no doubt, because of me. They charged into the apartment before their eyes could adjust to the dimness, and before they noticed I was beside the door behind them. Anna screamed as I attacked.

My belt struck like a snake at the back of one man's neck. The next swing of the buckle wrapped around one of the machine gun barrels. As the belt unwrapped, I kicked at the next killer. The other two were torn between shooting at me through their comrades and seeing to the screams in the kitchen.

When my belt was free, I ducked under a barrage of gunfire that cut the front door in two. The buckle clawed at the shooter's calves, then I used my own legs to swipe the legs of the fourth man from under him. The second and fourth men were quickly tranquilized, and I lunged into the kitchen to receive possible attackers from the back door, but none entered. The team had been unprofessional and obviously ill-advised as to whom their target was. I enjoyed being underestimated.

"Anna, shut up!"

My sharp words silenced her screaming. I knelt over the four sleeping men, heaped half on top of one another. After collecting their identifications, I took a moment to study them closely. Two were of Hispanic origin, perhaps local gangsters by the look of their baggy clothes. If Anna had called the old country, past clients of mine who didn't want their secrets known had surely tracked me down through her. They'd hired out instead of sending their own people, it seemed. Since I'd had dozens of powerful clients, I couldn't begin to figure out who'd sent these men.

"Who are they?" Anna wiped tears from her face. "Did I do this?"

"Do you see what happens when you do not follow my instructions? It would have been worse in Italia. You have only a few minutes to pack. We are leaving now!"

†

CHAPTER SIXTEEN

I had cut ties with many locations and people in my life, so leaving the duplex behind that I'd bought for Anna affected me little. My accounts were both sizable and numerous, my evils having paid bountifully. But my ghosts haunted mercilessly.

We drove north in my car. Anna's wheelchair was folded in the back seat and more than a few medical supplies and personal belongings crowded the trunk. I was as angry with myself as I was at Anna. She couldn't know my past well enough to be as wary of enemies as I was. Who was I to dream of a normal life for myself or for anyone near me? It was something Corban seemed to understand about me, and I understood about him. That he risked his own family was a burden we both carried. Janice and Jenna were in my eyes as my own sister and niece, though I'd spent only days with them in the last few years.

Anna tried to speak to me, but I didn't respond for two hours. She wept off and on while I contemplated more about Corban's well-being rather than my own. Corban needed me, and I was distracted by personal burdens I hadn't anticipated when I'd found my sister. In my position, what would Corban do? He would balance everything in his capable arms—and trust his God to faithfully carry him forward. I could try to balance things, but the trusting was still beyond me.

Where Highway 16 met the White Mountains of northern New Hampshire, I turned off the road before Pinkham Notch Visitor Center. The Appalachian Trail continued northward, but I drove my town car up a weedy access road where such vehicles didn't belong. When I noticed a patch on a tree where the bark had been peeled off in a peculiar way, I stopped the car.

"So this is it?" Anna dabbed at her eyes. "This is how you deal with your own sister? I knew you had a dark past, Luigi, but this is just pure evil!"

She weakly punched my shoulder once, and when she swung again, this time for my face, I caught her wrist.

"Would I have packed your medical supplies if I was abandoning you in the woods?" I released her wrist. "Anna, I am not killing you. This is a safe place for you."

"That is just what a murderer would say!" She folded her arms and pouted. I'd told her none of my past, but she obviously sensed the remnants of my old life. "Just do it quickly!"

Rolling my eyes, I took the keys and climbed out of the car. From the trunk, I fetched a shovel and a flashlight, then approached Anna's door. She locked the door and shook her head. Using the keys, I unlocked the door. Again, she batted weakly at me as I knelt before her. In the next seconds, she panted heavily between sobs and then gave up.

"Will you listen to me? Please?"

"I need a cigarette." She searched the glove box. "My last cigarette."

"Anna, I am taking you someplace safe!"

"Yeah, right! With a shovel!"

Frowning at the shovel in my hand, I then smiled and shook my head, suddenly aware of how terrible it must appear to her.

"Listen, Anna, I do not have time for this!" Frustrated, I threw down the shovel and whipped off my belt. With care, I took the buckle and lightly scratched her across one paralyzed thigh. She froze as two tiny spots of blood soaked through her gray sweats.

As Anna looked from her legs to my face, she seemed too confused to say anything more, finally. Her breath caught, then she slumped to the side.

With ease, I drew her over my right shoulder, picked up the shovel, and stood upright. Anna was lean, like me, and her legs had atrophied from her disability, so she wasn't too heavy. I started into the woods on a northwest heading, with no discernible path before me.

The trees thinned considerably as I ascended the mountain toward what I knew to be Tuckerman Ravine.

An hour later, I'd traveled two miles from the car. The rocky terrain was steep and patchy, as my route was winding. During rests, I'd tranquilized Anna several more times to keep her docile, but now I had arrived. Lion Head cleft was on my right, and Boott Spur was on my left. Tuckerman Ravine, where dozens of hikers, skiers, and climbers had perished over the years, faced me in a formidable shadow and haze.

Only a few days earlier, I'd stood at that very spot, searching for an opening I knew was there, but could rarely locate it right away, no matter how many times I'd been there. There, a crack in a boulder! I followed the crack until it ran off the side of what I guessed was granite. Well, it was cement meant to appear like granite.

Still holding Anna, with one arm I shoved the shovelhead into the bottom of the crack. I wiggled the shovel a little, shifted it, and felt the subtle resistance. There it was! Looking up at Lion Head and Boott Spur, I studied the Headwall over Tuckerman Ravine. Was anyone watching? At least no one was visible. Under most circumstances, I would access the hideout under cover of night, but I couldn't wait three more hours. As it was, I'd never tranquilized someone as much as I had already tranquilized Anna.

I twisted the shovel and levered it sideways. The resistance gave way and a rumble of gears trembled up through my feet. The crack in the boulder became a gap, then an opening that revealed a set of stairs. My hand still held constant pressure on the lever, but then I stepped into the stairwell, and removed the shovel. The opening began to close as I descended into darkness.

Above and behind me, the opening sealed shut with a heavy thud that reminded me of its strength even under several feet of snow during the winter months. I set the shovel aside as I reached a level concrete floor, then flipped on my flashlight. After following the corridor for a ways, I turned a corner. My fingers touched a digital keypad left from an era of military long past. The number I typed into the keypad was a code Corban had given me two years earlier when I was asked to train COIL operative Nathan Isaacson for individual agent status.

With the code entered, a steel blast door clicked and buzzed. I pushed through it into dim lighting from the ceiling, and slammed the door hard enough to cause an echo down the next corridor before me.

Fifty feet later, I reached a second blast door with a different code. After passing through it, I entered the core of the decommissioned Minuteman missile silo. I imagined a time when Corban had cleansed CIA databanks of the silo's location, and redesigned the exterior door outside to hide it from military officials who'd known the silo was there decades earlier.

Like many other silos across the continent, this one was an underground complex capable of sustaining a six-man crew for six months at a time. With the store rooms fully replenished, as they were now, two civilians could survive for several years, though I had no interest in testing that theory right then.

Before me, a rail guarded me from tumbling nine stories off the observation platform, now overlooking empty space except for several pulleys, winches, and lengths of chain. Opposite the empty missile shaft, another blast door opened and I recognized Janice as she smiled—then quickly frowned at my unconscious burden.

"Francis! What happened?" She still used the assumed name I'd once provided when guarding her and Jenna. Janice ran around the circular catwalk to reach me.

"This is my sister, Anna," I said. "She is unconscious."

"Let me help you. Gently now. I'll take her head."

Together, we carried Anna into brightly lit living quarters where music wafted from a modern-day speaker. Since Janice had a nursing background, I could think of no better company in which to leave Anna.

"Francis!" Jenna, Corban's adopted blind daughter, now ten years old, threw off a blanket and rushed toward me as if she could see the furniture in the room. I knelt and accepted her open arms in a rough embrace around my neck, though my hands were still carrying Anna.

"Easy, hon." Janice was straining under Anna's weight. "We're carrying a sleeping woman."

With some effort, we took Anna into a back room and set her on a narrow bunk bed.

"I didn't know you had a sister, Francis!" Janice gave me an embrace, her familiarity still strange to me. Jenna felt Anna's sleeping face for her features. "It's been two weeks. What's happening out there? Have you heard from Corban? I've been going sick with worry!"

"No word yet." We left Anna in the back room and I closed the door softly. "I spoke to a friend of Corban's who he went to for help recently. Corban may be under the presumption still that you and Jenna are . . . no longer."

Listening politely nearby, I noticed Jenna tilting her head to hear. I was reminded of her very mature approach to conflict. She'd endured not only the death of her own parents, but also several attacks from her adopted father's enemies.

"When you picked us up at Corban's funeral, I thought this would take only a day or two for you to help Corban solve everything."

"Corban is most elusive, but I must find him to help him further." Glancing around the living quarters, I saw it was no place in which to live indefinitely, though pictures of forests and sunsets in window-like frames helped dispel the claustrophobia. "I stand by my decision to fake your deaths, though I will need a few more days. No more than a week, I hope."

Before Janice could pressure me for more information about Corban, I had to change the subject.

"My sister speaks only Italian," I said. "And she is a paraplegic."

"What? A paraplegic!"

"In an hour I will return with her wheelchair and medical supplies, but I cannot spend the night. I have to return to the city so I can remain available for Corban, should he need me."

"What will you do if you can't find Corban?"

"If Corban cannot be found, I must continue as Corban would—work in his place, as a COIL representative."

"Francis . . ." Janice frowned. "No offense, but if I remember accurately, you're not even a Christian. How will you work for COIL?"

"Every moment Corban is in hiding, there are people in need of his help. How I will do it must be left in the hands of Corban's God."

†

CHAPTER SEVENTEEN

Back in New York City, I sat in the midst of a technological jungle of surveillance equipment as I considered my next move. Monitors around me flickered with video feed from cameras and streaming text from servers around the world. There'd been no sign of Corban traveling through airports or train stations, or using any name publicly he'd been known to use. All facts seemed to indicate that Corban was indeed dead.

The data banks and racks of hard drives recorded intel from secret agents in distant countries—programs I'd written myself, meant to be customized for that on which I was focused at present. They searched for key words that related to only a variety of my interests from public news feeds and secret wiretaps alike. But nothing on Corban anywhere!

When I'd traveled with Corban, he never seemed to be without a plan. Surely, he was up to something now, but why so invisible? I suspected I'd done such a clean job of making Janice and Jenna seem dead that Corban and the rest of COIL truly believed they were deceased. And though it seemed the enemies of Corban were restricted to government men like Karl Coleman and General Forglade, I wouldn't trust the COIL office with precious information until I spoke to Corban, or at least to Chloe, myself.

I punched a few buttons on a keyboard, then sat back and watched for a screen to report any findings. Karl Coleman, in my opinion, was the most dangerous man of the two, but only General Forglade was in the news as a wanted man. I understood Coleman to be a clandestine officer, one with connections and certain deadly skills. Forglade had been missing for a week, almost the same length of time since the supposed bodies of Janice and Jenna had been found.

Coleman seemed to be just one of the powerful masterminds behind whatever was happening with Corban. Thus, Coleman was keeping his name out of the news. General Forglade, perhaps not as dangerous, was getting all the attention. It had been over a week since I'd answered the post through underground methods for the hit against Janice and Jenna. Anonymous net accounts and proxy servers made such deals generally safe. Except I'd been waiting with tracer and chaser programs to hunt the hunters. I'd found Coleman and taken the job after discovering it was against Corban's family. But Coleman's hands were still clean, it seemed. Someone else always did the dirty work in Coleman's world. Somehow, I needed to pinch the man to do some lawless deed himself and trap him. But how could I do that to someone I couldn't locate?

My past reputation continued to work for me, though I now despised who I'd been. Hiding the Dowler girls had been easy; covering up their deaths with other recently deceased bodies had required a drive to a Pennsylvania crematorium and a sizeable donation for two bodies. It certainly hadn't been my first staged death scenario.

Karl Coleman was a devil, and I knew spiritual matters beyond me were at work. Corban could've surely explained it all to me, but for now, I was content to interrupt the dark vessels at work.

Perhaps Corban hesitated to surface until General Forglade was in US custody? Or maybe Corban was hunting Forglade and Coleman himself? Either way, I had time to pass until someone or something surfaced for me to pursue.

Leaning back in my soft chair, I inserted two more pieces of gum into my mouth. My eyes peered past one monitor at a weathered Bible on the shelf of my basement office. Months earlier, I'd secretly followed Corban to Europe on one of his missions. I was forever intrigued by his unorthodox methods and hazardous courage. Since I'd lost him at an airport in Romania, I had to backtrack to a hotel for clues. That was when I'd found the Bible in his room— with a note in it from Corban to me. The note had advised me to make better use of my time for God.

The note had been burned, but I still had the Bible, and it was this Bible that I now took off the shelf. Flipping through its pages, I wondered how a mere book could inspire countless lives to live or die for a God who died on a cross and rose again. If there was a God, would He help me since I wanted to help Corban, one of God's own ambassadors?

I stopped on a page that said Psalms. My gaze settled on three lines: "Vindicate the afflicted, save the children, and crush the oppressor." It seemed quite unreasonable to trust the chance words of a Holy Book for a particular problem, but the words fit quite nicely toward my lack of direction.

Vindicate the afflicted? Until Corban could freely resume his usual duties for COIL, I would assume those responsibilities for him, which might actually bring him out of hiding.

Save the children? Protecting the innocent from evil had become a pattern of my new life since meeting Corban. But which children was I to save? I guessed if God was leading me, I would find out, though doubt plagued me over such a coincidence of fate.

Crush the oppressor? That was closer to my line of work from my old life, but more than a few times I'd witnessed Corban crush oppressors in ways that brought justice without compromising his high moral values from the Bible. Therefore, I would also crush the oppressor, whomever that would be.

But first, I would vindicate the afflicted. How? When I wasn't watching Janice and Jenna, I was usually taking care of Anna or tracking Corban or Nathan's COIL activities— sometimes even following Chloe. COIL itself had a sophisticated network of international missionaries and Christian contacts I didn't have access to, so the afflicted I would vindicate would need to be from my own network.

I logged onto three proxy servers before I digitally stepped onto a bulletin board system in Singapore. Someone in Florida was looking for a timing mechanism for a washing machine. It smelled like a setup, maybe for a bomb, but I didn't inquire. A contact name was left for someone who needed carpet cleaning in Nevada. Definitely a body disposal job.

Then, I came upon a gardener job for two rows of vegetables in New Jersey. For certain, it was for a hit on two people—a job only a pro would take, since two targets compounded the particulars of any job. Since the bulletin was still posted, no one had accepted it yet. If it was a trap, there were precautions I could take. But if someone really were seeking to have two people killed, I had to intercede. It was exactly what I'd done for Janice and Jenna, and it something Corban would do: vindicate the afflicted. I was going to New Jersey.

...✝...

Three days later, I stood in the doorway of a messy office in Franklinville's police station. To my left were four desks, vacant except for one attractive blond policewoman officer about my age. To my right was a tall window that didn't appear to be bulletproofed, which faced the local library. I'd parked my rental car in the library parking lot.

"So . . ." A man with a white mustache and a big gut turned toward me. "What brings you to Franklinville's cyber crimes department?"

"This is the whole department?"

"Just me." He pointed to his nametag and offered me a form, stapled to a dozen pages. "Fill this out, state the complaint clearly, get it notarized, and send it to this office via the US Postal Service."

I didn't reach for the form.

"My . . . complaint, Officer Madison, is rather urgent." I glanced to my left. The blond woman sat at her desk listening, which wasn't helping my nervousness in a police station. But then she nodded and gestured with a hand for me to continue. "A man is threatening to kill his sister and her six-year-old son. I am reporting a serious threat to their lives."

"People say things." He still held the complaint form for me to take. "Cyber threats go in section two, page three."

"How long will the form take to process if I fill it out now?"

"Well, my office is backed up right now. If I deem it worthy of actually getting an urgent classification, I have the option of turning it over to the Feds or pre-screening it myself. Pre-screening takes time since I'm only in the field one day out of the week. Questioning the accused may take two or three visits if an arrest is not yet warranted. That could take a few weeks, depending on the judge who—"

"Never mind." I held up my hand, half-tempted to tranquilize the man purely for his apathy. "I am sure the threat is not worth all of that time."

He turned back to his desk before I left his doorway. As the blond officer rose from her desk, I brushed past her toward the exit. I'd tried the legal route to vindicate the afflicted. Now, I would do it my way.

As I unlocked my car door, I heard footsteps behind me. I reached for my belt by instinct and turned to ward off any aggressor.

"Whoa! Easy, there, cowboy!" It was the blond officer, her hand now on her service gun. "What did you have in mind, whipping me?"

I looked down at the belt in my fist, ready to swing it. There was amusement in her eyes.

"You caught me by surprise." I put my belt back through the loops. "My apologies, Officer. I've been tense lately."

"Madison's behavior probably didn't help, either." She leaned on my car hood, her hand no longer on her gun. Women didn't naturally approach me, so what was her angle? "Maybe I'm the one who should be apologizing. You're trying to be a good citizen and then you got the brush-off."

With an identity to maintain, I didn't tell her I wasn't a citizen of any country, not even my own any longer.

"Apology accepted, Officer . . ."

"Oakes. I'm the dispatcher mostly, but sometimes I'm on patrol when not doing desk duty."

"I see." Smiling, I wasn't willing to share even my assumed identity if I didn't have to. "Have a nice day, Officer Oakes."

"You know, it's about my lunch hour. Why don't we go to the deli?" She nodded her head at the highway, but I didn't see a deli. "We can talk about his Internet complaint you have."

"No complaint." I smiled again, feeling more uncomfortable by the second. "Officer Madison helped me see it's not important."

"So, that's how it's gonna be, huh?" Her face grew very serious, and I felt like a student about to be scolded by his teacher. "You're gonna handle this problem yourself since the people in blue did nothing?"

My eyes narrowed. This dispatcher was no fool. Was I so transparent? She didn't wear a wedding ring. Had she noticed that I didn't, either? Not only had I been uncomfortable about going to the police about a threat I could easily have handled, I was especially uncomfortable at the prospect of going to a deli with a police officer, pretty or not!

"Come on." She started for the passenger door. "If a girl can't trust a good Samaritan over lunch, who can she trust? I'll buy. What do you say?"

"I'm not that good," I said as she smiled, and we both climbed into the car.

But I wasn't smiling.

† CHAPTER EIGHTEEN

"**M**mm! This is the best sandwich shop from here to Atlantic City!" My new friend, Officer Heather Oakes, took a man-size bite of a pastrami sandwich. "So, Luigi Brugnetti, you've got that humorless mob face. Ever been a mob man? By your accent, I'd guess you weren't even born here. Lots of mob still in Jersey, mostly in the north. Retired, too. You going to eat that?"

My meatball sandwich sat untouched until that instant when I remembered to eat. I took more modest bites than Heather, though if I'd been alone, I would've been more ravenous like she was. Eating had never been a social matter for me.

"I have no mob ties. I can account for my accent by my mother's insistence on speaking Italian in her home in Queens."

"Queens?" She wiped her mouth, missing mayonnaise on her cheek. "You're a long ways from home to be looking out for someone you found threatened on the Internet."

"Civic duty." I shrugged, then remembered Corban. What would he say? Of course, I'd told the truth. I did just want to be a good citizen, but I was too used to padding my responses while under cover that now I felt the need to say more. "More specifically, my Christian duty. Do for others, as Christ said."

"Did Jesus say that?" She frowned, then smiled as if she knew I was bluffing. "So, tell me about the complaint that isn't a complaint. You said a woman and a six-year-old boy are in danger?"

At first, I thought about trying again to brush off the threat, but she'd already guessed I would only do that to handle the threat myself.

"There's a database in Southeast Asia where certain . . . wickedness is both offered and requested."

"I see." She was finished with her meal while I was on my fourth bite. "This is a site you frequent?"

"No! I mean . . ." Too late. I hadn't recovered in time. Her eyebrows went up. "Yes, to be honest. I do frequent this particular site."

She sat back in her chair and seemed to study me in a new light. I chewed slowly on my sandwich, tasting nothing because of my nerves. Though I hadn't been psychoanalyzed in person since my early French DGSE years, I was reminded of that discomfort now.

"Luigi Brugnetti—if that is your name—I read you wrong." She wagged a finger at me. "You're definitely not mob. You're the guy the mob calls to solve . . . family problems. You're dangerous, Mr. Brugnetti."

"If I am so dangerous, why am I helping people—and eating lunch with a police officer?"

"I didn't give you a choice, that's why."

Before I said something else without thinking, I filled my mouth with another bite. Who was this woman? I couldn't keep her from prying, and her intuition seemed better than her prying!

"There's a Canadian named Carl Dawson on his way to Franklinville to make sure his sister and nephew are killed."

"Killed by you?"

"No, I am just reporting the facts. Savannah Perkins and her son Adam are in danger."

"You took the job and now you don't want to follow through?" She folded her hands and leaned forward, as if she had conversations about assassins and conspiracies every day. "Did you get too close to the victims? Fall in love with this Savannah woman?"

"I've never met them." It seemed like I was defending myself too much. "But I'm only keeping them alive. To prove involvement on the part of Carl Dawson, I can email you the tracing information. That's all I'm here for. You do something, or not, but I'm not here to be questioned. I'm only helping."

Sliding from the booth, I drew a worn wallet from my slacks pocket. A twenty-dollar bill would be sufficient.

"Have a good day, Officer."

She was still seated when I left the deli, but by the time I reached the car, she was on my heels.

"Did you forget, Brugnetti, that you drove me here?"

Turning, I hoped to react cooler to her inquiries if I had to be around her for a few more minutes. Instead, she challenged me no further as she climbed into the car. When I climbed in, I noticed her service gun was unclipped and ready to draw. And she was left-handed.

No longer was I in a position that I could imagine Corban handling. Either I was about to be arrested in my own rental car—or at the police station where she would have backup.

Instead of starting the car, I rested a hand on the steering wheel and stared straight ahead. Using the mirrors, I checked everything around the car. Though I wasn't a veteran of doing right, I was aware, with some discouragement, of how much opposition I was receiving. Was doing right always this difficult?

"You have to start the engine for this next part." She chuckled, perhaps to remove the tension, but I could hear the uncertainty in her voice. She was the bravest woman I'd ever known—attempting to arrest a man she'd accurately identified as some sort of practiced killer. "Are we going? I have a shift to finish . . . sometime today."

"If you reach for your sidearm, this will end badly for you." I still gazed straight ahead, but her head was turned toward me now. Desperately, I wanted a piece of gum to help me relax, but if I reached for one, the movement could be misinterpreted. "You have been most perceptive in who you think I am, or who I once was."

A moment of silence passed. She moved her hand a little, and I saw her fingers shaking.

"I always do this to myself," she mumbled, perhaps directed at herself as much as at me. "Sometimes I leap before I realize what's at stake. You were a good man, I thought—a citizen reporting a crime."

"That was my intention," I said with clenched teeth, then I relaxed some. Nothing could help our situation if we were both tense. "I'm not a man to be arrested, Officer Oakes."

"No kidding. That's why I unclipped my holster, but you obviously saw that already." Her breathing had increased, probably matching her heightened heart rate. Years of predatory pursuits had toned my senses for such moments. But for her, it was just a job, and now she realized her job meant her life. "So, how do you suppose we proceed?"

"Perhaps you should walk back to the station." A map of the vicinity flashed in my memory. "The only head start I need is the one I create by getting you out of the car."

"So, you think you're that good, huh? In my town?"

"I know I'm that good."

"Well, I'm not content with getting out," she said softly. I was partially bothered by her stubbornness. And partially attracted. "But I'm not content with shooting you, either."

"And I'm not content with being shot."

"You're not leaving me much of a choice here, Luigi Brugnetti. I swore to protect, and what little I've learned from you, there are questions you need to answer. In the least, you're a wanted man. That's my guess."

"Having been in dozens of countries, I've faced countless enemies with varieties of weapons. You can't beat me, Officer Oakes. Now, I'll take your gun, and you'll step out of the car. I'll mail you your—"

She reached for her gun, but I was ready. The tight space hindered her speed, and the holster was high on her hip. Instead of grasping the gun myself, I reached across and clasped her wrist, then I drew the gun slowly with my other hand. I deposited the gun onto the floor behind her seat.

Now turned toward her in my seat, I watched her face turn from panic to surprise. She took two quick breaths, her eyes taking in my empty and exposed palms.

"What kind of crook are you?" She scoffed, as if disappointed I hadn't lived up to her accusations. "You just got rid of the gun."

"Get out of the car and walk away."

She frowned. Instead of reaching for the door handle, a smile slowly crept onto her face. It wasn't possible for me to hurt this strange woman. Her determination and fearless behavior reminded me of myself. Except her motives seemed pure, and mine seemed to have been tainted by myself.

"No. I don't think I will, Luigi Brugnetti."

"What? Go! I won't hurt you. When you look back, I'll be gone."

"That's exactly why I won't go. You won't hurt me. I believe you. And I don't want you to disappear."

I couldn't believe what she was doing to me. It made no sense!

"Leave! I have matters to attend to, lives that depend on me."

"Besides the lives of Savannah and Adam Perkins?"

"Good. You remember their names. Now their blood isn't on my hands. Go!"

"No, not until you tell me who you really are."

"Who I really am? You've already looked into my life with your detective eyes and exposed me wide open!"

"Yeah, but that's nothing. The faster you talk, the faster I'll walk away. Come on. You've made it clear that you're a good guy, so what have you got to hide? Out with it, Luigi Brugnetti."

"I . . . can't! You don't understand. This isn't happening."

"Hey, you came to us, remember. What did you think would happen?"

"You're right. This was a mistake. Leave!"

"Twenty years I've been a cop. I thought you were a good Samaritan. Then I thought I smelled a rat. Now, I think you're something in between."

"I'm a man with a bad past, but my present is intertwined with the life of a good man who needs me. I can't let him down."

"Who's this good man? Your boss?"

"No. Perhaps . . . my spiritual mentor."

"Where is this man? He told you to help Savannah and Adam?"

"No, but it's something he would've done." I shook my head. "This man is lost. I can't find him. He hasn't surfaced in nearly three weeks."

"Okay, so he's some sort of operative?"

"Stop doing that!" I growled under my breath and she watched as I fumbled with a gum wrapper and shoved a piece into my mouth. "Stop reading between my words."

"I can't help it." She laughed—at a moment like that! Now I seemed to be the one who was tense again. "All I do is read and file police reports that are barely legible sometimes. I have to read between the lines. So, you're some sort of operative?"

"Well, I was. Now I freelance."

"Are you a rogue agent?" She folded her hands. "Did you run away from your agency?"

"Years ago, yes. My mentor rescued me from that life. A terrible life. I've been spending my retirement watching over his family. He's retired, too, but he insists on helping people when all he gets is attacked for it."

"So, you're like his bodyguard?"

"His family's bodyguard, of sorts."

"Is his family safe while you're with me?"

"Yes. Please, let me go."

"Neither of us is a prisoner of the other. You've made that clear, Luigi. Drive if you want."

"No, I need you to get out. I can say no more. I insist. Get out now."

"Not without my Glock."

"I'll give it to you."

"When I get out? You better not mess with me, Luigi." She opened the door, thankfully reading the limit in my voice. "Okay, I'm out of the car."

Reaching into the back seat, I picked up the gun from the floor. After ejecting the clip and checking the chamber, I gave it back to her.

"You didn't have a bullet in the chamber, Heather," I said. "It would've done little for you to draw your gun earlier. Next time you're in the field, keep one in the chamber, even if it's against regulations."

"Okay, I'll keep that in mind. My clip?"

"I'll mail it to you. You'll protect Savannah Perkins and her son from Carl Dawson?"

"Of course, I'll do my best. Please, Luigi, you don't need to continue alone. I can tell you're torn. Let me help you. We can even meet privately. There are people who've done what you've done, and their records have been fixed legally. You don't have to live like this."

"Goodbye, Heather Oakes."

The passenger door swung closed as I drove away. Saving lives was so much harder than taking them.

†

CHAPTER NINETEEN

I wasn't so foolish as to trust the Franklinville station with the protection of Savannah and Adam Perkins. That's why I was parked on Pennsylvania Avenue down the road from their house later that night. Too much of my time and energy had already gone into the project to see the police bungle it.

Leaving my car hood raised, I crossed the street on foot and approached the house that had only one light on inside. Movement from within confirmed that Savannah was still awake, probably waiting for her brother, Carl Dawson, to arrive from the airport. From checking the airline arrival times, I knew he'd arrived in Newark two hours ago. He was due any minute.

After crossing the lawn, I paused behind a tree to peer at an unmarked police cruiser parked fifty yards down the street. Carl Dawson probably wouldn't know it was a police car. Was Heather in there? When passing headlights shined in the interior, I noticed only one person sitting in the front. I wondered under what circumstances the police would intervene.

My clothes were dark and shadows surrounded me. Nevertheless, I waited until another car drove toward the police sentry for my sprint behind the house and a high jump onto a propane tank. Operating on a predetermined route into the house, I leaped up, grabbed a thick windowsill, and drew myself up far enough to slide an upstairs window open.

Once inside, I stepped next to a clothes hamper and paused to close the window. I was in an upstairs bathroom. Upon leaving the room, I found myself in a short hallway, presumably leading to other bedrooms. In the other direction, I saw stairs and lamplight.

Moving toward the light, I discovered a balcony overlooking a cozy living room where Savannah Perkins sat in a soft chair reading a book. She could've looked up and seen me right then, but I stepped back until only my head was exposed. After a few minutes, it seemed she was doing her best to read, but her eyes kept drifting closed. Since all I knew about Carl and Savannah was restricted to Internet research, I wondered at Savannah's dedication to wait up so late for his arrival. It was nearly two o'clock. Did she fear him? Or suspect his intentions against her? I doubted it. Betrayal often comes from those closest.

As soon as she seemed to be asleep, I eased down the carpeted stairway and walked dangerously close to the twenty seven year old—close enough to touch her dark curls if I had wanted to. Instead, I moved behind her chair and slipped between the heavy drapes and the wall next to the window. Once in place, I realized the curtains weren't so thick and I was able to see through the fibers.

A few minutes later, headlights swept across the living room—revealing family photographs, a piano, and a collection of children's videos. Savannah was startled awake by a slamming door. She stood and stretched her five-two frame, then crossed to the front door near the kitchen. I took that instant to turn on my recorder—the wireless microphone disguised as a pen clipped to my collar.

Savannah opened the front door before Carl Dawson could knock. He was carrying a suitcase as he entered.

"Hey, Carl." She embraced him, but he didn't return the gesture. He only paused until she released him so he could continue into the house. "No flight problems?"

"Nothing important. Adam go to bed?"

"Hours ago. Don't you know what time it is?"

He walked past her to the kitchen and helped himself to a pitcher in the refrigerator. He drank straight from the container. After guzzling, he leaned against the counter. I definitely didn't like this man.

"We have to talk about Dad's inheritance."

"Carl, seriously?" She shook her head. "We already agreed. You and I are doing fine. We'll save it for Adam's medical, and then schooling if there's anything left."

"Things have changed, sis. I need a piece of it now, so I brought the papers for you to sign."

"No, Carl! We agreed already! Is this all you came down here for? You said it was about work or something. Are you gambling again?"

Taking a folder out of his suitcase, he set a pen on the counter.

"There's enough for Adam and me." He slid the forms toward her. "If you keep working, you'll earn enough for the two of you."

I stepped from behind the curtain before she could be persuaded to sign the forms.

"Am I interrupting?" I asked, already moving across the living room. Savannah drew back, terror on her face, but I caught her easily by the arm and covered her mouth from behind. "Don't make this difficult, Savannah."

She struggled, but I tightened my grip and held her in place.

"Nice timing, you idiot!" Carl hissed at me. He had reddish hair and a crooked nose. "She was about to sign the forms! That's how you get paid!"

"Well," I said softly, "now we make sure she signs, because I definitely want to get paid. How do we make sure she signs, Carl?"

"He'll kill Adam, Savannah," Carl told her. "Unless you sign. The money or the sick brat?"

I felt her tears on my hand that was still over her mouth. She reached for the pen and signed the forms so quickly, she missed the signature line completely.

"Look, you messed it up!" Carl snarled and cursed. He drew back a fist to strike Savannah.

"It's fine!" I moved her away a step, the guilt of my own actions bothering me, even though my part was a ruse. "Now what, Carl?"

"You know." He frowned at the papers. "I can make these work, I guess. Kill her and the brat, and wound me. Where's your gun? I told you this has to look like a robbery or something."

My recorder had enough. I spun Savannah from my arms and whipped off my belt. The buckle slashed across

Carl's cheek. The look of surprise on his face lasted two speechless breaths before he crumbled on the kitchen floor. Turning, I snatched a cell phone from Savannah's hands the instant she began to dial.

"Please, not my baby!" She clutched at my clothes, begging. "Whatever he's paying you, I'll double it!"

"Say no more." I held up her phone to silence her. "Savannah, I won't hurt you or Adam. Carl Dawson is a wicked man. I came to stop him."

She peered around me to see her brother lying on the floor.

"Is he . . . dead?"

"No, just sleeping." I drew the recorder from my pocket and plucked out the digital card. "This is for the police. Call them as soon as I leave. A police car is outside, so they'll be only minutes."

"You're a police officer? Was this a . . . sting or something?"

"Or something." I held up a gun clip. "And make sure Officer Heather Oakes gets this, okay? Say it. Heather Oakes."

"Heather Oakes." She took the clip and digital card and held them close.

Moving toward the stairs, I looked back. She wiped her eyes, then nodded and smiled at me. That was my payment, I realized. And that was why Corban did the work he did— for those tearful moments of thanks. I'd received much money from many jobs, and I never felt as good as I did at that moment, receiving no money at all.

...✝...

"Franklinville Police Department. This is dispatcher Oakes. How may I assist you?"

"Hello, Heather."

A moment passed, and I imagined she was checking the recorders to ensure they were recording our phone conversation. I was two miles away at Mud Lake, about to throw my pre-paid cell phone into the reservoir.

"So, you took the law into your own hands, Mr. Brugnetti."

"Oh, Heather, we both know that's not my name."

"Yeah, I know. I ran you. I ran everything there was to run on you, even facial recognition software from a perfectly framed photo of you from the deli shop. So, I guess I can say I met a ghost."

"I'm sorry."

"Me, too."

Closing my eyes, I thought of Anna. Even my own sister couldn't be close to me. Why did I expect to find any closeness with a stranger?

"I wish things were different," I said.

"Me, too."

"Others need me."

"We live different lives. I think I understand. But someday, you'll have to stop running."

"I wish I could. Even though you made me nervous, I did enjoy our time together." Emotion warmed my face. "Seldom do I feel anything, Heather, so I mean it as a compliment that you made me feel something."

"Something?"

"Something good." I sighed, wanting to talk longer, but having no words. "I must go now."

"Luigi?"

"Yes?"

"Call me again. I mean, someday. When you can. If you can. I think you're a good man."

With that, I threw the phone into the water. I had vindicated the afflicted, but it seemed to have cost a part of me.

†

CHAPTER TWENTY

Forty-eight hours later, I was riding up the Buriganga River in Bangladesh behind a sputtering motor. The vehicle was a wood plank boat as narrow as a canoe. Torrential rain had decreased visibility to one hundred yards, which reminded me it was the monsoon season in Southeast Asia.

I was still thinking of Officer Heather Oakes as I paid my driver five dollars—probably the largest tip of his life—then stepped out of the kheya nouka taxi onto a cement pier two inches under water. Like the residents around me, I splashed inland without regard for the wet weather, though I seemed to be the only one with five-hundred-dollar duck boots. The shore crowd moved about with umbrellas, but I wore a hood attached to my waterproofed windbreaker.

The cement pier ended at a sandbank where palm trees and higher ground weren't under muddy water like the rest of the island. Though this island looked like all the others, I'd been assured this one was indeed the char, or mid-stream island, I was looking for. Following memorized instructions from a Red Cross nurse who'd spoken English in Dhaka, I walked north through the palms. Around me, men and boys were tearing down their sectioned houses of corrugated metal to move to another char. Each char changed with every rainy season. With every rainy season, their home changed, but this was the only life they knew.

"Zabir Mobad?" I asked an elderly man who was supervising his multi-generational family as they moved his home toward waiting boats. He pointed with a smokeless pipe to the north, though the island that was only one square mile was under water to the north. I was about to do some more wading.

Three more halted conversations in Bengali led me to the deconstructed residence of Zabir Mobad.

"The Red Cross sent me to help you," I said in English. Zabir Mobad, naked to the waist, stood in a foot of water below me, tying a section of his dwelling to a floating island of hyacinth plants—which evidently doubled as their garden. Two other men, six women, and a dozen children climbed on the floating island or waded in the water to hold the island steady.

Zabir Mobad stopped working to look up at me.

"Two weeks ago, the Red Cross was here," he said in good English, confirming what the nurse had assured me. "They could not help me then, and they cannot help me now."

He lifted a bamboo table up to his family.

"The Red Cross sent me, I said." A boy of about three leaped from the floating island into my arms. He smiled and wiggled, but I wasn't in a playful mood. The flight had been long and the rain had soured my mood. I tossed the boy back onto the hyacinth plants. "But I am not a Red Cross worker."

"What does that mean?" The man stopped working again.

"I'm here to get your daughter back." A second child jumped into my arms, but I threw her back onto the island. "You may even know who took her, I was told. That could make my job easier."

When he stepped closer to me, I looked into eyes that knew pain and strife like few others.

"She was my eldest daughter. No one talks to them and lives." He drew his thumb across his throat. "Do you think I am a coward?"

"You're not a coward. You're a father who has many other children."

"Who are you?"

"I'm here to save the children."

On the floating island, there was now a line of children prepared for the same game. Their father watched as I caught and threw them back as rapidly as they leaped into my arms—until they were a laughing, tangled mass of arms and legs. To them, it was a game, but to Zabir, and to his missing daughter, life was not a game.

...✝...

The Dhaka slum called Korail spanned as far as I could see. The rain had stopped for now. Zabir Mobad piloted our boat up to a floating pier of other vessels in the sewage-stricken water that choked my senses. I'd been in terrible neighborhoods all over the world, but Korail was the worst.

"This is not a good idea, Luigi." Zabir remained in his vessel as I stepped from boat to boat to reach the fungus-ridden shoreline below the nearest bamboo-stilted dwellings. "They will kill us both. I should not have brought you. My family . . ."

"Are we expected?" I asked him. "Has anyone taken from them before? Do you know what a bully is?"

"Yes, but these are murderers, not bullies."

"Show me where to go." I waved at him to follow. He didn't know it, but I would force him to show me where his daughter was held captive if he didn't do so voluntarily. "You may wait outside."

He joined me on the shore and led the way through wet gutters and puddles between shacks on stilts. Normally, I threw myself at risky situations with nothing to lose, but for once in my life, I had much to lose. Janice and Jenna were relying on me, as well as Anna. Corban may not have known I had his family safe in the mountain silo, but he needed me as well, and I needed him. And there was Officer Heather Oakes, who'd asked me to call again. Someday. After Corban helped me more fully leave my past behind. I couldn't die today.

We wound through what seemed like hundreds of structures, filth everywhere, and people in the most desperate state of life, somehow surviving. Zabir shared how he'd grown up there. He'd raised enough money as a taxi driver in the city on the horizon where he learned English. Then he'd bought a boat and supplies to live upstream on a char.

"The chars always change," he explained, "but anywhere is better than here. People die here every day." He suddenly stopped and I moved beside him, expecting danger. "She may be dead."

"Keep moving." I pushed him forward, wishing I knew even one consoling word, as Corban would've had in my place.

Finally, we reached the other side of the slum district of Dhaka. The city's middle class apartment buildings were in sight through a span of polluted ground, trees, and bushes. Twenty-story office buildings stood beyond the apartments. But here in the slums, residents lived harsh lives and died in dank shelters that would tumble over during a strong monsoon breeze.

"Up there." Zabir pointed at a stairway to a shelter that appeared more stable than those around it. The diagonal bamboo poles that secured the structure on top of vertical bamboo lengths seemed new, and a window above was actual glass instead of plastic. "If she is still alive."

"How many might I expect?" I took off my windbreaker and handed it to Zabir. "Do they have weapons?"

"Three, maybe four men." He shook his head, his eyes not meeting mine. "I have heard the girls are kept in the back room. Weapons? Everyone has knives here. Some guns, but ammunition is difficult to find."

I confirmed that there was only one stairway up to the shelter.

"When I call for you, come upstairs." I adjusted my belt and started up, but Zabir grabbed my arm.

"Let me go with you." He nodded reassuringly, but his eyes were full of defeat already.

"No, wait here." I shook his hand loose. "I need someone trustworthy out here to keep watch."

"Luigi, I will do that for you." He stood up straighter. "I will guard the stairs. No one will attack from here, I promise you."

"Yes, I believe you."

He let me go. At the top of the stairs, I looked down to see he was indeed barring the stairs from anyone's entry. I couldn't let this father down. I had to save his daughter.

Since I wasn't a guest, I didn't knock on the plywood door. And since I'd never been inside a Dhaka slum residence, I expected less than what I saw when I stepped inside. It was actually a lavish apartment with rugs and chairs and light provided from scented candles.

Three men rose to their feet as I entered, and three remained seated at a card table. Six men. Cigarette smoke was thick. Another plywood door separated the main room from the back room where I heard women's voices. That door had a latch that could only be unfastened from this side. In the corner on my right was a bench with a hole in the center. The toilet.

With one sidestep, I moved away from the door. The other three men stood and spread out. Even without introductions, they seemed to guess my intentions after my eyes lingered on the door at the back. Or maybe they wanted my boots.

"Stop." When I held up my hand, they stopped moving. "I am not here for you; only for the girls. This enterprise is now out of business."

As often occurs when I'm outnumbered, my foes that afternoon chuckled and glanced at one another. One man translated for a couple who didn't understand my English, then there was more laughing. I wasn't disturbed by their underestimating of me. Instead, I drew out a colorful pack of bubble gum. After opening it, I took one piece, unwrapped it slowly, then began to chew it. Sensing their desire for a piece of gum, I tossed the rest of the pack to the one I gathered was their leader—an older man with a silver watch. He caught the pack and read the label. Little did he know, it was far from a normal pack of gum. Except for the top piece that I'd taken, the other five pieces were juiced with my most potent knockout blend. The first swallow of juice would enter the bloodstream within sixty seconds, paralyzing the victim for hours. I had only to wait.

However, the ruse I'd used many times before didn't work. The leader passed the gum to the next man, who passed it down the line of men, and the last one tossed it back to me. I pocketed the gum, recalculating my odds.

Six men. When in service for the French, I'd been trained to fight a superior force. Just days earlier, I'd taken down four armed men with nothing but my belt. But these six men were ready, and they were slum dwellers, familiar with police raids, competition, and fighting for every stolen taka.

To punctuate my thoughts, one man drew a butterfly knife and flipped it open.

Six men. When training COIL operative Nathan Isaacson on the finer points of international espionage, I'd learned he had skills as a soldier in the Marines that I needed to adopt. Like fleeing when it was time to flee. Or expressing humor to unbalance the enemy. But I wasn't one to run away, nor was I a man of comic relief.

Six men. I also considered Corban's thought pattern at such a moment. As a man of the Bible, he would certainly speak God's powerful words to the six ruffians. No doubt, he would warn them of their impending defeat, then soundly whip them with his craftiness.

Though I wasn't a man of Corban's God, I'd found direction from Corban's Bible. Did this not protect me? In Franklinville, I'd vindicated the afflicted. Here, I would save the children. Crushing the oppressor was my next mission, though I knew not whom that would be yet. However, the fact that my plan from the Bible was incomplete—I found confidence in this. I was an ambassador of Corban's God, was I not?

"You may flee now if you choose." I pulled my belt off. As practiced as I was with the belt, I didn't hesitate to let them see the weapon that would lead to their downfall. "Losing is not an option for me, even against these odds."

". . . old man!" One of the men hissed the insult through missing teeth, though his other words weren't in English.

"When you wake up," I said, "your faces will be in the sewer."

To swing my belt more freely, I stepped farther from the door. That one step saved my life. One of them drew a small gun the size of a derringer and fired at my head. But my foot broke through a weak spot in the floor up to my thigh as the bullet zipped by overhead.

The six were upon me in seconds. I had no time to swing my belt as I tried to pull my leg out of the jagged hole that had swallowed it. Instead, when a dozen hands laid hold of me, they ripped me from the hole with such violence that my pant leg was torn from thigh to ankle, matched with a gash outside my knee that instantly gushed blood.

I was thrown at the toilet bench and the beating commenced. After several blows, which I deflected without effect, I realized my death was imminent if I didn't respond offensively. The one with the knife was sure to wet his blade soon—my blood would surely not be the first to have wet it!

My belt was still in my hand! A fist bounced off my skull, but I remained conscious and wrapped my right fist with the belt strap, the buckle coming to rest over my knuckles. With my body absorbing most of the abuse, I was becoming exhausted. Thus, when I swung at them the first time, it was a weak attack, and the buckle shards scratched only two of the closest men.

As they pummeled my face twice more, I dared to drop my guard again for another swing. Two more were slashed on the forearm and hand. The first two fell, and the second pair staggered away. The last two backed away, one of them the man with the butterfly knife still in his hand. If he had used it, I hadn't felt it specifically, though I was aware of a number of wounds all over my body.

"You will die now," I said, and stretched the belt out, holding it by the end. Killing them wasn't in my mind, but it was my intention to generate fear in their hearts. The terror played on their faces as they acknowledged their comrades on the floor, assuming they were deceased.

Before I could attack, the remaining two fled through the door. By the sound of their feet on the stairs outside, Zabir didn't stop their departure.

I unlatched the door to the back room and flung it open. Twelve girls shrank against the back wall from my wavering frame in the candlelight.

"Take what you want and run for your lives."

One of them translated for the others, and I moved aside as the girls flooded the main room to pick it clean. In seconds, they'd left the shelter.

"Zabir!" I called, and found him outside as I'd left him. "Do you know how you will protect her now?"

"Yes, I do." He placed his arm around one thin girl. "We will move to another section of the river. They will never find us again."

Below the shelter, I used a rusty machete to hack at the bamboo poles supporting the structure on one side. After removing four poles, the shelter groaned, and with a nudge, it tipped to the deep sludge that covered the ground between the raised paths. I preferred to burn the shelter's remains, but fire had a tendency to spread in slum districts. The brothel and slaves were no more. For now.

I had saved the children.

✝

CHAPTER TWENTY-ONE

"**H**ey, pal . . ."

I woke to an elbow jabbing me. Sitting upright in the airliner seat, I surveyed the other coach seats in the 747-8 cabin. With a maximum capacity of four hundred and twelve passengers, I guessed we were only about twenty short of that on the flight from Tokyo to the US mainland. My seat was on the port side, a few seats behind the wing.

"You in some kinda trouble or something?"

The arm-jabber was a thirty-six-year-old mechanic from Detroit in the seat next to me. Upon boarding, we'd had a friendly conversation so I guessed he felt comfortable enough to startle me awake now.

"No, I'm not in any trouble." I tried a southern US accent to confirm my Native American cover. "Why?"

"That guy up there's been talking to the stewardesses for ten minutes. See the one with one eye? They keep looking back here at you. Earlier, he passed us and eyed you real close—no pun intended." My companion leaned close enough for me to smell his breath. "I'll bet he's an air marshal. You probably fit the description of some terrorist or Arab assassin. The airlines get their wires crossed all the time. But even I can tell you're no crazy person, even if you do have darker skin. You're an Indian!"

"This is just . . . crazy." I shook my head as if the idea were too absurd to consider, but in my life, there were no coincidences. If they were suspicious of me, they already knew who I was. Granted, most of my evils in my early years were sanctioned by France's DGSE corporate espionage department, yet I'd freelanced from Italy a number of jobs for sizeable deposits from numerous clients.

Checking my watch, I then adjusted my window's electro-chromatic dimming so I could see outside. We were still over the dark blue Pacific, which spanned to the horizon, but any minute we'd be over the US mainland. Perhaps I'd traveled far enough.

The one suspected of being an air marshal walked down the aisle toward us. My body still ached from the beating I'd received in the Dhaka slums two days earlier. I had no interest in another confrontation, but if it meant securing my freedom and preserving the Dowler family . . .

"Excuse me." The man was in his forties, wearing slacks and a polo shirt. He wore a patch on one eye, which made him seem more menacing. "Are you Aaron Runningwater?"

"Yes, sir." I nodded, anxious to please. He knew who I was well enough, but he was following protocol: step two, make verbal contact, and question the suspect. "Is something wrong?"

"It's probably nothing. A passport question. Seems Japan rearranged our seating parameters with an Airbus 380 and you were shown on that flight as well. Do you have your passport?"

"Of course." I reached into my breast pocket under my blazer. The air marshal tensed, perhaps even dropping his right hand an inch. The man was armed? That meant I had to consider not only my own safety, but also the safety of the other passengers if a trigger-happy marshal started shooting. "Here you go."

"Great." He smiled. "I'll bring it right back."

"Of course."

He walked away, his clumsy excuse for wanting my passport not settling my nerves at all.

"You don't believe that line of garbage, do you?" My friend elbowed me again, drawing my eyes from the marshal back to him. "Hey, Aaron, they're confusing you with some terrorist. I'd bet my life on it. You got to fight this!"

"Maybe you're right . . ."

Though my new friend didn't like that response, he started down the laundry list of FAA blunders since 9/11. Mistakes were certainly made, but this was no mistake. I smelled a rat from my past. The same party who'd tracked me to Anna's house was still tracking me—and probably more easily now since they knew what I looked like with my shaved head. That confirmed to me my foes were high enough governmentally to put me on a no-fly list, or a terrorist list. The same French government I'd served now wanted me dead with their secrets. Again, I wished I'd discussed these issues with Corban. He could've used diplomacy to clear my name rather than me taking avenues I was now considering.

"Where are you going?" my neighbor asked as I unbuckled my seatbelt and moved into the aisle. "Don't do anything stupid, Aaron."

I didn't respond. Perhaps because I was about to do something stupid.

The 747-8 was the longest passenger airplane built. It could fit three fifteen-hundred square-foot houses inside, with room to spare. Thus, it took some time to reach the back of the plane where a stewardess was mixing a cocktail in the small galley. After checking the passengers and the aisles, I found no one watching. I drew the curtain closed, then moved for the bathroom door. But I also grabbed the stewardess by the wrist. As my other hand covered her mouth, I realized I was far from reflecting Corban's sense of morals, but I was desperate, and a governmental explanation could take months—if I lived through the questioning at all.

Dragging the stewardess's hand across my belt buckle, I pulled her into the bathroom with me. Seconds later, she relaxed and I set her on the commode. From her belt, I took the galley elevator keycard. In twenty minutes, she would wake up, if no one found her first, and I would be a hunted man—more than I already was.

Outside the bathroom, I closed the door softly and inserted the elevator keycard into the slot for the elevator. The narrow door clicked open and I climbed inside. Trying to steady my heart rate as I descended to the freight level, I reached it with a bump—or maybe the plane was entering turbulent air. Before leaving the elevator, I discarded the cell phone I'd bought in Tokyo. For what I was about to do, I didn't want any technology on me that could be tracked by satellites.

A food storage compartment greeted me upon my exit of the elevator. Breaking a magnetic cupboard cover off its hinges of the food box, I wedged it into the open elevator lift. There were other elevators and hatches by which that level could be accessed, but I wasn't intent on making my capture easy on the air marshal. He had his orders to take me into custody, but I had no interest in hurting him.

Moving through a sealed door into the similarly pressurized cargo bay of the tail section, I rapidly moved through a narrow passageway past twenty tons of various packaged freight and over six hundred pieces of baggage.

Eighteen minutes until the stewardess would awaken.

Tugging off the canvas that covered a crate of freight, I tested the canvas strength by trying to tear it. It wouldn't tear. Farther down on the starboard side, I took a fire extinguisher off the wall. With a twist, I broke the metal lever off, then stomped it hard against the gangway underfoot. The result was a sharp jagged piece of metal on one end of the silver lever.

Continuing forward, I gathered two more canvas covers and a number of bungee cords. Finally, I reached a hatch on the floor, meant for entry or exit while the plane was parked on the tarmac. But for me, the tarmac was too far away. I knelt there and cut small holes around two canvas edges, then laced them together with bungee cords, their elasticity giving my homemade square parachute a bell shape.

But having a parachute and opening a parachute at thirty thousand feet was a death sentence—unless done just right.

I'd have to hold my breath and drop ten thousand feet through freezing temperatures, then open the chute where the air was breathable. This complicated matters—not being able to use the chute immediately, unless I could force the plane to lower.

Thus, I turned the third canvas into a chute pack, something that would hold the chute until the instant of deployment—sturdy enough not to rip off my shoulders when I yanked the chute from it. Since there was no time to find chute line, the four-corner bungee cords would have to do. Being taken into custody was out of the question. Under torture, while drugged, I could betray Corban and his secrets, or inform an enemy of Janice or Anna's whereabouts. I had to risk death rather than allow that to happen!

A crash from the back of the plane told me I was out of time. I needed five more minutes to get the chute into the pack to make it possibly workable when falling—even then, its deployment as planned was unlikely. Frantically, I folded the chute in sections, imagining how I would need to pull it out one section at a time while falling, until it opened fully to slow my descent.

"You can't be serious!"

My hands went to a double lever system on the belly hatch. I looked up to see the one-eyed air marshal standing on the gangway ten yards away, his gun in hand. The plane jostled more, tossing the man against the wall. Turbulence. It had to mean we were over the coast now—California or Oregon.

"Don't come any closer," I said, "or I'll open this!"

"Looks to me like you're planning to open it, anyway. But I do have one question for you."

"I'll answer your question if you put your .45 away. If you shoot me at this range, the bullet will pass through me into the instrument panel behind. Think of the passengers. Are you willing to risk their lives for me? I'm no longer who you think I am."

"Doesn't matter. You've been recognized." The man tucked his Eagle firearm into his waistband—a ridiculous caliber for an air marshal to have. "Now, my question. Is that a parachute you built there?"

Looking down at what I'd made, I wondered if he was criticizing me for what few men could build in ten minutes. It had only to be drawn over my shoulders, like a backpack.

"It is. I can't be captured. Many people depend on me."

"I believe you, Luigi Putelli."

"So, my past has truly risen from the grave."

"Putelli, I've got to take you in. A lot of people are saying they thought you were dead."

"While people need me, I'd rather die than face the possible failure of interrogation."

"You'll depressurize this compartment if you pop that hatch, Putelli. At this speed, we could both die just being sucked out."

"That risk I am willing to take."

"Are you sure your parachute will work? It looks questionable."

"It will work . . . in theory."

"And you'd rather bet your life against a hunch when you could use the guarantee?"

Frowning, I saw his single eye twitch to my left shoulder. Even as I realized that two actual factory-made parachutes were mounted on the wall, I simultaneously acknowledged the air marshal was charging me. There was no time to whip off my belt. I'd have to fight for my life—and the lives depending on my survival.

†

CHAPTER TWENTY-TWO

As the air marshal tackled me, I felt the fury boil within me—partially because I wouldn't have faced the air marshal at all if I'd noticed the two parachutes on the wall above the hatch in the fuselage!

One of the first fighting essentials is to assess your enemy. Though the man had only one eye and probably limited depth perception, he was a trained professional. This much I realized as he immediately tried to place my left wrist in a standard law enforcement submission hold, in preparation to handcuff me. My other hand was free, so I jabbed with stiff fingers toward his good eye, then his throat.

He used his heavier weight against me and climbed on top, pinning me to the floor against the wall, the actual parachutes within reach. As he batted my hands easily aside, his over-confidence from being on top worked against him. I didn't need my hands to win a fight. My legs worked in a pinch.

Behind him, I kicked my right leg up and hooked it under his chin. He clutched my collar and fell backwards. While he wrestled against my legs for an instant, I ripped one parachute off the wall. One second later, he broke free and rolled to his knees two arm-lengths away from me. The parachute was in my good hand, so I couldn't use my belt as a whip, though we were too close now, anyway.

His hand went to the gun still in his waistband.

"Don't do it!" I said, and he froze. "I'm not worth the bullet or the lives on this plane!"

"I'm arresting you, Luigi Putelli."

"Stand back!" I moved over the hatch. "My old employers have fooled the US government. I'm not a terrorist! Because I used to work for France, I know their secrets. That's why they want me dead!"

"Still, I have to take you in. Only then can I help you."

"No, I can't be helped by someone I can't trust."

"You just need to get to know me." He smiled, far too casually for our situation. Maybe under different conditions, I would've entertained his offer. A man who took his job this serious was possibly worth knowing.

After hooking an elbow around the first parachute, I took the other one in my hand. With all my strength, I turned the two levers of the hatch. An alarm sounded somewhere near and the plane jolted. Wind whistled from the partially opened hatch.

"It's wise for you to let me go."

"Who said I'm letting you go?"

Frowning, I was relieved he didn't lunge at me again. He couldn't stop me now, and he had no parachute because I had them both!

The plane's sensors had alerted the cockpit that the hatch was open. The plane was already diving for a lower altitude, which would help me. I imagined air masks had dropped from the ceiling in the cabin above.

Buckling on one parachute, I watched the air marshal as he waited on his knees. There was a smirk on his face that I found disconcerting, but if he didn't attack again, he could make any face he wanted.

Using my heel, I kicked at the hatch, held in place merely by wind force.

"You should hold your breath and leave this section," I instructed. "The plane will drop to breathable air in a couple minutes."

"Whatever you say, Luigi Putelli."

I took a deep breath and put more weight into my heel on the hatch. Suddenly, it hinged out and under the belly of the plane. For an instant, I thought I could hold my place without being sucked out. My homemade parachute slid toward the windy gulf, but the marshal caught it in one hand. He was visibly holding his breath and trying not to slide on the floor toward the hole.

But I was too close to the opening. Instead of fighting the force, I controlled my fall to plunge feet first, then a punch to my whole body tore me into the sky. The air marshal wouldn't get me today!

Heat that I hadn't anticipated thrust me in a direction I knew was horizontal in the slipstream. I opened my eyes as I tumbled, yet dared not breathe yet. My smile rippled in the icy wind as I located the plane far above me.

Then something stole my smile. A black dot was falling from the underside of the plane. Was that plane debris? No, the dot was a man—and it could only be one particular man.

The air marshal had followed me! How did he expect to survive? I had both parachutes! One was on my back and the other was flapping on my shoulder.

Having skydived many times in my youth, I knew I was still too high to breathe the air when my lungs could wait no longer. Slowly, I exhaled, then gasped in a panic as I tried to breathe the thin air slamming into my mouth. This desperation lasted ten seconds, until I sensed some relief and my mind grasped the situation afresh.

The marshal was falling nearly parallel to me now. Either he was suicidal, or he was depending on the graciousness of a man he believed was a terrorist. Three years earlier, I would've let the man fall to his death. But Corban had done something to my stony heart, and I cursed him for it at that moment.

As I drew close to my enemy, with my shirt whipping against me, I realized this man wasn't falling with suicidal tendencies. Rather, he was wrestling with my homemade parachute! It was already around his shoulders, and he was struggling to deploy the chute portion of my creation. The canvas flapped violently against his head. For not having received instructions on its deployment, he was doing remarkably well.

Finally, he had the chute out, and in the second I expected him to be jerked upward—with the canvas and bungee cords open as intended—instead, the canvas tore up one side of the chute and turned the air marshal upside down. He flailed, trying to reel in the torn section, when he noticed me falling a few feet away.

I slapped my chest, and he seemed to get the message—we would come together. Once he loosed the faulty homemade chute, he fell with nothing but his polo shirt, slacks, an eye patch, and a gleaming .45 in his waistband.

Moving closer, I misjudged my fall and collided roughly with him. He was cognizant enough to take the spare parachute I offered, but I didn't release my hold immediately.

"You . . . owe . . . me!" I yelled, though I wasn't certain my words reached his ears. I released my hold on the chute, then slid down his body to hold onto his legs as ballast so he didn't tumble while fitting the chute over his shoulders and tightening the chest strap.

When I released him, I intentionally drifted far from him in case he was tempted to use his gun on me. Then, I pulled my cord hard. The familiar jerk of a well-deployed chute yanked me up, then I settled into a windy ride. The air marshal continued to fall ten more seconds, then pulled the cord, his white chute like a flower against the green and gray earth.

Only then did I realize we were indeed over land. The solid color of green below told me we were over dense forest. The snowy white over jagged gray lines of ridges told me I was underdressed for falling into the mountains of California or Oregon where the cool fall season was heading toward winter.

Taking note of the afternoon sun on the western horizon, I glimpsed what might've been farmland far to the northeast. It was all I could notice before I watched the air marshal glide into a thick stand of tall trees. Had he not skydived before? As his white chute settled amongst the treetops, I drew on my own guidance cords to aim for a tiny meadow a couple miles east.

Cold wind whipped at my clothes as I flexed my knees for a gentle landing. I was already thinking how little I knew about wilderness survival, but somehow I would live. Corban's God seemed to be watching over me, even allowing me to help my enemies.

Hitting the ground, I rolled as I'd been trained decades earlier. As I came to a stop, lying on my back, I was reminded by the pain in all my joints of how old I now was. But I couldn't rest for long. With night closing and the air marshal nearby, I had to keep moving. Civilization was my first goal. Then, to Corban's family.

†

CHAPTER TWENTY-THREE

Twenty minutes later, I found the air marshal grappling with a tree trunk. He was still attached to his parachute harness, suspended forty feet off the forest floor. In his frustration, I heard him cry out in pain as he moved against the tree. For a moment, he was still, and I contemplated leaving him there. What kind of crazy person would follow me out of a jet, his only hope a homemade parachute?

And what did I have to do with a man who wanted to imprison me? Lives were in my hands, Corban's whole family in the balance. And just as importantly, my third objective from the Bible, to crush the oppressor, was yet unfulfilled. Was this man in the parachute harness the oppressor? I thought not. He was merely my personal antagonist who took his job too seriously.

"How badly are you injured?" I called.

Twisting frantically, he tried to view me directly below him. In his fumbling, he dropped something metallic. I barely dodged his heavy caliber handgun. Though I fancied myself as a man above using firearms now, I picked it up and stuck it in my own waistband.

"I'm still going to arrest you, Luigi Putelli!" he shouted. "I'm PRS Agent Wes Trimble, and you're under arrest!"

I'd tangled with PRS agents a few years earlier. The CIA's Pacific Rim Security Department was manned by veterans and experts, the best the Agency could provide, to address the volatile Southeast Asia.

"Do you need me to fetch you, or can you arrest me from where you are, before you climb down?"

He growled at my taunt and clawed at the tree, tearing bark off the trunk that fell on my face. Finally, he relaxed.

"You'll have to help me. I think my leg is broken."

I started climbing, ignoring my own soreness, surprising myself that I was risking my own freedom for the enemy. It was indeed what Corban would've done. So I drew myself high into the spruce tree, assured that Corban's God would deliver me from my enemies.

Reaching Trimble's height, he looked at me with his one good eye. His eye patch had flecks of bark on it, but there was no defeat in his gaze, and I was reminded of other hard men who couldn't be beaten by difficulties. It wasn't pride, I reasoned, but something more dangerous—it was honor and determination. Even with only one eye and wounded, this man couldn't be trusted to see things my way.

"Which leg?"

"My left."

"Hang onto me. I'll release your harness."

"And here I was just getting attached to it."

He grit his teeth and clung to my shoulders from the front as I unclipped him from the parachute harness. Finally free, he fell against me, and his rough breathing told me he was in great pain.

Ten minutes later, I eased him to the ground, which was strewn with twigs and pinecones. Trimble placed his back against the tree and clutched his thigh.

"That was the dumbest thing I've ever done."

"Trusting me?"

"No." He chuckled through a gasp. "I don't have a choice but to trust you now. No—jumping out of that plane was just plain stupidity!"

Looking at my watch, I then checked the sun. If I got started now, I could reach the—

"Don't even think about it," Trimble said. "It gets cold up in these mountains at night. That's snow over there, and you have at least one pass to get through before you reach Scott River. Besides, in the dark, you'll kill yourself on these mountain game trails."

"So, you know where we are?"

"Yeah, I got a good look around us before I slammed into this tree. Klamath River is to our west. We're in the Marble Mountains of northern California. A friend of mine lives about eighty miles that way." He pointed to the east. "In Shasta."

"Then, I'll leave in the morning and reach this Scott River. I'll send Search and Rescue to you by tomorrow night."

"Your photo is all over the country, Putelli, and after bailing out of that plane, the Feds will be all over the state looking for you. They'll shoot you before you can explain where I am, especially if you're carrying my gun. No, you're better off at my side."

"Certain people will get worried if I don't reach civilization within three days." I took a deep breath. Since my enemies had so seriously prompted my capture, I would need a plan. "How do you propose we both survive if I stay with you?"

"Build a shelter after you collect me some wood, then I'll build us a fire. It'll be a cold night. We could use that parachute to keep us warm."

"Impossible." I shook my head at the tree. "It's lost. But I'll get mine."

Conceding to this one-eyed man's instructions, I realized it wasn't in me to leave him for dead or even for several days alone. Why else had I come to find him instead of hiking straight for civilization?

We spoke little as I relocated us—with him on my back—to a steep mountainside that would shelter us from the wind. I found a depression in the wall and cleared loose rocks away to protect us more. After collecting dry wood, I turned to find larger fuel when Trimble stopped me with a hand on my arm.

"I'll need the gun," he said. "It's the fastest way to start a fire."

Understanding immediately, I ejected two cartridges from his handgun. He caught them and smiled up at me.

"Had to try." He shrugged.

But I didn't smile back.

"Get it ready. I'll ignite it when I return."

Shivering in my sweat, I dragged a number of sizeable logs to the edge of our camp. By sundown, the camp was surrounded on three sides with thick brush and fuel for the fire. With one gunshot, I ignited the gunpowder Trimble had pried from the two shells. Using paper scraps from his pockets and two gum wrappers from mine, the flames caught on twigs and grew.

Before I settled into camp beside the fire with an empty stomach, I took a torch to find my parachute, along with its pack. On my return, I selected two long, sturdy tree branches, and brought them back to camp. Trimble was busy peeling the inner meat from a green bough and laying it on a flat rock near the fire.

"Here I thought you'd left me."

"You would die without me," I said, and gestured at my two branches. "I'll drag you out."

As he watched me by the firelight, I worked on the parachute pack, fastening it between the two branches to make a rough travois. Sitting on the same side of the fire, our backs to the mountain, we shared the chute canvas for warmth. Trimble offered me a number of slivers of cooked tree flesh and I gathered a large ball of snow from a glacier that seemed to glow in the moonlight. With our stomachs gnawing on the tree skin, we drifted off to sleep, my body bruised and my mind too weary to strategize against the marshal. I guessed he felt the same.

I wanted to be rid of this life, this running. What of Officer Heather Oakes? Would there ever be peace in my life? Did Agent Wes Trimble have enough authority to keep me alive if I indeed allowed myself to be taken into custody?

Before dawn, I stoked the fire and roused Trimble. He seemed to be in worse condition, so before he was fully awake, I prodded his torso and ribs for other injuries.

"Leave me alone. I'm fine!" He batted my hands away, then leaned over and vomited. I offered him the last of our collected glacier snow, and he wiped his mouth. "It's just my leg. The bone marrow is making me sick."

"No, I think it was that meal you fed us last night." Before he could fully appreciate my attempt at humor, I pointed at the parachute pack. "This will help support your weight as I drag the poles, but you'll still have to hang on."

"You can't drag me, Putelli. I weigh more than you!"

"Let me worry about my strength, and you commit yourself to your own duty."

"Which is?"

"Watching for breakfast." I tapped the handgun. "But it must be of some size or after one shot, there'll be nothing left to eat."

We left the camp as the sun touched the tops of the trees below the cold mountains. I turned south and studied the range to my left for an opening pass to the east. Trimble was indeed heavy, and each step strained my muscles. His arms were wrapped around the pack straps, his knees bent so his heels didn't drag on the ground. My hands gripped the widest section of the branches, and parachute line was drawn tight across my chest as I pulled like a plow horse.

Within an hour, Trimble was mumbling a prayer, and though our situation wasn't terribly desperate, his injury concerned me more and more. I wasn't surprised when he became quiet behind me, and his hands fell off the sides. Stopping, I grabbed the thin chute canvas and wrapped it around him to hold him to the makeshift sled. Even while he was unconscious, I could maintain a steady if not plodding step through the gorges, across creeks, up ridges, and down ravines.

Several times, I fell to my knees, and at first, Trimble stirred, but by that afternoon, when I tripped or fell, he didn't waken. It was then I knew a bone infection must've set in, and now the man's life was at immediate risk.

That night, having eaten only berries and glacier snow all day, I gauged we'd covered only about eight miles. It was less than half of what Trimble had originally guessed we had to travel. Lighting the fire with a gunshot woke him with a start, and he was instantly alert—more alert than I expected a man to be who had an infection. For certain, he appeared to be more rested than I was.

"How long have we been here?" he asked.

"An hour. Here." I gave him a handful of huckleberries. "I collected them when I was out looking for wood. They'll revive you."

Lying back, I was barely able to extend my legs toward the fire. They trembled so badly that my whole body shook.

"You don't look revived." Trimble filled his mouth, and we stared at each other over the flames. "I have to admit, from the data I was given, Luigi Putelli wouldn't help a government agent through the mountains like this."

"I told you already: I'm not who you were told I am." With effort, I pulled up my pant legs to expose skinned knees from falling on sharp rocks. I plucked gravel out of the skin. "You may not think a man can change. Though I never thought it possible, I'm not the man I once was."

"Only God can change a man's heart." Trimble's eye looked fierce again, and I was reminded of Corban's challenging gaze upon me the first few times we'd met. "Do you believe in God, Luigi?"

"He's the reason I'm still alive. I've seen His work. The man I protect is a Christian."

"What's his name?"

"Eat your berries and sleep." I laid my head on a rock. "Tomorrow, I intend to reach civilization."

Trimble said something about his job overseas, but I had no energy to listen. I fell asleep thinking of Officer Heather Oakes. Would I ever be able to leave the reputation of my past behind?

†

CHAPTER TWENTY-FOUR

The next morning, I became distinctly aware that PRS
Agent Wes Trimble was not as injured as he claimed to
be, or even as much as I'd thought he was. The first
indication was when I returned to our second camp with
firewood and saw his footprints near a trickling stream.
They weren't the footprints of a hobbling man. I hadn't
made him a crutch or walking stick. Whatever poison his
bone marrow had leaked into his bloodstream seemed to be
no more. If his leg had been broken at all.

Next, as he labored onto the travois, with its parachute
straps over my shoulders, I participated in my own play-
acting and fell over. Intentionally, I elbowed his left thigh,
which should've been so tender that he would've screamed
or fainted—which I knew from having my own broken
bones. He reacted with a delayed gasp, but it was forced,
and he rubbed the injury instead of being afraid to touch it.

Yet, I began the trek, taking up the poles in my hands,
disclosing none of my insights into his facade. And again,
we spoke little, as men without common goals. I needed to
consider what this trickery meant. For one, I was already
exhausted and becoming more so. The best way to capture
me alive was to wear me down. It took a mile that morning

to work the cramps from my legs, and I admitted aloud that I was in no condition to continue without resting every half-hour. He responded with a snore, as if he were sleeping on the sled again. But I knew better now. Wes Trimble wasn't a very good actor, and I was no longer gullible.

Mile after rugged mile, I became more outraged at our situation. I'd been a spy for many years. What a man knows gives him an edge over his adversary. However, I couldn't find the edge I was gaining by hiding the fact that Trimble was well as I was becoming more debilitated!

Trimble's silence annoyed me as well. Though I was a man who appreciated silence, his silence made me feel like I was his project instead of me being his caregiver.

At midday, we rested at a river that was too deep and wide to cross. It flowed west, the opposite direction of our heading. After one more mountain range and the river's headwaters, we would view the cultivated land I'd glimpsed from the sky.

While drinking at the river, I slid Trimble's gun into the water, but kept two bullets, one in each pants pocket so they didn't jingle together. If we had to spend another night in the wilderness, the bullets would help start another fire. But the gun would only get me shot if Trimble was planning what I thought he was.

He was surely planning to arrest me, but how? At some point, he'd have to admit his acting and try to subdue me. The gun may have been keeping him at bay, so he'd played for sympathy to keep me near. Once he noticed the gun was missing, then what? A rock over my skull? A heavy branch across my brow?

I looked back at him as he tried to catch tadpoles from a pool of muddy water a few feet from the river. Whether he was cruel for treating me like an ox, or merely craftier than me, I didn't know. But the game would soon conclude since our journey would end after the next pass.

That evening, we reached the top of the last pass on the eastern side of the Marble Mountains. We gazed upon fields, homesteads, and even roads only a few miles away. By midnight, we would be in the midst of civilized conveniences. The money I kept in my belt would be enough to buy a few meals, but my identification as Aaron Runningwater could be used no longer. Reaching the East Coast could take days, or weeks, if I had to evade authorities.

Dropping the poles and easing the straps off my shoulders, I rested on a log. Trimble lay still on the ground for a few minutes, the travois under him. He gazed at the sky, and I looked up as well.

At that moment, I realized what I'd failed to notice a day earlier. There were no helicopters or search planes. Why not? A CIA agent and a wanted international assassin had jumped out of a jet over this area. The whole countryside should've been one massive manhunt. The only reason why the Feds wouldn't be looking for us, I decided, was if they already knew exactly where we were! But how?

Jumping up on my sore feet, I pointed at the brush above the pass.

"A rabbit!" I laughed and climbed up the mountainside. "We will eat well yet! You will see, Trimble!"

"Luigi, we can be in town in two hours! Come on!"

I made a good show of chasing a rabbit left and right, trying to stomp it, gradually moving farther away from Trimble. When I believed I was out of earshot, I ran west then south, and crept up on our back trail. From over a low bush, I watched this man who'd so outwitted me. Even knowing his craftiness, I was still surprised by what I saw next.

Trimble spoke in low tones on a cell phone! He watched the hillside where I had disappeared, and conversed for only sixty seconds or less. Many things began to make sense now. A cell phone had no coverage in a wilderness. However, perhaps he'd used the phone on the higher ridges. Or that morning when I'd seen his footprints, maybe he'd gone up to the hill above us. Somehow, at some point or points before, he'd placed a call. And with this latest call, the authorities were certain to be waiting.

Retracing my steps, I came out of the bushes empty-handed.

"Ah, it eluded me," I confessed, and wiped at blood from a new scratch on my arm. My clothes were ripped and filthy from the journey, while Trimble's clothes were wrinkled, but relatively unsoiled.

"Just as well." He positioned himself on the sled to continue the journey. "There's no use in eating a wild rabbit when a restaurant could be within walking distance."

Kneeling before him, I took the poles and straps in my hands. Then, I reached behind him for a hold on the parachute canvas as if I were adjusting his position. As he was eager to continue, he let me proceed by sitting upright.

Then I struck. A section of the canvas chute loosened easily, and I wrapped it around both of his arms at his sides before he could resist. Now that he was bound, I pushed him over and took his shoes.

"What is this?" he fumed.

I threw one shoe into the bushes, and another into a tree. Crossing my arms, I looked down at him.

"Should I bow perhaps?" I asked. "In which direction should I wave? I've known since this morning that you're not injured. Speak!"

"True, I'm feeling better. My leg wasn't broken, perhaps, but it was definitely badly bruised."

"Where might I expect your friends? Just below us?" I couldn't help but smile at his persistence. "Agent Trimble, I concede. You must also. And I know about the cell phone. How close are your guests?"

He looked down at his arms, as if he suddenly realized he'd put himself into a defenseless position. However close his people were, they couldn't help him before I hurt him.

"It's over, Luigi. They're already here."

"And now I'm too tired to run." I laughed at myself, the fool! "Only one other man has ever beaten me like this. You are very much alike."

"Your Christian friend?"

"Yes, the same."

"I'd like to talk to him someday, ask him why he associates with killers."

"He doesn't associate with killers!" Defensively, I felt my anger rising as he criticized Corban. Even if it were true . . . The thought of sullying Corban's reputation for God infuriated me. "He helps men with gifts find a new path. He was a wicked man himself once."

"Like I said, I'd like to talk to him. I'm a man who believes in second chances as well."

"Well, I'll not tarnish his name by sharing it with you. You've seen two days of my compassion, and you still ambush me like this!"

"Where's the gun, Luigi?"

"It's back in the river where we stopped at noon." I stepped over him, and his eyes widened, perhaps expecting a violent response after his treatment of me. Instead, I reached down his right shoulder and found the cell phone behind his arm in a hidden pocket. Trimble relaxed when he saw the phone was my focus. "Don't move!"

"Who are you calling?" he asked. "Your Christian friend?"

Backing away a few steps, I dialed the number I had memorized. As it rang, I considered who else I could've called. If I'd known where Corban was, I would've called him. And if I'd known her number, I would've called Chloe Azmaveth, Corban's right hand inside COIL. She would've provided a safety net for Corban's family. Chloe had been at Corban's side in Malaysia when I'd first joined Corban after he rescued me from death. But instead, I'd been selfish.

"Hello?" It was Officer Heather Oakes, on her private number.

"Heather, do you have a moment?"

There was a pause.

"Luigi. This is unexpected . . . under the circumstances. When I said you could call me, I didn't mean—"

"I don't have long." I closed my eyes. If I'd made different choices long ago, there would be no need to say goodbye to the only woman who'd caught my interest like this. "Heather, I wanted you to know that our time together was of immeasurable value to me."

"Immeasurable value?" She laughed, but it wasn't a nice laugh. "Luigi, having known you for just a couple days, I suppose those are the nicest words you've ever said to a girl. But having gotten to know you more through the news this week, I'm uncomfortable responding to that."

"Oh, I've really been on the news?" White-hot anger flashed through my mind, and I focused it on Trimble. My identity had never been known in full by the public. It had been my weapon against countless enemies. I'd been a phantom. Now, because of one vigilant PRS agent, I was surely a familiar face in all America, if not the world. "Perhaps your time with me proves what they say to be untrue."

"That's possible," she said. "You never hurt me. But that doesn't atone for what you've done to others in the past."

"That was for the government . . . mostly. I'm sorry, I don't mean to yell at you. So, all has come to light and I'm finished. Even the recent good I've done can't erase my past."

"It never does, Luigi. I wish things were different for you, even for us. I'm . . . sorry." Her voice broke, and she hung up.

Even for us, she'd said. Did that mean there was still a chance? If I could maybe get Corban to help me, somehow we could . . . ? No. Corban might not even be alive. It was a thought I'd been avoiding. There was nothing to be done now. My whole life had been a waste.

I tossed the phone at Trimble and it clattered on the rocks at his knees. Though I was furious at him for besting me, Corban had been right years before when he said we're limited to doing good by who we are. Trimble was a good man, and he was limited to doing good, however slyly he had accomplished his goal. And in years past, I'd been limited to doing only evil, for at heart, I was a wicked man. It was my nature. Where there may have been forgiveness for me, even for my worst acts, I wasn't willing to crawl and beg before Corban's God to lessen my woes. They were my woes, and I deserved to bear them forever.

Instead, I browsed the immediate landscape for a cliff, one high enough to guarantee me a quick death, rather than leaving me to rot in misery in a dark prison. Seeing the perfect precipice, I started to the south.

"Luigi, where are you going?" Trimble shifted his bound body to watch me. "Luigi, don't do it!"

Weak to the bone, I stumbled toward the cliff, my legs numb. I would end it all. Let them say what they wanted about me. It was hopeless to fight them all now. There were too many.

A masked man wearing fatigues and holding a rifle rose from the ground in front of me. Had he been there the whole time? Then another on my left. My way was blocked. I couldn't even kill myself with any sort of success!

"Get on your knees!" someone yelled. "Luigi Putelli, get on your knees, now!"

My gaze lingered on the edge of the rocks, twenty feet away. Was this another trick by Corban's God, keeping me alive to face my adversaries? Was my life to end like this—in captivity? If Corban was dead, then no one would care for me.

Though I wanted death, I knelt on the ground and placed my hands behind my head. As I lay flat, and a dozen screaming men rushed me, I tried to see the justice in my arrest. My enemies didn't care about the atrocities I'd accomplished for them so long ago. They only wanted me silenced in death, their secrets with me. Now they'd do anything to kill me, and I was at their mercy. With my only friend missing, they would surely come for me.

And yet, I'd done those atrocities. Would Corban's God still be with me? Or was I as alone as I felt?

The agents bound my wrists and ankles, then pulled a hood over my head. I heard a helicopter drawing near, and Trimble's voice giving orders for my safe delivery. And in that moment of despair, I identified a fraction of hope that came from Corban's God. If Wes Trimble was indeed the man I believed him to be, then my future wasn't as bleak as I'd foreseen. Now that I was in Trimble's hands, and after two days and nights together, I guessed he knew me as well as any man, besides Corban.

I simply had to trust in the goodness of Corban's God. My life wasn't yet finished. If I were granted freedom again, I'd find a way to make it worthwhile, and find a way to escape from under the weight of my sin. If only Corban were still alive . . .

PART III: CHLOE

I wished I were anyone but Chloe Azmaveth at that moment. But as soon as I saw the news update about Luigi Putelli being captured in California, my black mood dissipated.

Sitting before my laptop in my dining room in New York City, I played back the news coverage. The dark-eyed, tall man I'd seen at Corban's side nearly three years earlier—though now bald—was being called an assassin, a terrorist, a traitor, and a dozen other labels. In my business, that usually meant he'd been a patriot to his country of origin, and he'd perhaps abused that authority by freelancing his skills to third parties. Indeed, I remembered warning Corban about a killer named Luigi Putelli who may have been hired to kill him. This was the one, but why had I seen this same man with Corban?

At one point, the footage zoomed in on Luigi's face, and he turned to a cluster of reporters and cameras. He said something, just a few words, then he was taken inside a federal building in Lincoln, Nebraska, some sort of holding facility. A man with a patch over one eye waved the cameras away, then entered the building behind Luigi.

After playing back the footage eight times, I still couldn't decipher what Luigi had said. Nor were my lip-reading skills up to par, especially to pick up the nuances of a foreigner speaking English.

Sitting back in my chair, I put the footage on constant playback and let it roll. Yes, this was what I needed—a good mystery. Not that I didn't have enough mystery in my life! Quite the contrary. I was plagued with unsettling events recently that had shaken my life—both in my career and in my faith.

Initially, Corban's death had come as a shock. Murdered by a car bomb here in New York? But then he'd come in the flesh to my back door and I'd seen him alive with my own eyes under the bridge. Of course, the disappearance of his family, Janice and Jenna, had concerned me, but days later when their bodies were found, that had broken my spirit entirely. Things were out of control. Steps I could've taken hadn't been pursued. When Corban wanted only me to watch his back, I should've had fifty COIL agents prowling New York City!

There'd also been Corban's infiltration of the Tactical anti-Terrorist Division, the TaTD. That had ended very badly a week earlier. Demolishing an SUV and losing Corban's signal on my transponder had been devastating. From what I'd witnessed that day, Karl Coleman—still not in the papers as a wanted man—had made off with Corban.

On top of Karl Coleman escaping with Corban, Washington was still reeling from General Logan Forglade's involvement in the explosion of Flight 524, an event I'd heard associated with an alias of Corban's, Muhammad ibn Affal. And now this man, Luigi Putelli, was identified as an assassin in the clandestine world—arrested for charges that governments were apt to handle much more secretly, due to the sensitive intelligence the operative might have. He could even have COIL intel! It didn't take a detective to know Luigi's life was at risk if he fell into the wrong hands—or the wrong detention facility. My twelve years inside the Mossad, Israel's clandestine agency, had ingrained a suspicion within me of everything and everyone. And it was with this nature that I concluded that Luigi's arrest was suspiciously related to Corban's disappearance. The two had to be related, somehow.

"God, help me," I prayed at my table. "Help me help whomever I'm supposed to help. Don't let me waste away in a puddle of my own tears."

Corban was missing. Janice and Jenna were certainly dead now. No mystery there. The instigators of Corban's disappearance were on the run—the focus being on General Forglade, though I had every reason to believe that Karl Coleman was the primary instigator. That left me with Luigi Putelli on my screen. How tainted was he? Had he turned on Corban? If I made a move, my Mossad reputation with Israel would be on the line, but I had to have some answers!

Feeling like a fool, I realized I'd been watching the same footage repeatedly from only one news source. In two minutes, I had a list of other news agencies that had been at the federal building in Lincoln. The fourth one I tried had captured the audio of Luigi's words, since they were closer to him. After a few more repeats, I finally heard it clearly. He had looked straight at the camera and said, "I have J-J."

Stunned, I sat staring at the screen, not able to repeat the footage again. What was happening? Janice and Jenna were alive? Then who did the morgue have? Whatever crumbled in Corban's life affected my own, because we'd been so close for so many years. J-J could only refer to Janice and Jenna. Luigi Putelli had put Janice and Jenna somewhere safe. This Luigi was the bald man I'd seen at Corban's funeral! So Luigi's statement to the camera was a message for Corban, I guessed. Did that mean Luigi knew Corban was alive? Was Luigi helping Corban? I had to speak to Luigi! If Corban was alive, or if Janice and Jenna needed help, I needed to make contact. By not recognizing sooner that Luigi was the man who'd taken Janice and Jenna at the funeral, I may have complicated Corban's strategy. He'd said the bald man who took his family was a friend. That meant Luigi was my friend, an asset. So why hadn't Corban contacted me again?

Immediately, I went to the kitchen window that faced the back yard where Corban had left me a phone on my doorstep. My husband, Zvi, was out of the country. If the house was being watched, I was alone to face what happened next. My skills as a field operative were above average, but not as a housewife. It was time to move into the COIL office to live there as I often did during a crisis that required ongoing oversight.

A black town car followed me all the way into Manhattan. I believed it was an enemy, because of the timing, but sometimes agencies kept me under surveillance. Enemy or not, I had to remain focused on primary issues.

I prayed and planned until I reached COIL headquarters. I believed in a sovereign Lord, His mighty hand not distant from His people's activities. As such, I wasn't alone, even if COIL's founder was missing and no one but a suspected assassin had the answers to my questions. God wasn't being cruel, merely intent on His subjects being obedient as He worked all things out for His glory and our good. This was a mighty truth on which I needed to rest my faith.

The two suites above Times Square where COIL functioned had not paused regardless of the chaos in the lives of its administrators. The caseworkers at their desks, working in shifts around the clock, hardly noticed as I passed through security, then went into Corban's office instead of stopping at my own desk. To most of the caseworkers, I was merely Chloe, the public relations liaison. Or I approved a raise or holiday time.

Locked in Corban's office and seated behind his grand desk, I felt secure enough to begin what I was certain would be a marathon operation to recover from the damage done to us all. The armor-plated glass on my left and secure communication lines on my right were just a few perks of using Corban's office.

From a secret panel in the wall, I slid out a keypad and entered a code. This in turn gave me entry into a database of COIL's most secretive assets. Though I didn't know half the assets Corban had installed around the world, I knew one well enough to enter a codename at the prompt: SLADRICK.

Sladrick was hardly a codename, since Brody's real last name was Sladrick. Brody Sladrick was the only veteran operative inside COIL who'd saved more Christian lives worldwide than Corban had. Though younger than Corban by several years, Brody had been an independent operative for twenty years—fifteen longer than COIL had been in operation. The man was an expert at human intelligence, and he knew best how to exploit COIL's secrets, which I couldn't in Corban's absence. Corban had boasted that the man was a disguise genius, and he could retrieve anything from anywhere. He sounded like just the man I needed beside me, though I'd be working with him for the first time. Would he be able to come at a moment's notice?

My question was answered as he picked up on the second ring of my secure line.

"Sladrick."

"This is Mother Rahab."

"I'm listening."

"We have a Hezekiah Tunnel situation. I need you with me a-sap."

Hezekiah Tunnel was a code referring to an infiltration of our own fortress, like Jerusalem had been breached using its water tunnel under the Eastern Wall.

"I'm at the camp in Mexico. I'll be on a plane tonight. Rahab?"

"Yes?"

"Acting Chef is here with me. Do you want us both?"

"Please hold." I typed in the codename and discovered Acting Chef was Gail Benjamin, the actress, whose cover was often as a chef. "Affirmative, Sladrick. If she can make it, we're up to our ears."

"Understood." Click.

Without Corban in the office, several updates to the field agents' files had been neglected. I took a moment to include a comment that I , Mother Rahab, had recalled Brody Sladrick and Gail Benjamin from the COIL training camp in Mexico. I'd met Gail a year earlier at a COIL gathering, and knew she could be a great help on the case—besides just having another Christian woman my own age available.

Next, I dialed a contact of my own, not COIL or Corban's at all.

"Nice to hear from you, Chloe," Colonel Kalil Yasof said. He'd been Israeli Defense Forces' forward command in a dozen operations since I'd officially left the Mossad, but no one ever really left the Mossad. "You're not scheduled to call until next week."

"I have a situation, both personal and political." I used my native Hebrew so he would understand that I meant our mutual homeland directly. Though the colonel had proposed marriage to me before Zvi had, he wasn't a believer. Our relationship was strictly professional now, since he was my superior. "Agent Corban Dowler has been missing for a week, presumed dead by most. I'm not sure how much you've heard through your sources."

"I read it in a memo a few days ago. But Mr. Dowler, even in retirement from the CIA, has continued to represent Israel's interests and security against extremism worldwide. We'll miss him."

"Well, I've located a man he has worked with for some time, a rogue from Italy, once a French DGSE agent, the news is saying."

"Luigi Putelli."

"How did you know?"

"Every superpower in the world has hired this agent at one time or another—to do their dirty work, as you Americans say. What happens in America impacts Israel quite often. How is Luigi Putelli related to Mr. Dowler?"

"Corban trusted Putelli with the lives of his wife and daughter—also rumored to be dead. Putelli's distant past has caught up to him, but I can guarantee that Corban wouldn't have trusted Putelli without reason."

"If Putelli knows where Corban is, we need to know." Kalil hummed a few notes as he considered his options. I waited anxiously, hoping he understood without my asking that I wanted an IDF sanction to officially pull Luigi Putelli—or at least to access him through the US State Department. "This is muddy, Chloe. My sources say he's being held in Nebraska."

"Lincoln. That's correct."

"The French want him, and he has ten other agencies who want him after them, if he's still alive."

"Exactly my concern. If we don't get him out first, he could die with what he knows. Whoever has Corban, or wherever he is, could jeopardize Israeli security as well."

"Chloe, don't think I'm unaware that you're twisting the facts to your advantage." He chuckled, though I understood his warning. "I've assessed the threat to Corban's safety—to Israel and to your own enterprise there."

"Then you'll help?"

"Well, I can clear it on my side, but unofficially. Who are you working with?"

"I've called in a man named Brody Sladrick. He should be in your file. And a woman named Gail Benjamin."

"Good. She's one of ours."

"Mossad? She is?"

"A few years after you. Let me put you on hold." He was back a moment later. "There's a Senator Nettleton who's the new chair of the subcommittee for domestic oversight. He's sympathetic toward Israeli concerns and there's chatter he had contact with Corban in the past month.

"Corban has mentioned his name, but I don't know him."

"His authority should be enough to gain access to extract Luigi Putelli—if you go the distance, as they say."

"Okay, I understand. We'll make it look good."

"It still won't be easy, Chloe. That rogue, Putelli, has created a mess of his own. Don't reveal this to him, but we'll probably have to hand him over to face his current charges once we're done with him."

"I understand. It'll be strictly an information-gathering op."

"Just like the old days, Chloe. I'll get with Senator Nettleton's office right away."

"I'll keep you informed, Colonel."

Hanging up, I rejoiced that the IDF was on our side. A US senator was about to be brought into the game, and I had a prisoner heist to stage. But most importantly, God was on our side!

†

CHAPTER TWENTY-SIX

It was all business picking up Brody Sladrick and Gail Benjamin at La Guardia International Airport. Brody's face appeared as fierce as ever, and Gail was gorgeous, even more beautiful than on television. The fact that she was also Mossad gave me a greater respect for her.

The way Brody and Gail moved without communicating much with one another verbally, gave me the impression they'd been working together for some time. A quick moment when their luggage got mixed up allowed me to catch an exchange of glances that told me there was more to the couple than merely being a COIL field agent team, but I said nothing.

Gail wore a scarf and a beret to try to hide her identity, but I noticed a couple of bystanders still recognize and point at the actress. It was after midnight when we left the airport.

During the drive back to COIL headquarters, I detailed the situation. Brody, sitting in the back seat, reported having seen Corban weeks earlier during a North Korean operation in which Brody had been shot in the chest. He assured me he was almost fully healed, but admitted he wasn't so young anymore.

"Getting Luigi Putelli out of lockup is only half the battle," I said. "We have to secure Corban's family and recover Corban—if they're really all still alive."

"Who else are we working with?" Gail asked from the passenger seat.

"Homeland Security is unofficially sanctioning us to grab Luigi, but our other COIL field operatives are overseas, doing what they do, as Corban would say."

"First, we need to better identify our opposition. We can't fight a ghost." Brody held my gaze in the rearview mirror. He was an intense man; handsome in a hard way. Though he was no taller than me, he was much broader in the shoulder. "I'd say we need more people, some with muscle, not just credentials."

"Speaking of which," Gail said, "we need Luigi out now; credentials will take time. How is this supposed to work?"

"The details haven't been worked out yet." My eyes were burning. I needed to sleep, if I could. "I suggest we stay in prayer over all these things until COIL is patched back together. Regardless, we fly for Lincoln tomorrow."

Somehow, though, I knew things would never be how they once were. A sickening feeling hadn't left my gut in days—ever since losing Corban's transmission a week earlier in Maryland. Neither COIL nor its people seemed to ever be left alone. The pain of agents lost in the field still plagued my heart—Quin "Toad" LuDao and Nathan "Eagle Eyes" Isaacson, to name just two I knew personally. God's true servants were always under attack.

Brody and Gail bunked in the male and female "dorms" adjacent to the offices, used for these very reasons—secure sleeping quarters for layover agents or stop-over missionaries. I pulled out a narrow hideaway bed from a soft chair in Corban's office and stared at the ceiling where the lights of the city shimmered through the thick glass.

Prayer came with difficulty. There were so many things to pray for—and give to God: Corban and his family, Luigi's release, the enemies out there even now, hunting us. As spiritual as our enemies were, they were also physical. A real bomb had blown up Corban's car. Real bodies of Janice and Jenna had been found. With my worry, mixed with my lack of faith and my anticipation for the next day—I slept only two hours before there was a knock on the office door.

"We have a visitor," Brody said as I opened the door a crack. He looked rested. I searched his face for a sign of uncertainty, but he was much like Corban. He shielded his emotions so he wouldn't broadcast his thoughts involuntarily and give anything away. "I'll stall him while you wake up."

"Oh, right." I imagined I looked a wreck. "Be right out."

Dashing to the ladies' room, I straightened my clothes. Makeup had been weaned from my face during my early years as an agent on the move—unless for disguises—so cold water and a couple slaps on the cheeks had to suffice.

"Good morning!" I greeted Brody, Gail, and a forty-something Chinese man as they rose to their feet in the waiting room. "Let's talk in the office, okay?"

Leading the way into Corban's office, I prepared my mind for the day ahead. An agent had to be sharp and quick. Five seconds was all I'd had to study the Chinese man in the waiting room. Reading him early and accurately could protect me—and COIL—from any number of blunders. For one, I didn't recognize him. He held a briefcase that had passed through COIL security, which was as tough as any agency screening in the world. His suit was dark and expensive. COIL didn't pay for extravagances, so this man was an outsider. Was I expecting such a visitor? The fact that Brody had identified him as "our" visitor meant he was related to the case at hand: Corban and Luigi. Oh, Nettleton's office was here!

The three sat down before the desk and I sat down slowly, confidently, behind it, as I'd seen Corban host dozens of meetings. I folded my hands and smiled politely at the Chinese man, who sat between my teammates. In my peripheral vision, I acknowledged Gail's hair was in a tight braid and she looked like she'd gotten eight hours of sleep.

"I understand you're from Senator Nettleton's office."

"H-how did you know that?" He let his amusement show on his face, but I recognized him to be a careful man, a man who did important jobs for important people. "I hadn't introduced myself, but only asked for you."

"COIL's ears range farther than our grasp," I said cryptically, hoping I sounded more mysterious than ridiculous. An intelligence officer bluffs when she needs to or not—or folds unexpectedly to keep the other players on edge. Until Corban was recovered, we couldn't trust anyone completely. "How is the senator?"

"He's happy to oblige where American and Israeli interests merge. We're sorry about Mr. Corban Dowler. The senator met him only recently, but they had a connection. A man of intrigue—your boss."

"And much more." Another polite smile. I gestured to Brody and Gail. "These are my people on the case. What you say to me won't leave this room."

"Very well." He placed his briefcase on his lap and opened it. "My name is Rod Chang. I'm Senator Nettleton's closest advisor. As I told Mr. Dowler several days ago, I worked for the CIA's Subversive Logistics Division. The amount of pressure in your favor from Israel is phenomenal, and we're accommodating at their insistence to allocate your intelligence staff as lead on the investigation into Mr. Dowler's whereabouts. I'm aware of each of your foreign and domestic qualifications, though none of you are more than civilians as far as this department is concerned."

His words settled into my brain, but he didn't move, perhaps waiting for me to indicate I understood the stakes. He knew we were skilled. He knew we were human intelligence veterans. He knew we were not merely civilians, but there were limits involved.

"Mr. Chang, we understand the risks you're taking as well." I nodded once. "We won't let the senator down. My briefings will be forwarded to your office, including any national security concerns, as we come upon them."

"Any time we provide Homeland Security identifications to outside entities—three, as a matter of fact—it's already considered a national security concern. The authority you're being given . . ."

Our eye contact held for a couple more breaths, then he drew a manila envelope from his briefcase. Did I sense some hesitation, something deeper or even sinister with this man? He'd said pressure had put him up to this, so he wasn't here voluntarily. To confirm my assumptions, he frowned slightly as he placed the envelope on the desk.

"Only the senator holds the purse strings," Chang continued. "People jump when he says jump. A memo for cooperation was generated, but situations like these can quickly become bureaucratic, and you may run into opposition. Please be aware that Mr. Dowler may have information directly relating to the capture or whereabouts of General Forglade. We want the general in a desperate way for the Flight 524 catastrophe. Any information you may uncover is strictly confidential. Do I make myself clear?"

"We'll forward any information we get from Corban, when we find him, but about this opposition . . ." I glanced at Brody, and he nodded me forward. "Do we have license to address what may bar us from moving forward?"

"I thought you might ask this. The senator's words were, and I quote, 'You may project yourselves with subtlety and caution.' Does that give you the power to do what you must do?"

Again, Brody gave me a nod. Gail offered me a raised eyebrow, which I interpreted as affirmative.

"It does." I rose to my feet and offered my hand. "Thank you for your time, Mr. Chang. Do I have your contact info?"

"Yes, it's all in the envelope." He shook my hand firmly, not sparing when it came to me being a woman. I reciprocated. "Good luck, er, whatever term you Christians like to use."

"God's will." Brody said and shook Rod Chang's hand next. "We say, may God's will be done."

†

CHAPTER TWENTY-SEVEN

I paused outside an unmarked federal building before I entered its metal doors. The place was four stories high and covered an entire block on the outskirts of Lincoln, Nebraska. It was built like a bunker—no windows, all cement, and no welcome mat.

"Chloe."

Brody called my name, but I continued to study the outside of the building, including a row of cottonwood trees with cameras in them, and the parking lot complete with guards. We had unknown enemies, and if they were about to ambush us, I wanted to keep my eyes peeled for the slightest hint before the trap closed. The worst flashed through my mind. What if our enemies were closer than I realized? I felt like I was fighting for Corban blindfolded.

Finally, I turned to Brody and Gail, both in suits, as I was, and both armed with sidearms to play the role of Homeland Security agents. Brody wore aviator sunglasses. Gail's hair was up in a tight, professional bun. Just the right makeup had turned her from Gail Benjamin, recognizable actress, to Gail Forest, complete with crooked nose and bulky cheekbones. I wore no disguise since I'd be acting as myself as lead agent and under the most scrutiny.

"Just in and out," I breathed to Brody who held the door for me. "We get Luigi and then we get Corban. Right?"

"Right." Brody's stone face was reassuring.

Inside, I led the way, a single file in my hand, with Brody behind me, and Gail following.

"Agent Azmaveth." I held up my identification to a camera until a crash-door clicked and buzzed.

Through this door, we approached a tall counter with two uniformed personnel behind it, and two armed guards against the wall on my left, all men. I picked out the superior present, a squinty man behind the desk, and stopped before him.

"Homeland Security. We're here for a prisoner. Transfer of custody. Someone should be expecting us."

"Which prisoner?" Squinty asked. He wore no nametag.

"Luigi Putelli." I studied his face. He didn't move—not to check a clipboard or his computer screen at his elbow. "You have a lot of Homeland Security prisoner transfers arranged from Washington today or something?"

The question was a statement meant for him to respond according to protocol. Now they knew that any stalling would be considered deliberate, and heads would roll. Though I'd never worked within the US bureaucracy machine, Israel had her own inter-agency conflicts.

"What's the Homeland Security want with that piece of garbage?" Squinty glanced at his desk partner and chuckled. "A dozen other folks have come in here, too—all for him. Some didn't even speak English."

"He's nothin' but trouble, lady," the other said. He had a Southern accent. "The news keeps sayin'—"

"My name is Agent Azmaveth, not lady or missus!" I stated louder than necessary. "I don't care about the news. I don't care about your opinion of the prisoner, politics, or your grandmother's potted plants. We're here for a dangerous criminal who will answer for his crimes. Other agencies can wait in line. We're Homeland Security. Now, the prisoner, Luigi Putelli."

Squinty seemed to chew on the inside of his cheek. If he was considering a smart response, he chose against it, and turned to his computer. When checked, my name would show up as my true identity—an ex-IDF soldier, regular infantry. But there would be other credentials attached to it, if Senator Nettleton's office had considered the angles. After all, they wanted information from Luigi as well.

"The prisoner's not ready." Squinty didn't look at me, only sighed at his computer screen. "Says here he won't be ready for some time."

"I'm here at the exact time you were told to expect me!" I slammed my flat palm down on his desk, making him jump. "Why isn't my prisoner ready? If my prisoner is harmed, I'm holding you responsible! Take me to him now!"

"Visitors aren't allowed beyond that door." Squinty's sidekick nodded at another crash-door. "All prisoners are brought—"

"Do I look like a visitor?" I looked back at Brody, then my eyes drifted to the two armed guards. He didn't need to move closer to the sentries in order to cover them. Brody had two ceramic wrist rockets that fired a tranquilizer each, a non-lethal mechanism that had gotten him through customs gates and bad company alike. "I'm fully aware of the danger my prisoner is in. The accusations—unproven, I should add—are from terrorism to serial murder. But he's an object of national security and property of Homeland Security as of oh-seven hundred this morning. Either you bring the prisoner to me, or we go to the prisoner—now!"

"Lady, you're not going to push—"

"Agent Azmaveth!"

"Whatever. We're not on your timetable."

"I see." I backed away from the desk. These weren't government professionals; they were military grunts with a grudge against their own system. The next access door required a code. At that very moment, Luigi could be "accidentally" hanging himself, the officers hoping to spare the nation a drawn-out, shameful trial. Or, they were interrogating Luigi without due process, in some dark corner of the basement, hoping to get some horrible secret from him before anyone else did. Maybe even for pay. "Please, give me a moment."

With a signal to Brody to stay in the room, I exited the building alone and stepped into the sunlit afternoon. In thirty seconds, Rod Chang was on the line.

"Ran into roadblocks," I said. "They won't give me Luigi Putelli."

"Right away or ever?" he asked.

"They're stalling and I don't like it." I took a deep breath. "Mr. Chang, I don't like being bullied. Who exactly am I facing here?"

"Nobodies. Independent government contractors who handle certain detention facilities for us, even outside the States. These people are of no consequence. And they have no authority to tell actual agents to relax or take it easy. You're acting for Homeland Security, Ms. Azmaveth. Nobody says no to H-S. Push your weight around— assertively. Don't forget what's at stake for you. You want Corban Dowler, and we want General Forglade. Putelli may lead to both."

"But you told us to use subtlety and caution."

"That was part of my official instruction as the senator's spokesman."

"Okay, what's your unofficial instruction?"

"I sent those orders for Luigi Putelli myself, with the senatorial seal and signature. They have the bearing of the Oval Office. You've asked nicely, now it's time to not be so nice. Or whatever the Christian equivalent may be. Understand?"

"You understand I'm about to force their hand for our guy? Even Christians can be forceful."

"Well, that's what I'd do. Good luck, er, God's will be done."

†

CHAPTER TWENTY-EIGHT

When I marched back into the detention facility, I felt like a mother about to swat a few unruly boys on the playground. If the children couldn't play nice, they wouldn't play at all!

I nodded at Brody, then jutted my chin at the two armed guards. In that moment, I knew all the rumors I'd heard about Brody were true. He was built for conflict—short and powerful, and there was no doubt he'd do his part. When he turned toward the guards, I didn't concern myself further with his responsibilities since I had two men of my own to deal with. Though I approached the elevated desk briskly, my leap onto their counter was surprising and abrupt.

As I leaped, the toes of my right foot triggered a short, stout needle that sprang into place at the end of my boot toe. The needle hadn't been used for months, but I'd recently applied falaco tranquilizer to its length. My leg swept across the desk and jabbed hard into the shoulder of Squinty's partner.

Squinty leaped to his feet as I forced my presence upon him in his booth. I would've tranquilized him as well, but we needed him conscious. Instead, as he reached for his sidearm, I grabbed his hand on his gun, and jabbed with the heel of my other hand into his solar plexus. He wore no vest under his uniform, so my blow took his breath away. As he struggled to breathe, he sank to his knees, and I took his sidearm.

Before Squinty could recover, I accepted a pair of handcuffs from Gail—who'd taken the cuffs from the belt of the other man, now sleeping in a tranquilized state behind the desk. Only then did I look up to see that Brody was reloading his wrist rocket barrels, secured up his sleeves. His two armed guards were unconscious and cuffed as well.

"Please tell me this doesn't make us fugitives," Gail said to me quietly. As she was the least physical of the three of us, I was thankful she'd remained out of our way during the assault. "If we're attacking the good guys . . ."

"I called our man in New York. We're good." That was all I was willing to say in front of Squinty. With the heel of my left boot, I folded the right boot needle back into the toe. If needed, my left boot needle could be implemented from its heel. Both tiny weapons could be used a dozen times before the falaco toxin became too diminutive to plague a target's bloodstream. "Now, let's see what this guy can do for us."

Brody dragged Squinty out of the booth onto the cold floor and turned him over to lie on his belly. I was about to convince Squinty my own way, but Brody had been doing this much longer than me.

In front of Squinty's face on the floor, Brody placed his identification. He took a handful of Squinty's hair so the man couldn't turn his head to the left or the right.

"Tell me what you see there." Brody was calm, not furious, which seemed to terrify the bound man even more.

Instead of struggling, he whimpered, as Brody continued. "That's a Homeland Security identification. It says I'm Agent Brody Sladrick and I have the entire executive muscle behind me, so you're going to cooperate with this national security prisoner transfer. If you don't cooperate, I'll not have you reassigned to a facility in Alaska. I'll have you imprisoned in an underground chamber in Poland so deep you'll forget what sunlight feels like. You'll be termed a traitor, an unknown in the cog of the incarcerated. Only God Almighty will remember that—"

"Okay! Okay, I get it. What do you want? I'm sorry, okay?"

"What's the code for the door?"

Though I was impressed with Brody's effectiveness, I was equally impressed by the partnership he had with Gail. Gail was already waiting at the door, ready to punch in the code, as if she'd never doubted Brody's ability to extract it.

"It's, um, four-nine-two-six, then hit enter. Please, I'm sorry! I didn't realize who you guys were! I mean, I saw your—"

Nudging Squinty with my toe needle, I put him to sleep. Gail had already opened the inner access door and swung it outward on thick, steel hinges. We moved through together.

Closing the door behind us, we acknowledged that everything was electronically monitored in this place. And we couldn't leave a door open for an easy exit without lighting up someone's control panel.

Before us spanned a circular set of tiers, six deep, subterranean. The four stories above ground were crisscrossed with walkways and Plexiglas administration offices. The circular shape from top to bottom had the feel of the inside of an imagined flying saucer. A suffocating presence stole my breath for a moment as I studied the huge interior; there was only one way in or out of the whole building!

"Gail, stay here." Brody's order jarred my senses back to the present. "Chloe, you go up to get a cell number. I'll go down to fetch Luigi as soon as you gain access."

"On it," I said, and started up the ramp to the offices. I was more than happy to take orders from a more experienced agent, who was older than I was as well. Though he wasn't pushy, he was a man who gave even Corban advice on COIL operations, and Corban didn't listen to many people on how to run the Christian spy agency.

Personnel, in the same uniforms as the men in the entrance wore, noticed me approaching their nest-like offices. Below me, I saw Brody was about to face a number of guards on the circular catwalk. Fortunately, none of these on the inside appeared to be armed with firearms, since they all dealt so closely with dangerous criminals.

"Acquisition orders for prisoner Luigi Putelli," I stated as I approached the first official. "It's a priority order. Custody transfer."

"Everybody has priority." The first speaker was a mustached man with big forearms almost as thick as his legs. He crossed those arms and blocked my way up the catwalk. "How'd you get in? We just spoke to the front and told them that prisoner isn't ready . . . indefinitely. And you can't bring firearms in here!"

"Yeah, we get it. You want to oppose releasing a prisoner to anyone you think will treat him in a way less than you think he should be treated. But your thinking is irrelevant. I'm H-S Agent Azmaveth. H-S, as in Homeland Security. As a formality, I brought a copy for you, but I'm not obligated to give it to you. Should you further impede this explicit order, I'm obligated by the United States government to incapacitate you by any means necessary."

I adjusted my blazer so Mr. Forearms could better see my sidearm—merely a prop for me. Below, I heard Brody already in a scuffle with someone on the catwalk. As soon as Forearms leaned over to look, I took a step forward and got loud.

"Hey! Pay attention! Don't look down there! I'm speaking to you! Where's Luigi Putelli? Now!" My fiercest gaze seemed to hold his attention now. I figured a play out of Brody's own book would finish the job. "The next step is to lock down this whole facility. I'll do it for a week. Nobody in or out. We'll investigate every inch of everyone's lives here to sort out where this insubordinate attitude toward the US government originates. Who do you think signs your paycheck? Keep stalling. See what happens. Just see what kind of hole you find yourself in that you won't get out of without a presidential signature, and I'll advise the president myself not to sign anything with your name on it!"

Like a mother counting to ten for a spoiled child, I held up my wrist to silently count the seconds on my watch. I prayed his shifting feet meant he was getting the picture. If I had to call Rod Chang again, who knew how badly H-S would really drop the hammer!

"Cell four-oh-two," he stated.

"Is he hurt?" I dropped my arm to my side and covered my sidearm with my blazer. "There was no detail in his file."

"Well, he may have received a few bruises. The CIA dropped him off in less than satisfactory condition."

"Bruises, we can handle. Broken bones, and we start breaking careers. Get it?" I moved to the railing, but watching my back should Forearms attack. "Agent Sladrick! Cell four-oh-two!"

"Roger that!" he yelled back. "Okay, I'm there! Tell them to pop it! I have restraints in hand!"

"Open four-oh-two!" Forearms hollered toward the ceiling where a booth was suspended from the rafters, a single catwalk leading to it.

Only then did I notice how many uniformed men and women were above us, witnessing our exchange. The command was passed one more time, and the secure booth, with bars on its windows, seemed to be the focal point of attention.

"Got him!" Brody called.

"So, what're you gonna do with him?" Forearms asked. "I'm just following orders, too, you know. All of this. That's what I've been told to do."

"In one way or another, every wicked deed of every person will be judged." With a cold smile, I nodded at him. "There should be both joy and fear in that fact for you."

"What's that supposed to mean?"

Looking down, I checked Brody and Luigi's progress up the circular tiers. They were directly below me, their shoes loud on the metal grating.

"The Book of Acts, chapter seventeen, verse thirty-one, should make it clear enough for you. Have a nice day."

I wasn't about to linger with these people who'd already been inhospitable. After backing away two steps, I turned and walked quickly toward the catwalk intersection where Brody escorted a cuffed Luigi in front of me onto the walk. Luigi glanced back at me, and I felt a grave illness deep in my gut for two reasons. First, he'd been beaten recently, some of the wounds so fresh the skin on his head hadn't colored as bruises yet. And second . . .

At the inner access door, Gail punched the code and the door opened.

"Brody." I glanced quickly around us. We were alone. He paused before exiting through the door. Gail's face seemed to plead for me to leave, to flee, to escape while we could. But I couldn't. Not yet. "That's not Luigi."

He studied the man.

"Are you Luigi Putelli?" Brody asked firmly, his grip on the man's arm digging into the flesh.

The man rattled off sentences in what I figured were Italian, which I didn't know.

"It's not him," I said. "I've seen Luigi in the flesh almost three years ago. And then just days ago at Corban's mock funeral, and two days ago on the news. This guy's too meaty and short. Luigi is tall and thin. His face is bony, even gaunt."

"They intentionally gave us the wrong cell number." Brody clenched his teeth so hard his jaw muscles bulged. The detention officers didn't know what whirlwind they'd sown.

"Intentionally, they gave us a man they hoped we'd believe was Luigi." I looked from Gail to Brody. "This is more than two agencies clashing over jurisdiction of a prisoner. This is blatant subterfuge to mislead a government agency. The guy there said he was just following orders. Who knows how high this goes, who's at the top of this deceit? Luigi, the real Luigi, could even be dead, and this is part of the cover-up."

"Someone else is giving them orders, huh?" Brody's gaze went to the personnel I guessed were still watching us from above and behind me, hoping we took the bait. "If we leave now, we may never get another chance to get the real Luigi out of here."

"If he's even here," Gail said, then took a deep breath. "Okay, what do you want me to do?"

I could plan an op or stage a rescue with planning, but this was too much for me. We were at the door of a detention facility with no more than we had when we'd arrived. The most terrifying reality of all returned to roar in my skull: if we were captured, we could disappear inside this place before anyone could help or find us.

"Change of plans." Brody handed the fake Luigi to Gail. "They have one of ours, now we have one of theirs. Evidence. When vinegar fails, change to honey, for a minute. We make this painfully clear that unless the real Luigi Putelli is handed over, they will be executed one by one. We'll see how deep their loyalty goes to whoever is giving them orders to throw us this curve ball."

Drawing his sidearm, Brody checked the chamber. I did the same, realizing we were about to become an execution squad—of sorts.

"What weapons are we up against?" I asked.

"In here? Pepper spray and lead-tipped metal batons. Watch out for the control booth. They probably have a block gun. It shoots wooden or rubber bullets that'll knock you to your knees—or kill you with a head shot." He held a hand out to Gail. "Give me your gun. Secure the four guys at the front desk. Use your tranqs as often as you need to, to keep them quiet."

Gail looked to me for confirmation. I gave her a nod, knowing her hair bun held a half-dozen pins laced with falaco tranquilizer. She handed Brody her firearm. None of us carried an extra clip since the guns themselves—though real—were merely props.

Brody tucked the extra firearm into his waistband. Since we were COIL operatives, we were not accustomed to the heavy metal weapons of lethality. But there was a time in the IDF when I had no conscience for taking life, and the gun was as familiar to me as my COIL weaponry was now.

"We're looking for a blind spot," Brody stated to me. "We'll need at least two to play this right. I count nine guards in this place, not counting the guy in the booth. Gail, take the prisoner out to the front desk as if we're taking the bait. When you hear gunfire, open this door again, but just a crack. We won't be too slow in leaving, I'm guessing, when it's time."

"I'm ready," I said.

"It's time to smile." He squared his shoulders and put on his most pleasant face, which was still not too pleasant. "We'll see who's more loyal to whom: us to Corban and Luigi, or them to their paycheck."

We started up the catwalk.

✝

CHAPTER TWENTY-NINE

As Brody Sladrick and I approached the Plexiglas administration offices, Mr. Forearms came out to meet us again. Now that certain things were about to get physical, I remembered what Brody said about needing some muscle on the team. I was a one-hundred-and-forty-pound woman nearing fifty years old, and Brody was a middle-aged man who'd been shot in the chest a few weeks earlier.

"We came to make nice," I said with a smile and a shrug. "You gave us the prisoner without much grief. We don't want to leave on bad terms."

"It's no problem," said Forearms. He seemed to relax at my words. Apparently, no one had called the front desk.

"Is there somewhere we can talk?" I gestured toward the offices. Again, others above were listening. "It won't hurt anything if we share a little about what the H-S is planning to do with Luigi Putelli."

Forearms studied my face as I raised my eyebrows in expectation. It would be very suspicious if he wasn't hospitable at that point, and the bait to know what was to happen to their Fake-Luigi had to be tempting. Then he looked at Brody, a step behind me.

"Okay. We have a few minutes before count. Follow me."

Continuing up the catwalk ramp, we followed Forearms. The observers above dispersed to their own activities, the fireworks seemingly over.

The first office we came to, after one switchback of the catwalk, was labeled "Major Kesson." The highest walkway continued farther to the other offices. We entered the first office and Forearms indicated chairs for us to sit on, our backs to the door. Brody opted to stand in the corner, so I sat down, trusting him to watch my back.

"Which branch of the military are you, Major Kesson?" I asked, wondering if Rod Chang's intel was wrong about these people being private contractors for the Feds.

"No branch." He shrugged. "It's honorary. Twenty years worth of security details between Mogadishu and Afghanistan. Free enterprise and all that."

"Of course." I smiled, but I was thinking he just admitted to being a mercenary on US soil. "The truth is, Mr. Kesson, you've misled us in a most fatal way. Fatal to you."

"What?" He sat forward in his chair. His hands were in sight, no weapons at hand, but he was a big enough man that he wouldn't need weapons to hurt me. "Fatal? What do you mean? I thought we came up here to—"

"Someone has given you orders regarding Luigi Putelli, and we believe it's the traitorous organization that we're hunting." A little movement from the corner of my eye told me Brody had drawn his primary sidearm, and Kesson's eye twitch confirmed as much. "That makes you a traitor, and traitors don't lose their private enterprise jobs, or pensions, or respectability. They lose their lives. Traitors are shot. We're Homeland Security, which you know well. We're on the battlefield constantly. When on the battlefield, we don't hold hearings for traitors, because hearings may jeopardize an operation's timelines. So, a hearing may be superseded by direct execution. We're here to implement that to the last man here, if we have to, to find the real Luigi Putelli, and to determine who's working against the United States government."

The gun that Brody held against his side now appeared in a different light.

"You're going to . . . shoot me?" He chuckled nervously, but stopped when I didn't join him.

"We prefer the word execution. Lives are at stake, and you're stalling an investigation. I've seen Luigi Putelli myself. He speaks English well, and he's skinnier and taller than the guy you gave us. Why don't you call in your next in command? That might help your situation."

He licked his lips as he eyed me cautiously. Finally, he pressed an intercom button.

"Flesch, come in here."

I checked my watch. Almost twenty minutes had passed since tranquilizing the first man in the front entry room. The lightest falaco toxin lasted only twenty minutes. Gail would probably deal with a few conscious men very soon.

A stocky man with a neck tattoo entered the office. He stopped immediately inside. I turned to see he was staring at Brody's gun.

"Come on in, Mr. Flesch," I invited, and pushed the other chair a few inches away from me. "Mr. Kesson was about to explain to you why we're still here."

Flesch sat down with obvious concern over Brody remaining behind him.

"They know that wasn't Putelli."

"And what else?" I urged.

"If we don't give them Putelli and some answers, they said they'll start executing us."

"You're kidding." Flesch glanced at me. "Seriously?"

I may have played the cat and mouse game a moment longer, but Brody was the one with the drawn gun. When I saw Flesch flinch and start to rise from his chair, I knew Brody had shot him with a wrist tranq, which was barely discernable to me as I knew what to listen for. An instant later, Brody moved behind Flesch, where Kesson couldn't see the gun, and he fired into the floor dangerously close to my foot. Flesch slumped to the floor from the tranquilizer.

At the clamor of feet on the grate, Brody moved to the doorway, showing himself and the gun.

"Get back to your offices! Major Kesson will call you when you're needed!"

"Sit down, Kesson," I said calmly, my ears still ringing from the gunshot. Shakily, he stood, perhaps to flee or attack, but the desk was a broad obstacle. He stared at Flesch. "Why don't we make sure you understand the stakes. You tell us who you're working for, and where Luigi Putelli is, or you join your man Flesch here. And if you have no answers, you're useless to us."

"You guys are sick!" He swore and sat down, his nervous tic of blinking rapidly kicking in. "I don't know everything you want to know. This is sick! Just killing people for no reason?"

"We're at war, Mr. Kesson," I said, "and you're playing games for the enemy. Wartime policy has been enacted. Agent Sladrick here will execute the rest of your shift, then we'll come back to you."

Though I didn't like the fierce coldness in my voice, there seemed no other route at that point. The sooner I could convince this man of the magnitude of our demands, the sooner we could leave. Corban had implemented the same method to provoke men to straighten their lives. It could only be done by someone like Brody or Corban who could entirely control his environment.

"I was told to keep Luigi Putelli here unless the TaTD came to get him. Anyone else, I'm supposed to stall."

"The TaTD? We're talking about the Tactical anti-Terrorist Division?" I asked. "That branch of Homeland Security has been scrapped, just last week. It's being investigated for terrorist activities. Don't you watch the news? Flight 524 may have been brought down by them."

"Well, I guess they're back up and running, because no one came and shut us down. And we haven't been reassigned. All our prisoners are still dangerous terrorists and criminals, no matter what agency gets scrapped." Kesson seemed to swallow with a bit of difficulty. "I mean, that's who we have in custody here—terrorists and national security risks. The TaTD has been our link to Washington. We don't take orders from anyone else."

"But you understand what I'm saying, don't you?" I said. "General Logan Florglade is a wanted man. There's a manhunt as we speak."

"Uh . . . I'm confused." Kesson raised his chin, perhaps trying, but failing, to go down with dignity. "Who've I been talking to on the phone, then?"

Kesson seemed easier to read since he was afraid for his life, but I still watched him closely for any indication of a lie—such as looking down and to the left, or fidgeting with his hands or fingers. The TaTD did seem to be operational still, if this was a TaTD facility. Or at least someone was still using it to coordinate their retreat.

"Who's your contact in the TaTD?" I asked.

"That's what I'm saying. It's General Forglade's office. It's always been Forglade." He scribbled down an email and secure server address. "Several agencies have used us for years as a detention hub, so maybe no one really knew we're TaTD. I didn't think it was strange to do what Forglade ordered with an inmate two days ago when Putelli showed up. But I didn't know Forglade was in that kind of trouble."

Frowning, I pondered in silence for a moment. It was possible much of the public didn't know or care about what was happening with yet another crooked official in DC, but a mercenary whose lifeline was DC? I doubted it. Kesson was a small fish and I just wanted answers.

"What'd he order you to do when Putelli arrived?"

"Hold him until TaTD officials came for him specifically—a man named Karl Coleman. He's picked up prisoners here before. Coleman's not in trouble, too, is he?" Kesson laughed, then shut his mouth when he must've seen the answer on our faces. "Oh. Well, the order was to keep Putelli in isolation, make sure he didn't talk to anyone."

"And what about you?" I asked. "Did you talk to him, question him?"

"No!" Under my gaze, he shrugged. "Well, a few of us tried to get him to talk. We just wanted to know if he was a big deal like they were saying on the news. But he wouldn't say anything."

"So, you knew Putelli was a big deal from the news, but you didn't know Forglade was a wanted man, from the same news?"

"How could I know it was that serious? I just spoke to Forglade two days ago!" He gestured to a black phone on his desk. "Look at it from my point of view. The orders came from a man I've known for years. And I just met you guys, and you're telling me that it's all a lie, that Forglade is using us, or trying to hide Putelli here for his own gain or something."

"Now you're getting it." I sighed, though not fully grasping Forglade's motives myself. "You're not real quick, are you?"

"We need to trace that phone call from two days ago," Brody said quietly to me. "After we get Putelli on the road, then Senator Nettleton's boys need to tear this place apart."

"Am I . . ." Kesson cleared his throat and eyed Flesch again. "I mean, I cooperated, right?"

"You get the real Luigi Putelli here this instant," I said, "and no one else dies before we leave."

"Bigalow!" Kesson ordered on the intercom. "Take two and bring me prisoner Putelli on the double!" "Are we gonna get wasted by the suit with the gun?" a man asked on the comm.

Brody shook his head.

"No, Bigalow, just do it! They're Feds here for the prisoner!"

"Okay, Boss."

Three men ran past the office. They looked in and surely saw the supposed dead man. We listened to their feet on the grates, running down farther and farther. Kesson didn't meet my eyes through those long minutes, his gaze nervously staring anywhere else.

"Here they come," Brody announced, able to see the whole facility from the door.

"Tall and skinny. He'd be bald, but he hasn't shaved in maybe a week."

"Stay here," I told Brody. "If he's bonafide, I'll yell."

"It's him!" Kesson gasped. "He's the only Luigi Putelli we've got, the one everyone's been trying to prosecute—even the French!"

I met the three officers below at the intersection. Luigi's wrists were cuffed behind his back, but when his eyes met mine, I knew it was him. If I didn't know any better, I'd say I saw recognition on his face as if he knew me much better than I knew him. That was certainly probable if he'd been close to Corban the last couple years.

"Yeah, it's him, Brody!" I called. "Let's roll!"

Gail must've heard me, because the inner access door opened wide. Brody jogged down to me, the gun still in his hand. Bigalow and his two officers backed away.

"Boss, they're taking him!" Bigalow yelled.

"Let them!" Kesson said from the railing above. "Flesch has already been killed! Stay out of their way! They're Homeland Security!"

Taking Luigi by the arm, I led him into the foyer. Brody followed a moment later. Before we exited the only door out of the facility, I smiled at Brody. It had been no mistake calling on the veteran to help in my hour of need.

"How surprised do you think they'll be when they realize their buddy is still alive?"

"Honestly," he said, "I think they'll be mad."

"Why mad?"

"Wouldn't you be mad if you were convinced something was real when it wasn't?"

"That sounds like something Corban would do," Luigi said, as if Corban's approval would make everything okay. But it told me Luigi knew Corban enough to voice his opinion.

We left False-Luigi still cuffed at the front desk and exited the building. It was nearly noon, and the sun hit us in the face. I'd never been so happy to get out of a building in my life!

†

CHAPTER THIRTY

Outside Joliet, Illinois, we pulled off Interstate 80 for a pit stop. Brody and I had agreed that with everything going on with Luigi, we wouldn't risk the vulnerability of an airliner to fly back to New York City. The news of his stunt over Northern California was still worrying passengers and airplane security personnel alike. Besides, we could use the time in the car to debrief Luigi, which we'd been doing nonstop.

"Keep an eye on him," I told Brody. Standing next to the SUV as we refueled, we both watched Luigi through the windows of the gas station. Luigi, wearing an ill-fitting suit of Brody's, was picking out snacks and drinks for the trip, though his eyes were often on us. "This one has a tendency to disappear, from what the media is saying. They said he even faked his own death in Lebanon a few years ago."

"There's something about the way he looks at me." Brody frowned. "I don't think he likes me."

"Just don't bother to fight him if something starts," I advised. "Just tranq him. If you can."

Gail walked up then and tossed a spotting scope into the front seat.

"We seem to be clear." Her hair was still in a bun. None of us had slept much for two days, but she looked twice as fresh as Brody and me. "If someone's following or tracking us, it's from a remote location, like a satellite or drone."

"I think we got out of Lincoln before anyone could organize an intercept team." Gesturing for them both to come closer, I lowered my voice. "What do you guys think of what Luigi's told us so far? Karl Coleman hired Luigi to kill Corban's family. That explains why the TaTD wanted to get at Luigi first. No one else seems to have linked Corban and Luigi, though, like he said."

"He's still holding out on us," Brody said. "Do we all agree with that much?"

"Yeah." Gail crossed her arms. "He's not being direct. I've noticed his hesitation before answering questions, and his breathing increases when he seems to be lying."

"At least Janice and Jenna are safe," I said, reminding them that risking our lives in the detention facility wasn't a waste. "Guys like Luigi don't usually live long enough to make changes in their lives. He's a flat-out assassin—or was. But, he did find his sister in Italy, and he didn't kill that Agent Wes Trimble in the woods, and—"

"And he hasn't killed us yet," Brody said with a serious look on his face. I'd hoped Brody was confident to take Luigi if he attacked us, but we all seemed to secretly agree on the same thing: Luigi was in a league above us, even if he'd been arrested. He was in Corban's league, and it was ridiculous to think of anyone getting the upper hand on Corban.

"Well, we can't discount that this guy is in transition mode," I said. "I don't want to push him too hard. He's made steps to improve upon his past—if he was everything they're saying about him."

"He knows nothing more than we do about Corban's whereabouts, though." Brody shook his head once. "Does that complicate our operation with Homeland Security?"

"Not right away." Checking my cell phone, I saw there were no texts. "As soon as we get word back from Senator Nettleton's office, we'll know how to jump next, if they even tell us. I can't wait to hear what Rod Chang digs up on that detention facility still operating under TaTD jurisdiction. General Forglade is still running it while on the run!"

"That probably means someone over him is still playing puppet master," Brody concluded as Luigi walked up, his arms full of drinks and snacks.

"I should warn you," Luigi said, his face grave, which seemed to be his only face. "My eyesight is exceptional, and my ability to read lips is above average."

It took a moment for me to grasp what he was disclosing. From inside the gas station, he'd been spying on our conversation! He was indeed out of our league.

"Now, why would you admit that to us?" Brody asked, his tired face suddenly alive with amusement. "Normally, someone with those skills—speaking from experience— withholds that as a secret to get over on the enemy."

"But if we're all Corban's allies, we're not enemies of one another." Luigi's gaze seemed to be measuring my face. "Corban is still in danger, I fear. I'm certain I can help him. The questions you've asked me thus far have told me much. What we don't know collectively tells me what we must now discover—together or independently."

"No, no, no, Luigi!" I held up my hand. "You're in Homeland Security custody. There's no independent working now. If you care for Corban's reputation as you say you do, then you'll stay close. We took those cuffs off you because I thought we could work together."

"However well we may coordinate, we're still just a single unit." Luigi shifted his feet, and I wondered if he would try to run. His arms were full of food that he could throw at us for a couple seconds' head start. He looked weary, but I guessed he could still outrun the three of us on foot. "I think we need to split up. We could cover more ground, as you say."

"I didn't get this team together to split up!" I said.

"Wait." Brody narrowed his eyes, then glanced at me. "He does have a point."

"Brody!" Gail disapproved as well.

"If we worked in pairs, we'd cover twice the intelligence territory," he stated. "We'd stay in communication, but we can't go everywhere together and expect to discover what we could if we doubled our approach. Each of us has our strengths, even our own resources and skills. Gail and I have been doing this a long time, and working as partners, we can move faster and cover more ground than traveling in a pack. No offense."

"That pairs me with Luigi," I said with clenched teeth, not bothering to hide my aggravation with Brody. How did I draw the assassin who was on everyone's wanted list?

"You're Nettleton's contact, Chloe. Gail and I will be your support, run errands and stuff." Brody shrugged. "They expect you to be with him, not Gail or me."

"And we need more COIL agents involved," Luigi said, facing me, ignoring my uneasiness. "Who's available?"

"How much do you know about COIL?"

"Enough to know that we need to call in more agents to help us, at least to assist in what you may call the heavy lifting."

"We need muscle," Brody grinned, seeming to warm to Luigi by every passing minute. "That's what I keep saying."

"Everyone of use is in the field." Again, I mentally counted off the ones who could function domestically under such pressure. Johnny Wycke, Memphis, and June, even Scooter—they were all overseas in the middle of important operations. "We've lost top agents this past year. Our numbers are down."

"I've told you about Karl Coleman hiring me to kill Corban's family," Luigi said. "He probably incited my past enemies to kill me to cover up his own secrets. Because of this added danger, I advise we bring in one specific COIL operative, someone who knows Corban and COIL well, who can handle himself in an environment that requires strategic caution . . ."

"Who?" I asked. "Who am I forgetting?"

"A man I trained personally." Luigi looked from me to Brody. "Corban gave him to me to train in the art of human intelligence and solitary clandestine operations. None of you are aware of this person?"

"You trained an operator for COIL?" I laughed at him. "I don't believe you! Who?"

"Perhaps . . . I've said too much." He looked down at the pavement. "Yes, I've spoken wrongly. If Corban hasn't told you, then it's not my place to say any more."

"Luigi, we need more muscle," Brody pressed, "and we need everyone on the team. We're at an impasse unless we start busting down doors. Sure, we've got the brains and the tools, but we need brute, too. Ten, fifteen years ago, that could've been me, but now—"

"Oh, you're just right!" Gail said, elbowing him. "Luigi, what he's saying is if you know of an asset, we need him. What skills does he have?"

"He is, as you would say, the full package." Luigi's mouth turned up in what I guessed was a smile. "And he's younger and better than all of us."

"Do I know him?" I asked, still angry that Corban hadn't told me Luigi had trained one of our own. "Luigi! Do I know him?"

"You used to." Luigi set all his groceries in the back seat of the SUV. "Many think he died. I wouldn't have said anything, but I know that he's . . . local."

"Local?" I felt my temperature rising. "You mean he's in the States?"

"No. Local, as in, he's here. He's been following us from the detention facility." Luigi's gaze remained on my face, so I should've been able to read him, but he was more skilled at his craft than me. "I suspect he came to the facility to get me out, as you did. As I said, I trained him. We're close. You may even consider him already a part of this team."

"Who . . . is . . . it?" I fumed.

Luigi held out his hand.

"Give me your phone. I'll see if he wants to come in. He's been a lone operator for a long time."

When I hesitated, my mind spinning, Brody gave Luigi his own phone, and Luigi stepped to the bumper to dial, but still close enough that we could hear him talk.

"Chloe, it's okay." With a hand on my shoulder, Gail seemed to sense my uncertainty in all that we didn't know. "We have to try everything we can."

"Corban kept this from me!" I felt so hurt. Turning from Gail's hand, I studied the freeway and nearby lots for someone who'd been following us, or someone who was speaking on a phone at that instant. Someone I'd once known? Who? COIL wasn't even that old.

"It's me," Luigi said into the cell, his back to us. "If you're willing, we may need your expertise at this juncture. Chloe requests it . . . No, she doesn't know it's you . . . His family is safe, but whoever is trying to destroy him is still active. It could still be General Forglade and Karl Coleman, acting off-site . . . I understand. That seems wise. We'll proceed."

Luigi turned and gave Brody the phone.

"Well? Who is he?"

"I'm sorry, Chloe. He'd like to watch over us from afar, and I agree. Our enemies can't know who he is if we don't know, either."

My body went numb. Who was it? COIL was such a tight family. Who was in hiding? Someone I thought was dead? Who was now our greatest asset? At that moment, when I realized Luigi wasn't going to tell me who our loyal shadow was, I felt terrible shame mixed with an immense sense of helplessness. How was I in control at all? I'd been approaching the situation as if I had to remain in control. But it was God who was handling our lives and the events in them. Prayer and trust had even been lacking in my life ever since leaving the detention facility, as if God were only worth trusting when I was afraid or desperate.

Finally, I took a deep breath. I was calmer now.

"Okay, I understand the wisdom in splitting up, but only if we have precise objectives when we get to New York. We can begin making those plans as we drive. If we take turns driving around the clock, we'll be back at the office by tomorrow afternoon. Brody?"

"Yeah?"

"I need you to be the spiritual leader here. Corban always is, when he's with us on our team missions. We need to stay in prayer. More than anyone, I can easily forget we're fighting a spiritual battle here. In my heart I feel like Corban is in something deep, and I'm a worrier."

"Well then, let's pray now." Brody took Gail's hand, and placed his other hand on Luigi's shoulder. As I bowed my head, Gail took my hand, and I noticed Luigi staring at us. He didn't know what to do with his hands, or whether to bow his head like the rest of us. It was a sad reminder that he may have been included in our quick gas station prayer huddle, but he wasn't one of us.

Brody prayed.

...✝...

We made plans through the night. Our objectives were broad since our intel was scarce. But as Gail drove us into Manhattan, I felt confident we were moving in God's will and making steps to recover Corban. With few leads, the world became a large search grid.

But the leads we did have, and the resources we could muster, narrowed our search. We heard back from Rod Chang. Someone had indeed been continuing TaTD's claims on several of its past holdings, he explained, like the Lincoln detention center. This had been discovered by tracing the detention center's phone records to someone overseas, but Homeland Security had been unable to narrow it down to more than an East Caribbean sat-phone signal. Someone had put up some sort of jamming field, which would require high-profile access to top-secret resources to maintain. Homeland Security was waiting for further contact with the Lincoln center to trace the signal more precisely—if the jamming could be routed. Rod Chang agreed it was General Forglade still trying to direct operations in the States. Because of this, Chang encouraged us to pursue all leads possible.

The four of us reviewed Chang's conversation as we drove up Broadway, and we all agreed there was something disconcerting about the lack of attention toward Karl Coleman. After all, it was Coleman who'd hired Luigi to kill Corban's family. Brody made a few calls to his contacts, then he asked Gail to pull the SUV over so we could all look at the screen of downloaded data sent to him.

"This is General Forglade, a four-star general. An endurance runner and recognized outdoorsman and survivalist, even though he's getting up there in age. He taught at Fort Benning, and more recently, he's led some smaller operations in the Middle East. I think that's where he met Karl Coleman."

"It is," Luigi added. "They met in Cairo. Coleman instigated the Islamic nations to rise up—the Arab Spring. He was the spark that was meant to destabilize the area, but it seems to have become a hornet's nest."

"Well, the guy is as ugly as they get," Brody continued. "He's a killer, and that's just the stuff that isn't blotted out from black ops all over the world. Whole villages have been wiped out in Africa because of him—men, women, and children, when they didn't give up guerrillas he was hunting."

"Why wasn't he prosecuted?" Gail asked. "They have war crimes tribunals for men like him!"

"Who would testify? He killed all the witnesses. Some people spoke up from his unit, which is the only way we know anything about it, but even those people, his own teammates, have disappeared. Look at this! He was brought into the TaTD two months before the crash of Flight 524."

"He's a cleaner now," Luigi said. "Many paramilitary soldiers become domestically covert once they see how much money they can earn. Coleman is a killer for hire."

"And he was brought in to take out Corban," I concluded. "It has to be. People are so afraid of this guy that nobody is focusing on anyone but General Forglade."

"The question is, who brought them both in?" Brody asked. "Someone tied them together. Someone sanctioned the downing of Flight 524. A four-star general may sound high enough to do that, but that kind of call would require a panel or some sort of congressional approval."

"But General Forglade has been hung out to dry," Gail added.

"None of this would've come to light if Corban would've given them what they wanted." I took Brody's laptop and studied the screen myself as Gail pulled back onto the freeway. "We can't let Corban down, and we can't let these guys get away with mass murder. None of us should think too carelessly about these guys, either. Now that we know who we're up against, we know a little of what Corban is in the middle of."

It wasn't easy for me to split up the team, but it was necessary. By Luigi's instructions, Brody and Gail were to check on Corban's family and Luigi's sister in the mountain silo.

Meanwhile, I was to receive a pass by Luigi into the underworld in which he existed. He claimed he could trace around the satellite jamming process in the Caribbean, rerouting sooner than Homeland Security could. I had my doubts, but Luigi wasn't one to bluff at the expense of Corban's safety. This was something I'd learned during our weary drive from Lincoln: he cared for Corban like a brother.

I just hoped Corban was still alive.

†

CHAPTER THIRTY-ONE

In a sub-basement in New York City, I stood next to a very still Luigi in the doorway, scanning the room. Now accustomed to his long and awkward silences, I waited for him to explain beyond what he'd already shared with me—about his plan to find Corban.

Before us was a technological mess of cables and monitors, but the longer I studied it, I realized it wasn't a mess, but a type of surveillance nest. The ceiling light would've been inadequate for a human to function under, but the monitors were bright as they scrolled and parsed data.

After I listened to nearly two minutes of Luigi chewing bubblegum, he finally stepped beyond the doorway. I now identified the gum habit with the man who'd helped Corban's family before—according to Janice and Jenna's stories.

"It's as I left it," he said, and sat in a chair at what made me think of a gaming console. He immediately began to type, glancing from monitor to monitor.

There seemed to be no other chair available, unless it hid in the shadows beyond a rack of computer hardware, so I wandered to my left. My eyes were drawn to a tack board with a map of the world hanging between two locked cabinets. It had pins and lines drawn on it. The pins seemed color-coded. I recognized quickly that blue pins suspiciously marked places in the world that I had frequented in the last few years—Malaysia, Israel, Saudi Arabia, Iran, and others. White pins—many of them—were stuck in places where I'd arranged operations for Corban, and some I didn't know— North Korea, Germany, Sudan, Russia, Egypt, Lebanon, Malaysia, and many others. Red pins were the last color, and these were in Australia, Germany, Greece, Oman, and a dozen other places.

"Luigi, who are the red pins?" I asked before I realized my curiosity had won over my subtlety. I meant to retain some operative mystery, since I'd been a covert agent for many years. But every time I crossed one of Corban's peers, I was reminded of how little I knew but how happy I was that Corban had powerful friends.

Of course, Luigi didn't answer me, and I deduced what I could. The red pins represented the travels of the unknown COIL super-agent, the one Luigi had trained, the two of them being close, as he'd said. It was someone of such importance that Luigi, this suspicious intelligence agent, had deemed him worthy of tracking. But this pupil of his still evaded me.

"Nettleton's office isn't lying," Luigi said. I moved up behind him. "There's a satellite blackout over the East Caribbean."

"There must be other satellites you can access. Corban always does that. Russian or Israeli or Indian."

"Yes, I've tried those! Old access routes have new firewalls, as if this has all been planned." He blew a bubble and spoke around his gum. "Someone doesn't want to be found in the Caribbean."

"Could it be Corban?"

This caused Luigi to sit back and ponder in silence for a moment.

"I think not. Corban has other ways to remain invisible. This blackout is too conspicuous for him. It's General Forglade, I believe, as Nettleton's people think. He may have been the instrument to take down Flight 524, but now they are probably trying to take him out, too. And I wouldn't be surprised if Coleman has been tasked to kill General Forglade, and Forglade may know that."

"But no one can find Forglade with this blackout, not even Coleman."

"They will eventually. Wherever the general is hiding, it won't be for much longer." Luigi pushed away from one console, his chair wheels nearly rolling over my toes. "If we want to find Corban, we must find General Forglade first. There are satellites that can't be blinded."

"Weather satellites?"

"No, those are too obvious. Private satellites."

He typed on another console, drafting an email with such cryptic words that I couldn't follow it.

"It would take days to hack a private satellite system in space," I said. "What are you typing? What is CASS?"

"Custom Access Satellite Service." He stopped typing and turned to look at me. His dark eyes seemed to blend with the shadows behind the monitors. "I may be in your assumed custody at this moment, but you swore at street level that my activities would remain secret. This is for Corban."

"Of course. My lips are sealed and sewn. But we're supposed to be a team, and teammates communicate. You've got more secrets than I have questions."

"You may be right." He turned back to the monitor. "I'm still learning to accept how Corban's God intended me to be—not someone who's alone. For many years, I've indulged in the evil way. So I must adjust. Perhaps Corban was too patient with me."

"I think Corban's faith in God to change you from the inside out is proving itself." Pointing to a Bible that lay on a shelf, I saw it was opened to a passage in the Psalms. "Have you been studying?"

"Only for direction. Now, listen." He sent the email and launched his chair back to the first console. "In three days, CASS will launch a new satellite for us. It will—"

"Wait. What? Our own satellite?"

"That's the idea of a custom satellite. It weighs only four kilos and is the size of your fist. And it'll last long enough for us to look past the blackout and see what we're not meant to see."

"Why doesn't Nettleton do that?"

"Bureaucracy." He blew a bubble and popped it, making me think he was a teenager showing off for his next-door friend. "Lots of paperwork. Besides, a four kilo satellite requires only a small rocket, but a one-thousand-pound satellite for the government costs a billion dollars."

"Three days to build and launch a custom one?" I said a prayer under my breath. "We may not have three days. Corban may not have three days. He might still think his family is dead. Do you realize what this means?"

"You don't trust him to be faithful?" He looked me in the face. "By your silence, I would say you fear his love for his wife and daughter is greater than his love for his God. You have nothing to fear in that area. It's possible I know Corban better in this way. Corban won't compromise his faith, even if he believes his family is dead."

I was tempted to take offense. Of course I knew Corban better than this ex-assassin did! Or did I? The longer I hunted for Corban, the more secrets I discovered. In the back of my mind, I did think Corban would exact revenge on his enemies, after all the damage they'd inflicted. It wasn't a pleasant thought, but I knew Corban loved his wife and daughter very much. How would he, with his many skills, hold himself back from killing General Forglade or Karl Coleman? Though he was crafty enough to do it covertly, he'd never be able to live with himself afterward. He was a Christian now.

"But three days is still too long," I argued. "What if he's being held prisoner? If General Forglade or Karl Coleman have him, they could use him as a bargaining chip to buy their own freedom. Or worse yet, they could drug him and extract COIL secrets. There are a lot of countries that would pay good money to find out who in their governments are our Christian underground contacts."

He rose from his chair and peered down at me. His closeness reminded me that neither of us had showered in days—longer for him since he'd been in the Lincoln center.

"It is still our best direction," he said. "Someone like Forglade or Coleman had access to these systems to cause this blackout, and it is for a reason. A general is powerful, but not this powerful. Someone else, as Brody suspected, is still involved. Someone more powerful and in the shadows. That someone must be connected to them. No one else is claiming responsibility. If we find these two men, we find their contact, and we find Corban. But we can't rush into this web of lies."

"You really think we need three days? Was this your only plan?"

"I told you it was a satellite reroute!" He moved away and picked up his Bible. "Besides, my mission for Corban's God, in Corban's absence, is incomplete. Three days is enough time to meet with Senator Nettleton as scheduled, then complete my mission."

"Luigi, I don't understand." I was having trouble holding back a laugh by the way he continued to speak so impersonally of Corban's God. Yet, this devoted—or obsessed—friend of Corban's was committed. "What mission did you have?"

"Well, I'm not sure. This verse says to vindicate the afflicted. I did that."

"A COIL mission?" My brow furrowed. This man seemed loyal to Corban, but I felt violated at the idea of him hacking my COIL files at headquarters—even more violated than being tracked with the blue pins!

"No, my own mission. In New Jersey." He continued to look at his Bible. "I saved the children when I went to Bangladesh for that mission. On my return trip, I met CIA Agent Wes Trimble."

"The one-eyed guy on the news?"

"Let me tell you: he is crafty enough with one eye. I tremble to think what he would do with two!"

I laughed, but he didn't join me. My laughter became a cough.

"Okay, Luigi. You were interrupted from your third mission. How's the verse end?"

"Crush the oppressor." He held up a hand and made a fist. "Without taking a life, of course. Corban wouldn't approve."

"Neither would Corban's God," I added. "Which oppressor?"

He sat down at a third console and studied a grid of the world's continents.

"A database was compiled while I was away. Look. Nigeria is an exploding volcano."

Over his shoulder, I read as he whispered and scanned an English news report of Christians being slaughtered in the streets by Muslim militants in Dalwa.

"You want to help them?"

"They are oppressed."

"Yeah, but Luigi, we're talking about an operation that would take weeks to plan. Trust me, I've set up a lot of missions. Nigeria is no joke. You can't solve a whole region's hatred overnight. Or in three days."

"What would Corban do?" Luigi crossed his arms and stared me down.

"In your place, at this moment, after reading that news article . . ." I closed my eyes and sighed. "Corban would run off and risk his life to save the oppressed from the oppressor. He's done it before. Just please tell me you have a plan."

"A man in Maiduguri owes me. A powerful man."

"If he can help, why isn't he helping already?"

"He has no incentive. And he loves his money." Luigi shrugged. "Why would a wicked man help anyone? I only helped myself before Corban taught me true honor."

"But Corban doesn't work in your heart, Luigi. God does that. What incentive do you have for your contact in Nigeria?"

"His name is Pama. It's like I said—he owes me."

"You're in Homeland Security custody, and mine. You can't travel. For that matter, neither can I. We have too much to prepare here."

"Chloe, that hasn't stopped either of us before. These oppressors must be stopped. What would Corban do?"

Luigi returned to his screens, and I walked to the pin board.

"What would Corban do?" I mimicked quietly to myself, wagging my head. "That's gonna get old real fast!"

✝

CHAPTER THIRTY-TWO

I sat with Luigi facing Rod Chang in a mid-town restaurant in Manhattan. Each of us had ordered an iced tea, though Rod Chang hadn't touched his as he read my report to-date on tracking down Corban Dowler. Minutes ago, I'd spoken to Brody and Gail. Janice, Jenna, and Anna Putelli were safe and remained in the mountain silo. Brody and Gail were returning to New York to operate out of the COIL office, ready to deploy at a moment's notice, even without me if I wasn't back before they were needed.

Finally, Chang set the brief aside and took a sip from his glass.

"That Lincoln mess would've continued to fester if you would've been passive about getting Luigi out." Chang nodded at Luigi as if to apologize for speaking about him in third person. "From there, you informed us about TaTD, or General Forglade, still manipulating matters. Our net is closing around the Caribbean, but Luigi's customized satellite angle will beat us there. If it leads to the capture of General Forglade, I can get Senator Nettleton to cover that expense. I'll want those coordinates as soon as they come through, Mr. Putelli."

"We only want to find Mr. Dowler," Luigi said.

"So do we—make no mistake." Chang folded my report and placed it in his blazer pocket. The ex-agent-turned-advisor for the senator was wearing casual clothes today. "The senator had me dig up Corban's contributions to the free world for the last few decades, all to justify our involvement in turning this investigation for him into an official file. This country does indeed owe him. That's besides the national security risk we'd be facing if he's actually in enemy hands. According to our last conversation, Chloe, your final contact with Corban was when he was under TaTD custody. That doesn't leave much hope."

"You don't know Mr. Dowler." Luigi seemed offended by the way Chang kept using Corban's first name. "No one takes Mr. Dowler into custody unless Mr. Dowler allows it. The man is better than anyone."

"And yet . . . you both, two of his closest contacts, have had no contact with him." Chang raised his eyebrows. "Don't get me wrong. I liked the guy right away, and I like him all the more as I learn more about him. But he's just a man."

"He's a Christian!" Luigi grit his teeth for several seconds, not even chewing on the ever-present wad of gum. "God protects him. It's supernatural. You wouldn't understand."

I nearly laughed as Luigi looked away to stare out the window at the street, crossing his arms.

"Rod," I said, "we're optimistic."

"Well, I'm trying to be. I meant no offense. General Forglade is a traitor. I want him as badly as you want your friend back. This is still a government operation, though."

"Our CASS satellite will launch in two and a half days. We can share the geosynchronic coordinates with you when we get them, but if Corban is a captive, we're dealing with a sensitive situation. In the rush to have the general and Coleman arrested, I don't want Corban killed. I need you to guarantee Corban's safety, regardless of your politics. Corban's the key to all the secrets here—from Flight 524 to date. After all, they tried to pin that flight disaster on his Muhammad ibn Affal legend. You've acknowledged that much."

"Yes, I know. And we still don't know why Flight 524 was even taken down." Chang closed his eyes. "Okay. We need Corban alive as badly as we want Forglade. Until you confirm Corban's safety, I can hold off military or Agency intervention, but as soon as you guys are out of the way, we're moving in. I want your sat-coordinates, and you need to know we'll be on immediate standby. Wherever they are in the Caribbean, we'll scramble covert teams within one hour of notification."

"We'll keep you informed." I followed Luigi's gaze out the tall windows that faced the street. Was he watching someone outside? "Rod, I have some COIL business in Nigeria. Luigi will be going with me, but we'll be back in two days."

"Seriously? Nigeria is a mess!"

"COIL specializes in messes. It's our calling."

"Luigi's not to leave your side, if you have to take him. He's still ours. If he helps us, I can see about the trouble he's in internationally." Chang lowered his voice. "There are a dozen international agencies that want a crack at him. Even

Senator Nettleton's hands are tied. We're talking charges that go back years. France, his first employer, is furious we still have him and they don't. It's affecting our relations with other countries as well."

"They only want me dead." Luigi waved his hand as if it were a small thing. "Once Corban is safe, I'll do what you want."

I frowned at Luigi, then Chang and I exchanged glances. Neither of us seemed to believe Luigi would go that calmly.

"Get Corban," Chang summed up, "and we'll get General Forglade."

"And Karl Coleman," I pressed.

"Of course. Coleman. And then we'll worry about Luigi's status."

...✝...

Since the city of Maiduguri was such a remote distance from Nigeria's capital of Abuja—not to mention beyond a mountain range—I scheduled our arrival into N'Djamena, Chad. An eight-hour drive through the northern tip of Cameroon into Nigeria would put us into the desert region of Maiduguri. According to news reports, the slaughter of Christians was getting worse because it went on unchecked. Nobody cared.

Working with Luigi made me nervous, despite his assurances on the flight over the Atlantic that he wouldn't kill anyone, for Corban and COIL's reputations. He wasn't a Christian, and without the Holy Spirit's supernatural compulsion and protection, I doubted his integrity. However, I didn't doubt his devotion to Corban, for whom he pursued this mission. Luigi had some unearthly zeal to act in Corban's stead. That his zeal was inspired by a Bible verse gave me hope for him yet.

But I was lacking detail about who this Pama was who owed Luigi some favor. Since it was someone from Luigi's past, I had a great level of concern. When Corban had utilized non-Christians on previous missions, COIL had remained the chief handler, and so I continued to declare oversight on how we proceeded on our trips, even in how we were equipped.

We were traveling light, and since Luigi was an experienced agent, he required no extended instruction when I gave orders. From a stash in New York, he'd procured another belt buckle, and I wore my boots with falaco toe and heel needles. These were our only non-lethal weapons. They were so inconspicuous that we slipped through customs without a second look. If Rod Chang or others were tracking us, they wouldn't have had any trouble since Luigi traveled undisguised, as was I, with only a last name change to both of our fabricated passports.

It took an hour to agree on the price for the Jeep I'd called ahead for—the deposit draining much of my budget for the operation. But Luigi assured me there would be no other expenses once we reached his "friend" in Maiduguri.

But reaching Maiduguri was no small task. We had two border crossings, and Cameroon was having its own elevated civil unrest amongst Muslims—not to mention the occasional city work strike that created bandits far and wide. Fathers had families to feed—many with numerous wives. Crime was rampant.

Anticipating all this, I'd seen on one classified COIL report that we had an American man in the area who could possibly be our guide. The reports were classified for one of two reasons. Either the subject wasn't aware that COIL had run interference for his safety, or Corban wanted the COIL agent protected since he'd been involved in the operation. Whichever the case, I wasn't about to bring up the classified past. It was standard procedure to call upon other Christians when COIL needed assistance. And we often compensated in certain ways those who helped.

"Nigeria has not improved in years," Ron Colson explained. He drove our Jeep after joining us at Cameroon's eastern border. Well over six feet tall, he wore the shoulder-to-ankle colorful dress and headpiece of a chieftain. "Like recently, these extremists have been setting up roadblocks to force drivers to recite the Shahada, the Muslim confession of faith. If they refuse, they're killed, usually on the spot."

"What are their weapons of choice?" Luigi asked from the passenger seat. I sat in the back, my head covered with a loose scarf.

"Depends. Machete usually. Some have machine guns." He looked at me. "It's very dangerous in Maiduguri. I'd only do this for other believers."

"I know it's a risk, Ron," I said. "We think we can alleviate some of the Boko Haram problems, though. At least temporarily."

"Well, if anyone can, COIL can." He chuckled, as only a man with God's peace could in that environment. His file said he'd been in Cameroon's northern district for over a decade, and could speak French and the local tribal dialects. "That is, Christ through COIL. So far, I haven't needed to call on you guys for anything, but I know you're out there. There's not a Christian missionary in Cameroon as far as I know who doesn't have COIL's number on their sat-phone."

"We're happy to help." I smiled to myself. His words meant we'd helped him in the past, and he never knew it. But which COIL agent had helped on the operation? Corban's secrets never ended, and I was supposed to be the Primary Operations Manager!

The land was desert wasteland to me, but Ron explained it was prime graze land for the bony goats and thin cattle that we saw occasionally. The fine red dirt gave life to sparse grasses that grew knee-high. Without rain for days, the grass looked dead already.

The next border crossing, which took us into Nigeria, was more complicated. The border agents, in light green and white uniforms, spoke in good English to Ron. We were warned that our Christian names alone would upset any militant who stopped us. They asked if we had any literature, which we didn't, and how much of the Koran we knew by memory, in case we were questioned at gunpoint. The guards made it clear we were headed into a zone in which they couldn't guarantee our safety. And Ron made it clear to them that we were going through anyway.

"If we die in Nigeria," I told Luigi, as Ron handled our passports, "I'm blaming you."

"We're doing this for Corban's God." Luigi gazed to the distant west. His faith gave me an eerie chill. Was his faith just a superstition, or an infatuation with Corban, or was it real? "Unless He allows it, we won't die. This is what Corban has taught me."

"I can't argue with you on that one."

Back in the Jeep, the road became noticeably rougher, reflecting the broken infrastructure of a nation with decades of civil unrest and Islamic conflict. Tribal peoples still had an old mindset, and the government powers that ruled made little sense to them. They usually recognized local leaders from their own tribes. Even when those tribal leaders were Muslim, few had read the Koran for themselves as a practice, and many clung to witchcraft traditions handed down from their grandfathers.

"Oh, no. Start praying!" Ron said as he slowed the Jeep outside Maiduguri. A roadblock ahead couldn't be avoided. "Let me speak. And lock the doors!"

Locking the back doors, I made sure my head covering was in place. As an ex-Mossad agent, I knew parts of the Koran from several past undercover missions, but never could I in good conscience renounce Christ.

"Slow down more." Luigi's hand was on his door. "I'm jumping out. Never will I recite the Shahada! Let them chase me!"

"Do what I say!" Ron ordered. "Sit still and keep your mouth shut."

I set my hand on Luigi's shoulder. He looked me in the face.

"This is where you find out how real your faith is," I said. "Now, lock your door."

Luigi frowned, then complied. I felt his same fear. We both wanted to be outside the Jeep where we had a fighting chance.

The men at the roadblock were armed with machetes, but two had Kalashnikov machine guns. They were civilians, by the look of their clothing.

"There's no imam, that I can see," Ron said as he rolled down his window. "They may not be Boko Haram militants."

Once at a stop, the Jeep was surrounded by the men with machetes. They clacked their blades on the outside of the car. One man tried the door handle on my right, but found it locked.

Another man, this one with a machine gun, went to Luigi's window, and the other with a gun went to Ron's. In Ron's rearview mirror, I could see we weren't the only vehicle being stopped. This close to the city, other evening traffic was beginning to line up behind us. We couldn't even throw the Jeep into reverse and race back to the border.

"Travel tax!" the man with the machine gun told Ron. "One thousand nairas. Come on! Hurry up!"

The man's English—the official language of Nigeria—was so accented I could barely understand him.

"No, we're visitors." Ron shook his head. I noticed both his hands were on the steering wheel. "We're not paying. Move the car out of the way."

What looked like a rusted Cadillac blocked our way, a teenager at the wheel.

"Pay the tax. Everyone pays today!" The muzzle of the gun tapped on the window frame. "You drive a car. One thousand nairas is no problem for you because you are rich!"

"I'm not paying. The money I have is to help the people, not to reward you for your illegal roadblock."

"You pay me!"

"No!" Ron shut off the engine and took the keys out of the ignition. "I will not pay! It's an illegal tax for visitors to Nigeria!"

The men with machetes clubbed the outside of the car a couple times, but enough to make me jump. I couldn't believe Ron wasn't paying them, even when I'd told him we had a little more money! As if Ron could read my mind, he turned to Luigi and me.

"If you pay once, they demand more the next time," Ron said.

"But he has a gun," Luigi said. "He'll make you pay eventually."

"I've never paid, and I'm still alive." Then he addressed the man with the gun again. "No! I won't pay! Let us through!"

The gunman aimed at the sky and fired deafening rounds. Then he jabbed Ron's shoulder with the smoking barrel.

"Pay the tax or I shoot you!"

Closing my eyes, I prayed. Corban needed us. And my husband would be alone if I were gone. What was I thinking to trust Luigi on a mission into Nigeria?

†

CHAPTER THIRTY-THREE

The line of cars behind us honked and the bandit at Ron's window looked around. I wanted to scream at Ron to just pay the guy, but my mouth was too dry from my panic. Being shot inside a stopped vehicle wasn't how I wanted to die, not after all my training as an operative! This would be such a fruitless death. Luigi, looking frantically around the Jeep, seemed to feel as helpless as me.

"Next time, you pay the tax!" the gunman shouted at Ron, then signaled the blockade car. "Go! Go!"

Ron started the Jeep and crawled slowly forward. The machetes around us ceased their clanging on the sides. I chanced a look back and saw the bandits surround the next car as it moved forward.

"They're not Muslims!" I practically cheered.

"Oh, they're probably Muslims," Ron said, "but not extremists. They're just out of work. He wouldn't shoot us with so many to fleece behind us. It would be a mess."

"But you gambled with our lives!" Luigi pouted in the passenger seat. "You couldn't know he wouldn't kill us. The man at my window was about to shoot me. I saw it in his eyes. It's a look I know well."

"This isn't a life for many Westerners." Ron shrugged his big shoulders, as if that day were just another day haggling at the market with the locals. "It isn't a land you live in by the flesh."

"Faith." I laughed at my own fear as it faded, then punched Luigi's shoulder from behind him. "You want to serve Corban's God? This is the thick of it. Maybe you're rethinking helping the Christians here now?"

He didn't respond, but I hoped his eyes were opened. Too many men and women thought they were God's servants, but when the cost of service for His sake faced them, they balked and crept away. I prayed Luigi stuck around. A Christian Luigi would be a great testimony to our Lord!

It was after dark by the time Luigi guided Ron to a gated villa, north of the city. Luigi's memory was remarkable, yet mysterious. He'd been here before, many years before in less tumultuous times, he'd said. For what? That, he didn't say.

From the estate's gate, a thin black man with a sidearm approached Ron's window. Luigi leaned across Ron and spoke to the security guard.

"Tell Pama it's me. Luigi. I'm expected."

The guard shined his flashlight at me, then checked the rest of the Jeep visually. All we had were a couple of backpacks and jugs of water and fuel. He returned to the gate where he picked up a phone. I could see the mansion through the gate. We'd seen no other residence like this in all of Maiduguri as Ron had navigated through the city. And Luigi had merely given his first name to this guard?

The gate swung open and Ron drove through. A sports car and an armored limousine were parked in the shadow of an unmanned but mounted .50-caliber machine gun. Whoever this Pama was, no out-of-work rioters or looters were about to risk their lives against all that artillery.

As we climbed out of the Jeep and stretched our legs, a man in slacks and an open dress shirt emerged from the front door. Luigi walked toward him, then the two men stopped some distance apart. Ron and I glanced at one another. What were we expecting? A long lost brother? If this man was indeed Pama, he was black as night and as tall as Ron. They weren't blood brothers, at least.

"It has been many years, Luigi," the man said in a deep voice.

"I told you I would come one day." Luigi's hands were at his sides but I felt the tension. These men weren't friends. "Invite us into your house."

"But my family is home now." Pama peered around Luigi and saw Ron and me. The guard from the gate walked quietly up to my side. If he thought I was worthy pickings for a human shield, he was wrong. My toes were already feeling the button in the toe of each boot that flipped the falaco needles into place. "I do not wish to do business with you here, Luigi."

"Your house is my house," Luigi stated, which made Ron and me exchange looks again. I was again reminded of why Corban kept Luigi around, even if he did have a wicked past. The man was resourceful. "Because of me, your family is alive, and so are you. Invite us inside now. If I wanted to hurt you, I would've taken his gun already."

Without looking back, Luigi gestured with his hand at the guard who'd snuck up next to me. Hearing Luigi's words, the guard reached for his sidearm. Perhaps he was acting on some signal, or maybe he was merely resting his hand on the pistol grip. Whatever the case, my nerves were on edge, and we'd come far over horrible roads and tense streets. I wasn't about to die at the hands of a trigger-happy security guard.

The toes of my right foot pressed the button as I swung to face the guard. Having learned Krav Maga, an Israeli form of martial arts, at a young age, I wasn't one to grapple with men larger than me. As quickly as possible, I intended to end this conflict.

My right hand went to his face—not to claw him, but to blind him with my fingers in his eyes. Then my left hand went to his hand before he could draw the sidearm. Since he was half-blind and the gun was immobilized, I anticipated his retreat. Before he stepped away, I swung my left boot behind his calf. To him, it was but a bee sting. But for me, the five-second struggle was over. I let go of him, pushing away from his face, letting him trip over my foot as he fell.

Having witnessed falaco's effects many times, I confidently turned my back on the guard. Ron's eyes were wide as he stared at me, his mouth open. To him, it may have appeared that I'd killed the guard merely by pushing him over. By the fear on Pama's face, he may have thought the same. Luigi hadn't moved. He still faced Pama, as if Luigi expected no less from me. After all, we were a team.

"Enough." Pama held up a hand. "Come inside, please."

Luigi went first, following Pama. Ron started after Luigi, but I touched his arm.

"You should probably wait with the Jeep," I said. "If we're staying the night, I'll come get you. No one should bother you here."

"Of course, not now! Is that man—?"

"No. Just some COIL tranquilizer." I used the toe of my right boot to flip the needle back into the left heel. "We shouldn't be long."

From the front door, two household servants clothed in white ran down to the fallen guard. I passed them and caught up to Luigi. Leaving Ron with the Jeep was for his own conscience. Whatever Luigi's past was with Pama, I didn't want Ron exposed to that criminality. As for me, on the other hand—I was privy to more of the picture of how God was working in Luigi's life. A Christian had to be more tolerant of some extremes when waiting confidently on the Lord to work in the heart.

Inside the mansion, a nervous butler, who tried to act fierce, stood at attention, his eyes darting over us. Perhaps he'd seen through a window how swiftly the guard had fallen, for the butler had a concealed weapon in his housecoat—evidenced by a visible bulge—but he didn't draw it.

Quietly to not wake Pama's family at that late hour, we walked into a dimly lit study with a large oak desk overflowing with papers, but empty shelves lined the walls. An outdated computer monitor sat on one corner of the desk with computer cables strung across a worn carpet to a wall outlet. Duct tape held the cables to the carpet so no one would trip. Though Pama appeared wealthy, good technology support was apparently hard to find.

Luigi sat on a chair without being offered. I remained by the door, which was still open, and ignored Pama's hand signal to seat myself. Whatever relationship Luigi and I had, we were partners at that moment. If gunmen rushed in, I had no doubt of the steps that would follow: I would tranquilize a few to buy Luigi time, and I guessed Luigi would take Pama hostage. Then, we'd use Pama to escape. But I hoped nothing of that sort would be required.

Pama sat in a chair to Luigi's left, then turned to face him.

"I cannot pay what I owe you, Luigi, until the morning." Pama, though perhaps a stern man in the city, seemed intimidated by Luigi. "The banks are not open at this hour, and I do not keep cash in the house."

"Even if you had cash in the house and the banks were open, you still could not pay me what you owe me." Luigi sounded so cold, but I realized he was working from a script in his head. I'd seen Corban impersonate attitudes that had made me shiver as well. "But there is another way we may be able to settle accounts."

"What do you ask of me?" Pama stiffened. "You were sent to kill me once. But you let me live. Have you come to finish what none of my enemies have dared?"

No one spoke immediately. Luigi was obviously an expert at building suspense, chiseling the heart with cracks in which to wedge a seed to break down any potential resolve. I had the same ability, but only because of training, and I required planning for each occasion. Men like Corban and Luigi were naturals. Their confidence seemed unbreakable.

"I need your help," Luigi said.

His choice of words, after so much intimidation, were so precisely timed and voiced that I watched Pama melt. His face became softer and his shoulders once again rose. This man would now give Luigi anything, and Pama would be left thinking he was indeed in control as well as aiding Luigi.

"What do you need?"

"A man who has never converted to Islam, who can be trusted with a delicate task."

"Luigi, you know I have not converted. I was raised differently. Of course, I must live peacefully here, so I make some concessions, some gestures. You understand."

"Do you still control the cocoa market across Nigeria?" Luigi asked, though I knew we hadn't flown around the world to ask questions he didn't already know the answers to.

"Yes. My wealth has tripled because of it. Again, I owe you, Luigi."

"No, I do not want your money, but you will need it. Because I want you to stop the killings."

"The killings?" Pama frowned, then his face sagged as before—with fear. "Luigi! They would kill me if I interfered! My family would not be safe!"

"I remember who you were before you became a businessman." Luigi paused again, letting that piece of news sink in. "You control the cocoa market, which leads the economy in some kind of stable way. Before, you could have made a difference, but now you will make a difference this way. I need you to do it. I need you to stop the oppressors."

"It would take . . . so much, Luigi. There are so many to protect!"

"They are stopping citizens on the streets, and if they are Christian, they kill them." Luigi held open his palms. "You have the money many times over to hire security for this purpose, for those in danger, and for your family."

"Security? These are brainwashed extremists! They hate Christians, Luigi. Security alone will not work."

"Right, so you will use leverage as well. And education. And employment. And you will change this city. Then, you will change Kano, then Abuja."

"Leverage? What kind of leverage?"

"The imams are greedy, and they control the Boko Haram soldiers. Begin there. Stop the killing. Or I will return. Do you believe me?"

Though I couldn't see Luigi's face directly, his glare must've been intense, because Pama didn't seem able to speak until he opened and closed his mouth a couple of times.

"Yes, I believe you, Luigi."

"Why do you believe me?"

"Because you said you would be back once, and you are here. I will begin to help the Christians in the morning, but secretly."

"That is all I ask."

"Long-term, I will start programs with the Muslim youth and change the imam leadership to be compassionate and tolerant of other religions, perhaps modeling their minds like those in Jordan once were. I already have powerful friends in the capital. Yes, I have some ideas."

"If you do this until the end of your life, then I will not return."

"I understand. Thank you, Luigi. It is a good thing you ask me to do. And I will do it with diligence."

Luigi paused, then rose to his feet and looked at me.

"The oppressors will be crushed this way, a little at a time. Or maybe not crushed at all, but certainly swayed."

"It could work," I agreed. "Cocoa is their main crop."

"Pama, tell me where the washroom is," Luigi said.

"Through there and to the right. Do you not remember?" Pama pointed into the foyer, then stood as Luigi walked out of the room. "Are you his associate or his woman?"

Feeling my ring finger, I remembered I'd taken off the rock that Zvi had given me. Operations into Western Africa didn't require diamonds on fingers.

"We are acquaintances only, through a mutual friend."

Pama walked closer.

"And you kill so quickly for just an acquaintance?"

"He's Luigi Putelli," I stated, not inclined to explain the tranquilizer. They'd find out soon enough. "There are those not worth crossing."

"Yes, Luigi is such a man." Pama nodded. "I am not sure if I fear him or respect him more. He is older now, and his face bears more marks, but there is still death in his eyes."

When I heard a door close in the foyer, I wondered what was taking Luigi so long.

"There are resources we can provide you with for your work here," I offered. "Everything from covert advisors to educational materials. If you're willing, you can turn this country around. You could leave a legacy and earn the respect of the people, not just control the economy."

"Luigi has these resources to help me? He would do that?"

"Together, we do."

"Then I welcome it! Whatever you can send. What he has given me to do will not be easy with money alone."

Just then, the butler came into the room. He handed me a piece of paper.

"The man in the dark shirt asked for a pen and wrote this. He said to give it to you."

The note read: "C- I will send you the satellite coordinates when I locate Corban. I must walk alone. Corban would understand. –L."

Folding up the paper, I rose to my feet and extended my hand.

"Pama, I must go now. Thank you for your hospitality. I look forward to sending you what we have."

Though I wanted to run, I walked briskly out of the mansion and climbed into the Jeep. Ron was already in the driver's seat.

"Let's go home," I said. "Luigi won't be joining us."

✝

CHAPTER THIRTY-FOUR

The drive back through Cameroon was without event, unless my hidden tears of fear and frustration could be counted. As Ron talked, I often turned my head to the African wilderness so the missionary couldn't see my self-centeredness. He was a man who'd taken his wife and two sons to a strange land. He'd given up everything. He labored through dust and Islamic threat for each soul. His boys had since grown and returned to the States to raise families of their own in the ministry. So why was I crying?

The pain was tremendous, and the pressure inside was mounting. Corban had been like an uncle to me, and a brother to my husband. Janice had been as a close sister to me. Nettleton and Chang had taken steps to trust me with Luigi—and he'd vanished inside Africa. Of course, he had to leave me in Nigeria. It was a third-world country and I had no resources to find him. Short of calling Interpol, no one could sniff out Luigi now if he didn't want to be found.

Just as troubling, I wasn't sure I wanted him caught. A dark hole or a foreign execution awaited Luigi once the US finished with him. I wasn't so gullible to believe Nettleton was helping me out of honor and loyalty to Corban as a veteran operative of the CIA. No, Corban was a liability whenever the CIA didn't know his whereabouts. He'd actually used that liability as leverage over the years, holding aliases over the Agency's head that only he could fabricate, as he exercised his flawless Russian and Arabic languages, among others.

For an instant, I doubted Luigi would still help find Corban. Did Luigi care more for his own skin? I decided not. The Italian mastermind who chewed gum would still help Corban, but in such a way that didn't subject himself to an ambush, as I was likely to lead him into unknowingly. And once Chang found out that Luigi had taken flight, there were sure to be plans to net him again. It was disconcerting to think I'd offended Homeland Security.

At the Chad border, Ron and I prayed together, embraced, then parted ways, with Ron driving to the south where his village ministry awaited him. He'd been a gracious companion and an irreplaceable guide through the dusty roads and uncertain customs. In COIL's name, I promised him an aid package. But he rejected my offer with one of his own.

"I don't want money or supplies," he'd said. "Everyone sends me money and supplies, as if that's their way to appease their consciences."

"Appease their consciences?" I had asked. The light-hearted missionary seemed suddenly grim. "What do you mean?"

"Think of the widow's mite. That mite meant something to God because it meant something to the widow. People always send me their excess. Much of the time, it means nothing to them. I need hands and sincere hearts, and I need them here."

It was the sad plight I'd heard from other missionaries. The harvest was plentiful, but the laborers were few.

When I finally caught a flight across the Atlantic, I spent time in prayer with my Savior, and my woes were placed at His feet where they could best be addressed. I asked for His guidance, then I focused on the problems I was meant to work through. Unless Luigi flew back to the States on this same plane, he'd be late for the custom satellite launch. After walking the aisles twice and studying each of the other passengers with a guarded glance, I decided Luigi wasn't on that flight.

Exhausted, I arrived in New York and drove to COIL headquarters. I didn't want to see or speak to anyone, and only wanted to plant my head on a bunk until my body adjusted to the time zone whiplash.

But in climbing the stairs to the COIL offices, avoiding the frequented elevator, I sensed someone in the stairwell with me. My hand rested on the door handle leading to the COIL suites. In an instant, I could have COIL's twenty-four-hour security to back me up. My weariness left me, replaced by the awareness of danger.

"Who's there?" I said softly, for my shadow was but one flight below me, and it was a quiet evening. "Luigi? Is that you?"

Someone moved, and I was afraid I'd frightened the person away. Instead, he moved up to the next landing and stopped in full view, but his dark sweatshirt hood hid his face. He was a large man with muscled shoulders, light on his feet, except for the hint of a limp on his left side. Looking up at me, his face was still too hidden in the dim stairwell. This was him! I knew this was Luigi's muscle, his student, Corban's secret, COIL's shadow operator! I hardly dared to breathe.

"Friend or foe?" I queried.

"Friend." His voice was low and clear, maybe younger than I expected. "You've made a mess of things without me, Chloe."

I gasped. He knew me! My head was spinning.

"Your voice—we know each other?"

"Corban gave me the option to disappear, to use my death against the darkness."

"No. It can't be you . . . It can't be!"

"Luigi just called me. He said you needed me now."

"No. You died in Germany two years ago. You're dead!"

"It's been a long time since we argued on that water tower, Chloe." He chuckled—at a time like this! "I'm hesitant to argue with you again, but I'm very much alive."

Only Corban knew about my quarrel on the water tower in Malaysia during Operation Helena—a quarrel I'd had with Nathan "Eagle Eyes" Isaacson.

Somehow, I flew or dove down the stairs to land in Nathan's arms. He fell back against the wall, but he remained standing, holding me as I sobbed into his chest and clung to this miracle before me. I didn't know how he was alive, or how Corban had hidden his death from me, but God knew I needed him now.

"You're right, you know." I laughed, stepping away and wiping my face. "I've made a mess of things."

"Well, Luigi didn't help, splitting on you in Africa." Placing his hands on my shoulders, he was the same COIL commander I remembered, yet he'd changed. He seemed more weathered, and there was a new loneliness in his face. "Things are worse than you know, Chloe. While you were in Africa, I played with a little toy called a directional microphone."

"What've you found?"

"Senator Nettleton is working for the other team. He and Rod Chang are not our allies. Nettleton, Chang, and Coleman all intend for General Forglade to go down for everything."

"Really? Nettleton is dirty? He's given us autonomous Homeland Security authority!"

"Only as far as you keep them involved and do their dirty work of finding General Forglade. Luigi told me everything, and I've shared with him what I know. We're ready to go get Corban, if he's alive."

His words made my stomach muscles tighten.

"Do you know where he is?"

"If I know Corban, and I think I do, he's on the trail of the bad guys. With the satellite info from Luigi, by dawn we'll know where they are."

"Two things." I held up two fingers. "First, you have to convince Luigi to come in. He'll get himself killed if he keeps this up. Whoever he used to be, I don't think he's the same man anymore. And I think he needs us more than he realizes."

"Well, it's actually good he's not who he used to be, but that doesn't mean I can get him to come in. He'll tell you himself that he won't listen to anybody but Corban. What's the second thing?"

"You have to tell me everything from why you're wearing a leg brace to what you've been doing the last two years. I want to know everything!"

Waking Brody and Gail, we went to Corban's office and celebrated with tears and praise to God over Nathan's return. Though neither Brody nor Gail had met Nathan when he was team leader of COIL's primary extraction team, they'd heard of his past exploits. He explained how he was deathly ill in Germany after getting captured during the journey home, but he'd recovered miraculously. Corban hadn't been able to overlook the opportunity to train him as a solitary operative.

"I don't mean to be rude," Brody interrupted, "but if Luigi could call any minute with coordinates in the Caribbean, we need to know what you know, then get some sleep."

"Well, I'm still putting it all together myself." Nathan stood against the bulletproof glass, and I sat behind Corban's desk while Brody and Gail settled on the two chairs. The door was closed since the caseworker nightshift had arrived to coordinate COIL's field operations. "It was Flight 524 that didn't make sense to me, and in talking with Luigi before you two went to Nigeria, it hasn't made any sense to anyone else, either."

"That's the plane the TaTD took out, then they wanted to pin it on Corban's alias," Gail said. "It's bothered me, too. Why Flight 524?"

268 | D.I. TELBAT

"It's been right in front of us, and Senator Nettleton's been behind it the whole time. He's finished." Nathan shook his head. "See, it's personal for him. Corban and his old alias were just handy. The US has been tired of Corban for a long time. They feel he knows too much and still has too much power."

"Stay on Nettleton, Nathan," I urged, my hands shaking. This was it. We were getting close to figuring out the end of this nightmare!

"Nettleton's been abusing his authority for a long time. A congressional investigator was on Flight 524, returning with what must've been serious evidence of Nettleton's senatorial compromises." Nathan smiled, as if we were to applaud, but we were still lost. "It took me hours running that passenger casualty list, but I found it. Once I found that investigator's name, I looked him up. His office, once I got them talking, wasn't aware of the connection. Everything the guy had would've brought Nettleton down. Senator Shannon Griffin's death, Nettleton's predecessor, was even being questioned. A supposed heart attack was the initial story. Nettleton killed the previous chairman to get his hands on billions in domestic spending. He was either going to jail or he had to silence that investigator. My guess? The senator couldn't resist the military resources at his fingertips, just like he'd been abusing his power for years. He used General Forglade to take down Flight 524. It has nothing to do with Corban, but it has everything to do with Corban, because Forglade intended to cover it all up by blaming it on Muhammad ibn Affal. At first, it seems they didn't even know the alias belonged to him, but once they blew Flight 524, they had to pin it on someone plausible."

"Corban's in more danger than we realized," I said.

"The senator found the perfect patsy." Brody threw up his hands. "A Muslim name, a photo of Corban in disguise, and an ignorant public."

"I get Senator Nettleton and General Forglade's involvement, but what about this Karl Coleman?" Gail asked.

"According to what I heard Chang and Nettleton talking about, it sounds like Coleman is the worst of the whole lot. He's led execution squads into South America—black ops. I've known guys like him over the years. No conscience, walking death. That's why he didn't hesitate to order Janice and Jenna killed, but he hired the wrong assassin this time—our assassin, who's not an assassin any longer: Luigi Putelli."

"Who've you told this to?" I asked.

"Just Luigi and you three." Nathan took a moment to look each of us in the face. "At some point, I think General Forglade figured out Coleman was going to take him out. Nettleton used Forglade, but now Forglade knows too much. So the general is using military jamming tech to hide from Coleman, but it's a farce because Nettleton and Coleman are working together now. They both want Forglade. Apparently, General Forglade has bragged about a hideout in the Caribbean, but everyone is waiting to learn the exact location."

"It's a mess." Brody rubbed his sleepy eyes. "The public will never sit still to hear all the evidence, the twists and turns. Setting up an ex-CIA agent who had a Muslim alias? Without a confession, we've got nothing. Corban could still go down for Flight 524 if we don't take them all down in perfect order."

We were silent for a few moments, realizing how much we knew now, but also how far we were from finding Corban.

"I'm going to the Caribbean," Nathan said, "as soon as Luigi comes through with the coordinates."

"Me, too." I nodded at him. "And we're not sharing the coordinates with Nettleton or Chang."

"Not the correct coordinates, anyway," Gail said with a sly look. "Brody and I can take down Rod Chang with a little squeezing here on the home front. Now that we know the facts from Nathan's snooping, it's just a matter of presentation and recording. The flight passenger manifest ruins the senator. He killed the investigator. Besides all the other people on board!"

"Which is why the passenger manifest was buried," Nathan said. "It wasn't made public record since the crash investigation was supposedly still underway. It took some, well, impersonating to get my hands on that passenger list."

"General Forglade or Coleman could be holding Corban for collateral," I said, "to use against the senator or for their own freedom. Corban's still the king in this chess game."

"Good thing we've got another knight on the board." Brody winked at Nathan. "God's given us the muscle we need. Now, let's bring our man home."

"Right." I chuckled uneasily. "Unfortunately, everything now depends on Luigi to come through with those coordinates. It wouldn't hurt for us to start for the Caribbean, Nathan, just to be closer if Luigi calls."

"He'll call." Nathan frowned, as if he were trying to believe his own words. "I hope, before he tries to help Corban by himself."

PART IV: CORBAN

CHAPTER THIRTY-FIVE

I was struggling with murderous hatred. My family—the Corban Dowler family—had been slaughtered, and my heart felt like a volcano inside of me. Every impulse I'd been trained to exercise as a spy hunter compelled me to respond violently against my enemies: General Logan Forglade and Karl Coleman.

General Forglade was certainly a prize, and my sites were firmly set on him exactly where Karl Coleman said he'd be—somewhere in Gustavia, on the island of St. Barts. However, Coleman hadn't shown himself in the two weeks I'd been hiding out, shut off from the world, waiting for the killers of my wife and daughter.

My arrogance continued to swell within me. Many times a day, as I studied the general's cottage through my spotting scope, I asked myself, didn't my enemies know who I was? I'd been a ruthless CIA agent for many years, surviving countless missions through the end of the Cold War. And afterward, I mopped up loose ends, silencing enemies before they could become free agents for anyone else in the world once the Iron Curtain collapsed and the Wall crumbled. Was my reputation so ancient that new foes scorned me and dared to kill my loved ones?

This pride was ugly even to me. It was an attitude of self, and God was pushed to the recesses of my mind. I still knew the difference between right and wrong, but I was intent on doing wrong, and the patient fury in me made great effort to set aside my conscience. Had I served Christ so faithfully for so many years, only to fall to the level of darkness now, in my hour of greatest anguish? Did God not know my potential to hate and destroy? Bitterly, I knew God was rooting out this stronghold of sin in me, but it was most painful, and my animosity against His discipline had made me wish for the worst against my enemies.

Gustavia was a popular resort town built around a protected harbor. Coral surrounded the volcanic island. Green water reflected with clarity the vegetation beneath. Though winter was approaching, the moderate temperature was warm enough at that latitude for me to sleep for several nights on the hillside above the town that many called paradise.

In a matter of weeks, tourists from around the world would flood the island for its winter escape, its iced mango and grilled tuna steaks. But none of these luxuries intrigued me. Since I had no family to return to in New York, my only remaining objective in life seemed to be vengeance. COIL no longer needed me. Whatever I would do after my revenge was satisfied wasn't a matter of concern. These wicked men wouldn't live. If only I could get them both in one location!

General Forglade was the bait for Coleman. Coleman was the man I thought to be Roy Turpin. It seemed a lifetime ago when Roy Turpin and I had corresponded, me mentoring him for those two years. All the while, he'd been waiting for his plan, grooming me for destruction—my family, my livelihood, my faith. Roy Turpin, the man I'd thought would be God's vessel, had proven otherwise—a dark vessel. And he'd been a cancer to all those he'd touched.

All the details and all the unknown players in this nightmare were no longer important. I knew who had blood on their hands. If Coleman had been tasked to destroy me two years ago, and Flight 524 gave him a purpose—it no longer mattered. Coleman and others had found one another, and sealed their fate.

My last contact with Coleman had been in the underground bunker in Maryland outside Arlington. He hadn't known it was me, but he'd shot me with what he thought was a lethal toxin. After hearing he'd killed my family, I indeed wished he would've killed me. But since I was alive, he would pay. They would all pay. My skills were more than sufficient to obliterate those who all others seemed unable to take out.

It was a ten-minute climb up the steep hill from the town to the lighthouse that overlooked the eight-square-mile island. The scrubby bushes and trees on the rocky terrain were more than adequate to conceal my activities while hiding so far away from my target. Around the lighthouse and the nearby weather station, the Swedish ruins of Fort Gustav lay collapsed, but various sections remained, providing me cover from the town below. Occasionally, hikers ventured up the hill to check out the 360-degree view, but they were mostly tourists, unfamiliar with the hidden corners of the crumbled ramparts.

Using a high-powered telescope, I peered nearly six hundred yards down the hill, over the town with its few streets, across the harbor where sailboats bobbed, to the broad peninsula. The peninsula itself, lush with vegetation, had a wide road running down its length, ending at La Pointe. About four rows of cottages lined the narrow avenues on both the ocean side and harbor side of the peninsula. Then I focused on a particular red-roofed cottage across the harbor.

Though I couldn't see inside Forglade's cottage, my telescope was powerful enough to count every tile on the roof. At night, I watched mostly one lit window for movement, which occasionally went dark for a few seconds at odd times. Day after day, I watched the dwelling, occasionally spying on Forglade when he went around the bay to the Boulangerie Choisy, where I also picked up snacks for myself. And day after day, I waited for Coleman to show himself. The whole town and most of the island were in my view. No one could arrive in Gustavia without me noticing them.

When my stomach growled, I pushed the hunger away. I couldn't leave my post. Eventually Coleman would come for the general. The two men were enemies, weren't they? Hadn't I provoked Coleman to go after the general? Maybe Coleman didn't know exactly where Forglade was living, but he'd find him, as I had. He had to come!

Near sundown, I lowered my head from my scope and squeezed my burning eyes shut. I was standing vigil in the memories of my wife and daughter, wasting away, ready to exact what justice I deemed right from my own heart.

"I'm dying inside," I whispered, my own lips betraying the condition I kept denying.

Standing behind the ruins, I looked up at the lighthouse to my left. It flashed every twelve seconds, white, red, or green. It depended from which direction the viewer stood as to which color was visible, but this close to the lighthouse, in that lighting, I could see all three colors.

The lighthouse—it meant something to me right then. God was calling me, warning me, drawing me into the light, to see all the angles, but I continued to resist. My pain caused me to rebel. Could I give it up? Could I give up my hatred?

Looking away from the lighthouse, I considered what it would mean if I were to leave my path of revenge. Could I return to a life back at COIL, executing missions selflessly, knowing I was this selfish in my flesh? And what was I to return to—an empty house?

The pain of loss was immense, but my pain over avoiding the spiritual voice of my Lord and Savior was agony of a deeper sense. My own desires were killing me the longer I remained on that hill. There was a little water still in my dirty water jug, but I had no food left. I'd lost nearly fifteen pounds in two weeks, starving myself. If I didn't do something different, I'd die, with or without revenge. This way was clearly not working. How often I'd realized this in life, and yet I'd fallen into the same trap again!

"Father," I prayed from my heart, "I'm in sin, and I confess it before You. It's sin against You because I'm Yours eternally. Refine me, Lord, and give me the strength, Your strength, to live by the new nature You've given me. Correct my will, dear God, because I hate this evil that clings to me. I need You. Help me . . ."

"No revenge," I said aloud. My resolution seemed to come from outside my body, and yet it was immediately calming. I'd served God for too long to now turn and scar His mighty name by my selfishness. What a coward I'd been of what was holy and true! Even my Janice would've been ashamed of me.

I took a deep breath. If I was alone now, then I was alone. But I couldn't waste what God had built through me. And I wouldn't allow those men to blind me by their darkness any longer. A battle had raged, yet in my weakness, my Lord's strength had prevailed. Oh, I'd still get the enemy, but not for myself now. Vengeance belonged to the Lord. He always repaid the debts that were due. God would keep me from evil, and I would trust Him.

General Forglade hadn't left Gustavia in two weeks. He would await capture a little longer while I got food and rest. Regardless of the tragedies of my family, I had to believe God was still sovereign, that all things were moving in a direction for a singular end, for a good end. There was comfort in this thought, a thought I could only attribute to the Holy Spirit in me since I knew well my mind and my flesh.

A new plan began to take form. I wouldn't wait to capture Forglade. His time was over now. Coleman might never show, but if he did, I'd be ready.

Starting my descent, I went down the hill from the lighthouse to the town. Under my arm was my telescope. God had proven Himself in me that evening by saving me from my own depraved ideas. Now, I would prove myself for Him, as His servant and laborer once again.

Agent Corban Dowler was back. And I was ready for battle.

✝

CHAPTER THIRTY-SIX

I woke the next day around noon. It was the most sleep I'd had in days. The gentle rocking of my forty-foot Bavaria sailboat anchored in the bay hadn't bothered me. For years, I'd slept in the best and worst conditions. More than anything, I attributed my rest of body to my rest of spirit. Remaining in God's will was paramount. Where unease had persisted, I was now enveloped in a calm surety of my Lord's hand on my mission. This was no longer about me.

My brown hair was shaggy again, but I kept a baseball cap pulled low over my forehead. If General Forglade used binoculars on the residents in the bay, I guessed he wouldn't recognize me with a slimmer midsection and slightly hollow cheeks.

In the galley, I drew fresh pineapple from the fridge and marlin steaks I'd bought the night before. Chewing slowly, I read from Psalm 120, a prayerful song of deliverance. My body needed to be in the right condition for what lay ahead, but so did my soul. How easily I'd fallen into darkness! The Lord couldn't use me as a vessel for Himself to my fullest potential when I disregarded His purposes. Yes, I'd still grieve for my family, but there was work to be done. Dark hearts that had nearly drowned me would go after others.

They had to be stopped from killing the innocent, and destroying more lives. I'd been distracted from COIL business long enough!

Using the mirror in my stateroom head, I glued a droopy dark mustache onto my upper lip. My suntanned face with the mustache gave me a Mediterranean look, I guessed, or even Latino. St. Barts was part of the European Union as a French collective. Maybe I was now French. So be it.

On deck, I busied myself for ten minutes, re-rolling the mainsail and tightening the halyards. Meanwhile, I examined the shoreline. I was anchored midway up the peninsula, in the middle of the harbor. Though I couldn't see Forglade's cottage behind other residences, I could see the shoreline all around me. If someone were paying me particular attention, I didn't notice. The Bavaria had been at anchor for two weeks, since I'd sailed from Guadeloupe two hundred kilometers southeast. The boat wasn't new to the locals, or to the general, if he'd noticed it at all.

By means of an inflatable dinghy, I motored to shore. I had everything I needed in my vest pockets for the next stage of my new plan. Under the shadow of a bell tower clock, I exercised my French to rent a bicycle. The manager, a lad of fifteen, tempted me with every sinister and forbidden sin available in the shadows of Gustavia, but I paid him in euros for the bike and ignored his offers.

Riding the single speed bicycle, I first went up Rue de la Republique, away and across from the general's cottage. I was getting into character—smiling and waving, just being a citizen. For two weeks, I'd been the definition of an island castaway on the hillside, squatting in the bushes with a telescope, my heart hardening. Now, I was a French tourist, from Bordeaux, vacationing on my country's island territory. If anyone checked with the harbormaster, they'd find my sailboat registered to a dummy corporation out of Costa Rica. It would tell no one anything about Corban Dowler.

After I'd passed Shell Beach, I turned around and rode back into town. At the next available right, I sped down the end of the harbor toward the peninsula. Having watched the town for days, I knew well the local dangers—there were none. No US agents lurked, no government vehicles sped around with tinted windows. This was Gustavia, the ancient heartbeat of the Caribbean. The only risk was if it were discovered who I really was, and that was unlikely.

Next, I turned onto the straight road that ended at La Pointe of the peninsula. Slowing my speed, I sat up straighter, enjoying the sights as a tourist would. One, two, three, four—there was Forgalde's cottage. I dared not stop, or even pretend to crash, or visit with the locals in view of his windows. This was a man in hiding, paranoid already from years of clandestine maneuvers. He was a general, not someone to be trifled with—until I was ready.

Near the end of the road, I parked my bike in the small parking lot of the St. Barts Municipal Museum, which I knew from a brochure it also housed a library. It was a two-story building of stone, recently refurbished. I looked out at the mouth of the bay and saw a Predator speedboat arriving in town, motoring slowly toward the dockyard. Now that I wasn't up by the lighthouse watching the whole island, I couldn't analyze everyone coming and going. But I knew this motorboat was new, the driver unseen in the cockpit. So much for thinking there were no risks on the island. An unidentified stranger definitely raised my danger meter.

Having stalled long enough in the lot of the museum—with only one car in sight—I pedaled east, then took a right to cut behind the general's house. I knew the road led to the local military presence, the building founded on the site of old Fort Oscar, overlooking the sea.

I kept my chin down as I pedaled slowly up the lane. Someone opened a window on my right. A man used a handsaw to trim bushes on my left. Casually, I waved at him and he waved back. The islanders had nothing to worry about. But little did they know, a killer hid in their midst. True, I'd been selfishly dwelling on the loss of my own family, but now I thought of Flight 524 and that terrible loss of life. Forglade and Coleman had been behind those deaths and they would soon meet their justice in prison.

While applying the brakes, I took one final look around. There were a couple of dark windows on my right, but I saw no faces. Forglade's cottage was on my left. I drove the bike straight into an untrimmed shrub. With my transportation sufficiently hidden, I darted to the side of the house. Dark windows were on both sides of me. It had been years since I'd darted anywhere like this, due to my heavier midsection. But with the recent loss of weight, I felt lighter and more limber, even younger.

Edging my face up to the window, I realized with some anxiety that they weren't darkened windows at all, but were covered on the inside with tinting paper. Someone could still see out, but it would be impossible to make out details through the tint when looking in. There was a light on inside, but that was all I could see.

Ducking under the window, I approached the back door. Everything could end right here. One wrong step, and I could be shot. No doubt, Forglade was armed, and he probably wasn't too happy about the flame I'd held to his soaked lap a few weeks earlier, lighter fluid or not. What fugitive with military experience wasn't armed? He'd surely shoot me if he could.

The back door was locked. Kneeling there, I studied the lock, then the frame around the door. Technology on the island was modernized, except for residences. Communication satellites were bountiful, but I'd seen no evidence of alarm systems. Such a small community usually required only a neighborly, watchful eye. If Forglade had an alarm system, it was more sophisticated than I could spot from the outside.

From my right vest pocket, I drew a lock-pick set. The back door knob was an old foreign import, and its tumblers were rusty from twenty or more humid seasons. If Forglade hadn't bothered to change the main lock, I doubted he'd bothered with finer methods of security. It was a sign of arrogance. He was so confident in his own disappearance, leaving no trace behind, that he hadn't taken other precautions. Little did he know, Coleman had betrayed his general location when he thought I was about to die by my own poison. I'd figured out the rest by surveying Gustavia.

I pushed the door inward a crack, and moved aside quickly, my ear tuned for internal noises. Thankfully, no gunshot, no alarm, no footsteps.

Now, from my right pocket, I pulled a tranquilizer pen. I would end Forglade's secret reign in the next few minutes.

After nudging the door a little wider, I noted there was indeed no alarm. But the door hinges squeaked slightly. I couldn't risk opening it too wide. Barely eighteen inches would have to do. Turning sideways, I crawled into a type of coat room. Pivoting around, I eased the door closed, then locked it.

The enemy was in this house, but where? I prayed for calm, and for a heart free of vengeance. This was about justice, safety, and the preservation of life. Blood had been shed. If I weren't careful, my own blood would be next!

Somewhere, a door closed! Maybe it was a drawer. A rumbling of gears? Kneeling there, I felt something in my knees. Was it coming from beneath the floor? How was that possible? The island was volcanic rock. None of the houses had basements. All my days with the telescope on the hill flooded into my mind, searching for some clue that I'd missed. If this cottage had a sublevel, it had been carefully disguised, intentionally hidden.

I rose to my full height and stepped toward an open doorway. There was a dining table with food wrappers I recognized from meals purchased in town. Farther in, I saw the kitchen with a stove and fridge. Moving silently, I walked the length of the kitchen and stopped at a short bar where a rack was filled with French labeled wines.

The living room area was now in view. A sofa and card table were separated by a lamp. The lamp was on and oddly placed close to the window. I studied the scene for a moment, aware that there were two closed doors on my right—bedrooms, I guessed. The lamp was so odd that I couldn't look away. It was a reading lamp, which made it too small to adequately light the whole room. And it was too close to the window to be used by someone on the sofa. Where was Forglade? Had he left the lamp on?

From nights past, I recalled seeing—even through the tinting—the dim lighting that illuminated the window on that side of the house. The light had gone out at odd times, but only for a moment or two. If the light didn't illuminate anything while it was on, then it hid something when it went out. The tinted windows surely had something to do with this mystery; subterfuge was at play.

Moving carefully to the two bedroom doors, I stood with my back to the wall, a door on either side of me. Crouching low, I felt the air moving under each door. It didn't feel like cool air that a basement ventilation system would've produced. Perhaps I'd imagined the gears, or it had been a small tremor in the earth.

Gripping the doorknob on my left, I held my tranq-pen in my right fist. Gently, I turned the door handle and opened it. My senses were on high alert, my body and mind fully rested. But no noise met me, not even a rustle came from inside.

The bedroom light was off. Without moving in front of the door, I glanced inside the room—a bed, dresser, and window facing east. And a suitcase on the floor! The bed wasn't made. A bathroom door stood ajar, a small sink visible. But no Forglade.

That left the bedroom on my right, the only other space in the house I'd not seen yet. I closed the first door and adjusted my position for the next. He had to be in the last room. There was nowhere else he could be!

I turned the doorknob and readied myself to lunge inside. Suddenly, the lamp near the window went out. With the windows tinted from sunlight, the main room became remarkably dark. And next, the wall on my left began to open! A passageway was revealed! I glimpsed volcanic rock deeper within, but beyond that, I had no time to see anything else as I slipped into the second bedroom to hide. Cringing for fear of making noise, I closed the door behind me. If I couldn't sneak up on my target, then I'd have to hide until I could.

Had I been seen? I glanced over my shoulder to see I was alone in another empty room. Things were rapidly making sense. Of course there hadn't been security around the house. Why protect himself in an empty house when Forglade could simply enter an underground vault to hide? The light near the window now made sense, too, and the grinding of gears in the floor. The lamp was wired to turn off automatically when the hidden vault was about to open. That shrouded the room in shadows if anyone happened to be peeking through a window. And when Forglade was in the vault, the light came on, giving just enough indication that someone might be home. Ingenious!

Gears shook the foundation again, then ceased. The lamp blinked on, evidenced by lamplight shining dimly under the door that I hid behind. Footsteps on the floor! Were they coming toward me? No, they were going to the kitchen. I heard water running in the sink. Was it Forglade? Could there be others in the vault with him? That was certainly possible.

The unknowns caused me to pause. I couldn't tranquilize the man in the house. What if it wasn't him and I showed my hand? No one knew I was on the island, or alive for that matter. My secrecy was also my security.

A man hummed in the kitchen. He was cooking, I realized, when an exotic aroma wafted into my hiding place.

Thus, I waited. As a cautious spy, I couldn't close my net without knowing the angles. An underground vault changed everything. Forglade wasn't hiding in a standard cottage. This was a safe house, and such a gem wouldn't be only one man's secret. Forglade wasn't alone, even if I'd seen only him coming and going from the dwelling.

I had underestimated my enemy.

✝

CHAPTER THIRTY-SEVEN

Early the next morning, I was back on the brushy hillside with my telescope. The day before hadn't been a complete waste. True, I'd stood trapped in the empty bedroom for hours, but near sundown, the person who'd cooked the meal went back into the sublevel vault, and I'd slipped out through the back door to my bicycle.

Now, I studied the cottage with this new insight. In weeks past, I'd watched for people and approaches, as well as Forglade's movements. But I was tempting death if I missed again what should've been obvious to me earlier.

The cottage appeared perfectly rectangular from the outside. But inside, I should've noticed there was no apparent door behind the kitchen to access that space. Noticing such a fact would've saved me from standing around for hours.

From my vantage point on the hill, I noticed other things, and I pushed my mind past the sickening feeling of nearly making a fatal blunder—to focus with renewed intrigue on the blossoming puzzle before me.

The cottage directly east of Forglade's was remarkably close to it, as if the two had once been attached. Was there a passage underground that allowed Forglade to access the other cottage? Maybe under disguise, he'd even left from the other cottage. I hadn't paid much attention to the traffic there! And there'd indeed been traffic, now that I thought about it. Two or three natives—or so I'd assumed they were native Gustavians—had even gone fishing off La Pointe!

Just as perplexing, next to the second cottage was a satellite all but hidden in the tree next to it. From the ground, the dish probably couldn't be seen, but now that I knew the second cottage was probably joined underground to the other, that satellite could have special significance to Forglade's business on the island, or it might at least explain why he wasn't leaving the island. He was in contact with someone or something.

Suddenly, there was movement on the slope below me. Several paths led to the lighthouse. I could see them all, but no one was in sight. Yet someone had definitely been there an instant earlier, maybe crossing one of the paths, then moving into the bushes. Was one of the island boys spying on me? I'd ventured into the enemy's abode; it would be naive of me to write off a potential enemy. Forglade himself might know I was on the island—or at least that he was being stalked. Someone had evidently noticed. Assassins could be closing in on me.

Swinging my telescope to the water, I studied the area where my boat was anchored. It was my refuge of security, my only base of operations for the whole island. At the moment, there was no movement on board and it appeared undisturbed.

Folding up the tripod legs and tucking the scope inside my vest, I rose to my feet and immediately jogged east, down the spine of the island. I expected a silenced round to slash the shrubs around me, but I wasn't attacked. Had my enemy's noose not been sufficiently prepared? This changed everything. Forglade might relocate, if he knew someone on the island was onto him. It could possibly impact my primary hunt for Coleman, and my family's murderer would go free. And I had no immediate contingency. How foolish I'd been!

Still moving east as I left the vicinity, I moved around several red-roofed houses that sat above the town. A dog in a villa barked at me as I ran through low trees that scratched me, but I was quickly beyond the residence.

A small ridge gave me an elevated view of my backtrail. Not three heartbeats later, I spotted movement. Someone was actually tracking me, hunting me! Did they know who I was? My droopy mustache and shaggy hair wasn't a very elaborate disguise. I didn't wait around to be recognized, but soon, I'd run out of island. What then? Swim to the next volcanic island in the Lesser Antilles? The sharks would probably get me if I didn't drown first. No, I had to get back to my sailboat. Or did I? If someone had followed me that morning when it was still dark, he'd probably seen me leave the boat. The boat could've already been wired with explosives—by a scuba diver approaching on the stern!

I growled at myself. Now I was thinking crazy things, jumping to paranoid conclusions on little evidence. My emotions from the past month had made me pursue wild ideas already. It was taking time to settle back into my role as God's protector of His children.

Kneeling suddenly on the ground, I prayed through my panting breath. God was with me. He would guide me—one of His children. My heart was no longer filled with hatred for these killers. Now my pursuit was justice for my family, and a return to COIL where God had purposed for me to serve. COIL needed me, yes. Whichever enemy came after me now would get my fullest attention since my family couldn't be leveraged against me. They were already dead and I was alone. And since I was alone, I would use that liberty against my foes. Death wasn't my enemy. What else could they take from me?

Continuing on, I turned south, the ground sloping gradually toward what I knew was a steep hillside down to the water's edge.

One thing for sure, Forglade wasn't alone. He had resources, maybe even governmentally affiliated. Was he really hiding? It seemed not. The man had been reassigned. Perhaps he was too valuable to arrest or kill.

Over the next ridge, I ran until I came to the steep hillside, practically a cliff. The water was peaceful below, the leeward side of the island. I crossed a dirt path, then sidestepped down the slope. A chartered fishing boat was a mile off shore, beyond the reefs, but in plain sight. Were they also enemies? An expert marksman with a .50-caliber could've ended me right then.

Reaching the water, I slipped on the steep bank and fell into the gentle waves up to my waist. I climbed back onto the rock high-tide shelf where there was no trail. If I wanted to get back to Gustavia, my boat, or flat ground, I'd have to swim.

Looking uphill, I wondered if my enemy knew I'd turned south. I prayed he continued east. Otherwise, I'd be fair game for a shooter once I entered the water.

Taking off my vest and shirt, I wrapped the telescope up. With a grunt, I shoved the wad of clothes and scope into a crack in the volcanic rock. Then, diving into the water, I shed my pants and shoes, kicking them free as I swam under water for a dozen yards. After a quick breath, I submerged again, and went farther, my lungs expanding to the task at hand, my mind disciplining my body against panic in the open sea.

Instead of swimming along the shore, I swam toward a cluster of rocks that I couldn't see yet, too small on which to build a shelter, but adequate for me. In the past, I'd noticed the rocks several times through my telescope. They were high enough from the waves to grow sparse vegetation. But could I swim the quarter-mile beyond the peninsula to reach them? The waves around me were high enough that I still couldn't see them when I took another breath. But when I turned and looked back at the island, I established a better sense of direction and plunged ahead, still swimming under water so I didn't deliberately draw any eyes. From the right angle, I guessed I could still be seen since the water was such a transparent green.

Three breaths later, I took another reading of the island. I was on target, swimming away from it, and I saw no one on the slope or ridge I'd left behind. And no boats approached me from the sea. Had I really evaded a killer? Maybe. If that's what he was, my safety was temporary.

Gustavia was a small town. He'd come for me again, and I had to be ready. But right now, I was a man with no pants.

...✝...

Dusk settled over the island of St. Barts, but I still didn't move from my hiding place on the rocks offshore. I remained on the far side of my sanctuary, the waves lapping at my heels. The two tiny islands, if they could be called such, were a stone's throw apart, and each had barely the same surface area as my sailboat. They'd been my uncomfortable refuge all day, but now I was ready to return to the main island. My throat was parched and my stomach was beyond hunger.

An hour later, I judged it was dark enough, so I slipped into the warm water. A thrill moved through my being, appreciating the stealth with which I could now approach my boat. It was dark, and the island was lit up. That morning, I'd swum desperately through the water, but now I could take my time.

To save my energy, I floated on my back and kicked toward La Pointe at the end of the peninsula. As I neared the low cliffs, I found myself amongst anchored sailboats about fifty yards offshore, most of them monohulls. There was laughter and movement aboard some of them. Without disturbing anyone, I swam silently through the varied anchorages, and began to recognize buildings on La Pointe—the museum and gallery, even the local gendarmerie.

Gradually, I rounded the peninsula and started into the harbor. The water was warmer here since it was shallow with only one outlet. When I identified my boat from the others, I didn't approach it directly. I watched for shadowy movement across her bow, with the town lights behind it, but I didn't see anything alarming. Was she safe to board? An hour had passed since leaving the rocks and I was exhausted, so I climbed onto the stern step without any further caution.

No one met me with a silenced gunshot or glinting knife blade. Had I imagined an enemy earlier that morning on the island? The thought had plagued me all day as I was hiding. I'd seen no one exactly, only movement. Yes, I decided, there'd been someone. There was no room for ignoring signs of danger. During other operations, I'd been wounded for making that mistake.

Quietly, I moved across the deck. When I stepped down the dark companionway and inside, I smelled him. Someone had been there. A foreign smell, maybe cheap aftershave? Something sweet, but also something more natural—sweat.

Opening a drawer, I grasped a tranq-pen. If he was still on board, I might have a chance. The quarters were close and I knew the vessel well, even in the dark. But what if there were two men, or three? The pen could handle that many targets, if I could inject them without being killed first.

I sat at the navigation table aft the galley, and listened. Every touch of a wave, every whisper of loose canvas above, every creak of the hull made a unique sound. An hour I waited, and I heard nothing that signified the intruder was still aboard. To be certain, I checked the fore and aft cabins, the head, and both stowage spaces. No one was on board.

Since the danger hadn't been identified, I thought it best to leave the lights off and abandon my sailboat. My dinghy was on shore, but I had a second one that I could inflate and row ashore. There was much I had to take with me, but it was time to leave the boat permanently.

Feeling along the counter, I hoped to fix a sandwich, then pack. But my hand touched something next to the sink that made me freeze. I felt it with both hands to be sure I wasn't mistaken. Cylindrical and narrowing at one end, broader at the other. Glass on both ends.

Scoffing at my own confusion, I reached for the switch to illuminate the galley. There on the counter rested my telescope on top of my vest and shirt.

Many were my foes. Few were my friends. The likelihood of meeting a friend on an isolated island under my strained circumstances, with death trailing behind me—was slight. And yet, there were my abandoned possessions.

No one knew I'd come to Gustavia. How could anyone know? I'd left no trail. Not many knew I was even alive. Well, someone did now, it seemed. But who?

†

CHAPTER THIRTY-EIGHT

I awoke on the boat the next morning with a peculiar feeling. Someone on the island had acted friendly toward me, but I wouldn't go so far as to say I had a friend on the island. Not yet.

In the spy business, agents from allied nations and agencies frequently crossed paths. During the Cold War, British spies and American spies often stumbled upon one another. It wasn't so unexpected back then since we were vigilant in identical objectives to crumble the Berlin Wall, among other targets. Even if one expected to cross an ally in the field, it was still unnerving.

There was no one from my recent past on the island—I was fairly certain. So, I'd apparently been identified by someone from my distant past, someone intent on remaining unknown at this time. I was being watched, but not by an immediate foe. That was the message that the recovered telescope seemed to say to me.

Since I hadn't swum so far in years, my muscles ached in places I'd forgotten I had muscles. Nearing sixty, I took a few minutes to stretch my limbs before preparing a light breakfast. Moments like these excited me. God is ever active in the lives of His people, and I was startled at the idea of having a potential ally in the proverbial shadows near me. My mission for Forglade and Coleman's capture could continue unchecked.

My morning contemplations were further confirmed when I stepped onto the deck and found my dinghy tied to the stern. I stood on deck and chuckled at myself—and at the man who was probably chuckling at me right then, too. Sharks and drowning had been braved while running from someone who apparently meant me no harm. How much did my shadow know about my mission, though?

After motoring to shore, I rented another bicycle and rode it around the streets of Gustavia for an hour. Was anyone watching me? The town was busy in its relaxed Caribbean way. Merchants were buying fish from fishermen who'd been out on the sea all night. A couple joggers crossed paths with me three times, as they trained for that winter's Gustavialoppet, the Swedish Marathon, their shirts boasting their previous attendance. And tourists from the States were testing their French on the locals.

Satisfied with my surroundings, and with my cap pulled low, I cycled out to La Pointe to the St. Barts Municipal Museum. I'd heard the locals call it the Wall House, and I leaned my bike against its stone wall. Inside, I browsed the island's documented history—which included French, Swedish, and British occupation periods. Though I was looking for something specific, I wouldn't rush to discover it until I had a better context of what to ask for. An elderly man and woman, both with wire-framed glasses, glanced at me from their round reading table.

When I arrived at the display of ancient fishing boats, I studied them closely. It was of particular importance for me to make my attention to the boats concrete in the curators' minds, though I didn't care about the boats at all. But if someone came in and asked the elderly couple what I'd been interested in, they could say I'd paid special attention to the old fishing boats.

For ten minutes, I fostered this impression, then moved casually to a display of Creole houses. The models were detailed, and I collected as much information as I could in just a few seconds, my trained mind like a camera, filing everything away for later use. Then, I moved on, hoping to recall the architecture of the models. The houses were what interested me, of course, especially the older ones. Though Forglade's cottage was almost modern, it had probably been built on the site of an older Creole dwelling. Whatever basement or cavern existed there now was probably not new, or it wouldn't be an adequate covert hideout. It had probably been passed from those who sought hiding places to others who now also wanted to hide.

"Do you have a history of the Caribbean War?" I asked the curators in French. "The plaque says it was in the eighteenth century."

"About Gustavia exactly?" the woman asked. She stood and moved to a bookcase. "There is so much. We remained neutral during the war, you know. It was one of our wealthiest eras. Here it is."

"You can sit here, young man," the man invited, and moved a stack of brochures so I could sit across from them at their table. "Anything specific you're looking for?"

"Oh, I'm a writer." I didn't look up as I paged through fragile pages. My writing career was no lie. COIL operations were partially funded by my children's series penned under the name A.B. Leever. A cover is only good if it's real. "I may write an adventure involving Gustavia. The port and its fishing vessels fascinate me."

That set them both off, and I multitasked to read as I half-listened to them describe the fishing industry during the war—as if they had the history memorized, or had been there themselves. More books were brought to me, and I opened them, but I continued to actually read the one about the Caribbean War.

Two hours later, I found what I wanted, but not before learning facts about bonito and barracuda deep-sea fishing, which I guessed I'd never need, but one never knew.

Closing the history book on the war, I made a final effort to pay attention to a map of excellent fishing holes, the old man's bony finger pointing to each as he'd experienced them in his youth.

By the time I left the Wall House, it was noon. When I reached for my bicycle, I noticed someone had placed a jagged stone on the seat! Without showing too much regard outwardly, I stuck it in my pocket and pedaled away. But inside I was laughing. Someone was definitely watching me, even making a point to let me know I was being watched!

Was the rock a warning? I thought not, but my first glance had been insufficient to determine if the rock had a symbol or message scratched onto it. A skull and crossbones would've been an immediate signal. Even the word "GO" would've effected the impression I had in my mind about my shadow.

At Boulangerie Choisy, I stopped for a few edibles and to check the rock, risking a run-in with Forglade. It was a volcanic rock, I noticed, as I studied it over a mango drink. There were no markings on it, though. And it wasn't from the sea or from Shell Beach, with all its imported pebbles. This was a stone from the island, and I couldn't help but think I'd seen its color before.

Yes! Even the brief look inside the vault in Forglade's cottage was recent enough to recall the color of the cavern wall. Some volcanic rock changes color as it's exposed to the elements. The stone wasn't the color of exposed volcanic rock, but from rock that had been sheltered. Was I being told that my shadow was aware of the same cavern as me? That Forglade's cottage had been built over a cavern?

Indeed, I'd confirmed this much from my reading in the museum. Gustavia had remained neutral during the Caribbean War, but as the old woman had said, the port had prospered. They had traded in contraband. The Swedes had utilized a cavern on the peninsula, the journal had said, to hide gunpowder and whiskey. From the cavern, the underground merchants had taken their wares and lowered them down the southern cliffs to waiting boats—to avoid the eyes of spies in town. Noticeably selling to one side of the war over another could've changed the port's neutrality, so the secret was kept by all, for the sake of the merchandise. The cavern had been hidden, covered, and rumored to have been dynamited later during the rebuilding for a foundation. Apparently, the cavern hadn't been destroyed at all.

I guessed my shadow had left the stone to indicate he'd actually been inside the volcanic rock cavern.

Back on my sailboat, I tempered my excitement. Whatever clues I found to the mystery before me, the mission was still deadly. Men wanted me dead, and they'd mercilessly killed my wife and daughter when they couldn't kill or manipulate me. Such pressure on my shoulders required time with my Lord, precious time of solitude.

Since becoming a Christian and leaving the CIA, this priority in my life had been difficult to preserve over time—during missions, while on the run, or in hiding. But always, I knew my place, and it was with this attitude of submission that I sat at the navigation table with a Bible. I was a man of unclean lips, my flesh every bit at war with the Spirit as was any other true Christian. And the only way to remain in my Father's will was to commune with Him by prayer and reading from His Word. This wasn't a method that I'd discovered for success in order to achieve all my goals, as I'd heard false teachers of Christianity teach. Rather, I was a man who starved for my Lord's presence—and eternity with Him—now, more than ever. My family was gone, and my life was for God's purpose. Was I in His will now? These were things I examined at the heart level. If my motives were wrong to remain on the island, I believed God would impress upon me to sail away. But my path seemed straight, however narrow it was, and I finished my time of prayer refreshed.

The next stage of my operation was before me. I had to approach it with care, even if I did have a mysterious shadow who seemed to be watching my actions.

†

CHAPTER THIRTY-NINE

The hurricane was a surprise to me, but the island seemed to have had adequate warning. I'd cut myself off from the world—no radio, Internet, or even the sat-phone in the comm-room of the sailboat. The world was turning while I was toiling.

Because of the depth of the harbor, the other sailors familiar with Gustavia told me they usually crowded all the boats into the port and put out extra bumpers. The harbormaster had my trust to do as he deemed fit with my Bavaria, and I went ashore around noon as the waves began to roll and the rain began to sting.

There seemed to be too many boats even for the sizeable harbor. The largest vessels were moored at the mouth of the inlet, cabled together from Shell Beach to La Pointe. Several small boats had been dry-docked to give others more space. It seemed everyone in the Caribbean was seeking refuge in Gustavia's leeward harbor. Much of the island's income came from tourism, but fishing was a large part of the islanders' lives as well. Thus, the safety of their vessels in the harbor was paramount, drawing a huge crowd.

Numerous luxury hotels were open for business, but I didn't immediately go indoors. Instead, I took advantage of the crowd that came out to see the storm. This was my opportunity to see new arrivals on the island—and any potential enemies. With my rain slicker and hood tied tight against the wind, I shielded my face from the pelting rain.

That's when I saw him. It was just a glimpse, but I knew it was Karl Coleman. He was among others climbing from boat deck to boat deck to reach land. I wasn't sure which vessel was his, but he was among the last few to arrive and pay the harbormaster to include them in the sheltered waters.

I moved south, toward the peninsula, cautiously glancing in the direction of Coleman's entourage. In my right pants pocket, I felt the tranq-pen. A hurricane hardly seemed an appropriate time to abduct a killer, and it was with this thought that I realized I was ridiculously unprepared to take anyone into custody. Nor had I been in contact with the local law enforcement, the gendarmerie. Where would I even hold Coleman captive?

Hesitating on the crowded street, I looked back toward the center of town. I needed to get word to the mainland, to Chloe. Certainly, there were Gustavian officials in this crowd to whom I could explain my position—and the danger for their people.

A man in a dark green raincoat turned away from me and seemed to be watching the crowd as the boats began to take a beating. But I was certain he'd been watching me, maybe even following me. Was this my shadow? With Coleman on site, I couldn't be certain. The man who'd admitted with his own mouth to killing my family was trapped in a storm. There were too many variables to be careless.

Moving toward the man in the green raincoat, I approached from behind his left side. When he turned to look for me, it was obvious, and he immediately moved to his right toward the center of town.

With whom was I dealing? His hood had shadowed his dark face, and the boiling sky wasn't helping with visibility. I needed to look into this man's face to be certain whether he was an enemy or a friend. It wouldn't be possible to go after Coleman until I was certain I wasn't about to get a blade in my back from another quarter.

The people were mingling and conversing excitedly at the prospect of something happening on the quiet island, but the hurrying green raincoat was my only focus. He was easy to follow onto the second street away from the waterfront. The shop windows were shuttered, and since everyone else was at the harbor, the green raincoat and I were alone on the wet street.

No longer did he look back, which told me he was a professional. Amateurs always looked back; the nerves of a professional were more conditioned.

The tranq-pen was in my fist. Was I headed into an ambush? I thought not. The green raincoat hadn't meant for me to discover him.

He turned into a hotel that wasn't for the rich and famous—one that I'd considered boarding in while my boat was closely moored amongst the others. I jogged to catch up, and caught the door before it closed on his heel.

Inside the lobby, I stopped and braced for action, every muscle tensed for defending against an immediate assault. The lobby desk wasn't being tended, and I heard no sound of movement except the wind outside. The floor! Wet tracks and water from the man's dripping raincoat steered me to the stairway that led to the second and top floor of the hotel.

Following the tracks up the stairs, I was fully aware that he could double-back and attack. Though I'd noted the man was a pro, doubts entered my mind. What pro would risk being cornered in an isolated building? Something was amiss. I was being set up. But what speed he had! Though I'd been on his heels, he'd disappeared up the stairs without me even catching a fleeting glimpse of him.

On the second floor, the tracks led to the left. My heart sank with disappointment to see the window at the end of the hallway open and rain pattering the floor. Sighing at being outsmarted, I went to the window and gazed out. The man was there, standing not thirty yards down the street. Still, I couldn't see his face under his hood and through the rain. And his stance, looking back at me, seemed to be conveying a message. Who was this man? And what was his message for me?

I motioned for him to come closer. Looking down at the street below the window, I wasn't about to risk a hasty leap to follow this athlete. Instead, he reached under his raincoat. Withdrawing a little from the window, I guessed he had a firearm. Instead, he pulled out his closed fist. For a few seconds, he held his fist in the air. A signal? What was I to gather from the raised fist? Was it a salute to me? Or a warning?

His fist opened and a small piece of paper fell, then was quickly caught by the wind. Just as quickly, the paper was driven by rain to the ground where it was pelted as if by nails to a board. The man turned and ran around a corner.

Growling, I reminded myself at how fragile my knees and ankles were. True, I was healthy, but I'd lived a hard life, and my body was no longer young. But I wanted that paper! What had he left me? Finally, a clue as to the identity of my probable shadow, and the storm was about to wash the paper away!

Climbing out the window, I gripped the sill and hung for an instant before pushing away from the wall and falling. Though clumsily, I completed a three-point landing, rolled easily over my shoulder and rose to my feet unharmed. My heels felt a little bruised, but I had more important matters to address!

Plucking the paper from a puddle, I searched it for writing. It was a type of wax paper. There was French writing on one side. One word. Before studying it further, I turned in a circle, examining my surroundings. The paper could've easily been a diversion, but no one was approaching.

The word on the paper was Esprit, printed in blue and red lettering. It meant "spirit" in French, a type of local chewing gum. Chewing gum?

Smiling, I turned and walked down the street toward the harbor. How he'd found me, I wasn't certain, but I would spend no more time chasing Luigi Putelli around the island. I thrust the gum wrapper into my pocket, a souvenir for a time when I could reminisce on God's providential hand on my life.

...✝...

The storm was to my advantage, and with Luigi Putelli watching my back, I didn't waste another minute considering my lurking enemies—besides the two obvious ones, Forglade and Coleman.

By the storm's strength, I guessed I had no more than twenty hours to complete my mission. The storm would keep everyone on the island from leaving. Otherwise, if Coleman were there to erase the general, then he could do so and leave the island permanently. Now was my opportunity to catch them both.

Luigi's behavior toward me—or rather to avoid me—was completely characteristic of a weathered spook. That we were friends had no bearing during an operation. Even though I'd spared his life numerous times and he'd become my traveling companion once, the most effective way for him to watch over me was from the shadows; I didn't need to draw attention to him. Instead, he'd remain in the background, and any enemy who prowled near me would instead find Luigi prowling behind them. This allowed me to concentrate all the more on my targets. Someday, I'd learn how Luigi in his genius had discovered that I was alive and on the island of St. Barts. Whatever trail I'd unintentionally left, it might be followed by others, maybe even Chloe. But for now, with the storm raging, we were all isolated—my enemies and me.

It took two hours to find Coleman's entourage. They spared no expense in renting four suites in a new hotel west of town called Ville Natale, or Birthplace. The establishment was exquisite and directly overlooked Shell Beach and the entrance to the harbor.

Pausing at the lobby counter, I read an inscription stating the hotel was built on the site of a cannon placement that once guarded the harbor. It seemed oddly fitting, I reflected, that this killer and his goons were staying in the hotel that guarded the entrance and exit to the town. They were predators, and General Forglade was no doubt in their sights.

Coleman's men numbered seven. Four of them were healthy young men who carried themselves as if they knew their mercenary trade well. The deception with which Coleman had used against me was no small deception, nor was the downing of Flight 524 a matter of minor significance. A dark team had produced their intended results in my life: total havoc so I couldn't immediately recover and continue to help God's people.

With this understanding, I was reminded of the Apostle Paul's words: "We do not fight against flesh and blood, but against spiritual forces." Once again, my work for Christ within COIL had been halted. But I was a man of God, and He alone sustained me, even through the discouragement of deep heartache. The Lord's purposes would stand!

Though Coleman and his men had been located, I needed more information. What were their intentions against Forglade exactly? I'd assumed that, in watching Forglade, I'd eventually discover Coleman's arrival. But the unique safe house Forglade inhabited had to be government-linked, probably to my old agency, the CIA. Since I couldn't take Coleman while he was protected by his small army, I was limited to gathering intel, searching for a weakness—or creating one.

One of Coleman's men left the gift shop and started upstairs from the lobby. Near me, a stand of postcards mysteriously fell over, distracting the attendant. I quickly spied the computer screen guest database, discovering Coleman's suite number, then headed to the stairs after the mercenary.

Halfway across the lobby of marble flooring, the attendant started toward me. Maybe it was about the postcard rack. Whatever his intentions, I had to be swift to recover now. A concierge wasn't about to derail my operation!

"Excuse me, monsieur . . ."

"Oui? Ah, la, la! Thank you so much for the towels last night!" I took his hand in mine, smiling broadly. "My family is most grateful. A fat tip for you, my friend. Your name, s'il vous plait?"

"Uh, Marc."

"Sans blague! That is my nephew's name as well. Marc, you can see I am soaked. And my family needs me. Bonsoir."

"Uh, bonsoir, monsieur . . ."

Bounding up the stairs before he thought to ask my name, I caught up to the mercenary from the gift shop rather abruptly on the third floor. He turned defensively, and I flinched away from him, my hands up. Rattling off some French, whether he knew the language or not, I assured him that I was in a hurry for certain business. If he recognized my face under my cap from my past dealings for his employer, it didn't show on his face. Rather, he seemed to regard my local garb and age with little consequence, and moved aside for me to pass.

That was his mistake. I started to pass him, and at the instant that we were closest, I jabbed him hard in the hip with my tranq-pen.

"Hey!" He shrieked, and reached for me.

But I was already beyond him, checking the corridor. His friends were nowhere in sight. When I turned back, he was on his hands and knees, then he fell on his belly. Since he was halfway in the stairwell, I easily dragged him onto the landing to conceal his body. Fortunate for me, this mercenary was about my size and not heavily muscled.

Daringly, I left my subject alone for a few seconds, and ran around the corner of the hallway to gauge by the old-fashioned dial where the elevator car was parked. Due to the storm, the hotel was running on a generator for basic electrical needs only, and according to the sign downstairs, the elevator was off-limits due to safety concerns. A key would be required to make it operable. Only the door would open under standard power. The dial indicated the car was on the second floor, just one lower than me.

With my arms under my subject's armpits, I dragged his lower half thumping down each step to the next floor. I heard voices below and boots tromping up the stairs. Quickly, I pulled my sleeping mercenary friend into the hallway on floor two and pushed the elevator button. The doors opened to the elevator car. Perfect!

As guests were about to walk down the hall, I flopped the fellow into the car, and the doors closed—a sign outside the doors on this floor as well. The space inside the elevator was completely dark. From under my raincoat, I drew two flex-cuffs—a COIL favorite. I bound his wrists and ankles, then laid him on his belly, his hands behind his back. Touching the light on my watch, I estimated my patient's wakeup time to be fifteen minutes.

In those long minutes, I considered my own heart. Just a few days earlier, I had intended the worst for these killers. It would've been easy to kill them all without much bother. Maybe this was one of the very operatives who'd abducted my wife and daughter, then killed them. Did he hurt them first? Did he—?

No. Such thoughts were not healthy to contemplate. God would see to their final justice. I knew all kinds of laws had been breached, even by an agency with few bounds, when they'd brought down Flight 524 and killed my family. It was my business to end their reign so no one else could be harmed.

The man stirred a few minutes later. I placed a foot on his upper back, just below his neck. The weight was significant, and certainly terrifying as the man's senses returned to find that he was blind and bound. Now, it was time for a little Christian interrogation.

✝

CHAPTER FORTY

I let the mercenary squirm for a moment before I spoke inside the dark elevator car.

"You know, this is very bad for you," I said in English, though with a French accent. The man became very still. "Do not speak unless I ask you a question. Let your answers be yes or no. Do you understand?"

He didn't respond. More weight to my foot—painless to him, but threatening his ability to take a deep breath.

"Yes! Yes, I hear you."

His voice cracked from panic. He was worried. Good. I released some of the pressure from my foot to teach him the cooperation-reward relationship we'd now engage in.

"We are alone, you and I. Do you understand? Yes or no?"

"Yes."

"Do you understand you cannot see?"

"Uh, yes."

"Do you understand you are bound hand and foot?"

"Yes."

"Do you understand that the gun on your hip is useless at this moment?"

"Yes." This time he sounded more discouraged, as if he'd held out hope that I hadn't noticed it.

"Do you understand that my foot is on your spine?"

"Yes."

"Do you understand there is a storm outside?"

"Yes."

"Do you understand," my voice became softer now, "that I am aware of your seven traveling companions in suites 311 through 314?"

"I— Yes."

"Do you understand I am a veteran of many operations?"

"Yes."

"Do you understand that you will not be freed unless I free you?"

He paused briefly, his will slowly breaking.

"Yes."

"Do you understand that I am willing to go to great lengths to receive information from you?"

"Yes."

"Do you understand that you work for a man who keeps secrets for a living?"

"Yes."

"Do you understand that I intend to have you reveal certain information to me?"

He waited again, and my pressure increased.

"Okay! Ask what you want. I know nothing!"

"Yes or no!"

"Yes!"

"Good." I relaxed the pressure. "It is said that there is an afterlife. Do you understand that I believe this?"

"Yes."

"Do you believe in God?"

"Uh, yes."

"Do you believe God's standard is higher than man's?"

"Yes."

"Good. Do you have a family? Loved ones?"

"Yes."

"Do you care for them?"

"Yes."

"Will they miss you if you die today?"

He hesitated and seemed to squirm involuntarily under my foot.

"Yes."

"So, you mean something to them?"

"Yes."

"You are not just a worthless killer for hire?"

"No."

"Are you a man of honor?"

"Yes."

"Integrity?"

"Yes."

"Are you serving your country on this operation?"

He didn't answer at first, even when I applied pressure.

"Yes! I think so, okay? Yes."

"You think so?" My questions about the afterlife, his family, and morality were having the intended effect. My pressure lessened on his back. "You said you're a man of honor. Are you?"

"Yes."

"Is the man you work for honorable?"

A pause.

"No."

Good. A crack in his defenses. He'd compromised his loyalty to Coleman just a little, and he'd do so again. It was all over now.

"You understand I already know that?" I asked.

"Yeah." He scoffed. "I'm catching on."

"Good. Then you understand that I am specially commissioned to be here right now?"

"Yes." His voice sounded submissive now—a defeated, ashamed mumble.

"You served in the military before this?"

"Yes."

"Army?"

"No."

"Navy?"

"Marines."

"You're aware that your employer is in trouble?"

"Um, maybe?"

"Explain your answer."

"He's done things for the government. Sanctioned stuff. But my guess someone outside could be after him. Maybe ethics or something."

"That and much more. Much worse." I gave him that information to develop our relationship. "Were you part of the murders?"

"Man, I plead the fifth on that. I'm not going down for any of that stuff!"

"Keep your voice down!" I pressed on his back hard, then let up. "I know about the general on the island. Is he why you're here?"

"Yes."

"To take him out?"

"Yes."

"You need a whole team for that? He's one man."

"If you know what's up, then you should know he's not alone. He's got three with him."

"Right." The other cottage next door was indeed connected by the cavern complex! "When are you striking?"

"The boss wants to use the storm. We're planning it right now."

"What's your boss's name?"

"You don't know?"

"He has had many names." I chuckled and he grunted, as if he'd witnessed the same. "The most recent being K-C."

"Yeah, that's him. Coleman," he confirmed. His openness was helping me greatly, but I wasn't sure what to do with all the new information. "We know he's a rogue agent somehow."

This startled me.

"How do you know that?"

"Television. We know General Forglade is wanted, and we know Coleman was real close to Forglade. We're being paid a lot to clean up this mess for Coleman. This is what we do: erase problems, potential testimonies. None of us knows what he did, but we're hired by people in Washington, probably as corrupt as he is, to make a few problems go away. It's good money."

"Women and children?"

"Sometimes. Not recently." He shifted his weight. "Look, my shoulders are killing me in this position. I've earned the right to get some relief here. And I know you won't kill me."

It was true; he'd earned the right. I kept clear of his legs in the dark and helped him roll over to a sitting position. Standing close enough so he could feel my presence, I considered my next question.

"Whoever is with Coleman at this point will be prosecuted," I said. "That's why I'm here."

"Hey, I work for the highest bidder. I have nothing personal invested with this guy. It's just a job."

"Well, now you work for me for free! Unless you want to go down with the others."

"Like I said, I have a family. At least four of the others won't stand with Coleman if they know the law is closing in."

"You can turn them?"

"It's not about turning them. We watch each other's backs. Do a job, then we get out with what we can. It's in our contract. If agencies like Interpol come in, we're gone. We'll do anything until a prison cell is hovering over our heads. And it's too costly to live on the run anymore."

"Sounds like I won't be putting you in the US Marshal's hands after all." It seemed like a wise thing to say, since he already had the impression that I was the law, which, at that point, Luigi and I were the closest thing on the island capable of handling the likes of these men. Seven experienced mercenaries under Coleman's direction would be worse for Gustavia than a direct hurricane. "How soon can you and your guys abandon Coleman? That's all five of you who are in it just for the money."

"As I said, four are guys I know. The other two—I think they're loyal. We can't do anything obvious or we're dead. The storm won't let us leave the island. If Coleman wants to hit the general at dawn or earlier, we don't have a choice."

"When it comes to murder, you always have a choice!" I growled, thinking of my family.

"No, I mean, we won't have a choice but to go along. Look, you got my word we won't be part of the hit, okay? But I can't stop the others. I won't kill them. With you and your boys coming in, bodies complicate matters real fast."

"Good. Then I'll give you your orders to pass on to the others." I paused and prayed for God to be glorified through all of this. If this were just for me and my loss, then I was ignoring God. But dedicating my motives and decisions to Him, I remained in His perfect will. "You five will cut out of Coleman's team even if you have to do it one at a time. Just leave. There's a forty-foot Bavaria, a single mast—the only Bavaria in the harbor. That's your rendezvous. Her name is Visage."

"A sailboat?"

"If Coleman's two loyalists look for you, the island is too small to hide you for long. But the sailboat is private property. Stay out of sight. This will be over in twenty-four hours."

"Coleman probably won't hit the general without me," my captive said. "What guarantee do I have if something goes wrong, so I won't get prosecuted?"

"You want a guarantee?" I smiled in the darkness. "Letting you return to your family isn't enough?"

"Under the circumstances . . . I mean, to me, you're just another spook like Coleman."

"Well, let me put it this way: I'm not alone on this island."

"I figured that."

"And the sailboat is a personal possession. You can poke around. We're both risking ourselves by being a little vulnerable. It's what the good guys and men of honor do for God and one another when the lines have been drawn."

"So, we're trusting each other," he summed up.

"One last thing. Tell your boys to roll up the sleeve cuff of their left arm to differentiate who's with us. Get it?"

"Got it. You know, we haven't exchanged names or anything."

"Even if we did," I said, "they wouldn't be real, would they?"

"Probably not."

†

CHAPTER FORTY-ONE

That evening, as the storm battered Gustavia and turned visibility down to one hundred feet, I went to work for God's people. I say I worked for God's people because God's children had been harmed. And if God's children had been harmed by these dangerous men already, then God's children could be harmed by them again.

Evil and I had a history. In my own past, I'd been wicked, uncaring toward sin, declaring myself good by my own sinful heart. But then a miracle had occurred. Truth had spawned faith, and faith in Christ had borne a new heart by the Spirit of God.

Now, I was a man with a past, a Christian who no longer looked back with shame, but looked forward with joy. The blood of the cross covered my sins and set me on a path set apart for a holy purpose. My past dark life of espionage had now become a bright light for God's people. And it wasn't a crusade on which I ventured, but a discipline of love. Love for my Lord and His righteousness. Anything else would've turned my abilities into a systematic destruction of the wicked by my own determination. God had kept me from stumbling, even when tempted to be someone I was no longer meant to be.

It was with godly determination, rather, that I went to my sailboat one last time. Even with my wife Janice and daughter, Jenna, now gone, my life was still in Christ. COIL was still the vehicle for me to help the afflicted and care for the persecuted. General Forglade and Karl Coleman had to meet their end that night!

Though my initial plan had been for a stealth attack on Forglade's cottage, the storm assisted me in an armed assault. Thus, I pocketed several tranq-pens, but I selected two NL-2 fully automatic machine pistols as my primary weapons for the evening. The non-lethal tranquilizing guns carried two-hundred-and-fifty small, water-soluble pellets, the pistol grip extra-long to house the ammunition.

In other operations, when ranges were farther, I would select the NL-3 assault rifle, or even the NL-X1 sniper rifle, but I foresaw only close contact this night. I closed the hidden compartment behind the galley bulkhead.

Before going on deck, I strapped the guns under both arms inside my rain slicker. The temperature wasn't cold, so I left my vest behind so I could move about easier. On my belt, I laced a dozen pairs of flex-cuffs. Since the secret compartment behind the galley had no room for other equipment, I was without a flak jacket. I'd have to trust God as my shield when it came to bullets.

On deck, I hopped from one boat deck to another to reach land—the peninsula side. The wind whipped at my slicker and rain stung my exposed skin, but I moved toward Forglade's cottage with stoic fervor. First, the general. Then, I'd see to Coleman.

As I approached the cottage, I could've been overconfident in the protection of the storm and not bothered to disguise my assault. Instead, I took care and began to circle the cottage, prowling around it with caution. If I'd seen Coleman's mercenaries come ashore, the general's men were certain to be privy to their arrival as well.

My caution paid off as I nearly stumbled upon a sentry who stood on the downwind side of the shrub in which I'd first hidden my bicycle. Dressed in a black rain suit, he stood against the bush. I only noticed him because the bush swayed in the wind, and the taller shadow didn't move. He was certain to be armed, and if I hadn't been so careful, he would've hailed me, or shot me outright. Anyone out on a night like this could only be up to mischief.

But was this sentry the only one? I continued my circuit around the dwelling, and even included the cottage next door in my reconnaissance now, since I knew they were attached by the old underground smugglers' cavern.

Again, I nearly walked upon another sentry on the opposite corner of the house. From behind the second cottage, I watched this second man. Visibility was poor, but lights from town shimmered off glossy wet surfaces like their raincoats. Barely perceptible, this man turned his head as if to look in my direction.

I waited, unmoving. To him, I prayed I was just a shadow. From other operations, I knew well to use men's uncertainties against them. If he truly saw me, he might doubt, and then investigate—rather than first try to contact his friend around the cottage. They were sure to be wearing comm devices, maybe even wired to a third man, or an overseer inside the second cottage. Soberly, I considered the men I faced, as they stood watch over the general. These were men hardened by exploits that had earned them a place in paradise next to Forglade. Though this night was no paradise, they obviously still took their job seriously.

The sentry started hastily toward me, and I let him take a few steps. This man had an intimidating frame, much larger than my own. When his arm shifted under his raincoat, I knew he was more than merely curious. He was about to draw and aim a weapon. A gunshot now would ruin my surprise, even if I was intent on making a big splash in a few minutes.

Calculating my advantage, I waited until he was in the open, with me halfway behind the corner of the second cottage. He had a gun with thirty rounds maximum, and I had more than eight times that. But his rounds were live, and mine were only pea-sized pellets that stung the skin less than the rain did. His bullets would have an instant effect, whereas my pellets would require a couple heartbeats after the first breath of toxin. To win, he had only to wing me, but I had to fire with precision to get the tranquilizer near his mouth or nose—in the rain and wind!

My hand was already on my left NL-2, and since he seemed less certain that I was anything more than a shadow, I beat him to the draw. The barrel of my weapon poked out of my sleeve and peppered the man's face and chest with pellets. He recoiled with great flare, his arms flailing, his raincoat glistening from the rain and lights beyond. Hardly any sound had been made.

He fell and lay still. Not rushing into potential danger, I remained against the second cottage wall until I was sure I hadn't been discovered by someone else. Before examining the body, I set my wristwatch for twenty minutes. The tranquilizer toxin would last no longer.

Kneeling next to the man, I flex-cuffed his ankles to his wrists and took his sidearm from the lawn. I dragged him under the awning of the second cottage and left him there, his face against the building so he didn't drown from the rain. It was gestures like this, which I knew I had to do, that separated me from them. Life was a precious thing. Every soul mattered to God.

Continuing around the cottage, I stayed away from the small lamplight that shined through the tinted eastern window. If I passed before the window, the first sentry might easily see me. But as I neared his position against the bush, I realized he'd relocated!

Immediately, I dropped to a knee, my head low. The wind and rain hindered my senses, but I tuned my eyes and ears the best I could for anything amiss—a shadow out of place, a rustle of clothing . . .

My lips parted with a prayer on my breath as I identified a darker shade of black on the lawn not three paces from me. It had to be the sentry! But he was down. Were Coleman's mercenaries already attacking?

Carefully, I turned my head, ready to fire with either machine pistol at the next sign of danger. I felt exposed, alone, and outgunned. Without knowing who was around me, I couldn't prowl back inside the cottage. The light in the window told me the general was probably below, in the underground vault, exactly where I wanted to capture him.

"Psst! Corban!"

The call on my right so startled my nerves that my response was to open fire with a spray of pellets in the general vicinity of the neighbor's house. Just as quickly, I realized who must be out there—the only one who would know my name.

"Luigi?" I whispered over the rain. "Come out!"

A man emerged, and I was further convinced that it was indeed him when I wasn't shot dead. He held his empty palms out. My pellets thankfully hadn't tranquilized him!

I stood and ran a dozen yards to pull him down to a kneeling position. There were no words for my emotions at seeing him up close, joining me. My hand trembled as I reached up and gripped his shoulder. Did he know the pain I'd suffered the last few weeks with my wife and daughter dead? As a man who'd devoted the last couple of years to protecting them when I was overseas—surely, his sorrow wasn't slight, either.

"We don't have time to catch up, Luigi. I'm going in for General Forglade. Are you in?"

"Yes, but what about the others in the hotel across the water?"

"Right now, I'm focusing on this first target, but I've helped our odds against those others."

"Target?" Luigi wasn't one to question me, but I caught his tone. "You aren't killing, are you?"

"Killing?"

"This is why I've come out of hiding. We must be protected from ourselves at times."

It was an honest challenge, and one that would've troubled my soul more if I'd let vengeance have her wicked way through me. Luigi's question told me he knew about my family.

"I did struggle, but no, my heart is now pure in this."

"Corban, I must tell you about your family."

"There's no time." I checked my watch. "We have fifteen minutes before my first tranq starts wearing off on a guy on the other side. My plan is to lay in wait for Coleman after the general is subdued inside. Help me hide these two then follow me inside the back door."

"Use the north bedroom window. It's fixed to enter, Corban. I've been inside as well. Did you understand the rock I left on your bicycle?"

"That's a lot to grasp from a rock on my bike seat." I chuckled. This was a great moment, I felt, working with an expert who knew how to get the upper hand on his enemies. "You went below?"

"When Forglade went to town, I went in. I thought you did as well."

"Luigi, we don't have time." I held up my hand. "You hide this guy, and I'll hide the other one. Meet you on the northwest corner."

Crouching low, I dashed back to the man I'd tranquilized and left under the awning. Grabbing his hands, I dragged him directly north, between the two houses, and rolled him into a hedge. When I turned around, I nearly shot Luigi again as he carried his own tranquilized man to deposit him beside the other. I flex-cuffed Luigi's man.

"Lead the way," I said.

"Much has happened that may help you understand why I'm here." He started for the cottage. "We really must talk about things, Corban."

"You already made it clear you were afraid I was going to kill these men," I whispered as we reached the back window. "Do we need to take Forglade and Coleman down before they hurt others?"

"Yes, we should."

"Is anyone else here to do that?"

"No."

"Then we stay focused. Op-talk only. Get this window open. We're down to ten minutes."

Whatever lock the window had, it was basic, and Luigi had discovered so in better lighting. The window slid horizontally, and I climbed through. Inside the dark bedroom, I acknowledged the lamplight shining under the door. If the light went off, then we had to worry.

As Luigi climbed in, I stripped off my slicker. Luigi did the same as I slid the window closed.

"How many men underground?" I whispered. The silence of the house compared to outside had its own deafening feel.

"Forglade and one other are still unaccounted for. The third is probably in the other house." Luigi moved to the door. "He may have a warning system below. I couldn't determine that by what I saw. The living quarters below are simple, but the communication system is remarkable. Once we open the secret passage, he may escape through the other house, or send an alert through his technology."

"And just how could you know all that? It's taken me days to figure out half that stuff."

"While you read books in libraries about tunnels, I explore tunnels."

"So, the rock on my bike seat wasn't a message, it was a trophy? That you got in first?"

"Corban, are you jealous that I beat you?" We laughed under our breaths. "It's no matter. I only know the way. My plan ends there, so you do the rest."

He opened the bedroom door slightly, then listened for a few seconds. When he exited, I covered him from the doorway. The house seemed empty.

Treading softly, Luigi was certain to have in mind the sound of his steps below him. My heart pounded. Forglade was at the end of his freedom. When had we last spoken? His deceit still rang in my ears. It had been weeks before on another dark night. And on this dark night, Luigi and I had much to accomplish, against many adversaries. But we weren't alone. God was with us.

†

CHAPTER FORTY-TWO

Luigi faced the wall in General Forglade's cottage, his back to the strange lamp.

"We can't both go down." I handed him one of the NL-2s. "Stay up here in case someone else comes."

"Coleman?"

"Yes, I expect him."

"I'll stay up here, but I'll be turning off that light." He gestured at the lamp. "It's ruining my night vision."

He reached low on the wall and pressed a panel I hadn't noticed. To find such a lever, Luigi had obviously spent more time inside than I had.

Immediately, the lamp blinked out, and the feel of gears vibrated through the floor.

"That's pretty loud," I said with some concern. "He may be expecting me now."

"If you want to stay up here . . ." Luigi offered.

It was a tempting offer—to let the younger man go instead of me since he'd been below already—but this was my job. I had to finish this by taking the risks myself.

As soon as the panel exposed the cavern rock, and it was wide enough to fit through, I entered. My last view of Luigi was of him pressing the lever again to close the secret door behind me. I hadn't expected that! Was I now trapped underground? Where was the lever on the inside? These were matters I tried to push aside.

I descended steep stairs, my NL-2 aimed down the passage that turned left. The noisy storm outside could be heard no longer. Now, the mildew smell of perpetually wet rock and cement reached my nose, and the bright LED lamps along the walls made me squint.

At the bottom of the steps, I paused before peering around the corner. What awaited me? If I were Forglade, a man on the run and in hiding, I'd have a loaded gun at hand. He'd surely have no less. And if this was my moment to die, then I'd do so with a pure heart. Consciously, I settled my mind on the Lord, my complete portion in this life.

Quickly, I glanced around the corner, then ducked back, letting the view register in my mind. A computer console on the right. Living quarters and a kitchenette on the left. It seemed to be only one large room, the poured cement floor continuing to another passageway on the other side, where there was certain to be a similar staircase to the other cottage.

Forglade sat at the computer console. He had to have heard me enter—he was so close. Had the old man gone deaf, or did he have headphones on? Maybe he was making a final attempt to erase his records so—

"Quit messing around," he said. My eyes widened. Was he speaking to me? "Get your coffee and get back outside. I swear, Chang sends me the laziest men."

He was speaking to me!

Turning the corner, I watched him closely as I made my way to the kitchen counter running the length along one wall. Forglade never looked away from what he was doing on the computer screen, which allowed me to come up behind him.

"It's really blowing out there," I said, automatically disguising my voice by speaking a little deeper. "I figured a Caribbean job would be all sunshine."

I busied myself with the coffee maker next to a modern sink and a small fridge. My mind was spinning. Had he said Chang? As in Senator Nettleton's assistant? It could be. Rod Chang had been one of the first men I'd contacted to begin my investigation into the TaTD. It had to be a different Chang, though the intelligence world was a small one . . .

"Well, it's hurricane season," Forglade mumbled. "But if I were you, I'd be more concerned about an assault and less worried about the weather. Coleman's not here to pat you on the back."

Still, he didn't look away from the computer screen, and I took advantage of that to tap a spoon on a mug while I peered over his shoulder—fifteen feet behind him. It was too far to see words on the screen, but he was clearly in communication with someone via text boxes.

This was my moment. He was off his guard. How could I exploit it?

"You talk to Chang lately?" I asked, though still uneasy about the idea that it was the Chang I'd submitted to for DOD access.

"Earlier. As soon as the storm is over, he says he's got a boat for us to Caracas."

"Isn't Chang's first name Rod?" I dared. "Strange name for a Chang."

"He's your boss." Forglade pivoted his chair around to face me. "Why would you—?"

I raised my machine pistol. His mouth fell open. Calmly, I took a sip of the coffee and set the mug on the counter. The general gripped the armrests of his chair.

"Good to see you again, General."

"You! Corban Dowler? You're not dead yet?"

"Lord willing, not for a few more years. I have some work to do that you've distracted me from for a while."

Closing his mouth, he seemed to measure his options. His eyes twitched.

"We're alone, General. You can fight all you want, but it's over."

"There are worse things on this island than you, Dowler." I heard the fear in his voice, and it wasn't towards me. "A man named Karl Coleman has gone rogue and is here to kill me. If you can find me, he may be able to as well. What's in the past, is past. If he finds us, he'll kill us both."

"Is the death of my wife and daughter something in the past that you don't want to remember?" The anger in my voice was more than I intended, but I didn't mind seeing the concern on his face. "I've been on you for more than two weeks. Karl Coleman told me weeks ago to find you here. It's not a large town, you know."

"My bodyguards said he brought a whole team with him." Forglade sighed. "Well, at least he doesn't know about all this. Let them take the house. We're safe down here."

"I'm not here to be safe, General." I frowned. Was the man senile? "The reason I'm here is to take you back to the States. There's a lot of blood on your hands. Besides, Coleman's men know all about your little hideout here, and the cottage next door."

"What're you talking about?" He chuckled nervously. "I just reported to Chang. He said I was safe down here. They could bulldoze the house upstairs, and I'd be safe."

"Well, Chang lied to you. Coleman's men know you're down here. Besides, I found you, didn't I?"

Forglade rose quickly from his chair, and I raised my muzzle to compensate for his height, a few inches taller than me.

"Dowler, Coleman won't just kill me! If he's here, it means he wants my codes. I have the access to satellite blackout software. Coleman will torture me until I talk!"

"You don't seem to be getting this," I said. "Chang has betrayed you. He's betrayed me. Do the math. Coleman and Chang are working together. They're here to kill you. I don't know about satellite blackout software, but I do know enough about Flight 524 to say—"

"That was all Coleman and Nettleton!"

"Senator Nettleton." My jaw clenched at the memory of the young senator sending me into the jaws of death. He'd seemed so controlled the last time I'd seen him in his office. "Yes, more pieces are falling into place. Coleman will be here any minute, but these are for you." I unlaced two flex-cuffs. "As much as you deserve him, I'm taking you back to Washington."

"With Coleman on the loose, I can't go anywhere!" Backing up, he bumped into his desk. "You don't know him, Dowler! He's sadistic! No one can stop him. That man's an expert at killing. I know he'll torture me before I ever get—"

"Relax, General. I'm getting him in the next few hours, too."

"Pretty confident of yourself, huh?" His eyes widened, which was usually a sign of heightened adrenalin. "What do you have, an army outside? Your COIL troopers?"

"Toss the gun with your fingertips. Now." I gestured with my barrel.

"Chang said the next time you popped up, you'd disappear, too. You can't take us all on, Dowler. Don't you know who Senator Nettleton can gather with one phone call?"

"Do you have any idea who I serve? You know I'm with COIL. I'm not here for myself." Smiling, I felt the presence of Almighty God. "If you think Nettleton and Coleman are the muscle behind everything happening, you're mistaken."

His hand moved to his waistband where I could see a small caliber handgun.

"I know you won't kill me, Dowler." There was a glint in his eye that I didn't like. "You know I can't make this easy on you."

"That's okay. You didn't make it easy last time, either. It took some jalapeno juice squirted on you to get you talking. I'm used to your stubbornness."

"The lighter fluid? That was you? Of course. Then we have more history than even I knew."

"You're nervous about this, I see, General, so let me make this easy on you."

He scratched for his gun grip, but I was already pulling my trigger. A dozen pellets peppered his face, stinging him, then he collapsed to the ground. The gun was still in his waistband. I knelt to flex-cuff his wrists.

Suddenly, muted gunfire sounded through the cavern ceiling. Luigi was under attack! Coleman was striking sooner than expected, maybe hoping to use the storm to hide his treachery against the general. From Forglade's words—if I could trust them—I understood that Senator Nettleton was secretly using Coleman to take out the burdensome general. I'd thought both Forglade and Coleman were on the run, but the entire time, they'd been puppets of the very senator I'd thought was in my corner!

Rushing to the stairway, I realized I hadn't located the lever to open the hatch above! Frantically, I studied the volcanic rock wall. There! Punching the broad button, I aimed my NL-2 at the door as it opened. The gunfire thundered louder. It sounded like it was inside the cottage! No, probably the windows were shot out, and Luigi was making a stand. What would he have done without the NL-2?

"General! We have to—!"

Startled by another man's voice in the vault, I turned and fired at a young soldier at the bottom of the other staircase that led up to the second cottage. He had a carbine in his hands. Since he'd been intent on helping the general escape, he wasn't ready to fire his weapon. My tranquilizer pellets raked his chest twice before he slumped unconsciously onto the steps.

Drawing out two flex-cuffs, I took the general and guard's guns, and flex-cuffed the new man's ankles and wrists. The secret passage I'd opened closed automatically behind me, and the gunfire sounded more distant again.

"Hold on, Luigi," I mumbled, then bounded up the stairs of the second cottage, now that it was clear.

Upstairs, I ejected the magazines of both lethal weapons and tossed them in two different directions. I would've taken more time to dispose of them but the gun battle next door was calling me.

Picking up a lamp, I threw it at another to extinguish both lights in the furnished house. Darkness claimed the room, then I opened the front door. Immediately, I thought of my rain slicker in the other cottage. At least it wasn't a cold rain.

First, I ran straight north to the edge of the neighboring property nearest the harbor, then I charged west and hooked south. Muzzle flashes gave them away, their backs to me as I approached. Their cover wasn't ideal as they hid from Luigi. Luigi had only a machine pistol that had a limited range with pellets that could be deflected by a mere bush.

I, on the other hand, found myself in a particular dilemma. Now directly behind six men, with a seventh lying on the ground, I couldn't tranquilize them using the NL-2; they needed to be facing me before the NL-2 could actually be effective. But, I had other weapons in my arsenal.

Allowing the NL-2 to hang on its sling, I drew out two tranq-pens and crept up on the men engaged in the battle. Apparently, they could see Luigi, or something they thought was a target, because their firing continued without pause. Or perhaps Luigi was intentionally drawing their fire somehow, expecting me to do something.

Fortunate for me, the six remaining men were more or less in a line, shoulder-to-shoulder behind sparse cover, crouching or kneeling. Working right to left, I sprang on them, tranquilizing three through their raincoats before my presence was noticed. To make matters worse, I felt Luigi's pellets smack the side of my head, and I was forced to hold my breath lest I breathe in the vapor.

Kicking at the next man, I pushed him into the man on his left. As they grappled to recover, I dove over a hedge and used my sleeve to wipe the pellet remnants from my face. The rain seemed to do the rest, and I gasped for air.

Rolling over, I crawled away into the shadow of a tree and behind its trunk.

So much for my deal with Coleman's mercenaries. All seven seemed to have made the assault after all. But where was Coleman? He couldn't leave the island, so he had to be there somewhere!

"Hold your fire!" a man yelled. "Hold your fire!"

From behind my tree, I licked my lips and aimed the NL-2. Yes, there they were. Three of the seven were left. They were just within my range, but as soon as they located me again, I'd be in trouble. Hearing no more gunfire, not even the clicking of the NL-2, I wondered if Luigi was out of pellets.

"Hey, mister! The one with the sailboat!"

I recognized the voice of my mercenary-captive from the elevator. Responding would give away my position in the

338 | D.I. TELBAT

dark before I got a chance to take out one or two more of their number. By my calculation, there were only three left, but where was Coleman? He was the one I considered the most dangerous.

"Hey! We're coming out, guns raised, and our left sleeve rolled up. Tell your men not to shoot!"

My clothes were now soaked and I wiped rain from my eyes. Maybe I even had water in my ears because I thought he'd said "my men." In the wind, rain, and darkness, it was possible they believed I had a whole unit, as I'd alluded to in the elevator.

Sure enough, when I peered with one eye around the tree, I saw three men and their rifles with folding stocks raised over their heads. Was it a trap? In my business, it would've been rare for there not to be a trap. Thus, a little bluff of my own was in order.

"Cover me!" I yelled to no one but the wind. "If they move, shoot 'em!"

It was probable they hadn't figured out that Luigi and I had only tranq-guns, and Luigi was probably out of ammo after such a gun battle. If he was still alive.

Squinting through the rain, I stepped from behind the tree—though ready to dive back if one of them should aim at me. I didn't disguise my own weapon aimed at them.

The wind was still disorienting them, and even after my yell, they hadn't fully located me until I showed myself. Their faces were painted black, so I couldn't recognize the one I'd abducted earlier that day.

"You didn't keep our deal," I said across the thirty feet that separated us.

"We couldn't get out of it without getting killed." He was the one in the middle. "After I finished talking to you, Coleman and the others got suspicious. I'd been missing for too long. And Coleman moved up the timetable."

"He told us the deal," the one on the right said. His sleeve was rolled up, too. "Said the law was closing in. We made a point of not shooting anyone tonight, honest. Though I can't speak for the other two who are dead now."

"Mister, you've killed the opposition, and two of our own," the middle one said, his voice somber. "We're just looking to walk away. We got families."

"Where's Coleman?" My eyes surveyed the shadows for a threat.

"Probably back at the hotel. He'll run, I suspect."

"I doubt it." The man's interactions with me over the past two years came to my mind. "He's not the type to give up; he likes to get his hands bloody. You three want to leave the island? Bring me Coleman, alive!"

"Nah, we're done here, mister. We don't want any more of this."

"Well, you signed on!" I shouted. "There's a killer on this island, and you know what his resources are. If he's at the hotel, then you get him and bring him to the sailboat. This storm will be over before noon. You'll either vindicate yourselves, or you'll be in custody!"

"Will you keep the authorities off our backs?"

"If you come through. Now, go—before the authorities show up. We'll take care of this mess."

Lowering their arms, they looked at one another, then ran into the bushes. I relaxed, but only long enough to collect my thoughts. Luigi and I couldn't be placed in the local stockade at this point. We'd be killed by enemies still loose—either Coleman or Nettleton.

"Luigi! You still breathing?" I knelt in the bushes and flex-cuffed the four unconscious men.

"I'm still breathing, but I'm injured." He stood up inside the cottage, a wound in his shoulder. As I climbed through the broken window, I noticed he'd already used the NL-2 sling to make a sling for his arm. The NL-2 itself was in pieces on the floor, having obviously taken most of the impact of the bullet. "Corban, I can't see these authorities."

"The motorboat is yours, right? The silver Predator?"

"You knew?" He smiled. I loved impressing this master spy with my educated guesses that seemed like secret intel.

"My sailboat is now a rendezvous point for those three mercs, so it's not safe for you. I'll meet you at the Predator. I'm not finished here."

After I helped him out of the window, he headed toward the harbor. His was a life of narrow escapes and self-surgery; I didn't worry about his condition.

Inside the cottage, I opened the hidden door once more. While descending the cavern steps, I heard French spoken outside and behind me. The island police were there, surely overwhelmed with such violence. Their small force had probably waited down the avenue until the gunfire was over.

In the vault, Forglade climbed to his feet, which I'd not bound, though his wrists were still flex-cuffed. He turned expectantly to face me, then his countenance grew dark.

"Yes, General, I'm still here." Taking his elbow, I guided

him to the south wall, his nose to the volcanic rock. "Stand there and don't move."

"I have friends you can't imagine, Dowler! You're better off letting me go now."

"Is that right? You should know me better than that." Sitting down at the computer terminal, I wondered what the general had been working on. "I serve the God of a shepherd boy who took down Goliath. Doing right against the odds is now my nature. You can't dream up enough allies to defeat my God, nor my willingness to serve Him."

The general hadn't had time to close down his programs. The windows showed his travel plans and assets in three European accounts. The general seemed to be a wealthy man, so whose money was it? I'd captured enough fugitives and their blood-money accounts in the past to know where to deposit such funds instead. Accessing the three European accounts, with his passwords still active, I rerouted the funds to a COIL account in Iceland. Then I closed the sites.

As I marched the general up the stairs of the second cottage, he turned toward me, his voice weak and defeated.

"What'd you do with my money?"

"You just funded a medical ship to operate for two years off the Ivory Coast."

"Huh. I guess that's better than what I'd planned."

"Oh, I'm sure it is."

With barely a glance at the bustling activity outside the first cottage, I escorted the general to the harbor. I was thankful to still be alive, but I had an empty feeling in my gut. Karl Coleman had seemingly gotten away. And everyone I knew and loved could be his next targets.

†

CHAPTER FORTY-THREE

The storm passed St. Barts early, and by dawn, the harbor was being cleared of the fleet of boats packed into the anchorage. From the bow of Luigi's long Predator speedboat, I watched as the harbormaster and two assistants re-anchored my sailboat. I sipped coffee and acted like an innocent tourist enjoying the morning. Luigi was still asleep below in the stateroom, stitched by his own hand. His blood loss was minimal, thankfully. Since I'd arrived after midnight, I hadn't spoken to him yet, but I'd seen his blood-soaked rags. He'd survive and I looked forward to debriefing him soon. Anxiously, I waited for a sign that Coleman was still on the island and that the three mercenaries had proven themselves.

General Forglade was in the galley below, bound more loosely, but drugged more strongly to be less of a nuisance. The Predator itself was anchored just outside the mouth of the harbor, almost even with La Pointe on my right.

My appearance had changed again, with sunglasses, slacks, and a tropical shirt. And in the stern head, I'd even cropped my own hair. Once again, I was Corban Dowler, ex-CIA agent, founder of COIL, born again Christian . . . and widower. That last title was the most sobering.

Maybe Coleman would never be found. This idea needed to sink in. And there were other enemies out there, too, some who could come for me at any time. After several attacks against my family in past years, I'd been a fool to think that merely relocating them each time was the answer. I'd have to live with those mistakes. Their blood was on Coleman's hands, but I felt responsible. There was always a cost for walking the jagged edge for Christ.

Using Luigi's on-board DDS, I'd tried to send COIL headquarters a text, but there was no satellite signal. Many ashore said it had been that way for two weeks. In my grief, I'd not considered the ramifications of the manhunt on the island. Such an extensive computer system in Forglade's vault could've accessed certain systems in the States to black out a region—especially a small island. Surely, Forglade had done all he could to hide himself from Coleman, but he'd not known that Nettleton and Coleman were now working together, intent on Forglade taking the blame for Flight 524.

The peninsula was crawling with island officials. The night's gun battle and bound captives left behind was causing no small stir. A motor cruiser had arrived from another island to assist in the investigation, presumably contacted by island-to-island shortwave radio. And before dawn, I'd gone ashore to work some misinformation.

"Drug dealers, I heard."

"Oh, really?"

"From Mexico. And Columbia. Something with the cartel."

Because the storm had been such a dampener the previous day, everyone was in the streets again, especially curious about the gunfire during the night. The whole island of nine thousand seemed to be in Gustavia.

"It's strange for us to be together again, Corban."

Turning, I saw Luigi with his arm in a new sling. A small patch of crimson already stained the fresh shirt he now wore. Though he appeared rested, his jaw was unshaved.

"Well, it feels good, Luigi. I've been praying for you regardless of our separation."

"Yes, I need the prayers," Luigi said thoughtfully. "It's the reason I came to find you, though with all the weight you lost, I had trouble identifying you."

"Really?" I smiled. "You actually need me for something?"

"I wish to retire, but my enemies won't leave me be. You are the only one I know who can convince the authorities to leave me alone."

"That's the authorities." I frowned. "What about your other enemies?"

"My enemies are the authorities—those from other countries. One is France, as you know, from when I worked for the DGSE in an Italian office."

"Of course. You know all their secrets. They want you dead. It's the same for me to a degree."

"There's the matter of a woman as well."

"You?" I looked ashore, still distracted by unfinished business. "I hadn't thought of you as one who'd ever settle down, Luigi."

"She's a police officer in New Jersey. Heather Oakes. And then there's the matter of my sister, Anna Putelli." Suddenly, Luigi gasped, and his good hand fell hard on my right shoulder. He was a distant man, usually not personal, so the touch drew my full attention. "Your family, Corban!"

"Oh." I smiled through my aching heart. "It is well, my friend. A Christian knows that the ones who belong to God will meet him again in eternity. Tell me more of this Anna. She's your—"

"No, Corban! Anna is with Janice and Jenna! I took them to New Hampshire, to the silo where I trained Nathan!"

Turning my back to the shore, I faced Luigi directly.

"Luigi, I don't know how long you've been tailing me, but Karl Coleman admitted he killed them over two weeks ago, even when he didn't know it was me he was talking to."

"Then my plan worked!" Luigi's hand was still on my shoulder, as if he needed to convey the weight of his words. "I keep watch on the networks that are looking for cleaners. I took that job! Coleman hired me. I was hired to kill your family! It was me! I mean, they are still alive! I used other bodies. There's so much to tell you! You wouldn't listen in the storm last night!"

"You . . . protected them again? They're . . . alive?"

"Yes! With Anna, my sister, and Chloe and Brody Sladrick."

"Brody's in on all this?" Tears were flowing down my cheeks. "Luigi, I'm a man without faith!"

Falling upon Luigi, I didn't notice the pain I was causing him until my sobs subsided a few moments later. Withdrawing, I saw his pale face, but there was moisture in his eyes as well.

"As you can guess, Chloe has been in much despair." Luigi adjusted his sling and took a step away from me, probably not willing to tempt another embrace. "I thought it best to send her someone from the past who could comfort her, and help her like no one else could."

"Who did you send?"

"Nathan. She knows now he's alive. I spoke with her last night before I slept."

"How? The satellites are all blacked out. It's probably General Forglade's doing."

"Chloe and I launched a private satellite to trace Forglade here. That's how I found you. I knew you would be after him, close to him."

"You guessed right."

"But I came alone to the island to speak with you of my identity. I must become a new man, or I'll never be able to stop running."

"God is a just God, Luigi. I can clean your identity, but only He can clean your conscience, your heart, and your sins."

"That's another matter." His face seemed to harden. "Perhaps I'm closer to your God now. I served Him in your absence."

"From the heart?" I asked. "Or from your hands?"

He considered this, gazing down at the deck. Finally, he looked up.

"The difference is great?"

"The difference is heaven and hell." My directness seemed to check his zeal for me and the loyalty by which he'd served God. To tell him otherwise, without the warning of motive or eternity, wouldn't have been showing him love.

"Perhaps you should read more of that Bible I left for you. Do you still have it?"

"Yes." His face brightened as he seemed to remember when he'd followed me overseas and I'd left a Bible in a hotel room for him. "No one else has treated me like you have, Corban. There was a one-eyed man who tried, I think, but he wasn't like you."

"It's what brothers do for one another. The least I can be is honest with the man who continues to save my family from my foes."

"Without you, no part of your God would've touched my life. I'll try to—" He looked past me, squinting, then he smiled. "It's Nathan and Chloe! They got my message!"

I turned to see a giant catamaran with a towering mast approach the harbor. Nathan was at the starboard bow preparing to throw a deckline, and Chloe stood midships. Both were waving a greeting. They began to pull abreast north of our anchorage as Chloe dropped bumpers over the side to protect both hulls.

"They're both strong-willed, but still a good team." I said to Luigi. "It's good to see them together again."

He joined me at the rail of the Predator.

"That's Brody in the cockpit. I think he'll marry the woman—"

A loud PING pierced the morning air. We both ducked. An instant later, the report of a long-distance rifle reached our ears. The catamaran drifted past us and moved into the harbor. Dropping to the deck with Luigi, I pointed at the hillside above Gustavia.

"The shooter's up there!" I rolled over once, seconds after the first shot. Sure enough, the next bullet smashed into our speedboat, puncturing the deck and entering the stateroom below. "What weaponry do you have on board?"

Luigi stared into my eyes. I saw his lips moving, as if he were praying, but I knew he was counting as I was. The report of the gun following the bullet indicated the shooter was approximately one half-mile away. The rifle that covered that distance was probably a bolt action. We had five to ten seconds between gunshots to move around erratically and unexpectedly.

"Nothing. I have nothing on board," Luigi said, then we both shifted positions on deck. I lunged from my knees to one side, and Luigi went the other way, crying out as he landed hard on his bad shoulder. The next bullet tore into the deck exactly where I'd been an instant before. The shooter was for sure after me.

"Corban!" It was Nathan aboard the catamaran now well beyond us. He pointed straight up, above him. On his face was a ridiculous grin. His humor was always appreciated, but his timing was often terrible. "The mast! See the mast?"

"What?" I yelled back. "Keep moving! He's on the hill by the lighthouse!"

For now, the shooter probably didn't know the catamaran was with me.

When Luigi moved again, he dove down the companionway and tumbled below deck. My idea was similar—to get out of sight! But the shooter also needed to be stopped. My only firearms were hidden on my sailboat.

I leaped toward the starboard side before another bullet tore into the bow. The shooter was a skilled marksman, but I was determined to be an uncooperative target. He wouldn't keep missing once he figured out how I was dodging his rounds. Very soon, he'd adjust to aim where he guessed I'd move next, and then I would die.

Taking a deep breath, I tumbled over the side into the warm water. I shed my shoes and shirt on the far side of the boat, then dove deep, kicking toward the harbor. Two hundred yards of clear, green water spanned between my sailboat and me. Whatever else Nathan and Chloe might try to do, I had to act now or we'd all be killed.

Karl Coleman. It had to be him. There didn't seem to be multiple shooters, just one. So what did I know about this killer? Not much. What I thought I'd known, when I'd imagined him to be a vessel for God after intensive discipleship, was all a lie.

A bullet zipped into the water under my belly. It would've killed me if it had made contact, even if it had grazed me. I tried to memorize the angle of entry of the bullet, then rose for a breath.

After a quick lungful of air, I dove deeper, to the bottom of the harbor entrance, about fifteen feet. The shooter, Coleman, would still be able to see a shimmer of me, but I imagined it would be distorted, the water twisting and infracting the light.

Another bullet hissed bubbles ahead of me, then tumbled lazily through the water a foot from my head. I could've reached out and plucked the bullet from the water, but I was too intent on swimming. At least now I knew fifteen feet was a safe depth from what I guessed was a .308 sniper rifle, judging by the slug. Unfortunately, I couldn't stay at that depth forever; I needed air!

When I expected another gunshot, it didn't come, and there were no boats anchored in the entrance to the harbor for me to surface behind. I needed air now, but I couldn't surface directly. Somehow, I had to use the half-mile range against the shooter. With every shot, however, he seemed to be getting more precise. If I died now, Chloe or Nathan could be next. And if it truly was Coleman, and he got away again, he might really kill my family the next time. This had to end now!

I kicked off the bottom, and rose sharply for the surface at a velocity I didn't know I could swim. Perhaps losing all that weight was working for me still.

But a couple feet before my head burst through the surface, I launched myself to the right, and surfaced about a foot from where a shooter might have projected me to rise. Since I had exhaled during my ascent, I sucked in a lungful before splashing like an uncoordinated dolphin, and dived back to the bottom.

Had there been a gunshot? Maybe the shooter was studying me, knowing I'd need four or five more visits to the surface to reach wherever he imagined I was trying to get.

The noise of a motor rumbled nearby, then it was directly overhead. I guessed from underneath the hull that it was Luigi's speedboat. Thank the Lord! Surfacing on the south side of the hull, I took a breath while the boat drifted and idled, then I reached for the diving platform when the stern began to pass me. Even at about two knots, I was jerked painfully forward, but now I had a handhold. With my free hand, I slapped the hull.

"Go! Go!"

The speedboat launched forward, propelled by two powerful outboards not far from my elbow. Though I didn't hear the thump of a bullet on the cockpit as the shooter probably was aiming for Luigi at the helm, I did hear the report of the gunshot. The shooter had to know I was somewhere behind the far side of the hull.

Almost bodysurfing, I hung off the stern. The Predator turned to port sharply. I gulped a breath, then let go. Certain that the shooter would follow the Predator for a few seconds, I stroked wildly for the Bavaria sailboat, anchored and rocking in the wake-waves twenty feet away.

At ten feet away, I figured I'd tempted visibility long enough, and I dove under the water, propelling myself under the deep keel of my forty-footer. Now that I'd reached the boat, I needed another plan.

Surfacing at the stern, I caught my breath and imagined all that needed to be done.

To my left, the Predator had successfully completed its turn, and sped out of the harbor. As a tactical man, I knew Luigi, even wounded in the shoulder, would probably find a way to be useful. He might even try to approach the shooter from another angle, which would be suicide, due to the shooter's elevation. But no one knew what we faced better than Luigi. If the shooter had enough ammunition, he could last another hour before the islanders gathered for a successful assault, though many of their peace officers would die in the process.

"Corban!" It was Nathan to my right. At least he was still alive. The catamaran was wrecked against two smaller sailboats, and she seemed to be taking on water. Nathan slipped into the water and hid behind the hull of his own vessel. "He's two points southwest of the lighthouse!"

"Where's Chloe?"

"Brody got her to shore." He gestured ashore from where screams and stampeding crowds ran to and fro for cover. "I think I can take the sniper if I stay low and approach from the central ridge!"

"You bring any NL weaponry?"

"Just a flash and bang grenade, and my tranqs in my brace."

"There's a NL-X1 on board. Swim to me. I'll shoot, you spot."

He didn't wait for further instruction and his head disappeared. I knew he still wore a leg brace, but Luigi had taught the ex-Marine during training to adapt to any situation.

Nathan's head popped up at my side.

"Still no shot," I said. "He's either repositioning or he ran."

"Or he's still in the exact same spot waiting for a bull's eye." Nathan smiled mischievously. "I'll give him one if you need a minute to climb aboard, Boss."

I scoffed at Nathan's remark. Still the same Nathan—irreverent, yet irreplaceable.

"Just give me a boost and keep your head down. He may not know where we are yet. Luigi and his speedboat caused a little confusion I think."

After climbing over the starboard side, I belly-crawled across the deck to the hatch. A gunshot from the hill made me flinch, but we hadn't been the target. Either someone was attempting to assault the hill, or the shooter thought someone ashore was me. We had no time to wait.

In the cabin, I rose to my feet, only to look into the faces of the three mercenaries with black paint still smeared on their faces. Their eyes were wide, and the rifles in their hands were all aimed at me.

"Hands where we can see 'em!" one yelled at me. Another reached for my collar, presumably to force me to the floor.

Slapping his hand away, I turned to the galley bulkhead.

"Bad timing, boys. Lives are on the line. Coleman's on the hill below the lighthouse popping something long-range at us."

"It's my .308," said the one whose voice I recognized from the elevator. "He got the jump on us. This one's with us, guys."

They lowered their weapons, which helped me focus on the hidden armory that opened before me.

"What kind of guns are those?"

"A non-lethal series. Same stuff I used on your buddies last night."

"You mean Smitty's not dead?"

"He was just sleeping," I said, my secret out, "for about twenty minutes."

Plucking the NL-X1 sniper rifle off its padded cradle, I swung the long barrel across the galley, making the men duck. From the bottom of the hidden compartment, I grabbed two magazines of NL-X1 water-soluble explosive cartridges. The rifle had a range of one thousand yards. The shooter with the .308 had met his match.

"I'm Agent Corban Dowler," I told the three speechless men, "a Christian with the Commission of International Laborers. You boys still trying to figure out whose side you're on?"

†

CHAPTER FORTY-FOUR

Moments later, Nathan joined me in the sailboat, and the three mercenaries climbed off the stern into the water. I'd given them each a NL-3 rifle to assault the hilltop. The range of the NL-3 was limited, but they understood they were to draw fire from the shooter as Nathan and I targeted him.

The shooter continued to fire—not at us, but at townsfolk or authorities attempting to take the hill. People were surely dying. Coleman was a trained operator who had fooled me, a veteran spy. No common islander would take him down.

My Bavaria sailboat bow pointed northwest, so the windows on the port side were exposed to the hillside. With a wrench, Nathan knocked out three windows, and we cleared a counter in the galley for me to lay halfway across it. Using a spotting scope, Nathan leaned over my back and peered at the hill. We were each using different windows, a third broken window ready to shift to if we were spotted.

"He'll be looking for us after the first shot," Nathan said. His scope rested against the windowsill. "But his bullets will pass clean through this hull, Boss."

"Then I'd better get him with the first couple shots, right?" I took a deep breath and settled my eye in front of the 4x scope. "Range?"

"Range . . . 492 meters. Your grade's about fifty-percent."

"Got it." I adjusted my scope and chambered the first of twelve cartridges in the magazine. "Okay, where is he?"

Another gunshot thundered across the water. We heard other gunfire, which sounded like handguns, as men stormed the hill. I could see them now, about ten men, some in uniform, probably with varied paramilitary training. Their charge was reckless and useless, but for now, the shooter wasn't paying attention to my extra-long barrel protruding from the side of the sailboat in the middle of the harbor.

"The lighthouse," Nathan said, his calm helping my own unsettled nerves. Adrenalin was still rushing through my body from the swim, so my nerves were a wreck.

But my family was still alive, and one of the coldest adversaries I'd ever crossed was within my grasp. "Track down ten yards. A tan bush."

I followed the slope of the hill down a little, searching in my less powerful scope for a lighter bush than the deep green that covered the hill.

"Check."

"Track right about . . . eight feet. Look for a wall, like an old building."

"Okay, I'm there. I see it. It's the ruins of old Fort Gustav."

"Well, he's behind that wall."

It took me a moment to understand, then I lifted my head and turned to look at Nathan who was still leaning over my back.

"Are you serious?"

"Hey, I told you I'd located him." Nathan chuckled. "I didn't say I knew how to get him."

"I'll have to draw him out." My eye was back on the scope in time to see bushes moving, as if from a wind, then we heard the gunshot about one second later. With a more powerful scope, I might've discerned shapes better, but my view was obscured by bushes, and the shooter was directly behind an ancient brick and mortar wall. To make matters worse, Gustavia's harbor was normally sheltered and calm, but the hurricane to our west now was still sending occasional waves into the anchorage.

There was movement behind the wall as the shooter adjusted, probably to check for someone advancing his position. Then he fired downhill to the west, which was the best approach on foot. When I traced straight down below the ruins, I saw my three mercenaries tackling the steepest part of the hill. They had little actual cover, only shrubs and a few mounds of dirt. But so far, it seemed that the shooter hadn't noticed them. To see and shoot them, he'd have to expose his position to me.

"Firing to provoke," I warned Nathan.

"Ready. If he spots us, Boss, we're done."

"Understood."

Boom! My sniper rifle jumped against my shoulder. I imagined the cartridge flying at a velocity of eighteen hundred feet per second. At five hundred meters, the five water-soluble tranq-darts would have a spread of only two and a half feet.

Using the bolt action, I slammed another round into the chamber of the specialized non-lethal rifle. I peered through the scope about the instant the five non-infectious silicon ribbed darts peppered the ruins. Gently, I squeezed the trigger, ready for the final bit of tension to end this whole—

There! His head! Boom! Again, I chambered another round.

"It's a miss," Nathan said, "but he knows we're somewhere out here now. He's looking for us. Oh, he sees your merc friends. Fire, Boss! His head and shoulder are visible. Fire, Corban!"

I fired. The shooter, too far away to identify, moved slightly west at the last instant.

"Miss."

Another cartridge.

The shooter fired.

"Now he's shooting at the mercs. They're hiding. He's got them pinned down. Still out of their range. Take him, Boss. He's scoping for us!"

Exposed now from his torso and up, the shooter was in the open. I couldn't see his features well, but his bald head was visible enough. It was indeed Karl Coleman. The long barrel of his rifle swept across Gustavia, hunting for someone who was firing at him with a long-distance rifle.

The harbor water unsettled us, and at the last second, before I could shoot, the whole boat rocked. I lost Coleman completely from my scope.

"Fire, Boss!"

Again, I fired, but I knew it was off, and I regretted it an instant later. Such a careless shot, made while Coleman was searching for me, was an obvious tell of my location.

"Get down!" Nathan warned, his spotting scope still focused on the target.

He pulled me off the counter, and we fell in a heap on the galley floor. A bullet punched through the hull and passed down the length of the counter. A magnetic cupboard door splintered from its hinges.

Before I was completely oriented on the floor, Nathan was pulling me up and pushing me toward the rifle still propped in the window. Instead, I moved aside.

"Take him, Nathan."

Nathan met my eyes and nodded. He'd been a Marine sniper. The only reason he'd been spotting was because he'd known where the target was and I hadn't.

Instead of rushing into another hasty shot, Nathan removed the rifle barrel from the window altogether. He gave me the spotting scope.

"Do you have a boat hook on board?" he asked.

I rushed up the companionway to the helm. A bullet dashed into the deck, missing me by two feet. What Nathan wanted with a boat hook, I didn't know, but I wasn't about to question him at that moment.

With the long staff, its hooked end in my hand, I jumped down the companionway's six steps and gave the rod to Nathan. He and I crouched on the galley floor, uncertain where the next bullet would pass.

Licking his lips, Nathan gently laid the rod in the middle window of the three he'd broken. Then, he moved closer to the front window, the rifle cradled in his arms. Understanding now the decoy barrel he intended, I took hold of the end of the boat hook.

"You ready?" I asked.

The water of the harbor seemed to settle again.

"Do it, Boss. God help me . . ."

I thrust the boat hook two feet out the window. From the hill, it surely appeared like a barrel. Barely had I stepped back when a bullet tore through the window frame and slammed into the mini-fridge on the opposite counter.

Just as quickly, Nathan pushed the NL-X1 barrel through the first window. His eye seemed to focus for no more than one second through the scope, then he fired.

Breathing heavily, I waited, but after chambering another round, Nathan didn't move.

"Nathan?"

"It's a hit," he said, but he still didn't get up. "Use the scope. Check it."

Hesitantly, I leaned across the counter next to him and gazed up the hill. The lighthouse, the ruins . . . There was a hand resting over one section of the wall.

"Fire once more, Nate. His hand is exposed. See it?"

"Yeah, I see something." He fired again.

I watched. The hand didn't move as the tranquilizer darts hit the wall, maybe even the hand itself.

"He's down," I decided. "Our three merc friends are a short climb below him. They might reach him first, but the island authorities will take him into custody. Good shooting, Nate, as always."

Nathan stood and handed me the rifle.

"So, what now?"

"Well, I hear I have a family to return to."

"Don't worry about Senator Nettleton and Rod Chang, if you're even aware they were behind all this." Nathan went to the galley sink and washed his face. "Chloe, Brody, Gail, and I took them down in a little sting, then leaked it to the press. It was no mistake on Chloe's part to bring in Gail. As an actress and disguise artist, Gail had the four of us under a layer of makeup to fool Senator Nettleton." Nathan laughed. "And all these guys are going down for Flight 524. Your name is clear again. Actually, whatever happens in the courts, your Muhammad alias will go down as the instigator. You can use the publicity as an asset."

"Our God brought it all together, son." I shook Nathan's hand. "We both know our calling, as long as we're alive. It's moments like these that remind us God is ever before us."

"You don't know the half of it." Nathan grinned and turned, gesturing for me to follow him topside. On deck, he pointed across the short expanse at the catamaran mast. "Look at that bullet hole about thirty-five feet up the mast. The first shot Coleman fired was probably dead-on. You'd be dead right now, Boss, if we hadn't sailed past you on the port side at that exact instant. Think of all the details that had to be arranged for your life to be spared. A carbon fiber catamaran mast saved your life!"

"God's ways are remarkable." I gazed across the harbor. Chloe and Brody were waving from the western shore. Luigi motored the Predator speedboat up to the sailboat and threw Nathan the bowline. General Forglade, still in the speedboat, was probably ready for another tranquilizer shot, but I guessed I'd hand him over to the authorities. There were a lot of questions they'd want answered. As primary COIL agent on the scene, I would dismiss the others so they could return to their lives or missions. They'd proven themselves as keepers of their brothers and sisters yet again.

Once I tied things up on the island, it would take more than a storm and an army to keep me away from Janice and Jenna. I wasn't sure I could merely talk to them over the phone; I had to hold them in my arms.

"Did you hear me, Boss?" Nathan asked.

"What's that?"

"I said, people only see how remarkable God's ways are when they get out here and answer the call for themselves."

"They don't know what they're missing if they don't answer, huh?" Chuckling, I thought of the past weeks of life and death situations. "Nathan, I wouldn't want to live for my Lord any other way. Come on. Let's go see Chloe. I would've loved to have seen her face when she realized you were still alive!"

"It was something, Boss! But don't think I'm letting you fake my death again just to witness it!"

†

CHAPTER FORTY-FIVE

Two weeks later . . .

"Hello, I'm looking for Officer Heather Oakes. My name is Corban Dowler."

A young officer working the Franklinville Police Department counter turned to face several desks behind him.

"Oakes! Someone here for you."

A pretty, blondish woman in her early fifties looked up from her desk. I smiled and waved. She sighed, as if I were interrupting her, then she walked to the counter. Her smile seemed to be forced.

"Can I help you?"

"My name is Corban Dowler." I said no more, waiting for a reaction. Luigi had said he'd told her something about me, but she showed no recognition on her face.

"Well, Mr. Dowler, I have a pretty big pile of work to do. See that stack of reports there? That's all mine. So why don't you just tell me what I can help you with."

"Yes." Usually one to withhold my emotions, this time I couldn't hide my grin. "I see why he liked you. No nonsense."

"He?" She frowned. "Did I miss something? Someone likes me? I've got a secret admirer you're gonna tell me about?"

"Miss Oakes, I don't want to say too much here," I glanced at the younger officer, "but if we go for a sandwich at the deli, we can talk about it. I was told to ask you before your lunch break so you could schedule it in."

"The deli? I don't even know you. The last time someone— Oh! You're . . .?" Her eyes opened wide. "Who are you again?"

"Corban Dowler." I handed her a card. "Previously of Langley, currently with the Commission of International Laborers, COIL. Go ahead and run me. I'll wait."

I went to the wall and sat on a bench. Though she eyed me suspiciously, she also displayed a crooked smile as she studied her computer screen. Periodically, she glanced over her monitor at me, and I was reminded of what Luigi had told me. She was indeed witty, and maybe even intuitive. For certain, she knew I was there for Luigi, now.

A few minutes later, she grabbed a coat from her desk chair and donned it as she faced me.

"Can we go in separate cars?" she asked. "Meet you there?"

"Yes." I chuckled. "He told me you might say that."

"You're gonna answer all my questions, right?" she asked as she led the way outside. "Luigi is this great big mystery in my life, and I really don't like mysteries. After he was arrested, he dropped off the face of the earth."

"Oh, he's still around."

Once we were seated in the deli, she simply folded her hands and rested them on her wrapped sandwich. I took this as my cue to begin.

"It was my decision to come see you. I insisted. Luigi's tied up for a few weeks."

"Well, I guess that's what happens when you get arrested, huh? You get tied up?" She laughed. I liked her attitude.

"He's no longer in police or government custody. But he's debriefing with certain unnamed people who will ask him everything he ever knew or did for France while residing in Italy."

"Then he's not from New York originally?"

"No. He has on occasion misguided people to protect them—you included. Don't take that personally, if you can help it. At times, I've had to use misinformation as well, for the good."

"So, he's not in trouble now? The stuff he said he's done in the past is just—written off?"

"Oh, no. Nothing's written off. There's a long journey ahead of him. Luigi's a veteran spook of the highest caliber, so he has much to disclose—more than probably ten normal agents put together. But he wants this—to be, uh, legalized. Eventually, he'll be given citizenship in the States."

"What about his enemies?"

"Once the US adopts him, certain disclosures will be made to other governments. They'll be notified, in a firm tone, that Luigi Putelli is ours. Hands off."

"Putelli, huh? So then he'll be safe?"

"Safe? No, but safer, I suppose. He has a past. That doesn't go away. And that's more between him and God. But I could help him with his citizenship, so I did. Numerous times in the last three years, he's saved my family, and my own life. He's a good addition to the lives he touches, unless they're criminal masterminds or sadistically homicidal."

"Yeah, I got a report on something he handled here when we kinda dropped the ball. He's a bit of a wrecking ball, huh?"

"He's more subtle than a wrecking ball, but yes, he's a one-man justice system."

"So, you're here to explain things." She unwrapped her sandwich. "Is he mad at me? I kinda gave him the brush-off last time he called. Does he want to see me again?" Her cheeks turned pink.

"No, he's not mad, just sorry." I sipped my lemonade. "Luigi's a complicated man. Maybe with all of us working together, we can bring him to Christ, huh?"

"That's the other thing. I've been a Christian for almost thirty years and I'm not about to get involved with a nonbeliever. He did say you were his spiritual mentor, though."

"You mean more involved. I'd say we're both already involved. And I told him I wouldn't approve of him getting romantic with a Christian woman at this point."

"Have you checked up on me?"

"A woman who goes to Newark on her days off to help inner city mothers put their lives together catches my attention."

"It's not that big of a deal." She blushed again.

"Those single mothers think it is. You're helping them in the name of Jesus Christ. I'd say Luigi has good taste in women."

"Oh, you approve!" She laughed, still embarrassed. "So, when can I see him?"

"Well, that's up to him. I can't imagine he'll be done by Thanksgiving, but I'll let him know there's a green light on this end at least to contact you."

"That'd be nice." She frowned firmly. "But I'll make sure to put my foot down about not being unequally yoked. We'll get him in the Lord's army one way or another, huh?"

"My wife's name is Janice. She knows Luigi a bit. Luigi's circle of friends is pretty small, but he's going to need all of us in the next few months more than ever. I want you to be in contact with Janice. We can coordinate efforts with Luigi. Janice might even be of help with your work in Newark, too; she has connections."

"Thanks. You make Luigi sound pretty slippery still." She smiled. "Is he done with the spook life?"

"Guys like him and me—it's all we know."

"You didn't answer my question. I see you're slippery, too!"

"The world's an evil place. That's why I don't want Luigi going off on his own ever again. We're his family now."

"Thank you for telling me so much." She frowned. "A lot of times it seems I just drift from week to week. I can't tell you how special I feel that you've come to see me—and then I saw your file on the system. You're really someone, aren't you?"

"Just a man leaning on Jesus, Heather. Listen. I'd like you to consider a job with COIL. Look into us. Talk to Janice. No Christian should work a job where she drifts along week to week. The laborers are few. Christ needs you every day, not just on weekends. Besides, New York City is a lot closer to Newark than Franklinville is."

"You're offering me a job with this COIL place?"

"It's an organization. It's all on the card. Give that mountain of paperwork to someone else and join us. God's people have a different calling than what the world has."

"Luigi works for you?"

"No, not yet, anyway. He's more like a freelance shadow who doesn't think his sins should be dealt with by anyone but himself."

"There's a fiery place for people who hang on to their sins."

"True. And COIL only employs real Christians. There's an extensive screening process, too, so beware."

"As you know now, I've got nothing to hide. Wow, I can't believe this is happening to me." She blew her nose on her napkin. "I keep wondering if you have the right person."

"If it weren't for Luigi, I wouldn't even be here. You can thank him when you see him next."

"You two seem close. Only real friends care for each other like that."

"Only family." I smiled. "And since you're a sister in Christ, we can say without hesitation that you're family, too, Heather. I look forward to seeing you with COIL soon."

"Well, I'll definitely pray about it." She wiped her mouth. "But to be honest, it sounds exactly like what I need. God sent you guys to me. I know it."

"He knows what we need, Heather. We'll be in touch."

One week later . . .

"Agent Trimble?" I knocked on the doorframe of the office in the Pentagon basement. My visitor pass hung loosely on my blazer, but I had no escort since leaving the elevator. This was one of my old haunts.

"That's me." A powerfully-built man rose from a desk. He wore a sidearm, an eye patch over one eye, and an amused look on his face. We shook hands. "Corban Dowler, the legend, in the flesh."

"Corban, the ancient, more like it." We laughed.

"No, no," he said. "That's not what I hear. You're busier than ever with that COIL Agency. Good stuff. I'm a believer, so I keep tabs on you guys. Not much different than working where, uh, you used to work, wherever that was."

He blinked his one eye and I imagined it was his version of a wink, and we chuckled again as he showed me to a faded upholstered chair. Other agents of the PRS division were working at their stations without regard to us.

"I'm always glad to visit with a colleague, sir, but something tells me this isn't just a friendly visit."

"That's true, Wes." I folded my hands. "I'm here to talk to you about homemade parachutes."

"COIL needs a homemade parachute designed? What's wrong with a—" He stopped himself, stared at me, then understanding dawned on his face. "Ah, you jest. Homemade parachute. Clever, sir. I have chills up my spine as I speak."

"Yes, I thought that'd catch your attention." I smiled. "That was some stunt, diving out of that jet with whatever Luigi Putelli built for himself."

"Not my finest display of brain matter, I assure you." He shook his head. "Most of that wasn't in my final report, so I'm guessing you've talked to someone who's been questioning Putelli? I lost track of him a few weeks ago."

"No, I haven't spoken to anyone." I made sure he heard the seriousness in my voice. "Just Luigi. He's one of mine."

"Oh." He sat up a little straighter and even adjusted his eye patch. "Oh! Please tell me I didn't mess up something serious. I would've never tried to arrest him if he didn't have a lengthy sheet on him, sir. Just because I'm a generation after you doesn't mean I hijack operational priority from other agents, retired or not. You're one of the most respected men who's ever walked the halls of Langley, where I'd much rather be stationed, and I know, well, you can stop me at any time . . ."

"Wes, you're a good man." I smiled sadly. "Luigi said as much, and that's why I'm here. Maybe you're a little on the wild side, but we all are if we want to make a difference. Those days you spent with Luigi—who's not a believer, but is one of my dearest friends—should've been a time of investigation into what he was saying. Things he told you should've raised red flags about the nonsense you were reading on paper, but you ignored those flags. You made the mistake of being a company man before being a Christian man, and you handed Luigi over to traitorous men. He was just a day or two from being killed in their custody when my people pulled him out by force. My family would've died with him. God opens our eyes to see things our government training can't see. As Christians, we should look and listen through the lens of the Cross. Any of this jarring something loose inside you?"

He nodded slowly. At age forty-two, and the deputy director of the PRS division for the CIA as a liaison to the Pentagon, he was a respected agent as well as a known Christian. And knowing he was a Christian made it my business to get on his case.

"You're right, sir. I thought more of the arrest than of the man's soul—or souls he told me he was responsible for." He slapped his desk. "This is why you left, isn't it? The Agency demands from us more than we should give as Christians."

"It might be possible to work here as a Christian, Wes," I said, "but I couldn't find a way. I was forced to make too many compromises."

"Are you telling me to leave the Agency?"

"COIL could use you, sure. But no, I'm not telling you to leave. I'm telling you to check your priorities."

"Okay." He took a deep breath. "Yeah, priorities—I hear you loud and clear. So, Luigi's okay? I worked him over pretty good in the mountains."

"He's okay. I've got him debriefing for a few weeks so something like this never happens again, but he still has enemies and a past. If he were the old Luigi, and you wanted to really push him like you did, it would've meant the lives of everyone on that plane you jumped from. And Luigi probably would've still come out alive, somehow."

"Right. Well, I have some thinking to do on all this. But tell me, if I can't work it out, working for the government as a Christian and all—is COIL an option for me?"

"For you, COIL is always an option." I rose to my feet and extended my hand. "Call me any time, Wes."

Standing, he shook my hand, and our eyes locked. We were men who struggled with doing right against great odds. I saw in Wes Trimble a younger me, devoted to God, yet torn in many other obligations.

"Thank you for coming, sir."

"Call me Corban. And no more homemade parachutes, right?"

"Parachutes? I'm thinking about giving up flying altogether!"

...✝...

Two days later . . .

I was standing next to a kiosk in La Guardia International Airport just after midnight, sipping a strong coffee. The freestanding booth offered every imaginable blend. The owner kept clearing his throat, as if he wanted me to move on, or notice him, but I did my best to ignore him as I waited for Nathan. Chloe and I had arrived together to see Nathan off, but the solo operative hadn't shown himself yet.

Across the quiet corridor, Chloe was witnessing to two women with head coverings. In my heart, I prayed her spontaneous obedience to share Christ with the lost, even there, would produce saved souls. If nothing else, maybe Chloe's smile would attract a contact she could add to COIL's dynamic network across the Muslim world.

COIL was operating again without significant hindrance—for the moment. Dealing with Forglade and Coleman had to be viewed as a time of testing and refining for us all. Seeing the last few weeks in any other way could only bring fear and despair. No, we were Christians, and we knew God was at work.

"Another coffee, mate?" the kiosk owner asked in an Irish brogue. The man's voice was high pitched, which seemed uncharacteristic for such a large man with a bushy beard, but I didn't look him in the eye for long. More coffee would make me restless, so I waved the man's offer away.

"Nathan used to be more punctual than this," Chloe stated as she returned to my side. Sighing loudly, she waved one last time to the women she'd been talking to as they walked away. "What do you think? Is Nathan the same Nathan he used to be? He does seem different, more reserved or something."

"Well, he's engaged to Chen Li now. A good match, I think."

"That's true. The prospect of marriage will settle down the wildest heart, right?" She wrung her hands. "I can't help but worry about our guys out there. Just think—Nathan's been alone all this time, and we had no idea he was even alive!"

"I knew."

"Yeah, and you'll never do that to me again, right?"

"You don't have old Mossad secrets you keep from me?" I smiled at her. "The secrecy was for Nathan's safety, Chloe, not to spite you."

"Oh, I know. It's just overwhelming to think about. Now he's going back out there, alone again. He should've stayed with us longer, gotten to know some of the new recruits coming out of training. He could've really inspired them."

"He's still undercover." I glanced at the kiosk worker and saluted him with my coffee cup. He nodded back, and held up a magazine a little higher. "It was a brief homecoming. We needed him, and God put him at your side. But his skills are best used out there."

"His plane leaves in ten minutes!" Chloe checked her watch. She seemed more frustrated with Nathan's departure than I expected. "I don't think I appreciated him enough when he was team leader, and I don't know how to let him know—now that he's a hero to us all. Even if nobody knows he's still alive."

"I think he knows we love him." I winked at the kiosk owner, who peeked at us from around his magazine. "But that's not why he does what he does—to be a hero. He's a shepherd for the Lord."

A few minutes passed as Chloe paced back and forth.

"Well, we can't wait much longer for him," Chloe said. "We have to get you ready to leave for Gaza before noon. Nathan knew we'd be waiting here for him, right?"

"Maybe he's gotten shy in his old age. Nobody likes goodbyes, Chloe." I set the last of my coffee on the edge of the kiosk counter. "Nathan knows his job as well as we know ours. He doesn't need to cry with us before he leaves."

"It still would've been nice to see him off."

A final boarding announcement sounded from the ceiling. Nathan's plane was preparing to depart for Paris. The kiosk owner tossed his apron on a nearby bench and shouldered roughly past me. He did the same to Chloe, causing her to spill her hot drink.

"Hey! What's the big hurry, pal?"

But the man didn't look back as he jogged with a slight limp to the departure gate. He showed his boarding pass and disappeared down the ramp. The access door closed behind him.

"Seems he had a plane to catch." I chuckled as I stood next to Chloe. She frowned at me.

"What do you mean? He was running the—" She looked back at the kiosk. A new man was donning the apron and tending to the booth. "All right, what's going on?"

"The plane is rolling onto the runway."

"No, I mean—"

"Oh, you mean Nathan?"

"Yeah . . ." A smile slowly crept to her lips, but the grin on my own face felt as if it reached my ears. "He's still the same Nathan. That rascal! And you with him! He set this up! How long did you know?"

"A little while."

"Well, at least he saw us." Chloe had tears in her eyes as she hooked her arm around my elbow, as a daughter standing beside her father. "He knows he's not alone."

"None of us are, Chloe. Let's go." I guided her down the corridor. "We have work to do."

~

Dear Reader,

Thanks so much for reading *DARK VESSEL!* If you enjoyed it, I know you'll also enjoy the next book in this series, *DARK ZEAL*, Book Five! Visit books2read.com/b/ DarkZeal for a list of where you can get the next book right now!

DARK ZEAL takes us into the heart and heat of Gaza, Israel, where Agent Corban Dowler infiltrates the city for a routine medical op. He soon discovers an international plot by Hamas terrorists to destroy Israel, forcing him to respond as a soldier of Christ. Don't miss this action-packed page-turner!

If you enjoyed *Dark Vessel*, would you please help us get the word out by leaving a review? Perhaps a line or two about how the book made you feel or what you liked about the book. Thank you, reading friend!

You may want to subscribe to my biweekly D.I. Telbat Newsletter. You can find the signup form at ditelbat.com to receive FREE D.I. Telbat short stories, Author Reflections, or my novel news. I also have exculsive gifts for you! Come join the adventure!

Author David Telbat

~

ENDNOTES
VOICE OF THE MARTYRS

As in many of my novels, I desire to bring attention to ministries that come alongside the Persecuted Church world-wide. This time, I'd like to focus on two specific ministries of Voice of the Martyrs. (The information below can be found on their websites.)

VOM RADIO

VOM Radio is a weekly national program focusing exclusively on the testimonies of our persecuted family and on building fellowship between the Body of Christ in the United States and His Body in hostile and restricted nations. VOM Radio is the only program of its kind.

Each week, host Todd Nettleton shares testimonies from brothers and sisters willing to suffer persecution rather than deny their faith in Christ.

Visit vomradio.net/episodes and search for the following testimonies and conversations with a few of our persecuted brothers and sisters:

Sister Amber, arrested in Tibet: tibet-the-lord-just-held-my-heart. May 18, 2018

Gracia Burnham, missionary kidnapped in Philippines: Martyrs' Widows: God Takes Special Care. September 11, 2021

Gary Witherall, whose wife was martyred in Lebanon: In the Nightmare, God is Faithful. August 4, 2018

Nik Ripken, author of *The Insanity of God*: *Sheep Among Wolves*. February 2, 2019

Launched in 2014, VOM Radio now airs on more than 950 stations across the United States, in addition to worldwide digital distribution online and on every major podcast distribution channel. In 2016, VOM Radio was honored as "Radio Program of the Year" by the National Religious Broadcasters.

We praise the Lord for all that VOM Radio does—getting the word out about our persecuted brothers and sisters all over the world, and reminding us to pray. And we praise God for the freedom we still have in our country to have this type of programming available to all!

PRISONER ALERT

Another ministry of Voice of the Martyrs—Prisoner Alert (prisoneralert.com)—keeps us informed about Persecuted Christians who have been arrested for their faith, so we can pray, write, or petition government officials on their behalf.

There is much information on many prisoners from all over the world (prisoneralert.com/prisoners), including the reason they were arrested and the latest update on their cases. There is a page listing released prisoners as well, including the dates released and how long they were incarcerated.

The website offers tips on how to safely write to Christian prisoners. Prisoner Alert provides approved

DARK VESSEL | 379

phrases and Scripture verses, as well as translation into whatever language is necessary. Prisoners are most often not able to write back, but encouragement is greatly needed by those who are suffering.

Once you choose the prisoner you want to write to, there is a button where you can choose your desired phrases to write your letter. Their clear instructions make it easy to do.

According to the Prisoner Alert website, over 406,125 encouraging letters have been written. *Praise the Lord!*

Prisoner Alert is a great ministry of Voice of the Martyrs for those who wish to remember and pray for those who are suffering for their faith. Sign up for the Voice of the Martyrs free monthly newsletter to read stories of the overcoming faith of Christians living in restricted nations.

"Remember those in bonds as bound with them,"
Hebrews 13:3.

ABOUT THE AUTHOR

D.I. Telbat desires to honor the Lord with his life and writing. Many of his books focus on persecuted Christians worldwide—their sacrifice, their suffering, and their rescues.

After studying writing in school, David worked for a time in the newspaper field, but he is now doing what he loves most: writing and Christian ministry.

Through his website at DITelbat.com, you will find links to all of his books where you can read descriptions about each one as well as find retailer links for his ebooks and paperbacks.

His biweekly newsletter offers a short story, an Author Reflection, or his novel news.

Thanks for reading! Please leave your comments wherever you bought this book. Reviews tremendously help authors, and David Telbat would love to hear your thoughts. He takes reader reviews into consideration as he makes his future publishing plans.